H

PENGUIN BOOKS

Written in Bones

James Oswald is the author of the Inspector McLean series of crime novels. The first seven, *Natural Causes*, *The Book of Souls*, *The Hangman's Song*, *Dead Men's Bones*, *Prayer for the Dead*, *The Damage Done* and *Written in Bones* are available as Penguin paperbacks and ebooks. He has also written an epic fantasy series, *The Ballad of Sir Benfro*, which is published by Penguin, as well as comic scripts and short stories.

In his spare time he runs a 350-acre livestock farm in north-east Fife, where he raises pedigree Highland Cattle and New Zealand Romney sheep.

Written in Bones

A Detective Inspector McLean Mystery

JAMES OSWALD

PENGUIN BOOKS

PENGUIN BOOKS

UK | USA | Canada | Ireland | Australia
India | New Zealand | South Africa

Penguin Books is part of the Penguin Random House group of companies
whose addresses can be found at global.penguinrandomhouse.com.

First published by Michael Joseph, 2017
First published in Penguin Books, 2017
003

Set in 12.42/14.77 pt Garamond MT Std
Typeset by Jouve (UK), Milton Keynes
Printed in Great Britain by Clays Ltd, St Ives plc

A CIP catalogue record for this book is available from the British Library

ISBN: 978-1-405-92529-7

www.greenpenguin.co.uk

Penguin Random House is committed to a
sustainable future for our business, our readers
and our planet. This book is made from Forest
Stewardship Council® certified paper.

This one's for Janie, who gave
me the gift of reading

I

He is weightless, lost. He floats on the air like the lightest of feathers. Wind tugs at him, ruffles his hair like an affectionate aunt. Dimly he is aware of motion, of falling, but that is something from another time, another life.

Warm air caresses his skin like a lover's embrace. Like a womb surrounding him, keeping him safe from the pain and suffering outside. Only the slow tumbling upsets his calm, his fugue. He should be worried, he knows. Something happened, but for the life of him he can't remember what. The life of him. His life.

The wind is fiercer now, tugging tears from the corners of his eyes. He had not realized they were open, but now he begins to see things. Shapes of darkness, pinpricks of light, rolling and flashing and whizzing past him like fireflies, like angry wasps.

He wakes more quickly now, understands that he has been drugged. Sluggish thoughts try to make sense of his surroundings, but it is too dark, the wind too strong. He remembers the leather tourniquet and bulging vein, the prick of the needle in his skin, the flush of ecstasy as the heroin surged through him. But that was a lifetime ago. He found help, cleaned up, quit. How could he have fallen back into those old ways?

Fallen.

Falling.

He is falling.

The realization wakes him like a bucket of ice-cold water. Forgotten arms snap out from his body in a futile reflex. There is nothing to catch but air. And now he knows the pinprick lights are not fireflies but streetlamps, lit windows, the headlights of endless cars. The city.

Instinctively, he tenses, raises his arms to his face to protect it, even as he understands there is no protection from what is to come. Another lazy tumble brings him closer still to the ground, and now the lights are a thousand thousand fragile glass bulbs outlining the trees directly beneath him. Festooned through winter branches, they reach up to embrace him with fingers of brittle, stabbing wood.

He hits with an explosion of noise. A violence that drives the air from his lungs and the sight from his eyes. He is pierced, rent, ripped apart. The shock should have killed him, but the drugs dull the pain, make everything feel once removed. The final lurch brings him to a halt, forces his eyes open, even as he feels something hard slide deep into his guts. He is still high off the ground, staring down at a path scattered with broken branches and shattered lights. Wires fizz and pop close by as his mouth fills with warm liquid, an iron tang to it like electricity. The warmth leaches out of him quickly as he struggles to breathe, chokes and coughs out chunky dark blood. It falls to the ground in lazy slow motion, his vision tunnelling down to the point of impact. And as the darkness welcomes him, a flash of panic arcs across his dying mind.

He cannot remember his name.

2

'Jesus wept. It's brass monkeys out here.'

Detective Inspector Tony McLean stamped his feet and breathed steam into cupped hands, desperately trying to get some heat back into the tips of his fingers. February could be brutal in the city, and lately someone seemed to have rewritten the weather rules. Deep snow clung to the Pentland Hills, chilling the air as it fell down into the city and pooled in the Meadows. He'd remembered to grab his overcoat on the way out of the house, but in the rush to get here he'd forgotten his hat and gloves. He was regretting that now.

Standing beside him, Detective Sergeant Grumpy Bob Laird had managed to dress better for the weather, wrapped in a fluorescent green jacket that looked like it would double as a sleeping bag for an Arctic expedition. His balding head was enveloped in a garish woolly hat that he had to be wearing for a bet. Even so, the end of his nose glowed red from the cold.

'Least it's not raining.'

McLean followed Grumpy Bob's gaze up to the sky, palest blue in the early morning. The call had come through before dawn, waking him on what was his first day back after three months of suspension, psych evaluation and meandering interviews with Professional Standards. He'd hoped for a gentle reintroduction and a light workload, but that was wishful thinking. Instead, a control operative who sounded as tired as McLean felt had told him there was a dead body on the Meadows and he was the only senior detective available. McLean had considered telling him to check his rosters again, but he knew it wasn't Control's fault. Every team was understaffed and overworked, even Specialist Crime Division, and at least the scene was reasonably close to home. He'd been surprised to find Grumpy Bob already there when he arrived, but then the old sergeant lived even closer.

'What have we got then, Bob? Apart from chilblains, that is.' The two of them stood on the frosty grass of the Meadows, far enough away from the bustle of the forensics team to avoid being scowled at. The centre of attention seemed to be one of the ancient trees that lined the path from the site of the old Royal Infirmary. Jawbone Walk, if memory served. The whale jawbone arch that had given the path its name had been removed some years earlier for restoration, and McLean couldn't remember whether it had ever been put back again. He thought about going to have a look, but then remembered why he was here.

'Nasty one, sir. And odd. Best if you have a look for yourself.' Grumpy Bob nodded his head in the direction of the trees that lined the main road. A cherry picker was being reversed on to the grass, directed by a white-suited technician. The high-pitched electronic shriek of its warning buzzer sang counterpoint to the dull, omnipresent roar of the city, and only then did McLean notice the lack of traffic noise nearby.

'They closed the road?' He looked off towards the Lochrin end, then turned to Newington and Sciennes. 'That's going to be popular.'

'Didn't have much choice. Not going to get him down otherwise.' Grumpy Bob pointed up into the bare canopy of the tallest tree, and McLean saw what he meant. A wych elm like many of the older trees on the Meadows, it stretched upward thirty metres or more, branches piercing the morning sky like broken, arthritic fingers. Only these fingers had caught something bloodied and grisly.

His first thought was of childhood holidays in the Highlands, clumping, bored, behind his grandmother as she hiked over rough moorland, fishing rod in hand, to some remote loch or river. The land was given over to heather and sheep as far as the eye could see, only the occasional square of dark green conifers to break up the scenery. Burns ran through the gullies, chattering peat water over rocks and churning it into bubbles that looked like the glasses of Coca-Cola he was only very seldom allowed. Every so often they would come across the carcass of some unfortunate animal, drowned and swept away in a spate, left tangled in roots high above the stream, as if the trees had reached out and snatched it from the rushing water.

It wasn't the roots that had dragged this man into their deathly embrace, but the twisted, bare branches. He sprawled high up in the leafless canopy, twisted into a grotesque parody of a body so that it was hard to make out what was arm and what was leg. There was no mistaking his head, though, even at this distance. It hung down from a semi-naked torso skewered by the sharp point of a broken branch, features battered so as to be unidentifiable. Blood dribbled from what must have been his mouth and nose, slicking the trunk and spattering the ground.

'Good God. How on earth did it get up there?'

McLean looked around, recognizing the voice. Angus Cadwallader, the city pathologist, looked like a man who had been roused from too little sleep. Grey skin bagged around his eyes and his smile was tired.

'Morning, Angus. Been burning the midnight oil, have you?'

Cadwallader grimaced. 'Don't start. I'm getting too old for these early starts. And I really don't like heights.'

'You want to go up and see him? Can't just let the experts bring him down for you?'

'And miss a vital clue that cracks the case for you?' The pathologist slapped his friend gently on the shoulder. 'Don't worry. You can go up and have a look after if you want.' He turned away before McLean could respond. The cherry picker was in place now, a forensic technician already on board the lifting platform. A short pause as the pathologist scrambled in to join him, and then they were being lofted up into the tree.

McLean scanned the crime scene, pleased to see that, as well as closing the road, a wide cordon had been strung around the whole area. Uniformed officers were keeping the early morning gawkers away, although, to be fair, the frozen weather was helping. Not many people out and about, which at least made their job easier for now. Grumpy Bob had disappeared, no doubt in search of a cuppa. Heading to the road edge, McLean found a cluster of squad cars, forensics vans and a fire engine all parked in a line. Uniformed constables huddled around one large van bearing the Police Scotland logo. Chatting amongst themselves like schoolchildren in the playground, they didn't notice his approach until he was upon them.

'Who's in charge here?'

The nearest constable startled, slopping hot tea from a mug she had been warming her hands around. 'What the fu–?' She turned swiftly, angry face rapidly changing to fear as she realized who had spoken. 'Oh. Sorry, sir. Didn't know Specialist Crime were here already.'

'Aye, well, some of us wish we weren't. Any more of that tea going?' McLean nodded at the mug, trying to remember the constable's name.

'Here. Have this one.' She held out the mug. 'I'll get another and fetch Sergeant Stephen over.'

McLean took the mug more in surprise than greed, although he had to admit the warmth was welcome. Less so the four or five teaspoons of sugar that made the tea all but undrinkable. He slurped some down anyway as he waited for the constable to return. The others eyed him nervously, as if he were some kind of irascible headmaster, ready to hand out detentions on a whim. Was it his imagination, or were all police officers looking younger these days?

'Anyone know who reported the body?'

'Heard it was a dog walker, sir. Something about a kid, too. The sergeant knows all the details.' One of the young constables nodded at a point behind him, and McLean turned to see the female PC return, a sergeant at her side. He had met Sergeant Kenneth Stephen before, most notably in the case of a spate of hangings in the city a couple of years back. He was a good officer, as could be seen by the efficient way the crime scene was being managed.

'Morning, Kenny. See you're working the early shift again.'

'Aye, sucker for punishment, that's me.' The sergeant

smiled, then frowned as he noticed the group of constables with their mugs. 'Tea break's over, you lot. I need you all working the cordon. Keep the public back till we've got the body down.'

McLean took another swig of over-sweet tea to hide his amusement as the constables muttered and grumbled away. The female PC whose tea he was drinking made to join them, but Sergeant Stephen stopped her.

'Not you, Harrison. You can help the inspector here. Make a good impression and you might even get that transfer to Plain Clothes you've been after. Can't see why you'd want it, mind.'

McLean looked at the young woman. Her name didn't ring any bells, but then it had been a while since he'd had much direct contact with uniforms. That's what happened when you were out of the loop for three months, he guessed. There had been a lot of new faces at the station each time he'd been back for briefings, interviews and those dreaded counselling sessions. Some notable missing faces, too, as more than a handful of promising young detectives took the offer of severance pay intended for the older staff and quit to find less stressful jobs. Most of the new constables eyed him nervously or scuttled away whenever they saw him. Quite what scurrilous rumours the junior officers spread while he was away he had no idea, but he was used to being the station pariah. PC Harrison didn't seem to be as scared of him as most, holding his gaze, her expression one that would win her many a game of poker. He broke first, turning back to speak to the sergeant.

'What's the story then, Kenny? Who's our man up in the tree, and who found him?'

'As to who, I've no idea. We've not been able to get a good look at him yet and he's pretty badly smashed up by the branches. Young lad found him. Out walking his dog before school. Apparently, he heard something crash into the trees, thought he was being attacked.' Sergeant Stephen pointed at the spot directly beneath the man, where a nest of broken branches scattered around the frosty tarmac.

'And he called us, this boy?'

'Christ, no. Poor wee thing ran home, terrified. His mum called us. After she'd come out here and had a look for herself.'

'Where are they now?'

'Back home. They live in one of the tenements up Marchmont Crescent.' Sergeant Stephen pointed across the road to the rows of buildings that lined the south side of the park. 'Family Liaison's with them at the moment. We'll get a proper statement as soon as we've got this place sorted.'

McLean looked up at the tree. The cherry picker had lifted Cadwallader and one of the fire crew up into the bare canopy and was now edging towards the point where the man's body shifted in the breeze. Someone had been thoughtful enough to roll out an inflatable safety bag directly beneath them, and the whole operation looked like it really didn't need him getting in the way right now.

'Constable Harrison, is it?' he asked of the young PC. She stiffened slightly at her name.

'Sir.'

'Have you done any Family Liaison work?' Even as he asked it, McLean realized how crass the question was. Just because she was a woman didn't necessarily mean she'd have FLO training.

'Not much, sir. Just what I've picked up on the beat. Domestics, that sort of stuff.'

'Probably more experience than I've had in the last few years.' McLean turned back to Sergeant Stephen. 'Mind if I borrow your constable for a while, Kenny?'

'Be my guest. She's more trouble than she's worth, anyway.' The sergeant smiled at his own joke. 'You going to see that kid, then?'

'Aye. Might as well get it done. This lot'll be here for hours yet.' McLean pointed up at the tree, where the cherry picker was now lodged firmly into the canopy, Cadwallader leaning out across the void as he inspected the body in situ. 'Unless he comes down by himself, that is.'

3

'He should be in school and I should be at work. You any idea what a nightmare this is? What it's costing me?'

McLean understood the hostility in Ellen Johnston's voice, but it annoyed him all the same. She had a pinched face, as if she had spent too much of her life sucking lemons, and a haggard expression that suggested mornings weren't her natural habitat. She had dressed, that much was apparent, but her choice of clothing wasn't much better than pyjamas. Her sweat pants looked like they'd been washed a thousand times, shapeless and grey; a pity the same couldn't be said for the hoodie, which sported an interesting collection of stains across its faded green front. It was somewhat at odds with the expensive tenement flat where she lived, and her assertion that she should be working.

'I'm very sorry, Miss Johnston. We'll try to be as quick as possible, but this is a very serious situation. The more information we can gather, the better. Especially this close to the event.'

'It's Mrs, actually.' Johnston shrugged. 'You'd better come in, then.' She stood to one side, letting McLean and Harrison into a hall cluttered with furniture just a little too large for it. No offer of tea; she simply led them over to another door, opening it to reveal a good-sized living room. A young boy sat on a sofa, huddled in close to one of the arms, his eyes darting nervously to the door as they entered. Beside him, a uniform constable first looked up, then stood swiftly.

'Inspector. Constable.' She straightened her uniform as she spoke, a look of hope in her eyes that she was about to be relieved of her family liaison duties. McLean so hated to disappoint people.

'John, there's more polis wanting to talk to you.' Mrs Johnston addressed her son brusquely, her irritation at the way her day had started clearly not aimed just at the police. The boy who looked up at him was younger than McLean had been expecting. Too young, surely, to be out walking the dog on his own before it was light. He had some of his mother's features about his thin face, but mostly looked worried. He flinched at the word 'polis' in a manner McLean would have found more understandable in a council flat in Restalrig or Sighthill than in this expensive part of town. There was something about Mrs Johnston's accent, too, that suggested wealth was something she had come to only recently. Looking around the living room, McLean could see no obvious evidence of a Mr Johnston. There were photographs of Mrs Johnston and her son on the mantelpiece, but no father anywhere.

'Is there a Mr Johnston still around?' He had tried to make the question sound innocent, but the scowl that was Mrs Johnston's response told him he'd missed that particular mark.

'Tommy's been dead these ten years now. Not that youse lot ever did anything to catch the bastards responsible.'

'Tommy?' McLean had to say the name out loud before

the penny dropped. 'Tommy Johnston? The nightclub owner? He's John's father?' He looked at the boy with more sympathetic eyes. Not just because he'd lost his father but because the boy must never really have known him at all. The family liaison officer obviously understood the situation, too. She stood up, put a gentle hand on John's shoulder. He looked from her to McLean and then to his mother, eyes wide with fear.

'Hi there, John. I'm Tony.' McLean crouched down so that he was at eye level, suppressing the urge to wince at the pain that shot through his hip. The cold weather didn't do much for his old bones, particularly not the ones that had been broken.

'You gonnae arrest me? I dint do nothing.'

'I don't know what they've been telling you about the police, John, but we don't arrest people for no reason. And you're right. You've not done anything wrong. But you did see the man in the tree, and I'd very much like to find out how he got there. So anything you can tell me about it would be helpful.'

The boy stared at him, silent. McLean could see his thoughts playing across his face, the frown deepening as he struggled to decide whether the polis could be trusted or not. Given what had happened to his father, John's reticence was perhaps understandable.

'What's he called, your dog?' McLean asked.

'She. And she's Tilly. Short for Tillicoultrie. Where she came from. Granny and Grampa live out there. I like going to visit them.'

'Where's she now? In your room?'

'Aye. She's happy there.' John's gaze flicked momentarily

13

from McLean's face to where his mother was standing by the door.

'Perhaps I could meet her. But first, tell me about this morning. You were taking her for a walk in the Meadows, is that right?'

'I take her every morning, 'fore school. She likes to chase the squirrels. Only this time she stayed close. She was whining and shivering like she was scared or something. Then I heard it flying. Sounded like a bird only much bigger, see? It was up high. Too dark, so I couldn't see it proper like, but I could hear its wings. Tilly did, too. She pulled so hard I dropped her lead. I dint know what to do. Thought it was gonnae swoop down and catch her. She's only wee, wouldn't a stood a chance. Only I couldn't call for her, or it'd have heard and come after me. Seen on the telly how they do that. Swoop down and *bam*! So I hid under that tree right up against the trunk, like. And then there was a scream and the tree shook and all these branches came down on top of me. I ran home without her. Only when I got here she'd run home herself. She was up against the door, shivering. Couldnae get in quick enough.'

'He watches too much rubbish on the telly, so he does.' Mrs Johnston spoke as if her son wasn't in the room with them all. McLean ignored her. He'd have much preferred it if he could have talked to the boy without her there, but that would have been inappropriate at best.

'What was flying, John? What did you see? Did it have lights on it?'

The boy paused, as if reliving the events had terrified him into silence. How old was he? McLean wasn't that good at gauging these things, but he couldn't be more than ten.

'Couldn't see well enough, could I? Only heard its wings. Reckon it must have been big, though.'

'You heard wings, you say? Not a plane? A helicopter?'

John looked up at him again, and McLean could see the fear in his eyes. Not fear of the police but something much deeper. 'You're gonnae think I'm stupid. Just a wee boy making up stories. But I think it was a dragon.'

'Tommy Johnston. There's a name I'd not thought to hear again.' McLean clumped down the stairs, PC Harrison beside him. The family liaison officer had left while McLean was busy being introduced to Tilly, an elderly little Jack Russell terrier who seemed to be just about the only friend in the world poor John Johnston had.

'Should I know who he is, sir?' Harrison asked.

McLean stopped mid step and turned to face the PC. She was young, perhaps early twenties. Slim, maybe an inch or two shorter than him, and her round face had a rosy-cheeked tint to it that suggested she was someone who spent much of her time outdoors. Beyond that she was a PC, he knew absolutely nothing about her, least of all how long she had been in uniform. It was perfectly possible there was a generation of officers out there who had never heard of Tommy Johnston, unlikely though that seemed.

'Thomas John Johnston was one of Edinburgh's more colourful characters. He ran a string of lap-dancing clubs across the city. A few in Perth, Dundee and Aberdeen, too. Always just the wrong side of the law, but he never did anything so obvious we could put him away for it. And he was better than the alternative, which I guess means we tolerated him.'

'So what happened to him? He's dead, right?'

'Oh, very. Being shot in the head will do that.' McLean resumed his trudge down the stairs. 'Seems while Lothian and Borders tolerated him, others were less forgiving. It was a very professional hit. We found him in his car in a back lane at the south end of the Pentlands. Never did find out who killed him.'

'And the clubs?'

'His whole empire was built on tick. Creditors came and took the lot. We ended up with some fairly unsavoury Glaswegians running things for a while. People trafficking, drugs. With Tommy it had been pretty much just prostitution, and he looked after his girls, unlike most of the pimps we have to deal with now.'

'And that makes it OK, then? He's nice to the sex workers so he gets a free pass?'

McLean stopped just by the front door, pulled up short by the vehemence in PC Harrison's tone. 'I'm not sure a bullet between the eyes is that much of a free pass, Constable.'

'Aye, but that wasn't us, was it?' She held his gaze perhaps a second too long, then dropped her head. 'I'm sorry, sir. Not my place to say.'

'No. You're right. And don't be scared to speak your mind. Not to me, at least. There's other officers in CID may not like it, but that's their problem. Come on.' McLean pushed open the door to a blast of ice-cold air from outside. PC Harrison stood in the hallway, mouth hanging slightly open, the door almost catching her off guard as it swung closed on a heavy spring. She leapt forward with surprising grace and agility, ending up perhaps closer to

McLean than was comfortable or appropriate. He stepped back reflexively, foot slipping on the ice-slick flagstone, and only saved himself from sprawling on his arse by grabbing the nearby railing. When he pulled his hand away again it was covered in something dark green and sticky.

'You OK, sir?' PC Harrison asked as McLean sniffed whatever it was that was coating the railings, wrinkling his nose at the meaty stench. A smear of something greenish-brown carried on up the outside wall of the building, too, some of it splattered on the door. He'd noticed it on the way in and thought it a well-aimed seagull dropping, but the sheer quantity and the smell of it suggested mischief rather than misadventure, canine rather than avian. He scraped what he could off his palm, then pulled out a clean handkerchief and wiped away the rest.

'Bloody kids throwing shit at the door. Reckon there's a story in that, but not ours to investigate.' He considered putting the handkerchief back in his pocket, then settled for just bunching it up in his soiled fist. There'd be a bin somewhere he could chuck it in, and one of the forensics vans would have antiseptic wipes. 'Come on, let's go and see if they've finished fetching our man down out of that tree.'

It wasn't far to walk back to the scene, and PC Harrison said nothing the whole way. McLean could see long before they arrived that the operation to safely extract the body was still underway. The cherry picker reached into the leafless canopy and a couple of men in hard hats and climbing harnesses were halfway up the tree itself. At least the pathologist had finished his inspection. McLean found him sitting on the passenger seat of his muddy green Jaguar, door open as he pulled off his white paper overalls. Far from his normal cheerful self, Cadwallader looked even paler than he had before, but he brightened a little when he saw them approach.

'Tony, I was wondering where you'd disappeared to. And who's this new friend you've made?'

'PC Harrison's been helping me interview the boy who found the body. Here, you haven't got any wipes in there, have you, Angus?' McLean held up his grubby hand. 'Touched something I don't really want to think too hard about.'

Cadwallader leaned into the car, came back with a pack of supermarket own-brand baby wipes. 'There you go. Got through a fair few myself. Poor chap didn't just bleed out up there. Branches have ruptured his guts, and more besides. Not going to be much fun doing the PM, I can tell you.'

McLean took one of the wipes and set about his hand with it, unsure whether the pungent synthetic lavender smell was any better than the dog-mess odour. He scrunched the whole lot up into a ball along with his soiled handkerchief, then looked around for somewhere to put it all.

'Here.' Cadwallader held up a small plastic bin and McLean dropped the lot in.

'So, what's the deal with our dead man, then?' he asked.

'He's dead. That much I can confirm. Superficial injuries are consistent with him being dropped into the tree canopy from a considerable height above. It's only bad luck that he didn't carry on straight through and end up on the path there.' Cadwallader nodded in the direction of the inflatable safety bag rolled out across the tarmac track.

'Any idea if it was the fall that killed him? Or was he already dead?'

'I'll have a better idea once I've had a chance to examine him somewhere I'm not in danger of imminent death myself. But given the amount of blood on the branches directly beneath him, I'd have to say it was the impact that killed him. That and being gutted by a broken stick.'

'Any idea who he is?'

'Not a clue. His face is pretty badly beaten up. They sent the crime-scene photographer up in that contraption of theirs after I'd finished, so I've no doubt someone'll put a name to the face soon. That's your department, though, Tony. Not mine.'

'Well, at least I won't ask you for a time of death. Not yet, anyway. If it was the fall that killed him, we've got a fairly good time for that already.'

'The boy?'

'If he's reliable, aye. Says he heard something crash into the trees when he was out walking his dog. Mind you, he also says he thought it was a dragon come to get him.'

'A dragon, you say?' Cadwallader raised a sceptical eyebrow. 'I'll be sure to keep that in mind when I'm examining him.'

'Think that's them bringing him down now, sir.'

McLean turned away from the pathologist, looking in the same direction as PC Harrison, up at the tree. Sure enough, the cherry picker had manoeuvred itself in under the body, a stretcher strapped to the box. The two climbers were in place, too, perched on branches McLean thought couldn't possibly support their weight. He had scrambled higher up trees without any ropes or heed for his safety when he'd been a boy, but watching them now gave him an uncomfortable sensation in the pit of his stomach.

When it came, the noise was like a rifle shot, echoing out across the Meadows. For a moment McLean thought that was what it was, and then the realization dawned. He saw a brief scramble as the operator in the cherry picker lunged for the stretcher. The two climbers sprang back, their training kicking in instinctively as the branch that had been holding up the body snapped.

It fell like a dead weight, rapid and ungainly, hit head-first into the inflated safety bag with a sound like a box of eggs dropped on a supermarket floor. For long moments there was only silence, underscored by the chuntering noise of the pump as it struggled to reinflate the bag. Then, with an audible creaking of joints, Cadwallader hauled himself to his feet and began pulling his soiled white overalls on again.

'Well, that's one way of doing it,' he said.

4

'What I want to know is how the fuck he got up there in the first place.'

McLean sat at the large table that dominated one end of Detective Superintendent Brooks' office, trying not to be distracted by the view out of the glass wall. The cold, still morning had turned into a bright day, a weak sun struggling to warm a sky of blue so pale it was almost grey. Behind the window it was pleasantly, almost soporifically warm, and the meeting so far hadn't been all that stimulating. There was something about the detective superintendent's tone that struck a nerve, though.

'Really, sir? That's your first thought? Not, who is this guy? Why was he killed? What message is this meant to send?'

'Now now, Tony. Those are all important questions, it's true. But you can't deny it's unusual to find a body high up in a tree like that.'

Sitting opposite him, face shaded by the sunlight streaming in behind his head, Deputy Chief Constable Steve 'Call-me-Stevie' Robinson made his usual half-hearted attempt at pouring oil on troubled waters.

'In some cultures, that's a standard method of disposal. Leave the cadaver out for the birds to pick at. Something about returning the body to nature once the soul's departed.' Acting Detective Inspector Kirsty Ritchie chimed in with an observation that was probably only slightly more useful than the deputy chief constable's. 'Not that I think that's what we're dealing with here,' she added, the hint of a smile playing across her lips.

'It's a bloody nightmare is what it is,' Brooks said. 'Closing the Meadows like that. We shut down the whole city for most of the morning. No way we can keep the details under wraps. Press are already sniffing around like dogs.'

'Why would we want to keep the details under wraps, sir?' McLean sat forward, finally committing himself to the meeting. 'The sooner we can get an ID on the victim, the sooner we can find out who killed him and why. The press can help us there, if we let them.'

'You'd know, of course, McLean. Heard you were like this now, you and that reporter Dalgliesh.' Sitting next to Brooks like a lovesick puppy, Detective Chief Inspector Mike Spence held up his right hand, index and middle fingers twisted together. McLean suppressed the urge to sigh; it was partly his fault Spence was DCI anyway. If he'd not been so reluctant to accept the post, then things might have been very different.

'You know what they say, Mike. Keep your friends close, but your enemies closer. Classically educated man like you, I'd have thought you'd know that.'

Spence twitched at the insult, notoriously prickly about his poor background and state schooling. McLean found it hard to care. The man could be a good detective when he put his mind to it, but these days he seemed to be interested only in criticizing all his colleagues. That and brown-nosing the higher-ups in search of promotion.

'Gentlemen, none of this is getting us any closer to

an answer. And Christ knows, we need one soon.' Brooks laid his pudgy hands out flat on the table like a couple of strings of badly made sausages. 'McLean. What's the situation with the crime scene? Forensics finished up, have they?'

'Apart from a small area at the end of Jawbone Walk, yes. Melville Drive's open again and the traffic's getting back to normal. We've not managed to identify the body yet. His face was badly battered before he fell out of the tree on to his head. Afterwards, well . . .' McLean left it hanging, much like the string of entrails ripped from the victim's belly that had been still up in the tree when he had left.

'And he was dropped there. From a good height? An airplane, perhaps, or a helicopter? Has anyone spoken to Air Traffic Control?'

'DS Laird's on it. We spoke to a potential witness, too, but I'm not sure he'll be much use to us. He's only ten, it was still dark, and he reckons it was a dragon coming for him and his dog.'

DCI Spence laughed, Brooks glowered, but the DCC sat a bit more upright. 'A dragon? How so?'

'He said he could hear its wings beating, which makes me think it was actually a helicopter, possibly with some kind of stealth technology. What the hell it was doing flying over the city in the dark I've no idea, but if it was throwing people out I doubt it would have bothered with flight plans.'

'Stealth technology? Isn't that a bit far-fetched?' DCI Spence asked.

'So we're going with the dragon, then?' McLean couldn't

help himself. 'I'll have Grumpy Bob stop by the zoo once he's finished talking to the control tower at the airport.'

'This is no joking matter, McLean. A man's dead, and in highly irregular circumstances. We've got a major enquiry on our hands. Last thing we need is you not taking the job seriously.' Unlike his boss Brooks, whose fat face tended to redden as he angered, blood draining from cheeks and forehead was a sure sign that Spence was about to lose his temper. The little tic about his left eye was another tell-tale. Both were clearly evident now.

'I'm deadly serious, Mike. Reckon we should probably call in some experts on dragons, too. I think Tolkien's dead, but I'm sure there's some other fantasy writers out there who'd be happy to help.'

The tic worsened, his left eye narrowing as if he were trying to suppress a cheeky wink. For a moment McLean thought Spence might be about to have a stroke, then the DCC cut in.

'You know the both of you are acting like schoolkids. No, Mike. You are. And Tony, you're not much better. I don't know what's going on between the two of you, but park it or I'll find a nice beat assignment for one or other of you over in Glasgow. Maybe even both of you.'

McLean kept his mouth shut, knowing better than to provoke Call-me-Stevie's wrath. Spence had clearly missed that particular lesson.

'Sir, do I need to point out that I am senior to Detective Inspector McLean? If he had any respect for the job, any respect for the chain of —'

'Oh, do shut up, Mike. It's not a pissing contest. You said it yourself, a man's dead. He seems to have been killed in a very messy and public way. That means we're going to have to work damned hard to solve this quickly and cleanly. If your ego can't cope with McLean being in charge, I suggest you go and make yourself useful elsewhere.'

Spence sat back in his chair as if he'd been slapped, but not before shooting a look at McLean that suggested trouble in the near future. For his own part, McLean was trying to work out what the DCC's angle was. He'd been played by Call-me-Stevie before, after all, and an innocent woman had died because of it.

'You want me heading up the investigation, sir?' he asked.

'Yes, McLean. I do. No point anyone else going over the same ground.' The DCC looked pointedly at Spence. 'And besides, this has a whiff of the strange about it. I believe that's your area of expertise.'

If McLean hadn't known the DCC had a rubbish poker face, he might have thought it was meant as a joke. However, the look Robinson gave him was one of pure sincerity.

'OK. But I'm going to get it in the neck when I get home.' McLean paused for a moment, savouring the unusual taste of those words in his mouth. It was a very long time since there had been something, or someone, worth hurrying home at the end of the day for. 'What about resources? We're stretched pretty thin as it is, what with Carter back in uniform, half the detective sergeants gone and Kirsty here getting the boot up to DI.'

'Acting DI.' Brooks laid heavy emphasis on the first word, cutting into the conversation before the DCC could respond. 'You can work with McLean on this one, Ritchie. You've got Grumpy Bob still, and DC Gregg. I'll see if we can't poach a couple of uniforms, too. There's been a few applications come across my desk recently.'

'Just keep an eye on the budget. We're all having to tighten our belts.' The DCC pushed his chair away from the table and stood up; meeting over on that happy note. McLean stood as well, keen to get out of the room before Spence started whining again.

'There was just one other thing, sir,' he said. 'Not sure if it's relevant to the case or just a coincidence. But the boy, the one who was there when the body fell into the trees, who thought it was a dragon.'

'What about him? Thought you said he wasn't exactly a reliable witness.'

'What he thinks he saw or heard isn't relevant, no, sir. But I was surprised when I found out he was Tommy Johnston's son.'

'Tommy Johnston? You sure?' The DCC shook his head. 'No, course you're sure. You wouldn't have said it otherwise. Bloody hell. I didn't even know he had a son.'

'Came as a surprise to me, too. But like I said, I don't think it's relevant. The boy's just ten, so he can't have known his dad. Just a weird coincidence.'

'Aye, well. I hope you're right, McLean. Last thing we need is that can of worms opened up again.'

The major incident room on the second floor had been rewired and given a lick of paint since last McLean had been in it. The carpet still bore the same stains, though, and the ceiling was missing a few acoustic tiles where extra network cables had been run. He had been expecting a bustle of noise and busyness, but when he pushed open the door there was hardly anyone about. A couple of technicians muttered under their breath as they fought to connect up a long line of elderly computers, and a lone detective constable was going from phone to phone, picking up the receiver and checking for a line. She turned as she heard the door open, smiled when she saw who had entered.

'Heard you were back, sir. Is it true we're hunting down dragons now?'

Once again, McLean was amazed at the speed with which gossip could spread across the city's police force, although, on reflection, if anyone was going to know exactly what was happening when, where and with whom, then it would be DC Sandra Gregg. Once she started talking it was often difficult to get her to stop, but somehow she managed to be a good listener at the same time. It was a powerful combination in the interrogation room. He'd watched many a hardened criminal crumble under the onslaught of words, saying anything just to get the mindless chatter to stop, then finding themselves trapped by their own desperation.

'Thought there might be a few more bodies in here. Grumpy Bob not back from the airport yet?'

'Don't think he's even been, sir. Said he had to phone and make an appointment. Last I heard, he was negotiating with the duty sergeant over staffing. You know as well as I do how thin we're all spread.'

'Aye, well. I work best with a small team.'

'There's small and there's ridiculous, sir.' Gregg made a

slow pirouette, taking in the whole of the room. 'How are we meant to get anything done? We should be collating all the crime scene reports, going over the interviews, speaking to next of kin.'

'Slow down a bit, Constable. We don't even have an ID on the dead man yet.' McLean held his hands up as if Gregg were running towards him and needed warding off. Then a worrying thought occurred to him. 'We don't have an ID, do we?'

'Not that I've heard yet, sir. But a man's dead.'

He checked his watch. Past lunchtime, but not by much. 'Yes, a man is dead. And by our best reckoning he died sometime between half five and six this morning, so only about nine hours ago. There were no witnesses as such. Nothing more we can do until we've got an ID at the very least. So instead of fretting about the reports and checking the phones, why don't you chase up the crime scene photographer and see if we can't find some decent mug shots? Get an artist's impression drawn up, though; he was too badly injured to release a photo to the public. Especially after he fell out of the tree.'

'He fell?' So there was a bit of gossip Gregg hadn't picked up on.

'On his head, yes. There was a safety airbag underneath, but it was still messy. Not much in the way of identifying features left, apparently.'

Gregg went pale, what was going on in her imagination writ large across her face. McLean struggled to think of something to distract her, but was interrupted by his phone before he could come up with anything. A simple text message flickered across the screen, and he thumbed it away before slipping the handpiece back into his jacket pocket.

'That's Angus. He's scheduled the post mortem for an hour's time. Apparently, being dropped out of the sky by a dragon gets you bumped up the queue.'

'You heading over there then, sir?'

McLean looked around the incident room, slowly coming to life as more officers filtered in. 'You know me, can't keep away from the place. It shouldn't take long, though. Meantime, have a word with Sergeant Hwei, set up a press conference for teatime. God help us, but we're going to need their help on this one.'

5

The walk to the city mortuary was one McLean had made far too often in his career. Not many detectives attended post mortems any more; you could get all the information you needed from the report usually, and it wasn't exactly the most pleasant of experiences, watching the dead being opened up. Bad enough to have been killed, in an accident, by a jealous partner, in a blind rage or, more infrequently, in a cold and calculated execution; worse still to have all your most personal secrets revealed by the pathologist's knife. And yet he couldn't help but believe he owed it to these people. He was charged with finding the truth of what had happened to them, however extraordinary or banal. Not to witness their final examination in person felt like a betrayal.

His grandmother had been a pathologist, too. That helped. The smells of the mortuary didn't turn his stomach in the same way they did those of other detectives. Sometimes he even found comfort in the whiff of formalin, the tang of antiseptic and the butcher's shop dead-meat stench. They reminded him of childhood, in a slightly macabre way. Not that he would ever admit that to anyone. Not even his old friend Angus Cadwallader.

'Good of you to come, Tony.' The pathologist greeted him with a cheerier smile than he had managed early that morning. He was all togged up in his scrubs when the inspector arrived, and for once didn't bother with the small talk. 'Just waiting for Tom to come back from the loo and we can get started.'

As if on cue, the door to the examination theatre swung open and Dr Tom MacPhail came in. 'Tony.' He nodded a greeting, then hauled himself on to a small stool set up by the X-ray viewing light boxes on the back wall, ready to observe his boss at work and corroborate any findings.

'Subject is male, Caucasian, approximately 170 to 180 centimetres tall. Impossible to give an exact height due to damage caused to the skull by a post-mortem fall from a tree.' Cadwallader worked his way around the body, poking and prodding and peering close at times, speaking to the microphone that hung above the examination table. His assistant, Dr Sharp, stood close by, but not so close as to get in the way. She seemed to know exactly when to hand over each shiny steel instrument of torture or hold up a dish for some removed organ to be placed into. No need for words as they danced around each other like lovers. McLean found himself fascinated by the performance, barely paying attention to the examination itself, or the mess of the dead man's injuries. It wasn't until the pathologist stopped mid-sentence and bent down to the body again that he was pulled back into the reality of the situation.

'Ah, now that is interesting.'

'Interesting?' McLean took a step forward, then stopped, unwilling to get too close.

'Poor fellow suffered some horrible damage when he hit the tree. He's got multiple lacerations from broken

31

branches. They really ripped him up. I've seen less damage from car crashes.'

'Is that what killed him?'

Cadwallader gave McLean a toothy grin. 'Technically, I'd go with massive blood loss but, effectively, yes. He's got at least two large punctures in his abdomen. The shock of hitting the branches might have killed him, but if it didn't he would have bled out in seconds anyway. That's not what's interesting, though. Well, not from your point of view, I don't think.'

'What have you got, then?'

'Two things, really. Come here.' Cadwallader beckoned McLean forward, and he reluctantly complied. Closer up, it was easy to see the extent of the damage inflicted on the body. Enough to make him glad he'd missed lunch.

'What am I looking at?'

'There's a couple of tattoos. Here and here.' Cadwallader lifted a shattered arm and pointed to some dark swirls on the shoulder, then traced his finger across to the opposite chest, where more markings showed through the mess, broken up by rips in the flesh. 'We'll get them cleaned up and photographed. Might help in identification.'

McLean tried to get a better look without stepping any closer to the body, but the markings on the dead man's skin were too indistinct. 'Was that the two things, or just one?'

'You know me too well, Tony. No, the tattoos were just one thing. The other is more puzzling. See here?' Cadwallader pointed to the man's sides. Unlike his arms and the front of his body, which were ripped and torn as if he had been set upon by a plague of hungry rats, his sides were only lightly scratched. Dark bruises mottled the pale skin, tingeing yellow at the edges.

'These bruises are from something that happened to him before he died. Not long before, but at least a few minutes. Maybe half an hour. I'd say he'd been lying on the ground and been given a good kicking. Seen plenty of bodies with bruising like that. Too many, really.'

'I can sense a but coming.' McLean tilted his head sideways, the better to see what the pathologist was talking about. If he squinted, he could see a regular pattern to the bruises, not the amorphous mess more normally associated with a punishment beating.

'Sadly, yes.' Cadwallader leaned in close, pointing with his gore-smeared gloved hand. 'There are distinct areas of discolouration, and the bruising is very uniform. It's more like a ligature mark than an impact.'

'You think he was tied up?'

'Something like that, though it's quite extensive for rope. More like he's been crushed in something. Oh, and he shat himself.'

McLean looked up sharply, expecting a cheeky grin on Cadwallader's face and not being disappointed. '"Shat"? Is that a technical term?'

'Not really, and it's not unusual when someone's terrified. Bowel sphincter loosens, stomach muscles contract and out it all comes.'

'Charming,' McLean said, but the image sparked a memory and he found himself looking at his hand. 'The waste bag in your car, Angus. Where you chuck all your used overalls and gloves. You emptied that recently?'

Cadwallader stared at him, bemused, then over to his

assistant. 'Tracy?' he asked, hopefully. Her shrug suggested the bag was probably still there.

'I can go and check,' she said. 'Why?'

'My handkerchief. I used it to wipe something foul off my hand. It splattered on a tenement door in Marchmont Crescent, where the little boy who found this bloke lived. Thought it was local kids playing pranks with dog mess, but what if it was the victim's?'

'I was beginning to worry you'd not got the memo, sir. Can't have a press conference without the chief investigating officer present.'

McLean tried to give DC Gregg a reassuring smile, but his heart wasn't really in it. He'd gone back to the crime scene after witnessing the post mortem, hoping to find inspiration in the long walk from the Cowgate to the Meadows. Nothing had come of it except a long list of questions that wouldn't be answered easily. Even more frustrating was the discovery that some helpful person had cleaned the muck from the tenement door, wall and railings. He'd need to find out if there had been a history of such vandalism in the area. It might simply have been a coincidence, same as it was probably a coincidence that the dead body had been found by Tommy Johnston's son. He didn't really believe in coincidences, though.

'Everything set to go, then?'

'Aye, we're on at half four. That should give them plenty of time to get stuff out on the six o'clock news.' Gregg produced a sheet of paper, fresh from the colour printer, and handed it over. 'We've just got this through, too. I'm running off enough copies for everyone.'

McLean took the sheet and looked at the picture. Artist's impressions were always a bit hit and miss, and this time there hadn't been much in the way of detail to work with. He stared at the face of a late-middle-aged man, with short greying hair and featureless eyes. It could have been anyone's dad, somewhere in that indeterminate decade between mid-fifties and mid-sixties. Bulky around the cheeks and chin. The artist had given up with the nose. Understandable, since falling into the tree canopy hadn't left much to work with.

'Ring any bells?' Gregg asked, and the more McLean stared at it the more he felt that perhaps the image did. This wasn't some random stranger but someone he had met. Had shaken hands with and looked in the eye.

'I've a horrible feeling he might have been one of us once.'

'One of us?' Gregg asked.

'A copper. Possibly even plain clothes, but before your time.' McLean tilted the page back and forth, struggling for the memory. Then it came to him, a spreading sensation of cold in the pit of his stomach. 'Oh fuck –'

'They're all ready and waiting, sir.' Sergeant Dan Hwei, the station's senior press liaison officer, popped his head around the door to the conference room, interrupting McLean as he stared at the picture with horrified fascination.

'What? Oh. Right.' McLean handed the page to DC Gregg, not quite ready to share his suspicion with the rest of the world. 'Get on to the labs, will you? See if they can't prioritize the DNA screening. I've a horrible feeling I know who this is, and I really want someone to prove me wrong.'

*

Something about a room filled with journalists always brought a chill to McLean's heart. He understood the need for reporters, at least on an intellectual level, but faced with the reality of a mass of them congregated in one place, his first instinct was to run, his second to hide. It was childish, really, but then so was the behaviour of Brooks, Spence and Robinson, none of whom had deigned to turn up to the press conference. Ritchie and McIntyre at least had an excuse, having been called to HQ, but that didn't make the lack of support any easier to deal with. Beside him there was only Sergeant Hwei and a couple of uniform constables who had strayed into the wrong room by mistake. Even Grumpy Bob had found somewhere else to be, but then that was his particular skill.

'OK, then. I guess we'd better get things started.' McLean cast his eyes over the assembled crowd, looking for familiar faces. He wasn't sure he recognized anyone at all, the only unifying theme being that most of them were too young to have been out of school long.

'As you're no doubt aware, we had to close Melville Drive, the A700 Meadows road, this morning, following the discovery of a body.'

'Is it true the body was found in the top of a tree?' The first interruption of the press conference came from a male reporter at the front of the room sporting the most ridiculous beard McLean had ever seen.

'If you'll let me finish, I'll take questions at the end. Now, where was I? Oh, yes. We had to close the A700 for a period of seven hours this morning, following the discovery of a man's body. And yes, it was lodged high in the branches of a tree, overhanging Jawbone Walk. As I'm sure you're all aware already. The body has been retrieved and an initial post mortem carried out. Obviously, given the nature of the discovery, we're treating this death as very suspicious.'

'Who is it, Inspector? Whose body?'

This time the question came from further back in the room, a woman's voice that McLean thought he might have recognized. The sea of faces yielded no clues. It suggested that none of them knew the victim's identity either, which was some small relief. That cold dread hung heavy in his stomach, the implications of who he thought the dead man might be still percolating through his mind. Perhaps best he kept it to himself, at least for now. He could always be wrong, after all.

'We haven't identified the victim as yet. Due to the nature of his injuries and the difficulty of retrieving him, his face has been badly damaged. Well, if I'm being honest, all of him has been badly damaged. We've put together a basic description, and there should be an artist's impression in your press packs.'

'How did he get in the tree?'

This voice McLean did recognize. Looking to the back of the room, he saw the familiar leather-coated figure of Jo Dalgliesh grinning at him like a cadaver. Her near-death experience after eating a couple of slices of poisoned cake had left her even thinner than before, the bones of her skull threatening to force themselves through the ruddy, chapped skin of her face. The shock had turned her straggly hair grey and, in response, she'd hacked it brutally short. He was under no illusions that she'd paid a hairdresser for the shearing; more likely a lonely shepherd.

'That is one of the questions we'd like to answer, Ms Dalgliesh. But since the first officer only arrived on scene around half five this morning and it's . . .' McLean checked his watch '. . . not gone five in the afternoon yet, I think we're doing well to have recovered the body, reopened Melville Drive and done the initial post mortem. Don't you?'

Dalgliesh didn't answer, but the predatory smile she gave him was not reassuring.

'Is there a danger to the city, Inspector? Do you think there'll be more killings?'

'More killings? Is one not enough?' Sergeant Hwei answered the question before McLean could get a word in.

'Gentleman, ladies. Let's not jump to conclusions when we've so few facts to play with. I'll grant you, this is a very unusual case, and I can assure you we're exploring every avenue at the moment. Wild speculation isn't going to help us here, though. We need to gather the facts before coming to conclusions. I think it's safe to assume the skies aren't about to start raining down dead bodies on us.'

A smattering of nervous laughter spread across the room, dying away no sooner than it had begun. McLean couldn't blame them; he was almost as much in the dark about the situation as the collected reporters. Who was to say that there wouldn't be more bodies falling from the sky? And what if they hit something other than a dormant tree in the middle of a wide, open space in the wee small hours? He could just imagine the chaos if a corpse smashed into the roof of a car on the Lothian Road during rush hour.

'Any more questions, please see Sergeant Hwei. And

please, if anyone has any information they think might be useful in our investigation, do share it. That's why you're all here, to be honest. We need to identify this man, find out how he came to be where we found him. Then we can worry about why he died and who was responsible.'

McLean sat down hard, hiding behind his papers and the row of microphones on the table in front of him. He knew that such candour was frowned upon; best to keep the press in the dark as much as possible, that was what the senior officers always said. But the senior officers hadn't bothered showing up, and these people could help him, help the investigation. And if they wanted to make life difficult, they'd do it regardless of anything he did or didn't say.

6

'You got a moment, Tony?'

McLean thought all the reporters had left. He'd watched them file out of the conference room after the questions had dried up, disappointed faces occasionally looking up at him as they passed, in the hope he might have some little exclusive crumb for them to appease their editor with. He kept his own suspicion to himself, still processing the implications of him being right. No point falling down that rabbit hole if it turned out to be a bad hunch, though lately his luck hadn't been so good. He looked up from the report he'd been reading, knowing full well who would be standing there. He'd known Jo Dalgliesh more than fifteen years now. Hated her for most of that time, although that loathing had muted with the years. Too much effort, and too much shared experience.

'If you're hoping I held back some tasty nugget of information just for you, I'm afraid you're going to be disappointed.' Of all the reporters he might have shared his thoughts with, Dalgliesh was perhaps the most likely, but he wasn't that desperate yet. McLean folded the report closed with a weary sigh. It hadn't been exactly the most stimulating read, anyway.

'Ah, there, and I thought we had something going. A special relationship.' Dalgliesh pulled an electronic cigarette the size of a Cuban cigar out of her pocket and shoved it in her mouth. McLean was about to point out that she couldn't smoke inside, even if it wasn't really smoke she was inhaling, but she hadn't switched the thing on. After a couple of seconds of frantic chewing, she pulled it out of her mouth again.

'Trying to quit?' he asked.

'Doctor's orders. Bastard. I tell you. A month in hospital almost killed me. Not going in one of those places again.'

McLean studied the journalist a little more closely than before. She had always looked like something that had been preserved in a peat bog for thousands of years, skin leathery from exposure to the cold climate of the north-east and cured by the smoke of an endless stream of cigarettes. Some of the less caring officers had joked that it was hard to tell where she ended and her ancient leather overcoat began, and for a while he had laughed along with them. She'd dug the knife into him plenty of times, after all, and made public the sordid, terrible details of his fiancée's final hours simply to make some money selling books. But at the end of the day she was a human being and, loath though he was to admit it, not a bad investigative journalist when she put her mind to it. And there was the small matter of that time she had saved his life when he'd been faced with a crazed serial killer. He had to give her that much.

'You're back at work, though. So it can't be all bad, aye?'

Dalgliesh coughed so hard her whole frame shook, and for a moment McLean thought she was going to hawk and spit on the conference room floor. Instead, she thumped her chest a few times to dislodge whatever was left of her lungs in there, swallowed hard and gasped for air.

'Rent's got to be paid. And anyway, sitting on my arse all day's no fun. Much better seeing what you're up to. Which brings me to your body in the trees. You really got no ID on him yet?'

McLean shook his head, feeling the tips of his ears heat up at the half-lie. 'Why? You think you know who he is?'

'Mebbe.' Dalgliesh narrowed her eyes. 'Then again, how do I know youse lot aren't just covering it all up?'

'Covering what up? It's not like we can pretend we didn't find a body in a tree on the Meadows this morning.'

'Aye, well. There is that.' Dalgliesh picked at her fingernails. 'An' I've seen the pictures. No' exactly much left of his face. Still, it's getting so's I don't know who I can trust these days.'

'Trust?' McLean raised an eyebrow. Dalgliesh was notoriously paranoid, but this was a bit much even for her.

'Poisoned, remember?' The reporter pointed a finger at herself. 'And the stuff I've been looking into recently? Let's just say, you'll no' find me in the phone book any more.'

'So who do you think it is, then? Our mysterious man in the trees?'

Dalgliesh peered at him, a glint in her sunken eyes that reminded him of his old adversary. 'You reckon you know anyway, don't you?'

'I've a suspicion.' McLean held up his hands in a gesture of surrender as Dalgliesh's scowl deepened. 'Only since I saw the artist's impression we handed out at the press conference. That's all we've got to go on until the DNA comes back. The pathologist might have been able to put the face back together enough for a likeness, but getting him out of the tree didn't exactly go to plan.'

'Aye, I heard youse lot dropped him on his head.'

'Angus said the skull was already fractured, which would explain why it went the way it did when he landed on the airbag.' McLean tried not to remember the sound the body had made as it hit the inflated canvas. Failed.

Dalgliesh fished around in her bag until she came out with a folded sheet of paper. She went to hand it over, then stopped.

'You're no' going to ask me how I got this, are you?'

'Know how you got what?' McLean snatched the paper from her before she could react. That was the most telling thing, he realized. The old Dalgliesh, before the poison had almost killed her, would never have let him take something from her without a fight. Now she just stared at him with a look on her face that was part disbelief, part resignation. He unfolded the sheet, revealing a photograph he recognized as coming from the crime scene. Dalgliesh had sources everywhere, after all. It showed a close-up of the dead man's face, battered and torn so as to be almost unrecognizable as human.

'Don't imagine many folk would see this, but then there's not many know him as well as I do.' Dalgliesh carried on guddling around in her bag as she spoke, finally producing a battered old iPad, which she poked and prodded into life with fingers that shook more than perhaps they should. The screen was thick with greasy prints but, after a few moments of swiping and pinching, she held it up for McLean to see. The photograph was surprisingly clear, a paparazzi shot of a man's head and shoulders as he stepped out of some building or other. Probably a restaurant, if the glass reflection behind him was anything to go by. McLean recognized him; there weren't many police-men his age who wouldn't, although, depressingly, many of the newer intake might not know him.

'Bill Chalmers.' McLean took the iPad from Dalgliesh, laid it down beside the printed sheet. He didn't really need to see the face any more. 'What makes you think it's him?'

'That not who you thought it was?' Dalgliesh nodded at the photographs.

McLean looked from one picture to the next, seeing absolutely nothing in them to suggest they were the same person beyond the fact that both were male and had short-cropped salt-and-pepper hair. And piercing blue eyes – or at least one eye that had survived the fall. And a particular set to the jaw. And a shape to the ear. 'Aye, it was. But why? Who'd want to kill him? And why so obviously?'

'Kind of think that's your job, is it no'?' Dalgliesh shrugged. 'And before youse ask, I called his office and nobody's seen him in the last twenty-four hours. He lives alone, but he's no' answering his doorbell either.'

McLean stared at the photographs, side by side. Ration-ally, it was almost impossible to say whether they were of the same man, but the more he looked the more similar-ities he saw. Many thoughts ran through his mind; how, why and who would do such a thing. But chief among them was a formless feeling of dread, accompanied by a cold weight in the pit of his stomach, as if he'd just swal-lowed a bag of ice. Nothing was ever straightforward where sudden death was concerned, but this had all the hallmarks of a nightmare in the making.

'You spoken to anyone else about this?' he asked.

'Do I look like a rookie to youse?'

'Well, do me a favour, will you? Keep it under wraps for now. Least until we get it confirmed by DNA.'

'What? So you can get your cover-up sorted?' Dalgliesh snorted in disbelief. 'An' what's in it for me?'

'I don't suppose the undying gratitude of Police Scotland Specialist Crime Division's going to be enough?'

'Undying gratitude? That pays the bills, aye?'

'OK, OK. You'll get confirmation before anyone else. Christ, what a mess. Bill bloody Chalmers. You know what that means, right?'

Dalgliesh's answer was confined to a single raised eyebrow as she gently took back her iPad, leaving McLean with the crime scene photograph.

'It means I'm going to have to ruin the DCC's plans for the evening.'

The lower levels of the police station where McLean worked were all that remained of a much older building, demolished in the 1970s to make way for the unlovely concrete block that now rose above the street. The air temperature never seemed to change down here, which made it a welcome retreat in the rare hot weeks of summer, but less pleasant when it was frosty outside. The Cold Case Unit he had briefly been in charge of had its main office in a room that must once have been a storage vault, which was fitting, since most of the time it was piled high with dusty archive boxes. Most of the time it was empty, too, a victim of the staffing cutbacks and a lack of enthusiasm for digging over old ground. It was still a good bet that you would find retired Detective Superintendent

Charles Duguid there three days a week, though. And today was one of those days.

'Wonders never cease. Thought you'd given up on us for good.' Duguid looked up from a desk strewn with piles of papers, the mess almost as chaotic as McLean's office two storeys up. Only these files were long past being urgent, unlike the overtime sheets and crime scene reports that multiplied day by day on his desk.

'Wasn't sure you'd still be here.' McLean looked at his watch and wondered whether he shouldn't be somewhere else, too. Somewhere warm, and with pleasant company.

'Aye, well. Mrs Duguid's away on some junket with the Guiders and I don't much fancy rattling around at home.' Duguid sat up in his seat, flexed his shoulders and stretched. 'Guessing you didn't come down here just for a wee chat, mind.'

'Things aren't that bad. Least, not yet, anyway.' McLean paused. There was no good way to ease into this conversation. Might as well hold his nose and jump straight in. 'You knew Bill Chalmers, back when he was in the force, right?'

Duguid's face darkened. He leaned forward, elbows pushing aside the papers on his desk, overlong fingers interlocked as he jammed his hands in under his chin. The scowl on his face said it all.

'Chalmers. Aye. We both came through training together. Why? What's the wee eejut got himself caught up in now?'

'You'll have heard about the body in the tree. Over on the Meadows.'

Duguid nodded his head, the scowl easing a little.

'Well, I've a horrible suspicion it might be him. Chalmers.' McLean held out the photo of the dead man, taken

46

while he was still in the tree. Before gravity had done its best to make visual identification impossible.

'The fuck?' Duguid was on his feet far more quickly than should have been possible for a man of his age. His chair rocked alarmingly, its back smacking into the wall and sending a precariously piled stack of reports toppling.

'Not confirmed yet. But the more I look at this, the more I reckon he's our man.' McLean paused a moment before adding: 'You know if he had any tattoos?'

Duguid's scowl deepened, the skin of his temple twitching. 'Why the fuck do you think I'd know a thing like that?'

'Just asking. It's something that came up in the post mortem.' McLean held up his hands as if the retired detective superintendent had a gun on him, which at least seemed to calm Duguid down.

'Jesus Christ. You're a bloody bad news magnet, aren't you?' He pulled his chair back from the wall, tumbling yet more reports, and slumped into it, reaching out to snatch the picture from McLean. 'Bill fucking Chalmers. Dead. Fuck me, that's going to upset the apple cart.'

Duguid searched around the mess of his desktop until he found a pair of spectacles, shoved them on to his nose and peered closely at the picture. Then he reached for the desk lamp, dragged it over and switched it on.

'Looks like he took a hell of a beating, whoever he is.'

'Best guess is he was thrown out of a helicopter. Just lucky he landed in a tree and not on the road.'

'Lucky?'

'OK, poor choice of words, but you know what I mean. If he'd hit solid ground, we'd be mopping him up with sponges and it'd take months to ID him.'

'Not if it really is Chalmers.' Duguid put the picture down, ran a massive hand over his thinning grey hair before rubbing at his eyes and dislodging his spectacles in the process.

'How so?'

'You'll have sent a sample off for DNA testing already, I assume. Chalmers will be in the database, just like every other Saughton inmate. Shouldn't be hard to match him.' Duguid tapped the page with a heavy forefinger. 'It's him, though. I'll give you good odds.'

'Aye, that's what I thought, too.'

'So why'd you bring this to me, then? I mean, it's not exactly a cold case, is it? The man was jabbering on about his charity on the news just a couple of nights ago.'

McLean leaned against one of the other desks in the room. 'I guess I just wanted a second opinion. You know, before I go to the DCC with that.' He nodded at the photograph.

'And you can't wait for the DNA? Case like this, they'll turn it around in twenty-four hours. I've seen the way you sweet talk the forensics girls. You'd probably get it quicker than that even.'

'No.' McLean shook his head. 'Dalgliesh has seen this, so others will have, too. You know what coppers are like. The older sergeants will be rubbernecking even if they're not on this case. Won't be long before a few more start to recognize him, start letting their chums in the press know. Only a matter of time before it goes public.' He pushed himself up from the desk, snatched up the photograph and folded it into his pocket. 'I'm only putting off the inevitable. Probably best if he hears it from me rather than some gossip website.'

Duguid looked at him with an expression McLean couldn't quite read. He held the gaze for a moment, then picked up the nearest report and went back to reading it without a word. Knowing when he was dismissed, McLean turned and left the room, confused more than anything else. Retirement and the chance to work on old cases had mellowed the detective superintendent somewhat, but it was still hard to forget the decades of animosity between the two of them. So it was with some surprise he realized that what Duguid had been showing him was sympathy.

7

'Bloody hell. Must be something important if you felt you had to come all the way over here to tell me in person. Come in, Tony.'

The deputy chief constable beckoned McLean into his office, pulling the door closed behind him. The last time he'd been in here, McLean had been covered in blood, traumatized by the death of a young woman. The DCC had protected him from the fallout of that tragedy; by all accounts, McLean should probably have been fired. But he had also made him complicit in something much darker, dragged McLean part way into something that wasn't so much a conspiracy as a network of favours owed and blind eyes turned that had grown so complex as to be almost sentient. Three months' suspension while the story went away hadn't been nearly enough to process the implications of that, and now here he was, straight back in at the weird end.

'It's the body we found in the tree this morning, sir. Think we might have an ID.'

'Come now, Tony. No need for this "sir" nonsense. Call me Stevie.' The DCC pointed to a chair on one side of the wide, polished desk. McLean stayed standing.

'I'm not sure I can, sir.'

'Suit yourself.' Call-me-Stevie shrugged, then dropped into his own chair on the far side of the desk. 'So you've got an ID, but you didn't want to tell me on the phone and it couldn't wait until tomorrow morning's briefing. I'm intrigued. Who could possibly warrant such unusual procedure?'

'Bill Chalmers, sir. And I've a suspicion it'll be all over tomorrow's press, so I thought everyone needed to be prepared.'

The DCC said nothing, and for a moment McLean thought he might already know. And then, slowly, the full import of what he had said began to slide over Call-me-Stevie's features.

'Chalmers? Dear God. Are you sure?'

'I've asked the mortuary to fast-track the DNA sample and cross-check it against what we've got on the database. We should have a definite answer first thing tomorrow. For now, it's just someone thinking they recognize him from the crime scene photos, and the fact that nobody knows where he is.'

'And you think the press are going to go with it anyway?'

'You know what they're like. It was Jo Dalgliesh who suggested that was who the dead man might be. The more I look at the photographs, the more I'm inclined to agree. She can't be the only journalist to have made the connection.'

'And you think they'll run with it tomorrow, even if it's not confirmed?' The DCC leaned forward to where an expensive-looking laptop sat on his desk, tapped his fingers on the desktop beside it.

'I'd be very surprised if it wasn't already doing the rounds on social media. Nobody waits for the print press these days.'

The DCC paused for a moment, a frown creasing his forehead as he stared at the laptop. Then he shook his head, closed the machine and stood up. 'I'll make some calls. There's people who need to be warned and a hell of a lot of prep work to do. We'll have a briefing at six tomorrow morning.' He gave McLean a hopeless smile. 'Too much to hope it's not him, I suppose.'

'My grandmother always told me to hope for the best and prepare for the worst. Stood me well so far, sir.'

'She was wise, your grandmother. Didn't think much of Bill Chalmers either. And that was before his little problem came to light.' The DCC picked up the laptop and shoved it under his arm, shuffling around the desk to leave. Clearly the meeting was over. McLean crossed the room and opened the door.

'I'll double check on those DNA results. Make sure we can say definitely that it's him tomorrow. Or that it isn't.'

'You do that.' The DCC strode out like a man used to having underlings open doors for him, then stopped mid-stride. 'Oh, and Tony?'

'Sir?'

'Thanks for bringing this to me first. I appreciate the forewarning. Chalmers . . . well, he destroyed the careers of many fine officers, but he'd gone a long way to making up for that with his charity work. This isn't going to be an easy case to manage from a public relations point of view. Looks like some interesting times up ahead.'

Darkness enveloped the front of the house as McLean pulled up the driveway, parking next to the back door beside Emma's battered old rust-brown and blue Peugeot.

He was still buzzing slightly from the late evening meeting with the DCC and hardly noticed that the kitchen light was off until he reached for the switch. Mrs McCutcheon's cat blinked at him from the middle of the table, her head bobbing gently as she tasted the air to make sure it was him.

'Just you and me again, eh?' He glanced up at the clock, surprised to see that it was past ten already. Given how early he'd left that morning, he should have been more tired. Instead, he had a restless need to move around. No, to get out there and start asking questions – that was what he really wanted to be doing.

He pulled out his phone, checked the screen for messages. Nothing. Hardly surprising, really; he'd only spoken to Amanda Parsons at the forensics labs a couple of hours earlier. She was a miracle worker, true, and she'd promised to get the sample from the mortuary sequenced for DNA matching as quickly as possible. But it would still take time to compare it with Chalmers' records. First thing in the morning they'd know for certain. Until then he could only speculate; no point heading off on that path until they knew.

Frustrated, McLean opened the fridge in search of something to eat. There was food aplenty: leftovers from past meals; an assortment of cheeses; salad; vegetables. Over on the counter, fresh fruit piled high in a polished wooden bowl he'd given his grandmother for her birthday ten years ago. Beside it, the bread bin would doubtless contain a freshly baked seed loaf or sourdough. All good, healthy stuff, and a welcome change from the reheated curry or cold pizza that had been his diet for too long. He pulled out the last bottle of beer, found a clean glass on the draining board where he'd left it the night before, poured the one into the other and slumped down in a chair. All the while, Mrs McCutcheon's cat stared at him with her shiny black eyes.

'Gone to bed early again, has she?' He reached out and scratched the cat behind her ears. She rewarded him with a deep, rumbling purr, something she had only started doing recently. Possibly because there was someone else around to make sure her food bowl was kept filled.

Taking a long sip of his beer, McLean looked at his phone again. Still no confirmation from Forensics. Damn, but it was going to be hard getting to sleep with that question still hanging. He thumbed the screen until it brought up a news feed, scanned it for stories about the body found on the Meadows. There was plenty about the traffic chaos caused by closing one of the city's main arteries for half the day, a bit about the discovery of the body, even some lurid speculation as to how it might have ended up high in the branches of a tree. How the hell *had* the body got up there? Dropped, clearly, but why? There had to be easier ways to kill a man. Unless it was a freak accident. But then someone would have come forward, surely.

'Thought I heard noise. Long old day, then.'

McLean looked around to the kitchen door, where a pale-faced Emma Baird leaned against the frame. Her long hair was tangled and askew, as if she had slept on it awhile, and she wore a mismatched set of jogging pants and hoodie that looked like they might have been stolen from a teenager. She stretched like an arthritic cat, yawned and then padded across to the table on bare feet. She wrapped McLean in a warm hug and planted a kiss on the top of his head before recoiling in mock horror.

'You smell like a police station. Go take a shower.'

'In a while. Just need to get my head straight first.'

'And beer helps?' Emma nodded at the glass. 'When was the last time you ate something? You know, actual food?'

McLean frowned, not really quite sure. There'd been some biscuits with his coffee in the morning, and he'd probably had some lunch at some point, though he couldn't exactly remember what or when.

'You're hopeless, you know, Tony McLean?' Emma went to the fridge and pulled a few things out, fetched bread, a plate, a knife. Soon she was busy making cheese sandwiches. McLean's stomach grumbled in anticipation. Maybe he'd missed lunch after all.

'How was your day?' he asked through a mouthful of sourdough and Brie, peppered up with something green he suspected might be rocket.

'Busy enough. Dusted down a couple of burglary scenes, photographed some broken glass. You know, glamorous stuff. Mostly, it's filling in bloody forms. And I thought it was bad before they hived off half the forensics jobs to private industry.'

McLean smiled, which probably wasn't the right response. It was good to hear someone else's woes for a change though, and Emma had been put through enough hoops just to get her old job back.

'Likely to be pulling a few long days for a stretch. This is a weird case, and you know how they can end up.'

Emma sat down opposite him, pushing her hair out of

her eyes as she did so. When first they had met it had been short, spiky and black as the night. Now it hung past her shoulders in a great, tangled swoop, streaked with grey despite her youthfulness.

'Well, maybe I'll be able to help out with that. I finally got signed off on the retraining, even though I've not learned anything I didn't already know. Should be letting me loose on the more serious stuff next week.'

'That's great news, Em.'

'Aye, well. It's not the same as it was. Still can't get my head around the extra admin. I mean, I thought it was the public sector who were meant to be all about red tape, but this new lot monitor everything. You need a work recording code to go and have a pee.'

'You don't have to work for them, you know.' McLean found it hard to wipe the smile off his face for some reason. 'Don't have to work at all if you don't want to.'

'It's no' so bad, really. Just used to doing things my own way, I guess. And I can't be a kept woman all my life.' Emma yawned again, then rubbed at her forehead, shoved the heel of her hand into one eye socket with a grimace.

'You OK?' McLean asked, aware that it was a stupid question even as he said it.

'Ach, it'll pass. Stupid headache. Probably should have got out for a bit of fresh air today rather than staring at a computer screen.' Emma swept hair out of her eyes and looked straight at him. 'You going to be long with that sandwich?'

McLean shoved the last bite into his mouth, savouring the salty goodness of the cheese, washed it down with the last of his pint of beer. 'All done.' He suppressed the belch that until a few months earlier he wouldn't have thought twice about sharing with the kitchen. 'Thanks.'

'In which case, come with me.' Emma stood up, reached across the table and took McLean's hand, dragging him towards the door. 'Time to wash that police station stench off of you.'

8

'. . . unconfirmed reports that the body discovered on the Meadows yesterday is noted philanthropist and recovered drug addict Bill Chalmers. Mr Chalmers, founder of the drug rehabilitation charity Morningstar and campaigner for drug-law reform, could not be contacted . . .'

McLean switched off the radio as he pulled his car into a narrow space between two riot vans, reasonably confident that neither of them would be going anywhere that morning. One of the few benefits of driving the Alfa was that its 1960s styling meant it could fit in spaces most modern cars wouldn't even look at, but he still felt a twist of unease in his gut every time he left it parked somewhere. Quite why he'd not bought himself a new car during his three months off McLean couldn't really say either, but now they had started salting the roads in earnest again he was beginning to wish he had used that time a bit more wisely.

The station was buzzing as he pushed in through the back door, despite the ungodly hour. The night shift wasn't over yet, but a lot of day-shift officers were in early. Nothing like a good bit of gossip to get things going. Not that any of the uniforms and plain clothes milling around knew what he knew. The email had pinged on his phone at half two that morning; Amanda Parsons burning past the midnight oil to process the DNA and run the comparison with the sample on the database. A good enough match to confirm what the press were still only hinting.

'Morning, sir. Ready for the firing squad?'

McLean looked up to see Grumpy Bob approaching. He had a crumpled brown-paper bag shoved under one arm and carried a paper cup of coffee in each hand. From the smell, it was his own secret supply, not the boiled burn-water they served in the canteen.

'Morning, Bob. I hope one of those is for me.'

Grumpy Bob started to hand over one of the cups, then realized he'd drop the bag if he did. A quick shuffle and he handed the other one over, catching the bag with his freed hand before it slipped any further. 'Don't want to break the pastries.'

'Pastries? There something going on I don't know about?' McLean followed the detective sergeant down the corridor to the major incident room. Grumpy Bob paused before pushing open the door.

'You tell me, sir. This place was empty yesterday. Now look at it.'

A sea of uniforms filled what was one of the largest spaces in the building. Dozens of hushed conversations amplified into a buzz that must have made life very difficult for the officers trying to use the phones banked along the far wall. At the top of the room by the whiteboards, McLean saw Detective Superintendent Brooks, Detective Chief Inspectors Mike Spence and Jayne McIntyre, Acting Detective Inspector Kirsty Ritchie and a half-dozen detective sergeants. DC Gregg was shuttling between them all, handing out sheafs of paper.

'You're here, Tony. Good.'

He swung round to see the DCC come through the door behind him. The city's two ACCs were deep in conversation in the corridor outside, and it occurred to him that a well-placed bomb would effectively wipe out Edinburgh's policing capability in one messy bang. Everyone was here.

'Morning, sir. Thought the briefing wasn't till six.'

'It's not. And most of these officers aren't even assigned to the investigation. Wish I could get them to be half as enthusiastic every day.'

'I've got the DNA results. It's a confirmation, I'm afraid.'

'I know. Got the email, too.' Call-me-Stevie squeezed out a painful smile. 'Knew before then, actually. I made a few calls last night. Bill's not been seen in the last forty-eight hours, and there were places he was supposed to be, people he wouldn't have stood up unless he was dead. Important people.'

'I'll need to speak to them myself, sir. Probably have to interview you too, if I'm still in charge of the investigation, that is.'

The DCC's smile hardened into something more sinister for a moment, then softened. 'There'll be time for that in due course. For now, I think we'd better get this briefing started. Make sure everyone's on point before the press really get their teeth into us.'

'You think that's likely? I mean, it's not as if we've done anything wrong yet.'

'Yet?' Call-me-Stevie slapped McLean on the back in what might have been a friendly gesture from anyone else.

60

'I admire your confidence, McLean. Come on. Time to address the troops.'

'Some of you will have met Bill Chalmers. Some of you might even have served with him; he was a detective constable with Lothian and Borders until twenty-five years ago, after all. There's at least one of us here who was present at his arrest, too. But most of you probably know him as the man who looks after the drug addicts and gives the politicians a hard time. Gives us a hard time too, if I'm being honest. None of that is important right now.'

The deputy chief constable addressing a morning briefing for a suspicious death enquiry was unusual enough. Seeing the ranks of uniform and plain clothes police standing silently while he spoke was even more surprising. McLean had suffered enough talks from the top brass to know that most of it was either arse covering or management bollocks. This was different, though. You could hear it in Call-me-Stevie's tone, and the whole room was caught up in it.

'I'd say that what Chalmers did, the thing that got him thrown off the force and into an eight-year stretch in Saughton, I'd say that was all water under the bridge. Long since past. Hell, it's been nearly twenty years since they let him out. But that doesn't mean the press won't dig it all up again and shove it in our faces. Even if he'd died in his bed after a long and uneventful life, they'd dig it all up again and shove it in our faces. That's what the press do. But this is different. Bill Chalmers died violently and his body has been discovered in a manner that is both unusual and sensational. It's a gift to the tabloids.'

Sitting beside him, DCI McIntyre nudged McLean

gently on the leg. 'Reckon he's going to start slavering at the mouth any minute,' she whispered under her breath.

'Now, I know a lot of you speak to reporters. Sometimes it's just idle chit-chat, sometimes they maybe buy you a drink or slip you a little something. If it's not too serious, I'm usually prepared to turn a blind eye. We need the press, after all, for all they like to stab us in the back every now and then.' The DCC paused in his monologue, looking first over the bulk of the room, then turning to stare at the senior officers sat behind him. His gaze lingered on McLean for perhaps longer than was polite, though his face remained unreadable. Then he turned back to his key audience, his tone suddenly hard.

'But so help me if I hear of any officer talking directly to the press about this case. So much as a squeak. That officer will rue the day he put on a uniform. There'll be no disciplinary action. No moving to a rough posting in Strathclyde or a stretch in traffic patrol. You'll be out quicker than you can say "union rep". Do you understand?'

Silence filled the room. Even the city outside paused for a moment, as if it, too, was afraid of talking out of turn.

'I'll take that as a yes, then. Consider yourselves warned.' Call-me-Stevie pushed himself away from the lectern. 'Now I'll hand you over to Detective Inspector McLean, since he's the one who knows the most about what's going on.'

Compared to the quiet that the deputy chief constable commanded, the murmur that spread over the room as McLean took his place at the lectern was deafening. Looking around, he could see few faces he recognized and fewer still who met his gaze without turning away or staring back with undisguised hostility. He knew he was a stranger in his own station; three months off would do that, and the months before when he had been on secondment to the Sexual Crimes Unit over on the far side of town hadn't much helped.

'First off, I can confirm that the body we found on the Meadows yesterday is that of Bill Chalmers. DNA matches his entry on the database. I can also confirm that the death was not natural, and indeed we're treating this as a murder enquiry. So what the DCC just said about talking to the press? Well, just don't, OK? Not this time. Everything through a senior officer first. If you're approached for information, come to us. We'll do our best to keep the jackals fed so you're not being pestered for more, but this is going to be a high profile investigation, and it's been a slow month for news.'

McLean shuffled the papers he'd brought with him, more to give himself time to gather his thoughts than to remind himself of what needed to be said. The sooner the briefing was over the better, as far as he was concerned. There was too much to get done. Too little time.

'OK, so most of you will have heard about the body being in a tree. We're working on the assumption that it was dropped from a light aircraft or possibly a helicopter.'

'Not a dragon, then?'

McLean scanned the room, looking for the source of the comment. It was inevitable that the young boy's claim would have spread like wildfire, although he was at a loss as to how anyone who hadn't been at the interview or in the senior officers' meeting the night before could have known. Maybe that young PC had let something slip, or it could just have easily been DCI Spence.

'If anyone has evidence of a dragon in the vicinity of the city, please let me know. I'll be happy to put them in charge of a team tasked with arresting it. In the meantime, let's not get distracted from the crime here. A man's been killed, and in a very unusual and public manner. Who did it? Why? What message are they trying to give by dropping the body like that? Is it a warning? A message? If so, for whom? How Bill Chalmers ended up in that tree is an important question, yes. But it's only one of many.'

The rumble of voices from behind the closed door to Detective Superintendent Brooks' office suggested that at least someone was not happy with the way things were turning out. McLean could distinguish the different tones of Brooks himself, Mike Spence and the deputy chief constable, although individual words were harder to make out. There were at least two other men in the room but apparently DCI McIntyre had been excluded from the discussion, as she was sitting on one of the low, comfortable chairs that clustered around the meeting area just outside. For his own part, McLean stood, unsure whether he should wait for the meeting to finish or just knock on the door and go in.

'Ants in your pants, Tony?' McIntyre closed the crime scene report folder she had been leafing through and laid it down on the table beside her.

'I just need to get started. Sort out some actions, get people assigned to their teams and, well, just do something.' He looked at his watch; it was still early in the morning, but late enough for normal people to be at work. 'It's more than twenty-four hours since Chalmers was killed. You know as well as I do how important those hours are, and we've lost them already.'

'I know, I know. Detective chief inspector, remember?' McIntyre hauled herself out of the chair with a groan. 'But trust me, Tony. You'll just give yourself an ulcer fretting while those old women bicker among themselves. What's the real problem? Why can't you just get on without them, like you always do?'

McLean stopped mid-pace. McIntyre was right, of course. Time was he'd have just ploughed ahead with his own investigation, and hang the consequences. But that was when he had some officers to help him.

'You know as well as I do how short-staffed we are, Jayne. I need more detectives, but we've damned few sergeants and all the constables are running around at Mike Spence's beck and call. None of them dares work with me, either. They all think I'm some kind of pariah.'

'Well, you do have something of a reputation, Tony.' McIntyre smiled as she spoke, smoothed down the creases in her jacket. 'You've got Grumpy Bob and technically Ritchie's available, if you need her. I'd suggest if you need some DCs you'd be better off talking to the duty sergeant. See how many uniforms might like a temporary transfer. I can't see any of this lot making too much of a fuss, as long as you keep a tight lid on overtime costs.'

'Brooks actually suggested I steal some constables from uniform. Thought I'd better make sure he was OK with it before I went ahead.' McLean nodded half in agreement with McIntyre's suggestion, half in the direction of the closed door. 'What are they all nattering about in there, anyway?'

'Christ knows. Probably trying to work out what their response to the press will be. They all worked with Chalmers before he fell from grace. Well, except Mike. He's too young. Brooks was on some drug-law-enforcement liaison committee that dealt with Morningstar, and Stevie just likes to be in control.' McIntyre put a reassuring hand on McLean's arm, looked him straight in the eyes. 'Go talk to the duty sergeant. Get yourself a half-dozen constables to play with and get stuck into finding out who did this, OK? I'll square it all with the boys.'

9

'Oh, excuse me, sir. Sorry.'

If she hadn't said anything, McLean might not have noticed the PC as she walked swiftly up the corridor in the opposite direction to him. There were so many new faces in the station he hardly knew anyone in uniform these days. And yet they were still understaffed, almost to breaking point; as many experienced officers had left as new recruits come in. All that skill and expertise gone to waste. Or to highly paid IT and finance jobs.

'It's Harrison, isn't it?' He was fairly sure he recognized the young woman who had accompanied him to interview John Johnston the morning before. Her smile suggested he'd got it right.

'Just heading up to the incident room, sir. Got the latest reports from Traffic.' Harrison held up a sheaf of papers that would tell McLean, in intricate, dry detail, exactly how much closing down one of the city's central traffic arteries had buggered up everyone's day. Information that would move the investigation on no further at all but which had to be collated to tick a box somewhere on someone's performance appraisal.

'I've a better idea. You serious about transferring to Plain Clothes?'

Harrison's eyes widened. 'Yes, sir. Completely.'

'Right, well, come with me then. We'll see how you get

on with looking for evidence.' He set off down the corridor without waiting to see if the constable was following. It was stupid, perhaps, taking a complete novice along with him. But then everyone had to start somewhere, and it wasn't as if there were any seasoned detectives around to help.

'Where are we going, sir?' Harrison asked as they reached the door that opened on to the parking lot at the back of the station. McLean stuck his hand in his pocket, felt the keys to his Alfa nestling there. Did he really want to take it across town at this time of day?

'The West End. Up near the National Gallery.' He shoved the keys deeper down into his pocket, looked around the car park in vain for a pool car. 'Don't suppose you know anyone on patrol who could give us a lift?'

'Who exactly is Bill Chalmers, sir? I mean, I know about the charity work and stuff, but everyone keeps going on about prison? And he was a detective?'

McLean stared out the window of the squad car that was taking them across the city, glad of the warmth on what was a bitter cold and grey day. Constable Harrison's question surprised him; he had assumed everyone knew the story and those that didn't would have been swiftly brought up to speed as soon as the dead man's identity had been confirmed. Then again, Chalmers' history before his charity work was old news, and there weren't many serving officers who would remember him as a detective.

'He was one of us. CID, as it used to be called back then. Lothian and Borders. By all accounts he was a good detective, too. For those times. But he took a bad beating

68

working undercover. Nearly died. The way I heard it, he started taking drugs to help with the pain, then moved from being a user to being a dealer. Only he didn't stop working for CID all the while. Gave him a bit of an advantage. I can't remember who took him down; that was before my time. He spent five of an eight-year sentence in Saughton and came out a reformed character. Set up Morningstar while he was still on licence and he's been running it ever since.'

Harrison sat silent for a while before speaking again. 'So who'd want to kill him?'

'That, Constable, is the million-dollar question. And if we're lucky, we might just find one or two answers here.' McLean nodded in the direction of the windscreen as the squad car pulled to a halt. In front of them, the road dipped and curved away towards Douglas Gardens and the Water of Leith. To the right, a narrow cobbled street disappeared into the shadows. Rothesay Mews sat in a quiet spot of the city's New Town, a row of stone buildings originally designed to house the coaches of the well-to-do Georgian and Victorian gentlemen who lived in Rothesay Terrace, higher up the hill. Modern garage doors filled most of the wide carriage entrances now, but it was easy to see what the place might have looked like when horses were still the main way of getting around. Walking down the hill from the spot where the squad car had dropped them off, McLean could almost smell the manure on the cobbles, treacherous under slippery ice.

'How the other half live, eh? This is a bit nicer than my folks' place in Restalrig.' Constable Harrison's head moved in a series of swift jerks as she took in the scene, like a nervous bird looking for predators. Given that his own home had a coach house larger than any of these, dedicated solely to the storage of empty cardboard boxes and the ever-multiplying wheelie bins, McLean decided it was best not to answer. Instead, he led her down the street to where a bored uniform officer was guarding a white painted door. He looked up as they approached, and McLean recognized Sergeant Don Gatford. He wondered what he'd done this time, to be handed such a menial duty. Then again, it might just have been a ploy to get out of something worse.

'Afternoon, sir. Wondered when someone might turn up. Bloody freezing just standing around here.'

'Christ, is it afternoon already, Don?' McLean shook his hand out of his sleeve and looked at his watch. Lunch missed again. He wondered if Harrison had managed to grab a bite before bringing the reports to him and being dragged off on this errand. Ah well, if she wanted to be a detective, then interrupted eating patterns were something she'd have to get used to.

'Got yourself a new sidekick, I see.' Gatford grinned at Harrison. 'You want to watch yourself around the detective inspector, lass. He's got a reputation.'

'Would that be why I'm an inspector and you're still just a sergeant, Don? What you doing here, anyway? Shouldn't this be the sort of job for PC Carter?'

'What? And have him fuck it up?' Sergeant Gatford almost spat on the cobbles, then seemed to remember his company. 'Sorry, lass.'

'Like I haven't heard worse in the station every day, Sergeant.' Harrison smiled. 'Is Carter really that useless?'

'Well put it this way,' McLean said, 'he was a DI six months ago. You got the keys then, Don?'

'No keys. We had to get a locksmith in to open it up ready for you. That's another reason why I'm here.'

'What about the alarm?' McLean looked up to see a familiar logo on a squat metal box screwed to the wall. Similar ones marred the sandstone façades of half the houses in the street.

'Penstemmin system. We gave them a call and they disabled it for us. Chap's coming round to set a new code. Be handy if you can find a set of spare keys while you're in there. Save us the bother of fitting a new lock.'

'I'll see what I can do, Don,' McLean said, then pushed open the door and stepped inside.

A blanket of warm air swept over McLean's face as he took a couple of steps up the stairs immediately inside the front door. PC Harrison was close behind him like an obedient hound. He waited while she shut the door, watching for what she would do next. Her eyes were every where, drinking in the details, but she kept her hands by her sides. Then she jerked her head back slightly a couple of times, nostrils flaring as she breathed in through her nose.

'What is it?' McLean asked. He'd not noticed anything in his hurry to get in out of the cold. Poor old Don Gatford, still standing out there.

'I'm not sure.' Harrison did the sniffing thing again, more like a cat than a dog. She had a small nose, turned up at the point slightly. 'Smells almost like burning wires, or . . . I don't know . . . like when you bash two rocks together at the beach?'

McLean sniffed, still not getting anything. 'Can't smell it myself.'

'Sorry, sir. I didn't mean to –'

'Don't apologize. You did good. Pay attention to everything you see, smell, feel. I'd caution against tasting, but it can be useful sometimes. And sound is important, too.'

'What sound? I don't hear anything.'

'Exactly, which would suggest that the neighbours are out, or very quiet. Or the walls are too thick for noise to get through. I'm going to risk assuming they're out, but we'll be knocking on doors and asking questions soon enough. Find out if anyone saw him, when and what he was doing.' McLean headed up the stairs, stopping on a landing.

'What are we looking for, sir?' Harrison asked as she climbed slowly behind him.

'Anything that might give us an insight into who Bill Chalmers was.' He shoved his hand into his jacket pocket and brought out a couple of pairs of latex gloves, handed one over. 'Don't think this is likely to be a crime scene, but just in case.'

A door off the landing led to an open plan kitchen and living room with windows front and back. The designer furnishings looked expensive, and the walls were covered with modern art that, while not to McLean's taste, must have cost a bob or two. One corner of the room was dominated by a large flat-screen television, surround-sound speakers discreetly hidden on bookshelves. A Persian rug partly covered polished floorboards. The room looked more like a showcase for a trendy interior designer than somewhere someone actually lived. Clearly the charity business was doing well for Chalmers. Or at least it had been until someone had tried to make him fly without wings.

'Think I've found some keys, sir.'

McLean looked around, expecting to see Harrison dangling a keyring off her finger. Instead she was pointing to a small wooden bowl on the granite-topped counter that separated the kitchen from the living area. A jumble of pens, loose change and other rubbish filled it almost completely. He picked things out one by one, laying them on the spotless counter. A pair of keys at the bottom, one for a mortice lock, one for a latch, looked like they would probably fit the front door. He put them in his pocket, then pulled out another set from the bowl. Four this time, they were wound on to a faded leather 'Welcome to Fife' key fob.

'Holiday home?' Harrison asked.

'Could be. Let's have a look at the rest of the place. See what else we can turn up.'

The rest of the place turned out to be two bedrooms and a small bathroom. Both bedrooms were neat, the beds made. The one to the front of the house was clearly where Chalmers slept, if the cupboards and drawers full of men's clothes were anything to go by. The one at the rear had a small desk shoved into one corner, but there was nothing on it.

McLean found what he might have expected to find in the bathroom: toothbrush, toothpaste, combs, soap. Chalmers used an electric shaver, it appeared, and he liked expensive cologne. Or maybe he was given it by an admirer. An empty plastic prescription jar stood beside a box of ibuprofen tablets in the mirrored cabinet over the basin, but the label on it was worn away so he couldn't read what pills had been inside. The name of the pharmacy was still legible, so they could find out easily enough; another action to be followed up.

'Impressions?' McLean asked as they stood once more at the top of the stairs. Harrison paused a while before answering, her head moving more slowly now as she looked around the walls, up at the ceiling, down at the coconut-fibre carpet.

'It's very clean, for a bachelor pad. Either he was obsessively organized or he had someone come in here and tidy up after him – I'd say at least three times a week. Or he didn't actually stay here much.'

'A fair point. But if he didn't stay here, then where?'

'Fife, maybe?'

'Possibly. Add it to the list of questions still to be answered.' McLean clumped back down the stairs and opened the door to see Sergeant Gatford deep in conversation with a uniformed constable. The winter air was cold enough, but McLean felt the chill deepen as Constable Carter, formerly Detective Inspector Carter, looked up to see him. How the man had kept a job at all after what he had done was beyond McLean, but it was clear from the look of pure hatred on his face that he held the detective inspector responsible for all his ills. Then Carter's gaze slid past McLean to Constable Harrison behind him and the temperature dropped even further.

'You find any keys then, sir?' Sergeant Gatford broke the uncomfortable silence. 'Only, the constable here's come to relieve me, and not a moment too soon. Don't

74

think I'll ever feel my toes again.' He stamped the cobbles in his heavy police-issue boots for good measure.

McLean was tempted to pretend he didn't have a set of keys in his pocket, but realized that was just being petty. He took them out, handed them to Harrison. 'Give them a go, will you?'

They all watched as the constable tried first the mortice and then the latch. Both keys clicked round the well-oiled locks.

'Looks like you're in luck,' she said as she turned back and held the keys up for McLean. Carter was already moving up the street.

'Not so fast, Constable Carter.' McLean pitched his voice as a command and, reluctantly, Carter stopped, turned back to face him.

'Sir?' It was more of a sneer than a word.

'The technician from the alarm company's not been yet. Someone has to wait here for him.' He took the keys from Harrison, threw them to Carter, who caught them, fumbled and then dropped them to the ground. 'Lock up when he's been. Then deliver those back to the incident room, along with the new code.'

McLean stopped at the top of the street to catch his breath. A squad car had turned around just off the main road, no doubt waiting to take Sergeant Gatford back to his station. He could probably pull rank on the driver and get a lift across town to the major incident room, but he didn't much feel like sinking into that melee at the moment. Neither did the endless paperwork in his office appeal at all. The afternoon sun was almost gone, just catching the tops of the taller buildings and painting the sandstone orange. Soon the streetlights would flicker into life as darkness descended, another day winding down. Winter was a cruel season this far north.

'Where to next, sir?' Constable Harrison asked as she caught up with him. McLean had already pulled out his phone and was tapping away at the screen in search of information.

'Your shift must be ending soon, right?'

'Not till six.' Harrison tugged at the airwave receiver attached to her uniform. 'I should probably call in and let Control know what I'm up to, mind.'

'It's been taken care of, don't worry.' McLean found what he was looking for: a confirmation of his suspicions. The offices of the charity Bill Chalmers had set up were just a few minutes' walk away. He needed to talk to the assistant director, but probably not with a young uniform constable accompanying him, nervous and full of her own questions.

'Cadge a lift back to your station with Don, why don't you? Control already know, but you can tell Kenny Stephen I've poached you for Specialist Crime. We'll have a catch-up briefing in the major incident room before shift end. If you can make it to that, then great. If not, tomorrow, seven sharp. No uniform.'

Harrison nodded her understanding, then trotted off to the car like a child who's just won a prize from the teacher.

'You be careful with that one, sir. Ambitious, she is.' Sergeant Gatford grinned as he wheezed up the steep hill towards the car. At least the exertion would have warmed him up a little.

'Ambitious is good. Better than being lazy and useless.' McLean tried not to be too obvious about where his comment was directed. Constable Carter was already flapping his hands and stamping his feet to ward off the chill a hundred yards further down the mews. Idiot hadn't worked out he could go and stand in the hallway. He had the keys, after all.

IO

The offices of Morningstar occupied the bulk of an old town house in Melville Street, in the heart of the city's West End; the same street where McLean's solicitors were based, he noticed as he walked along the pavement looking for the right entrance. Some of these old places were being bought up and turned back into residences by the new rich now. The one percenters, he had heard them referred to, often with scorn, by his fellow officers. McLean found it best not to comment, since his grandmother had left him a house on the other side of town far grander than any of these, and more money than he could ever imagine spending. His wealth sat uneasily with his chosen profession; so much simpler if he'd been a banker or a lawyer, perhaps. Or followed his grandmother into medicine. He couldn't really remember why he had chosen the police as a career, all those years ago. Probably because someone had told him he couldn't do it. That was the only reason why he carried on, after all.

It was good to be reminded from time to time that many people lived barely scraping it together day by day. Too easy to fall into the trap of thinking everyone else was just like him, that fifteen or twenty quid wasn't really much to worry about when, for some people, it was the difference between survival and despair. Morningstar was just such a reminder, dealing as it did with the people who had succumbed to that despair and sought relief from it in a needle or a pill. McLean had a lot of time for that kind of charity, even though he had often dealt with the other side of the equation. The pushers and dealers who preyed on the hopeless, sold them the promise of a way out of the drudgery of their daily existence, then squeezed them hard when the addiction kicked in.

Bill Chalmers had been one of those men, of course. Policeman turned drug lord. McLean found himself chuckling mirthlessly at the thought as he climbed the stone steps to the front door of the charity office. Chalmers had been before his time, at least in CID. But from what he'd heard about the man, there were few people less lordly. Gamekeeper turned poacher was more like it, working the land rather than owning it.

'Can I help youse?' The receptionist sitting behind a low desk in the entrance hall was a young man. Clean shaven and well enough presented, he still had the skeletal, sunken eyes and prominent cheekbones of a recovering addict. His face was the colour of sun-bleached cardboard, smooth as a baby's except for the ugly red pocks of acne. When he spoke, he revealed cracked, brown teeth and a heavy accent. North of the city, if McLean was any judge.

'Detective Inspector McLean. I was hoping I might see the assistant director? About Bill Chalmers.'

The young man looked McLean up and down slowly before turning to the slim computer in front of him and tapping away at his keyboard for a moment.

'Aye. Ruth was expecting one of youse lot. I'll gie her a shout.' He picked up the phone beside his keyboard, tapped in a number. 'Tha's polis here tae see youse, aye?' A brief pause while something was relayed down the line, then he replaced the handset and looked up at McLean again. 'She'll be right doon. Youse want a coffee or summat?'

McLean tried to remember the last time he'd had a drink, found he couldn't. 'Thanks. A coffee would be grand.'

'Won't be a minute.' The young man got up, shuffled around the desk and headed for a door that opened on to a small kitchen area. McLean looked around the reception hall while he was gone. It was well furnished, expensive leather sofas arranged around a low glass coffee table. The pot plants looked real and well tended, and the walls were lined with photographs showing notable events in the history of the charity. He stepped up to one, a large image showing Bill Chalmers shaking hands with a member of the royal family. The background was blurred, but it was probably some reception or other in the grounds of Holyrood Castle. All smiles and laughter and white bread sandwiches with the crusts cut off.

'Bill always did like to move in high circles. Reckoned he was getting the last laugh.'

McLean turned to see a woman standing close behind him; he wasn't quite sure how she had managed to creep up so quietly.

'Ruth Tennant.' She extended one hand, her face wrinkling into a friendly smile as he took it. 'And you're wee Tony McLean. Well, well. Wasn't sure when I heard the name, but now I see you . . .'

'Do I know you?' McLean looked more closely at the woman. She was perhaps the same age as him, neither tall nor short, particularly, greying blonde hair cut just above shoulder length. Dressed in a dark tweed suit, she could have been a teacher in one of the city's better private schools, or running one of the little boutique shops that lined Morningside Road. Or running a charity that helped recovering drug addicts reintegrate into society.

'Ach, I doubt you'd remember. Must be, what? Near enough forty years now? And I was Ruth McPhee then. Long before Mr Tennant came along. Rest his soul.'

'Ruth McPhee.' McLean realized he was still holding the woman's hand and let go of it, searching his memory for the name, although it didn't immediately spark anything. Forty years was a long time, though. He'd have been, what . . . ?

'Big Pants Ruthie? No way!'

'Aye, bring that up, won't you? And with Malky just listening in.' The hurt tone in Tennant's voice was betrayed by the smile on her face, a face McLean couldn't quite square with the young girl in pigtails and ridiculous dungarees he'd known at primary school a lifetime ago. Strange how the past kept on resurfacing just when he was least expecting it. Looking around, McLean saw the young receptionist standing in the doorway with a mug in one hand, eyes wide and uncertain.

'I kind of lost touch with everyone from back then when Gran sent me off to boarding school down in England.'

'Aye, and you lost the accent, too. More's the pity. Who'd a thought it, Tony McLean a polisman.' Ruth shook her head in disbelief, the smile ebbing away. 'Still, you're no' here to catch up on old times. You're here about Bill, right enough. Come along to the office.'

*

81

'When was the last time you saw Chalmers? Bill, I should say?'

Ruth Tennant gave McLean a look he'd not seen since primary school. 'Oh aye, know him well, did you?' Her office was a large room to the front of the building, on the first floor, so that it looked out across the wide street rather than being overlooked by lost pedestrians and bus passengers. Her desk was tucked into one corner, as if the space itself was too overwhelming. It would originally have been a fancy reception room for a well-to-do family, a place to receive visitors and impress them. Now the large fireplace had been boarded up, a series of mismatched armchairs arranged around a battered wooden table in the centre of the room. A few faded pictures hung from the walls, mostly obscured by piles of sagging cardboard boxes and battered old filing cabinets. Looking up, McLean saw cobwebs hanging from the ornate cornicing that suggested maintenance wasn't high on the charity's list of priorities.

'I met him once, at some horrible reception, round about the time Police Scotland came into being. He didn't seem much interested in talking to anyone lower down the greasy pole than a superintendent. Spent most of his time with the politicians.'

'That sounds more like Bill, aye.' Tennant waved a hand at the collection of armchairs. 'Have a seat, Tony. Or should I call you Inspector?'

'Tony's fine.' McLean looked at the seats, picked the one that looked least likely to burst a spring and lengthen his already long odds of ever being a father. He placed the mug of coffee the receptionist had given him on the table, then carefully lowered himself down.

'As to when I last saw Bill, it would have been, what, three nights back? We worked late on the new funding campaign, getting it all ready for the big launch next week. He was going up to Fife the next day. Day before yesterday that'd be. Something about meeting a new sponsor. He was quite excited about her, actually.'

'She have a name, this sponsor?'

Tennant frowned. 'Sure she does, but Bill never told me. He liked to keep that sort of thing to himself until he was sure of the money.'

'But he was meeting her in Fife. So that's where she lives, I take it?'

'Possibly. Or she might have been visiting him. He has a house in Elie. Had, I suppose.' Tennant shook her head gently. 'Can't believe he's really dead.'

'Elie?' McLean remembered the keys in Chalmers' flat with 'Welcome to Fife' on them. 'You got an address? We'll have to pay a visit.'

'Aye. I'll dig it up. I say Elie, but it's no' in the town. Out in the countryside. Nice place. Good for getting away from it all.'

'You been there much?'

'Me?' Tennant shook her head. 'Once or twice. Never stayed over though. Bill's . . . was . . . a very private person. Liked his private space.'

'What about his place down the road?'

'The mews? Aye, I've been there a few times. But with the offices being so close, more often than not we'd meet here. I think he preferred it that way.'

'Which would explain why you didn't have a key. No one else we could track down, either.'

Tennant frowned, as if something had just occurred to her. 'Now you mention it, I can't think of anyone he was close to, really.'

'Maybe not close how you mean it, but what about a cleaner?'

'A cleaner? Christ, no. You really didn't know Bill, did you? He'd never let someone else tidy up after him. Think he'd rather die than have someone else go through his stuff.' Tennant's eyes widened as she realized what she'd just said. 'Oh God! I didn't mean . . .'

McLean tried to square that with the stories he'd heard about the man, and with the state of his house in Rothesay Mews. It didn't quite fit with the profile he had been building in his head. He took a sip from his coffee, which was surprisingly good despite being served in a cracked mug, and studied Tennant from behind it. Her face showed the same shock and bewilderment he'd seen a hundred times and more. The news of sudden death took people different ways, of course, but there was always that underlying mixture of sadness and at the same time excitement, if that was the right word. Everything changed in that one, final instant of death. Those left behind to pick up the pieces either crumpled at the task or rolled up their sleeves and got on with it. Both were kinds of grieving, and Ruth Tennant looked like she would favour the latter approach.

'This launch, the new funding campaign. Is that still going ahead?'

'Guess so, aye. We put that much work into it. And besides, we need the money to keep this place open.' Tennant looked around the room as if only just noticing it for the first time.

'Things not going too well, then?'

Tennant laughed mirthlessly. 'We're a charity working with recovering drug addicts, Tony. Hardly sexy like cancer research or treating sick kids. Raising funding's hard enough at the best of times, and this is the age of austerity, right? Problem is, that's what drives folk to taking drugs in the first place. So you could say we need money now more than ever.'

'So who would want Chalmers dead, then? Does anyone stand to gain? He have any family?'

'Family, no. Not that he ever talked about. I assume he left a will with the solicitors, but it's not something he ever discussed with me. Christ. There's no question he was killed, then. This wasn't some kind of accident?'

'At this stage, we've pretty much ruled it out.'

'Aye, I guess it's not so easy to accidentally end up in the top of a tree.' Tennant shook her head again. 'But no. I can't think of anyone who'd want Bill dead. Maybe wish he'd go away, but no' dead. And to do that? To what . . . push him out of a plane? Was he, you know, still alive when he was falling?'

'Best not to dwell on it.' McLean was slightly taken aback by the question. Details of Chalmers' death had leaked out, of course. Along with the imaginative description from the young boy of a dragon swooping down to take him and his dog. He'd have to get someone on to tracking which particular journalist it was who had ferreted that story out. Add him to Dan Hwei's blacklist.

'Could I get a look at his office? Where he worked?' he asked, more to break the train of thought than through any great desire to see anything there.

'Sure. I'll take you through.' Tennant stood up, leaving her own untouched coffee on the table as she headed for the door. 'I might have to leave you to whatever it is you do, though. I've a group coming in this evening and I need to get set up for them.'

'You're still open for business?'

Tennant gave him a look that suggested she thought him an idiot. 'What, you think just because Bill's dead no one needs our help? The show must go on, Tony. The show must go on.'

11

If he had thought he was going to find any great insights from standing in Bill Chalmers' office, or even from sitting at the great man's desk, then McLean was bitterly disappointed. As perhaps befitted the boss of the outfit, the room Chalmers had taken for himself was at the rear of the house, overlooking a substantial private garden and the back of the next row of terraces. It was smaller than Ruth Tennant's office, but it also lacked the circle of armchairs where whatever counselling or self-support sessions the charity ran could be carried out. Chalmers clearly liked to work alone.

The room might well have been a study when the house was first built, or perhaps a private library. Dark oak bookcases lined most of the walls, stacked with an eclectic selection of titles and endless forgotten folders. There were more photographs of Chalmers posing with the great and the good, although fewer in here than in the more public parts of the building. These were presumably the ones that meant more to him personally than to his sense of self-promotion, so it was surprising to see one showing him posing with a small group of people, his arm around the shoulder of a younger Jo Dalgliesh. McLean peered closer, recognizing a couple of other journalists he'd had run-ins with in the past, all employees of the *Edinburgh Tribune* at one time or another. Maybe that explained how she'd been able to identify him from the badly damaged mess in the crime scene photograph. It was something he'd have to remember to ask her the next time they met.

Looking around the room, McLean couldn't shake the feeling that this was a place where very little work happened. Like the mews flat, it was meticulously tidy, in sharp contrast to the organized chaos of the other offices he had seen. Apart from the photographs, it had no feel to it at all, almost as if it were a film set; somewhere to be seen, but not a place any real business was done.

Turning to leave, he caught sight of something incongruous out of the corner of his eye. Stopping, McLean looked again, not quite able to put his finger on what it was that had jarred. He scanned the room once more, eyes settling on the ornate, leather-topped antique desk. An elderly computer sat beside one pedestal, but the monitor and keyboard had been pushed to the side, the clear space where they had been suggesting that Chalmers had used a laptop for most of his work.

The chair was as ancient as the desk, another reason to think that Chalmers spent little time in here. McLean pulled it out and sat down once more, letting his arms fall where they were most comfortable. As he suspected, the clear space of desktop was where he would expect a laptop to be set up, although slightly off centre, biased to the left. He had no idea if Chalmers had been left-handed, but the space to the right was just about big enough for an A4 pad, and there to the right of that was a cheap black ballpoint.

McLean reached out for it, then let his hand drop to the drawers in the right-hand pedestal. They were unlocked, filled with more pens, and business cards from dozens of people they would have to interview and who would turn out to have nothing to do with the investigation at all. A slim silver cigar cutter nestled in amongst the pens, flecks of tobacco around the blade suggesting it was regularly used. McLean picked it up, turned it over. He'd never been a smoker himself, and couldn't understand the fondness some people had for cigars. The smoke made his eyes water, the smell turned his stomach far worse than anything he'd encountered at the city mortuary. But each to their own.

The back of Chalmers' cigar cutter had a neatly engraved symbol on it, round and abstract and almost impossible to make out in the low light. Beneath it was an inscription:

For Bill
~ 22 July 1992 ~
'Chasing the Dragon'
J D

A cold sensation spread through his stomach as he read the words. On the face of it, there wasn't anything strange about them. The date didn't mean anything to him, but it could have been around the time Chalmers had been injured in the line of duty, a few years before he was arrested. The quote immediately made McLean think of opium dens and cheap seventies karate movies, but it also reminded him of the young boy and his overactive

89

imagination. The initials might have been meaningless, but the photograph and the connotation of smoking linked up in his head. J D. Joanne Dalgliesh.

Or it could have been someone else entirely.

Shaking his head to dispel the thoughts, he put the cigar cutter back with the rest of the detritus in the drawer, pushed it closed. The other drawers yielded nothing of any interest, just empty boxes for electronic gadgets a generation or two out of date, cables that might have come in handy sometime, power transformers. He could go through the drawers in his desk in the library back home and turn up pretty much the same stuff.

He put his hands down in the space where Chalmers would have had his laptop, added it to his mental list of things they needed to track down, along with his phone. Neither had been with him when he was found. He had the address of the house in Elie from Ruth Tennant; perhaps a drive up to Fife would be more productive than wandering around here. Standing, McLean took one more look around the room, but nothing new drew his attention. The answers lay elsewhere. Perhaps with a certain reporter.

The major incident room was distressingly quiet as McLean stepped in through the propped open door, still staring at his phone and its inability to put through a call to Jo Dalgliesh. He'd been trying her sporadically all the way back from the offices of Morningstar, but the number kept coming up unobtainable. He'd call the *Tribune* later, get a message to her that way. Or she'd turn up when he was least expecting her, like she always did.

Looking around the room, he could see the shift was winding down, another day coming to a close. A line of uniform constables sat at computer screens, phone headsets and hands-free microphones on as they typed up all the information gathered so far. A few spoke to the wall as they answered calls to the helpline number that every newspaper had printed that morning and every TV and radio news bulletin had mentioned all day long. It wasn't the most efficient way of conducting an investigation, but at least it made them look like they were doing something. And who knew? Maybe a tiny snippet might prove key to unlocking the whole mystery. An early riser looking out of a window to see a helicopter fly by too low, perhaps. Or even half a dozen sightings of a giant dragon's lair somewhere in the Pentland Hills.

'Ah, sir. You're back. How'd the interview go?' Detective Constable Sandy Gregg approached from the top of the room where the whiteboards were. Black smudges on her fingers suggested she was probably responsible for most of the scribbled words taking up half of them.

McLean remembered Ruth Tennant, his surprise at meeting someone he'd lost touch with a lifetime ago. 'We'll need to get the assistant director in for a formal statement. Couldn't really do much there on my own, but Chalmers hadn't been in for a couple of days. I don't think he was taken from there. More likely he was at his house in Elie. Get on to Fife and have them check no one's there. I'll head over in the morning and have a look myself.'

Gregg nodded, turned away to get on with her tasks, then stopped. 'There's a bunch of constables waiting to be told what to do, sir. DCI McIntyre sent them over, apparently.'

McLean looked in the same direction as Gregg and saw three people standing around looking bored. They were all impossibly young, but then he'd been that age once. For a moment he thought he didn't know any of them either, but then one turned around, saw him and gave a nod of recognition. Constable Harrison had managed to get back in time for the evening briefing after all. He crossed the room to meet them.

'Welcome to Specialist Crime Division. I'm Detective Inspector McLean, as some of you already know. This is Detective Constable Gregg. I'd suggest you do whatever she tells you to.' McLean smiled to let them know it was a joke, but judging by the expressions on the faces of the three of them he couldn't be sure they understood. 'Harrison, I've already met. You two are –?'

'Constable Stringer, sir.' For a moment McLean thought the shorter of the two young men was going to salute, but somehow he managed to suppress the reflex. 'And this is Constable Blane. We both came through Tulliallan together.'

Judging by the look of them, they'd come through life together. There was an easy familiarity between the two, almost as if they were brothers. If they were, then their genetics had been mucked about somewhere as physically they were poles apart. Constable Stringer stood a half a head shorter than McLean. Thin and wiry, he had a piercing stare and an unsettling way of holding your gaze just a little too long. He'd probably be very good at interviewing suspects. His friend Blane, on the other hand, was tall, broad-shouldered and had that way of hunching in on himself that large people often do. An attempt to avoid drawing attention, perhaps. Undoubtedly he had been given the nickname Lofty at some point in his life, and was probably still trying to work out why. It was perhaps a little unfair to make such snap judgements, but McLean couldn't help himself sometimes.

'Welcome to the team.' He looked around the room briefly, seeing the uniforms and support staff all about their business. 'No one given you anything to do, then?'

'We only just got here, sir.' Harrison answered the question swiftly, talking over her colleagues before they could say anything. McLean noticed Stringer take a breath to speak, then close his mouth, a flash of annoyance quickly fading from his face. Blane hardly moved.

'Well, I've no doubt DC Gregg will bring you up to speed. DS Laird will be here in a minute, too. He can take you through the processes. It's early days yet, but we've several different strands to follow. There'll be an evening briefing in about half an hour. Should have a better idea of who's doing what by then.'

Nobody said anything, which suited McLean just fine. He raised one hand, half-heartedly pointing to the door. Not quite sure why he had to justify his actions to these youngsters. 'If anyone needs me, I'll be in my office.'

Tucked behind his desk, McLean was about to reach for the first in what would be a long series of boring manila folders when the phone interrupted him. He stared at it for a moment, surprised that it was actually working, then snatched up the handset before it could switch itself to voicemail. Messages disappeared into some arcane space deep within the electronic heart of the machine. McLean knew they were in there somewhere but to date he had never been able to find them.

'McLean.'

'Oh. Tony. You're there. I wasn't expecting to catch you. Was just going to leave a message.'

McLean recognized the voice. 'Miss Parsons. Amanda. How can I help you?'

'You? Help me?' A pause, followed by a short bark of laughter. 'Well, you could lend me the keys to that lovely car of yours so I can make my boyfriend jealous. But no. That wouldn't be right. Sorry. Where was I? Oh, yes. Thought you might be interested to know we've got the preliminary toxicology screening results back from the body in the tree. What's his name? Chalmers. That's it.'

McLean took a moment to parse what the forensic technician had told him, such was the speed and stream of consciousness of her speech. For a moment. all he could extract was that she had a boyfriend, and he wondered what kind of saint could put up with her endless, exhausting enthusiasm for her job.

'Toxicology? Already?' He finally distilled the conversation down to its salient point.

'What can I say? Miracle worker.' Even though she was on the other side of town, McLean could see Parsons shrug.

'I'm guessing they're interesting. Otherwise you'd not bother calling me.'

'Interesting, aye. And unusual. He was drugged when he died. Quite heavily. Aff his tits, you might say. Reckon he'd be conscious but hardly aware of what was happening. Probably thought he was flying. Then again, I guess he was flying, for a while, at least.'

'What was he drugged with? Had he taken something himself?' McLean found he was sitting forward, elbows leaning heavily on the desk. He'd managed to knock a pile of folders to the floor without noticing.

'That's the interesting bit. See, at first we thought it was just heroin, but the signature wasn't quite right. It's very similar, though. Has much the same effect, only you need a lot more of it. Not so easy to take, either, which is why it went out of fashion, I guess.'

'Amanda, are you going to tell me what he was on?'

'Sorry. Sidetracked. There's some other stuff in his blood that we're still waiting on confirmation for, but what was really doing his head in seems to be opium.'

'Opium?' McLean struggled to remember much about the drug, other than it wasn't something he could remember ever having come across outside of a history book. 'You sure it wasn't heroin? Or, I don't know, just morphine or something?'

'Heroin leaves a different trace in the bloodstream, Tony.' Parsons put on a tone that reminded McLean curiously of his old English teacher explaining the more esoteric rules of grammar. 'There's all manner of other alkaloids swirling around in the mix. Modern opiates and opioids tend to be purer, they break down into fewer compounds. The key ingredient here is certainly opium, but there's more besides.'

'Any idea how he took it? Injected, smoked?' McLean paused, then added: 'Ate?'

'Might even have been poppy-seed tea, for all I know. That's more a question for the pathologist, don't you think?'

McLean stopped short of asking Parsons how she could possibly know so much about opium and its many means of ingestion. 'I'll have a word with Angus, get him to look at the body again. Might be tricky, though; most of his guts were ripped out in the fall.'

'No need. I already did. Soon as the results came in, I could see we needed more information. I mean, your man there could have injected it, smoked it or maybe even popped some pills, but whatever he did he did it lots. The levels we've detected, well, he wouldn't have been walking anywhere, that's for sure.'

McLean stared out of the window at the windowless stone wall to the back of the station. Darkness had fallen while he wasn't paying attention, as it so often did at this time of year. A quick glance at the clock on the wall reminded him it would be shift change soon; time for the catch-up meeting, and one more piece to add to the puzzle.

'Thanks, Amanda. That's really useful stuff.'

'Well, don't get too excited. I mean, we get positive results all the time and they're not all drug addicts. Some are on pain meds or have a weird metabolism. This one, the results just look a bit strange is all. There's chemical signatures I've not seen before, and I've dealt with plenty dead addicts. We'll get a more in-depth analysis back soon. I'll let you know when it's in.'

'Your instincts are usually good. Did Angus say when he was going to have another look?'

'In the morning, I'd imagine. Though knowing him he might be at it right now. Anyway, my shift's about to end and I've got the day off tomorrow. You sure you don't want to lend me that car of yours? I'll take good care of her.'

McLean couldn't stop himself laughing. 'You're never going to give up on that, are you?'

'Not a chance. Oh, there was one other thing. About your dirty laundry.'

'My –?' McLean struggled for the joke, then it dawned on him. 'The handkerchief. Dr Sharp found it then?'

'Aye, she did. Sent it over to me, since apparently I'm the expert on that kind of thing. It's shit all right, but it's not human. I think that was what you were hoping?'

'Just an idea I had. Thought it was worth checking. Let me guess, kids throwing dog mess at the neighbour's door.'

Parsons didn't answer straight away. 'Not dog, no. At least not any dog I've encountered.'

'Any idea what it's from?' McLean tried to remember the stuff he'd wiped from his hand, the quantity of it spread across the door, the wall and the iron railings. Edinburgh had a seagull problem, much like any other city close to the sea, but there was no way a bird could have produced that quantity.

'Not a clue, I'm afraid. You want me to send some off for DNA?'

It was McLean's turn to pause before answering. Technically it was too far from the crime scene to warrant forensic analysis. It was just a hunch that it had something to do with the case. And if it wasn't Chalmers' terrified bowel-emptying, then chances were it had nothing to do with the case at all. On the other hand, a DNA test could easily enough be covered in the budget for the investigation, and it would ease his mind at least a little if he could confirm it was nothing but coincidence.

'Aye, do that please. But it's not priority. Just whenever the lab can get around to it.'

12

'Remind me who it is we're meant to be talking to?'

Morning rush hour, and the traffic backed up on the Gogar roundabout as McLean and Grumpy Bob drove out to the airport and an appointment with a representative of Air Traffic Control. The detective sergeant was at the wheel, and McLean was glad they'd managed to grab one of the few remaining pool cars. His Alfa might have been lovingly restored and brought up to the twenty-first century in terms of its heating and cooling, but it was still made from Italian steel and to a design not much concerned with salt on the roads.

'Lady by the name of Emily Bannister. She's one of the head technicians at the tower, apparently. Looks after all the flight records.'

'It wasn't her you spoke to before, I take it.' McLean peered through the grimy windscreen, willing the cars in front to start moving again. As if to mock him, an airliner dropped slowly down from the sky on its approach to the runway, unencumbered by such inconveniences as traffic lights and poor road design.

'No. She was off yesterday. I spoke to some officious wee scrote who got all defensive when I suggested they might have missed an aircraft over the city. Seemed to think I was questioning his professional integrity.'

'Sounds like someone with something to hide. Let's hope Ms Bannister is more forthcoming.'

The traffic flow eased a little as they passed the hulk of the Royal Bank of Scotland Headquarters at Gogarburn, then slowed to a crawl at the airport turning. Sitting in a car like this was perhaps not the best use of his time, but McLean knew he would be just as unproductive back at the station, surrounded by the organized chaos of the major incident room. At least here he could think without being constantly interrupted.

'Do you reckon it's a coincidence, where we found the body?' he asked, as they finally inched on to the slip road and approached the first of many roundabouts leading to the airport. Grumpy Bob paused a moment before answering, although whether that was because he was considering his response or trying not to drive into the car in front of him was anyone's guess.

'Coincidence how?'

'Well, if he was just chucked out of a plane, he could have landed anywhere. On a road, maybe, or more likely smashing through somebody's roof. He had to have been dropped from some height to sustain the damage he did.'

'You think? He can't have been going that fast or he'd've gone straight through the tree and been splattered all over the path.' Grumpy Bob mistimed a gear change, crunching the lever in a manner that made McLean very glad they weren't in the Alfa.

'Another thing to run past Forensics, I guess. Someone's bound to have some way of working it out. Doesn't really change things that much, though. Except that the closer to the ground he was when he was dropped, the more deliberate the choice of point of impact, wouldn't you say?'

Grumpy Bob mashed another gear change in his hurry to make it through the last set of lights. 'I guess so. Still doesn't explain how he got up there to be dropped.'

'No. Nor why. I can think of easier ways to kill a man.' McLean lurched forward, hands instinctively catching the dashboard in front of him as Grumpy Bob slammed on the brakes in response to the car in front stopping without warning. 'Driving in rush-hour traffic, for one.'

Emily Bannister turned out to be a shy, nervous young woman, quite overwhelmed by the presence of two police officers in her tiny office. It didn't help that she kept apologizing for her colleague's bad behaviour in giving Grumpy Bob the brush-off the day before, or that it had taken her more than two minutes to meet them at reception after they had arrived and that was clearly a terrible mistake on her part. McLean wanted to sit her down and fetch her a cup of tea before she broke with the strain of it all. Instead, he tried to keep his tone neutral and work around her anxiety.

'Must be a busy job, dealing with all the flights coming and going from this place.' He nodded in the direction of a small window that overlooked the main terminal building. Ranks of jet liners and smaller propeller-driven planes lined up, awaiting their passengers, or disgorging them on to the tarmac like so many blinking ants.

'Busy doesn't begin to cover it. But it's not like it's just me working it all the time. I mean, we have shifts, you understand. And different teams for different parts of the job. Like, there's a controller for the plane when it's on the ground, and he'll hand over to another once it's in the air, and then when it's ten miles away Prestwick take over. And –'

'Prestwick?' McLean interrupted. He wasn't sure it was important, except that if Ms Bannister didn't stop talking and start breathing she would probably faint.

'That's where the main ATC – sorry, Air Traffic Control Centre – is located. There're two for the whole of the UK. One down in Swanwick in Hampshire. That does the south, Heathrow and all the other London airports. Prestwick covers the north of England, all of Scotland, and out into the Atlantic. Everything's coordinated so that we can hand over flight control automatically, or receive incoming flights, and –'

'All very interesting, thank you.' McLean interrupted again. 'But not strictly relevant to our current enquiry.'

'Oh. Sorry. I get a bit carried away sometimes.' Ms Bannister dipped her head nervously, shrinking in on herself as if she'd been told off. 'What was it you needed to know?'

McLean paused a moment to gather his thoughts. The office was obsessively neat, a necessity perhaps because of its tiny size, but also the sign of a mind fixated on details. The spotless desktop held two flat-screen monitors, a keyboard and a trackpad, all lined up with millimetre precision. Even the cables appeared to have been coaxed into neat, straight lines rather than the unruly tangle as on his own desk. A three-tier system of trays labelled 'in', 'out' and 'pending' was empty except for a single brown paper folder on the top.

'Yesterday morning, sometime between five and six, we

think a light aircraft, or maybe a helicopter, flew over the Meadows. Probably not all that high up at the time. I'm guessing it's too much to hope there's a flight plan and pilot's name logged somewhere?'

Ms Bannister tilted her head like a confused dog. 'A plane? Over the Meadows. Is that why the road was closed yesterday? But I thought the papers said you'd found a . . .' She fell silent, eyes widening as the thoughts tumbled into place. 'He fell from a plane?'

'That's what we're trying to find out. And any records you might have to help us track that plane down would be invaluable.'

'I . . . I see.' Ms Bannister pulled her chair out from under her desk, pointed at it. 'May I?'

'Of course,' McLean said, then waited while the young woman seated herself, carefully pulled her keyboard into the perfect operating position and began to type. The screens had been blank before, but at her first input they lit up with a half-dozen windows, each showing reams of numbers or graphics that meant nothing to him at all. She typed, swiped at her trackpad, typed some more, bringing up screens and flicking through windows of impenetrable gobbledegook with a speed and dexterity quite at odds with her awkwardness when interacting with the two detectives. This was clearly her preferred space.

'Yesterday. Between five and six?' She looked up at McLean briefly, not waiting to see his nod before turning back to her beloved computer. 'Let me see, let me see.' A couple more windows popped up on to the screens, then disappeared again.

'There's no lodged flight plans for an over-city journey.

But that's hardly surprising. Flights into the airport were over the Forth; those going out heading towards Livingston before turning to whatever course. Nothing commercial would have been over the Meadows. Then again, I don't suppose you're looking at commercial flights, are you?'

'Not exactly. No.'

Another furious tapping at the keys and swiping of the trackpad. 'So, let's look at the radar for yesterday morning. Should be here somewhere. Yes. Here we go.'

The left-hand screen opened up into one window, showing what looked like a child's drawing of the night sky to McLean but which might have been a radar tracking image of a dozen or so aircraft. 'What am I looking at here?'

'See this?' Ms Bannister pointed a slim finger at the screen, where a dot was moving slowly from one side to the other. Meaningless numbers moved with it. 'That's a freight 747 from Stansted, headed for Detroit, I think. Here, this is probably easier.' She tapped the trackpad a couple of times and the screen changed to a more recognizable map of Scotland, the North Sea and some of the Atlantic Ocean. Icons shaped like tiny aeroplanes overlaid themselves on the map, flickering on and off, moving slowly across the electronic sky.

'This is real time, what's happening at the moment. All non-military flights are tracked. You can just click on a plane to see the details.' Ms Bannister did just that, showing an Iceland Air flight from Glasgow to Reykjavik.

'What about that one?' McLean pointed at the screen, where an icon much smaller than most of them hovered over an area to the east of the city.

'Ah, you worked it out. I'm impressed. Yes, light aircraft.

Probably heading for East Fortune.' Ms Bannister clicked on the aircraft and a window popped up with its details. McLean squinted at the tiny writing, but it didn't mean much to him.

'This is live, though?' he asked. 'What about yesterday morning?'

'Sorry, I only have the flight numbers and tracking, not the nice mapping graphics.' Ms Bannister clicked back to the black screen with its pinprick lights, each followed by numbers. 'See, this is the airport here in the middle. The city's down here, and the Meadows would be around here.' She pointed again and again, delicate finger almost touching the screen. McLean followed her directions but couldn't see anything.

'There's nothing there,' he said.

Ms Bannister turned to face him, a triumphant grin on her face. 'Precisely.'

'So . . . There were no flights?'

'Not between five and six. Not an aircraft with a commercial transponder, anyway. Unless it was too low for our radar to see.' The grin faded to her more normal worried frown. 'But that would be breaking the law.'

McLean stared at the screen again. It still meant very little to him, but the hope there would be a flight plan and name had always been a slim one. It made sense that whoever had dropped Bill Chalmers to his death wouldn't have left such an obvious clue.

'I don't think whoever was flying cared much about the law, Ms Bannister,' he said. 'They pushed a man out without a parachute, after all.'

*

The forensics services might have been mucked about by the bureaucrats, cut back, cut back again, and moved from pillar to post in the name of something mis-sold as efficiency, but some things always stayed the same. Dr Jemima Cairns, for instance, was still short and round and fierce, ruling over her lab with a mixture of terror and encouragement, but mostly terror. McLean couldn't help liking her; she didn't suffer fools at all, let alone gladly. She'd helped him on more occasions than he cared to admit, not least with a surprising knowledge of knots that had helped in the investigation of a bizarre series of apparent suicides by hanging that had plagued the city a few years earlier. His reward to her had been the discovery of an ancient, unauthorized graveyard in the grounds of an abandoned mental hospital, and while for some the work involved in identifying dozens of long-buried victims might have been seen as onerous, for Dr Cairns it had been birthday and Christmas rolled into one.

Which was perhaps why she tolerated his idiot questions, and the very fact of him cluttering up her lab when she had work to do. Either that or she just liked him. He couldn't be sure.

'Bill Chalmers. Have you had a chance to look at the evidence from the scene yet?'

Cairns had met him at reception, for once insisting that he sign in and wear one of the plastic visitor badges he always forgot to give back on leaving. The walk to her office had been blissfully lacking in idle chit-chat, something for which McLean was very grateful. He was on a tight schedule, but he needed to speak to the technicians who were actually doing the analysis. Too often the important details got lost in the report, or in the Chinese whispers of getting the message passed to him through half a dozen people.

'Your man in the tree? Aye, we've had a crack at it. Early days, mind.'

'I know. And I'm sorry to put you under pressure, really. But this is about as high profile as it gets, given who he is.'

'The drug man. I saw him on the telly a while back. Made quite a good argument, really.'

'Aye, well. Be that as it may, what I really need to know is how high up he was when he was chucked out of the aeroplane.'

'More likely a helicopter.' Cairns opened the door to her office and beckoned McLean in. 'Unless you're going with the dragon option.'

'I think we can rule that one out, don't you? The wee boy's only ten years old. I probably had just as vivid an imagination when I was his age. And he was right about one thing. Chalmers was dropped into that tree from a ways up. Must have been approaching terminal velocity to do the damage we saw.'

Cairns gave him a look that reminded him of his primary-school teacher. 'Do you know how fast terminal velocity is, Inspector? How long it takes to get there from a standing start?'

'Why do I get the feeling you're just about to tell me?'

Cairns gave him a half-hearted sneer. 'Somewhere between four and five hundred metres, at a best guess. Gravity accelerates a falling body at 9.8 metres per second. That's in a vacuum, of course. In the real world you've got to deal with air resistance, and that depends on the profile of the falling object. You've seen those idiots with the wing suits jumping off big buildings and stuff, right? They're maximizing their surface area, and so their resistance. Your man Chalmers weighed about ninety kilos, stood a shade under five foot ten. Sorry, I'm mixing my units again.' Cairns shook her head. 'About one seventy-seven centimetres. That was before his head got stoved in.'

'So how fast was he going, then?'

'A branch approximately five centimetres in diameter pierced his gut and pushed right through him, exiting to the right of his spine. It's broken, dead wood, so effectively pointed like a spear, but that still takes considerable force. I'd estimate he was probably falling at around twenty metres a second when he hit the canopy. Terminal velocity for a man of his size would be around fifty metres per second, a good bit more if he was head down like a skydiver, though my best guess is he was either spreadeagled or tumbling. Doesn't make much difference either way. He fell from no more than a hundred metres. Probably less.'

'You're sure of that?' McLean shook his head apologetically. 'Sorry. Of course you're sure of that.'

'It's all a bit open at the moment. But it's going to be somewhere in that ballpark. Not terminal velocity, for sure. He'd have to have been dropped from about five hundred metres to reach that speed. He'd have gone straight through the tree and smeared himself all over the tarmac if that had been the case.'

'Praise the lord for small mercies, then.' McLean slapped his newspaper against his arm. 'Fifty to a hundred metres. How high's that in comparison to the buildings around the Meadows? The old Royal Infirmary site up the hill?'

Cairns cocked her head like a terrier. 'You think he was . . . what? Catapulted out? Maybe someone's built themselves a trebuchet?'

'No, nothing like that. It's just something the air traffic people said. They've no record of anything flying over the city when it happened, but if it was low enough, then it wouldn't show up on their radar anyway.'

13

It should have been a perfect evening. McLean had managed to leave the station at what was for him quite an early hour. Emma had been waiting for him and, if she hadn't quite managed to have his supper ready and on the table, she had at least ordered something from the takeaway when she'd got in from her own work, so he didn't have to. By the time he'd showered and changed, the pizza had arrived and the wine was poured. As they sat opposite each other at the kitchen table, he tried not to notice that she had already drunk half a glass of it, but his observational skills were hard-wired by two decades of plain clothes police work.

'Still getting used to the paperwork?' McLean waved a hand at his mouth, the tomato on his pizza hotter than any lava. Emma wasn't eating much, just cradling her glass of wine. Maybe she was just waiting for the pizza to cool down.

'Does it show?' Emma grinned at her joke, but somehow the smile didn't reach her eyes. 'I guess it's just difficult adjusting after being my own boss for so long.'

'It can't be that bad, surely.' McLean risked another bite, feeling the roof of his mouth burn. It was always the same with pizza. He never learned.

Emma slumped back in her seat, her head lolling as if it were too heavy to keep it straight on her shoulders. 'Worse. We all went out to a warehouse in Broxburn for a team-building exercise this afternoon. Bloody exhausting, running around like we were schoolkids doing PE.' She yawned, just in case McLean didn't understand what she meant. 'Team building's all good and well, but there's a backlog of samples a mile long. Don't seem to be anything like as many technicians as we used to have, either.' She rubbed at one eye with the heel of her hand. 'Damned head feels like it's going to explode as well.'

McLean put down his half-eaten slice of pizza and looked more closely at Emma's face. Her eyes were sunken, almost bruised. The grey streaking through her black hair now looked more like black streaking through grey. Far from the vivacious young woman he'd known, now she looked frail and shrunk in on herself. How long had she been like this? A week? A month? She'd complained of a niggling headache before, but he'd not thought much of it. Stupid really, given what had happened to her because of him. Was it before she'd gone back to work, or after? So much for his finely honed observational skills.

'Have you been to see a doctor about it?'

The question went unanswered, but Emma stopped trying to push her eyeballs into her brain and fixed him with a stare that was at least a tiny spark of her old self.

'It's a headache. Time of the month. It'll pass.'

He didn't believe it, and neither did she, if her sullen pout was anything to go by. 'Em, you had a nasty blow to your head. You were in a coma for months. Something like this? You have to take it seriously.'

Emma opened her mouth to say something, but at the same time McLean's phone started jangling away in his pocket. He'd been upgraded on his return to work, and all the ring tones had reverted to one monotonous and unconvincing copy of a fifties Bakelite handset. He had no idea who was calling, so he had to pull it out and check the screen just in case it was important. It was.

'Got to take this. Control.' He half expected Emma to complain that he never paid her any attention, but instead she seemed to perk up, interest piqued at last. She leaned forward while he talked to the operative, inquisitive eyes locked on his face. He didn't have time to speak once he'd ended the call before she cut in.

'Something happen? You going out again?'

McLean looked at his wine glass. He couldn't remember whether he'd drunk any of it or not. If he had, it was only a mouthful; even with the new limits he wouldn't be over. For a moment he wished he'd already had half the bottle, but then they'd just have sent a squad car round. Too much to hope that an on-duty detective might be able to deal with things.

'I have to. Sorry.' He rolled up the rest of his slice of pizza, cooled enough now, and shoved it into his face. Emma reached across the table and helped herself to his wine glass. Hers was already empty.

'What's happened? Reckon you'll be long?'

McLean pushed back his chair, stood up and walked around to Emma's side of the table. She smelled of wine and sleep, of comfort and warmth. He should just call Control and get them to assign someone else, maybe ask them why they'd called him in the first place and not someone on the night shift. But he couldn't do that. Not now he knew what had happened. He bent down, kissed Emma on the top of her head, then set off for the back door.

'I wouldn't bother waiting up. Some bugger's gone and broken into Bill Chalmers' house.'

In the dark and late at night, Rothesay Mews was a far less welcoming place than when McLean had first visited. He was for once grateful that the Alfa was so small compared to modern cars as he manoeuvred it into a space between a massive Mercedes off-roader and some sleek-looking black thing he didn't immediately recognize. Only when he got out, saw the T-shaped emblem on the bonnet and the electric cable snaking away from it and in through a cat-flap in the front door of the nearest house did he realize that it must be one of those new Teslas he'd heard some of the constables chatting about in the canteen. He'd have given it a bit more of a once-over, always on the lookout for something better for day-to-day driving than an Alfa Romeo that was approaching its fiftieth birthday, but there were more pressing reasons for him being here.

Ice slicked the cobbles as he walked down the mews towards the front door to Bill Chalmers' house. A squad car was parked outside, its blue light spinning a lazy strobe over the street. Pity the poor bastards trying to get some sleep tonight. Closer in, he could see a couple of police-men at the front door, itself hanging open. One of them looked up as he approached, and McLean recognized Constable Carter again.

'Who called it in?' he asked. No point wasting time on pleasantries. At his words, the other officer turned to face him, one of the young lads from the Chalmers crime scene.

'They set off the silent alarm, sir. Penstemmin called us. It was like this when we got here. No one inside.'

'You've been in?' McLean looked at the constable's hands, clad in black leather gloves against the cold. Well, that was something at least.

'Only to the top of the stairs, sir. Didn't want to upset anything, but we needed to be sure there was nobody still inside. Just the one door in and out of these mews houses, and nobody's been through it in the hour we've been here.'

'Good work. Anyone call Forensics?'

'Aye, they're on their way.' Constable Carter's voice grated on McLean's nerves, even though he wasn't being particularly offensive. There was just something about the man. Still, at least he knew how to manage a crime scene. Or he should have done.

'OK.' McLean racked his brain for a moment. 'Wallace, isn't it? You stay here. Carter, you're with me.'

'You what?' Carter asked.

'Come with me. You've more experience of crime scenes and what not to do in them. I was the last person in there besides whoever set the alarm off, so I'm going in to have a look. I need someone to come with me. Understand?'

Carter's face was a war zone of conflicting emotions, not helped by the lazy flashing blue light of the squad car. Whereas earlier in the day he had held McLean's gaze with unconcealed contempt, now he seemed reluctant to meet the inspector's eye.

'Fine. Stay here. I'll go on my own.'

He slipped past the open door carefully, anxious to touch as little as possible. This might just have been an opportunistic burglary, but McLean had been around long enough to know better than to rely on that. Inside, the flashing blue light was muted somewhat, the shadows hiding any clue as to how the lock might have been forced. For a moment he wondered if Carter had actually locked up after the alarm technician had been, shook his head at the thought. Useless though he was, even the constable wouldn't be that stupid.

Pulling a slim torch from his jacket pocket, McLean played it around the tiny hallway. There were no obvious marks on the mat, no tell-tale footprints up the stairs. If the two constables hadn't made any marks on the coconut-fibre stair runner, then it was unlikely the burglar had either. Still, he trod carefully, keeping his feet as close to the edges as he could as he climbed to the top.

All the doors leading off the landing were open, even though McLean distinctly remembered he and Constable Harrison closing them as they left. He ran the torchlight over the two bedrooms and the bathroom, seeing nothing immediately different from before. Peering into the main living room showed a different picture altogether.

It looked like someone had thrown a grenade into the room and stood back while it exploded. The furniture was all ripped apart, turned upside down, piled against the walls. Pictures hung askew or lay smashed on the floor. Flashing his torch over the kitchen area revealed the contents of all the cabinets strewn over the tile floor, pots and pans tossed into the sink and up against the window. The bowl he had emptied before was nowhere to be seen, although most of its contents were scattered over the countertop. Looking through them, he recognized the keyring with the 'Welcome to Fife' fob on it and four keys, mashed up against a cracked jar of mayonnaise taken from the fridge. McLean stuck the end of the torch in his mouth while he fished around in his pocket for some latex gloves, cursing silently as he realized he'd given his last pair to Harrison. There were a couple of clear plastic evidence bags in there though. He pulled one out along with a pen, lifted the keyring carefully into the bag and sealed it up before putting everything back in his pocket.

'Jesus, this is some mess.'

The voice was so sudden, so unexpected, McLean almost tripped over his feet spinning around to see who it was. A much more powerful torch than his own swept over the room, then into his face, dazzling him, before it swung out of the way.

'Sorry about that.' The beam pointed upwards to reveal in underlit profile the face of Dr Jemima Cairns. Unlike McLean, she was dressed in the full white paper bodysuit, overboots and hood. The play of the light on her features made it hard to tell whether or not she was scowling, but McLean was prepared to bet she was.

'Could you no' have waited five minutes before charging in here in your fancy suit and those grubby shoes?' Cairns played the torch over him again.

'If it's any consolation, I was the last person in here before whoever stopped by and did this.' McLean indicated the devastation wrought upon the room.

'Bloody hell. Looks like someone took a sledgehammer to the place.' Cairns grinned, and this time McLean was sure of it. 'Should keep us busy for days.'

A friendly face greeted McLean as he stepped back out of the mews house and into the cold dark street. Acting DI

Ritchie was wrapped up warm for the occasion, the cold, chapped glow of her cheeks obvious even in the blue flashing light.

'What brings you over, Kirsty?' he asked, eliciting an instant furrow of the forehead where her eyebrows had never quite grown back after she'd lost them pulling him out of a burning building. 'Not that it isn't always good to see you,' he added hastily.

'Aye, well. Could do without being woken up and dragged off to a crime scene only to find there's already a senior officer present.'

'Control sent you?'

Ritchie pulled her phone out of her pocket and waved it in the air. 'Brooks.'

'Why the hell did he get in touch with you? Control had already assigned it to me. They knew I was on my way.' McLean shook his head at the stupidity of it.

'Well, I'm here now. What's the story?' Ritchie looked up at the houses, lights on in almost all of them now. 'Apart from a lot of pissed-off people?'

'Looks like a burglary, only far as I can tell nothing's been taken. Whoever went in there just trashed the place.'

'Burglary? Why the hell are we involved, then? I'd have thought there'd at least be a couple of bodies to drag two DIs out of their beds on a cold night.'

'It's a bit early for bed, isn't it?' McLean raised an eyebrow, the expression lost in the dark. 'Though I guess that depends on who's already in there waiting for you.'

'You know me and Daniel split up, right?' Ritchie said.

McLean felt his ears burn. 'Sorry. No. I didn't.' He stepped off the cobbles and on to the narrow pavement as a forensics van backed down the mews, its reversing siren adding to the already disturbing noise levels.

'It's no biggie.' Ritchie shrugged, then looked up at the window where the lights had just come on. 'So why are we here then?'

'Nice of Brooks to tell you. This is Bill Chalmers' house. One of them, at least.'

Ritchie's scowl returned. 'Chalmers? Fucking marvellous. Guess that explains why the world and his wife are here. Why Brooks has got his panties up his crack, too. No expense spared for the DCC's old pal. Anything we can actually do? I mean, Forensics are here, and they could be all night if there's a whiff of overtime. They'll not want either of us getting in the way.'

'I know. Already got it in the neck from Cairns for going in without a bunny suit on, but I needed to see the place before anyone touched anything. Looks like a bomb went off in there.'

'A bomb? Must've been noisy.' Ritchie turned on one heel as she looked around at the brightly lit windows, the flashing blue lights and the general bustle in the street. 'You think we should ask if anyone heard it?'

'Do you think they'll be out there long? Only I've got to get up at six and it's getting on.'

Perhaps inevitably, there had been no answer at the house immediately to one side of Chalmers' and, of the upper windows in the street, it was the only one that had remained unlit. To the other side, the door had been answered by a young woman in saggy jogging bottoms, an Aberdeen University hoodie and bare feet. Her face was slightly puffy, eyes rimed with sleep and hair all skewed to one side, but she invited McLean and Ritchie in with only a cursory glance at their warrant cards. She had introduced herself as Lesley Spencer, then led them upstairs into a house laid out similarly to its neighbour, if decorated in a completely different style.

'I really can't say. Sorry.' McLean cradled a cup of instant coffee that wasn't as bad as he had feared when offered it. 'Your neighbour, Mr Chalmers. You know he was killed the day before yesterday?'

'The body in the tree. Yes, I'd heard. We're an insular bunch here, don't talk to each other much, but two of my neighbours have popped round to tell me.'

'Did you know Mr Chalmers at all, Miss Spencer?' Ritchie asked.

'It's Mrs, actually, but Lesley's fine. And no, I didn't know him. I mean, I knew who he was, yes. I'd say hello if we passed. He'd nod if he was going into his place as I was coming out of mine. But like I said, we're an insular bunch here. Keep to ourselves. Probably something to do with being in these glorified converted lofts. Most of the garages downstairs are either rented out or belong to someone else. I work in the city. No need for a car.'

'What about this evening? Have you been in? Did you hear anything?'

'Can't say that I have, no. But then I've had the telly on since I got in at six, and I was in bed by nine.' Mrs Spencer glanced across at the mantelpiece, where a surprisingly ornate carriage clock said that it was a quarter to eleven. McLean had got the call at about half past eight and Penstemmin Alarms had notified Control no more than fifteen minutes before then. For once, someone had done their job properly, it would seem.

'Do you get much noise from next door?' Ritchie stood up, put her coffee mug down on the small table in the middle of the room and stepped over to the party wall. McLean strained his ears to hear anything of the forensics team on the other side.

'You don't get much through those walls. There's a good two foot of sandstone there, with the fireplace. Plus the dry lining. I hear more on the other side, in the bedroom,' Mrs Spencer said.

'So someone could have been turning the place over and you'd not have heard?' McLean asked.

'Sorry. No. And if it happened after nine, well, then I'd have been asleep. There was the car, mind you. But that was earlier.'

'Car?' Ritchie and McLean both spoke together, like an old couple.

'Aye, that's right. Would have been just before nine. I heard a noise through the window as I was getting into bed. Had a peek out the window and there was this big, shiny car trying to turn around at the end of the mews. Difficult enough doing that with a push bike, let alone something as long as that. It ended up backing all the way up the hill. Skidding its wheels on the cobbles and all. They're lethal with a bit of ice, you know.'

'You OK taking the lead on this, Kirsty? Only I've got quite a lot on my plate already as it is.'

They stood in the mews, McLean shivering slightly as the cold seeped up through the thin soles of his shoes and into his bones. Ritchie seemed unaffected, but then she was wearing something that wouldn't have looked out of place on the side of Cairngorm in a blizzard.

'Aye, I've got this. Not a lot we can do mind, not till the forensics guys are finished anyway. I'll get a few constables to go door to door and talk to the rest of the houses, but if the neighbour didn't hear anything . . .' She looked up at the window of the house they had just left, where Mrs Spencer was most likely trying to get back to sleep now.

'Might be worth having a look at CCTV in the area. Follow up on that big car that thought this was a two-way street.'

'I'll give Control a call, get a copy of everything made and sent to the station. We can look over it in the morning.' Ritchie forced the last of her words out through a wide yawn and McLean couldn't help sympathizing with her.

'Look, there's nothing we can usefully do here tonight. The place isn't going to get any more burgled with this many uniforms swanning around. We can pick it all up in the morning when there's a few detective constables to delegate the heavy lifting to.'

'We've got Mrs Johnston coming in first thing tomorrow, remember?' Ritchie shoved her hands deep into her pockets. The cold air hadn't seemed to bother her, but the thought of interviewing Tommy Johnston's widow clearly did. Probably something to do with the way her cosy anonymity had been blown away by her son's discovery of Bill Chalmers.

'I know. Don't imagine that's going to be much fun. She blames us for telling the press about her, after all.'

'Did we?' Ritchie's eyes glinted in the reflected lights of the buildings. At least the squad car had turned off its flashing light now. 'I mean, they had to have found out from someone.'

'I don't know. It's possible. Not much we can do about it but apologize.' McLean shook his head, partly to cover up the shiver that ran right through him. 'Come on, Kirsty. Let's both of us go home. Get some kip. Things'll look better in the morning.'

14

A huddle of newly plain clothes detective constables clustered around a computer workstation at the far end of the major incident room as McLean walked in the next morning. He'd slept surprisingly well, despite the extra complication to the investigation added by the previous night's burglary. That was something he'd still have to get his head around. Or at least let Ritchie get her head around.

'Morning, sir. Wasn't expecting to see you for a while, what with last night and all.' Detective Constable Gregg bustled over from the big whiteboard that dominated one wall of the room. It was beginning to fill up with writing, most of it followed by question marks. A few photos had been pinned up as well, so that any senior officer entering the room would think work was progressing.

'Ah, you know me. Can't keep away from all this.' McLean opened his arms wide to encompass the almost empty room. 'There's nothing gets me fired up so much as a busy investigation.'

'Aye, well. It's early days yet. Still mostly calls from well meaning idiots with too much time on their hands.' Gregg nodded towards the banks of computers and phones where uniform constables were busy taking down details of every strange thing that might possibly have happened in the city over the past few days. Pleas to the public for information tended to bring out the crazy in people.

'Ja— DCI McIntyre about?' he asked, noticing that there were no senior officers in the room apart from himself.

'She's away to Glasgow, or so I heard. Something to do with Organized Crime and Counter Terrorism. No idea when she'll be back.'

'Brooks?' McLean asked. Too much to hope that the detective superintendent would have shown any interest, and Gregg's minimalist shake of the head confirmed as much.

'What about that lot? They settling in?' McLean nodded in the direction of the new detective constables.

'They'll work out OK, I reckon. Just need a bit of hand-holding to get started. I've got them working through the CCTV footage from the West End last night.'

'In here? Don't they have to go over to the media centre for that?'

'If we want the full image, yes. But we can get a lower resolution playback through the network. All part of the upgrades going through. Makes our lives a lot easier, I can tell you.'

McLean had to agree, even if the technology made him a little queasy at times. He walked over to the workstation, peering over the heads of the three constables. Unfortunately, Blane's head was so big it blocked any view of the screen.

'Any luck?' he asked, and was rewarded with all three officers flinching. Stringer and Blane were both standing, and turned around so swiftly he thought they were going to fall over. DC Harrison had managed to commandeer the only seat, and swivelled around at a more leisurely pace before getting to her feet.

'Sorry, sir. Didn't know you were there,' she said. 'We're still getting the hang of the new system, but it doesn't look very promising.'

'No? How so?'

'Perhaps easier if I show you.' Harrison sat down again, swivelled the chair back around and started to work the mouse. McLean stepped closer as Blane made room for him, and saw a screen split into images from four cameras. The pictures weren't all that good; mostly dark shadows and the occasional bright point of a car headlight sweeping past.

'Coverage isn't that brilliant around the mews itself, sir, and there seems to be an intermittent glitch with the recording, see?' Harrison pointed at one of the four images just as it turned into a flickering mass of grey and white. The timestamp stayed solid, seconds ticking away, and then the image came back unchanged from before. A moment later, one of the other images did the same.

'Are they all like that?'

'All the ones I've looked at so far, yes. They've been upgrading the whole system across the city. Higher resolution cameras and all-digital recording. That's the only reason we can access it here at all. There's still a few glitches though.'

'And no sign of a big black car coming or going between eight and nine last night?'

'Nothing conclusive, no.'

McLean straightened up, feeling the stretch in his spine. 'Ah well, it was always a long shot. There's still the door to doors to do. Someone might have seen something a bit more clearly than Mrs Spencer last night. See Detective Inspector Ritchie when she gets in. She's going to be lead on this part of the case.'

As if on cue, a voice carried over the soft hubbub of the major incident room. 'Did I hear my name being taken in vain?'

McLean turned to see Ritchie and Grumpy Bob, both holding mugs of coffee and looking like they were getting ready for a long day of not doing very much at all.

'Only if you've not brought me one of those, too.'

He'd meant it as a joke, but DC Harrison was on her feet in an instant. 'I can get you a coffee, sir. No bother.'

'At ease, Constable. The day I start ordering junior officers to fetch drinks for me is the day they have my express permission to tell me to fuck off.' McLean noted the horrified expression on DC Blane's face at the swearing and wondered how the big lad had managed three years in uniform if he was so sensitive. 'Having said which, if you three wanted to nip off to the canteen and just happened to bring back a coffee when you're done there, I'd not complain.'

Harrison nodded her understanding, and the three detective constables headed off for the door.

'That the CCTV footage?' Ritchie nodded at the screen they had left behind, still showing images from four camera angles intermittently blanking out and reappearing.

'Yes. For all the good it's worth. What's next on the list of things to do?'

'We're waiting for Mrs Johnston and her boy to come in and give a formal statement. PC McRae from Family

Liaison's bringing them over in about an hour. Should be fun, given that she blames us for telling the press all about them.'

McLean grimaced. 'Can't say as I blame her, really. Way I heard it, some journalist pretended to be from Social Services and blagged his way into an interview, but he had to have found out where to go from someone. High-profile case like this, the press'll be pestering every police contact they've got.'

'Tell me about it. Christ, even I've had to fend off a few calls.' Ritchie pulled out her mobile phone, swiped the screen and held it up to reveal half a dozen text messages received in the past hour.

'Whereas nobody's called me at all.' McLean hadn't thought about it before, but there was one person whose silence was deafening. 'Don't you think that's odd?'

'Dalgliesh?'

'Aye. She was at the press conference, asking awkward questions. Being paranoid even for her, now I think about it. I've been trying to call her, but her old number doesn't seem to work any more.'

'You think she's gone off you?'

'Chance'd be a fine thing.' He pulled out his phone, checked it for messages and found none. 'Still, it's not like her. Think I'll maybe see what she's up to. Journalists are like kids, you know. If there's noise, it's fine. It's when there's nothing but silence you know you have to worry.'

Ritchie raised an eyebrow. 'Thought you said she wasn't speaking to you. How're you going to see what she's up to?'

'How do you think?' McLean grinned. 'I'm a detective, aren't I?'

The offices of the *Edinburgh Tribune* took up one floor of what had once been a tenement block down near the parliament building in Holyrood. As it wasn't far from the station, McLean had thought the walk would do him good after a morning spent stuck inside. He had changed his mind after the first couple of hundred yards, the air so cold it rasped his throat and lungs. Stepping into the warm reception area was blessed relief.

'Jo Dalgliesh in?' he asked the receptionist before blowing on to his hands and rubbing them together.

'Not sure. Can I ask who's looking for her?' The receptionist picked up the phone on her desk and tapped out a number without even glancing at the keys, her eyes fixed on him.

'Tony McLean. Detective Inspector,' he added for good measure, although he didn't bother to show his warrant card. He hadn't visited the newspaper all that often, tended to avoid it if he was being honest, and he certainly didn't expect the receptionist to know who he was.

'Take a seat please, Inspector.' The receptionist smiled at him as she pointed to the slightly grubby sofa squeezed into one corner of the room. A low table in front of it held a half-dozen fresh copies of that morning's *Tribune*, artfully fanned out in a manner that suggested both that the newspaper didn't have many visitors and that someone had a lot of time on their hands.

'Is she coming down?' McLean asked, but before the receptionist could reply the door to the office clicked open. It wasn't Dalgliesh who emerged.

'Inspector. Good to see you. I hear you're looking for Jo.' Johnny Bairstow, editor-in-chief and Jo Dalgliesh's boss, was a young man prematurely aged. He had the gaunt frame of an ultra-marathon runner, close-cropped hair receding swiftly from his shiny forehead. He held out one hand as he spoke, the other firmly closing the door behind him.

'Mr Bairstow.' McLean shook the proffered hand without much enthusiasm. 'I take it Jo's not here then.'

'No, she's not. Actually, I was half minded to call you and ask if you'd spoken to her recently. I've not heard from her in days, and she's not answering her phone either.'

'Have you been round to her house?' As he asked the question, it occurred to McLean that he had no idea where the reporter lived.

'I may be little more than a glorified office manager these days, but I was a journalist for ten years. Of course I've been to her house. No one there, and her neighbour's not seen her in a couple of days. Says it's not unusual, though. And to be honest, I've long since given up trying to keep track of what she's doing. Long as she keeps on filing the stories, I'm happy.'

McLean looked past Bairstow to the closed door. It was possible Dalgliesh was behind it, hiding from him, but he couldn't imagine why. There was something the senior editor wasn't telling him, though.

'You know what she's working on right now?'

Bairstow gave him a look more old-fashioned than his years. 'What's everyone working on right now? Chalmers, I'd have thought.'

'She knew him, right?'

'Knew him? Whatever gave you that idea?'

McLean studied the senior editor's face for signs of lying, but he looked genuinely surprised. 'I don't know. Something she said, maybe. Sure I saw a photo of them together somewhere.'

'First I've heard of it. Don't remember her mentioning him ever before this whole sorry business started.' Bairstow shook his head slowly. 'I don't suppose you've any idea how he got up into that tree?'

McLean paused a while before answering. Bairstow had been, and probably always would be, a journalist first. 'We've a couple of theories. Pretty sure it wasn't a dragon, though.' The expected smile at his joke didn't appear, so he continued. 'The how would be useful to know, of course. But I'm far more interested in the why.'

That got Bairstow's attention. 'How do you mean?'

McLean smiled. 'Ask Dalgliesh, why don't you? And while you're at it, tell her to answer her bloody phone, too.'

15

The massive concrete towers of the new Queensferry Crossing rose out of a heavy fog to his left, the squat iron cantilevers of the rail bridge to his right, as McLean drove across the Forth Road Bridge and on into Fife. In the passenger seat beside him, Acting Detective Constable Janie Harrison sat upright, nervous and excited at the same time. He wasn't quite sure why he had asked her to come with him and not Grumpy Bob, except that Detective Sergeant Laird was spending most of his time in the Cold Case Unit these days, tucked away from sight and the demands of the Chalmers investigation. He could have asked Ritchie along, but then that would have meant two detective inspectors turning up on another force's patch, which would almost certainly have put someone's nose out of joint. Except that there weren't other forces any more; they were all one big, happy Police Scotland.

'Something on your mind, Constable?' McLean had been trying not to laugh all the way across the city and out to the bridge. Harrison kept trying to say something and then stopping herself. She had asked about the case, about where they were going and why, but there was something else. He reckoned he knew what it was, too, and was quite happy to let her sweat for a while, summoning up the courage.

'Your car, sir. It's very . . . old.'

'First registered in 1970, so yes, it is. Built before I was born, for one thing.'

'Why do you have it? Why do you use it? I mean, wouldn't it be better to have something a bit more modern?'

'Believe me, that's a question I ask myself every day.' McLean dabbed the brakes gently as he pulled off the motorway just past the massive Amazon distribution hub. Not quite the original intended use of the industrial site: Dunfermline had expected a massive boost in technology with the arrival of a vast semiconductor plant. Instead, it had got service jobs for box-packers, but then, these things rarely went to plan.

'I did have a modern car, another Alfa Romeo. Couple of years back.' He hadn't thought about it for a while, but the only long journeys he'd ever made in it had been out on this road to Fife. 'Some of your colleagues thought it was amusing to play little jokes on me. One was phoning up the local Bentley garage and arranging for them to bring a very expensive Continental Coupé to the station for me to test drive. Fortunately the salesman saw the funny side, and he had something a bit less pricey he'd taken in as part exchange.'

'So what happened? You didn't get on with it?'

'Oh, I liked it just fine. It just ended up underneath part of Rosskettle Psychiatric Hospital.'

Harrison fell silent for a while, eyes straight ahead as they pushed on past Cowdenbeath and Lochgelly. 'That was my first assignment after I passed out from Tulliallan, sir. All those bodies.' She shivered theatrically. 'But that was ages ago. And you've still not got a new car? Surely you can afford . . . I'm sorry. None of my business.'

'Don't worry. I can guess what the junior officers say about me. It's probably true, too. Most of it, anyway. I could have bought the Bentley when the salesman brought it round, but I didn't want to draw attention to myself.' McLean slapped the steering wheel gently with one hand. 'As if this old girl doesn't do that.'

A few more miles disappeared under the wheels in as close an approximation to silence as was possible at seventy miles an hour in a car over forty years old. It was only as they were approaching Glenrothes that Harrison spoke again.

'If you were looking for a new car, sir? Well, I might be able to help you. My uncle works in corporate sales for one of the big franchises. They sell all sorts. And he can get you the best price.'

McLean laughed out loud. He couldn't stop himself, at least not until he turned to see Harrison's face. She looked like a puppy that's just been kicked.

'Sorry. I'm not laughing at you. Well, not directly anyway. It's just the reaction I get whenever someone's a passenger in this car. You, DS – sorry, Acting DI Ritchie, Emma Baird and Amanda Parsons from Forensics. You all come up with helpful suggestions about her, recommendations for an alternative, that sort of thing. Grumpy Bob just complains the seats are too hard for his back, and don't get me started about Dagwood.' McLean shook his head, smiling despite himself. 'No, I'm not laughing at you. Thank you. I may well take you up on that offer. I just need to find the time to look into what would be suitable.'

Harrison said nothing, but she settled back into her seat a

little more comfortably as they left the dual carriageway and headed out on the ever-narrowing roads into darkest Fife.

McLean had been expecting Bill Chalmers' Fife retreat to be close to Elie itself, but the satnav on his phone took him through the picturesque fishing village and on out into the wilds of the East Neuk. He knew the area vaguely from trips to St Andrews with his grandmother back in the day, but even so he was glad of the map when he finally turned the little Alfa up an unmarked gravel track seemingly to nowhere. It led through mature trees, past an old stone cottage and finally to a sleek, modern, single-storey building set in open parkland. A squad car sat to one side of the wide gravel turning area, and as he pulled to a halt a couple of uniform officers stepped out. One stretched like a man unworried by the new arrival; the other strode over to the car.

'Can I ask what you're doing here?' The officer was young and wore the uniform of a constable. McLean didn't recognize him, but that was hardly surprising. They were a long way from Edinburgh.

'That you, Keithy?' Harrison piped up from the passenger seat, causing the constable to bend down lower and knock his head against the edge of the car door.

'Ow.' He rubbed at his temple, peering into the gloomy interior, past McLean. 'Janie? Janie Harrison?'

'Perhaps this would make things clearer, Constable.' McLean pulled out his warrant card and held it up for the young officer to see. There was a moment's pause, and then he straightened up, stepping backwards so swiftly he almost tripped and fell on his arse.

'I'm sorry, sir. I didn't . . . No one said . . .'

'No harm done.' McLean opened the door and stepped out, feeling the chill in the air. He'd brought a coat, but it was on the back seat.

'You found the place all right then, Inspector?'

McLean turned to see the other officer approaching at a more leisurely pace. This man he did recognize. Sergeant James Logan was a contemporary of Grumpy Bob and had worked in Lothian and Borders for most of his career before transferring to Fife just before Police Scotland had come into being.

'Aye, in the end.' He looked around the gravelled area, walled in by the house on one side, a garage block beside it and thick trees to the back. 'Not an easy place to get to, mind.'

'Reckon that's why Bill would've bought it. He always was one for his privacy.'

McLean frowned. Someone else had mentioned that about Chalmers recently. Then he remembered his chat with Ruth Tennant in the offices of Morningstar.

'You knew him then, Jim?'

'No' really. We came up through the ranks together, but he was CID and I was Traffic. Then the daft bugger got himself hooked on drugs and, well, you know the rest.'

'Don't think anyone really knows the rest. That's why we're here.' McLean turned back to where Harrison and the young PC were chatting away like old friends. 'You been watching the place, I take it?'

'Aye, since before dawn. Night shift were here before then. No one's come or gone since we got the call day before yesterday. Took your time getting here.'

'Sorry about that, Jim. We're short-staffed, same as

everyone. I'd've sent Grumpy Bob, but he's always had a knack for being somewhere else when the assignments are being given out.'

'Aye, that sounds like Bob.' Logan nodded in the direction of the two constables. 'That you breaking in his replacement? She's kinder on the eyes, I'll give you that much.'

McLean ignored the comment. Sure, Logan was old school, but there was only so much age could excuse.

'Anyone been inside yet?'

'Not as far as I know. I've had a wee shuftie in through the windows on the other side, but you can't see much wi' the blinds down. The door's locked and I've no' got any keys. We've been waiting for your lot to come out before trying to break the door open.'

McLean pulled the 'Welcome to Fife' keyring out of his pocket. 'That might not be necessary. As long as he doesn't have an alarm.' He shouted over at Harrison. 'You done chatting yet, Constable? Only there's work to do.'

The acting DC stopped her talking instantly, snapped to attention like an infantryman on parade and then hurried over. 'Sorry, sir. It's just, Keithy . . . Constable Petrie and I came through Tulliallan together. Didn't know he'd moved to Fife.'

'Well there'll be plenty of time for reminiscing later, I'm sure. For now we've got a house to search. You remember your gloves?'

Harrison nodded her head, extracting a pair of white latex gloves from her jacket pocket.

'Right then, let's see if we can't get in.'

16

The house was a modernist design, all tall, narrow windows and raised-seam zinc roofing. The front door, if that was the right name for an entrance at what was clearly the back of the property, was almost as wide as it was high, heavy wood in angled planks with a thin strip of wire-reinforced glass running vertically down the middle and a long stainless-steel bar in place of a handle. At least the holes for the keys matched those on the keyring. The mortice had been left unlocked, and for a moment as McLean turned the key he thought he had been wrong about it. Turning it the other way gave a satisfying clunk, and he let out a sigh of relief before unlocking it again.

'This might be noisy,' he said as he slipped the Yale key into the latch, but when he turned it and pushed the door open, there was no wail of an alarm. Not even the beeping of a keypad waiting for the code to be tapped in. 'Then again, maybe not.'

Acting DS Harrison stepped into the surprisingly small entrance hall behind him. Once again, she stopped and sniffed, her head doing that cat-like jerking motion.

'What?' McLean asked.

'Nothing.' Harrison shook her head. 'Well, for a moment I thought I smelled something, but it's gone now.' She sniffed a couple of times more. 'No. Nothing.'

McLean shrugged; he'd not noticed anything himself. Perhaps the acting DC was trying to impress him.

'You want us to come in and help?'

McLean looked back out the door to where Sergeant Logan and Constable Petrie held back, uncertain as to whether or not they should enter.

'Give us a chance to check it over undisturbed eh, Jim?'

'Right you are, sir. We'll be waiting in the car if you need us. Too bloody cold to stand around outside for long.'

McLean nodded at the sergeant, then turned to Harrison. 'Touch nothing. Observation only.'

'What are we looking for, sir?'

'I don't know. I'll tell you when I see it.'

It was all open spaces and high ceilings. From the back, the house didn't look much, but inside it had an airiness that suggested a skilled architect had been involved in the design. A long corridor, lit by grimy skylights, linked several guest bedrooms to the main living area. McLean opened each door in turn, revealing rooms that were perhaps a little smaller than he was used to, each with its own tiny bathroom en suite. Their windows were the tall, narrow ones that looked out from the back of the house on to the driveway, and each had a blind pulled all the way down, casting a gloom over the rooms. The beds were made, the furniture simple and expensive, like the house itself.

At the end of the corridor they found a utility room complete with deep stainless-steel sink, washing machine and tumble-dryer. An empty basket sat in front of the washer. Opening the machine, McLean pulled out damp sheets that were beginning to smell of mildew.

'Looks like he put on a wash just before leaving,' Harrison said.

'Or someone else did.' McLean shoved the sheets back where he'd found them. 'Begs the question why he'd want clean sheets if he'd only just got here, though. Come on, let's see what else we can find.'

Two doors led off the utility room, one to a concrete-floored shower and toilet that would probably be described in an estate agent's brochure as a 'wet room' but to McLean just looked like somewhere it would be easy to clean off after getting covered in blood. The other opened on to the garage block, where two cars sat side by side in the darkness, and beyond them a door that must lead out to the garden.

'Anyone spoken to Traffic about Chalmers' cars?' he asked.

Harrison looked blank for a moment, then pulled out a heavy, standard-issue airwave set. 'I'll get on to it, sir.'

'You do that. I'll have a wee look at the front of the house.'

The more he walked around the empty, silent house, the more McLean became convinced that someone had been here before him. Not Chalmers in his last few hours alive; this was something else. A violation, perhaps. The way a house felt after a team of trained detectives had been through it, only neater.

Nothing was out of place, or at least not obviously so. It didn't help that Chalmers was obsessively clean; there was no dust to leave tell-tale marks where things might have been moved. There was very little to be moved at all, for that matter. No little personal effects, no photographs of the man shaking hands with rich, famous or powerful friends like the ones McLean had seen in his office in the city. There weren't any of what his grandmother had used to call dust collectors: little keepsakes; china figurines; wooden carvings given as gifts. Nothing to suggest that a person actually lived here.

And yet, even so, it felt changed.

He walked slowly around the vast open-plan area that was the front of the house. Floor-to-ceiling glass panes made up one entire wall of the building, and the wintry light played in through blinds that had been pulled down over them. He carefully opened one, flooding the room with so much brightness he had to squint until his eyes adjusted to the glare. He might have expected motes to swirl and dance in the sunlight, disturbed by his actions, but it was cleaner than a laboratory. Spotless.

The great space had been split into three zones by the careful placement of furniture. At the end where he had entered, kitchen units and a shiny granite-topped island looked remarkably similar to the fittings in the mews house, expensive and unused. A dozen chairs surrounded a large dining table, but only one place had been set. An empty glass sat on a coaster to the right of an empty plate, knife and fork neatly placed together at six o'clock. This and the laundry basket were perhaps the only evidence that anyone had been in the house at all. Apart from that feeling in the pit of his stomach, and the scent he kept catching on the air. Only it wasn't so much a scent as a taste, so faint he couldn't be sure he wasn't imagining it. Wasn't imagining the whole thing.

McLean found the master bedroom suite through a door at the far end opposite the kitchen. As he stepped into the room, he tasted that bitter note in the air, that faintest hint of something unpleasant. It was almost like there was a blocked drain somewhere, but by the time he'd crossed to the open bathroom door and looked inside, the smell was gone. The bathroom itself was clean, unremarkable. The cupboard under the basin held an assortment of toiletries and some small hand towels. Above the basin, a mirror-fronted cabinet yielded toothbrush and toothpaste, soap tidied away in its own little plastic soap box, an electric razor and several empty prescription pill bottles. He was about to reach for one, take it out and read the label, when he noticed something strange about what he was seeing. A tiny detail – perhaps nothing – but everything in the cabinet was placed neatly at the right-hand edge of the shelves, a clean, empty space to the left. Had someone been through the contents already, not putting them back exactly where they had been before? Or had there been more toiletries in there?

Closing the bathroom cabinet, he went back through to the bedroom. The bed had been stripped, the duvet folded neatly over the end of the bare mattress, uncased pillows at the head where they should have been. There were two bedside tables, one with a book, a reading light and a folded leather wallet on it. The book was interesting enough, a first edition of Thomas De Quincey's *Confessions of an English Opium Eater*. McLean didn't know much about antiquarian books, but he'd guess it must have been worth a couple of thousand pounds. Not your typical bedtime reading either.

Picking up the wallet, he found credit cards in Bill Chalmers' name, along with a thin wad of twenty pound notes that looked like they'd not been touched since they'd come out of the cash machine. A couple of receipts were neatly folded and tucked away, no doubt for sending to the accountant. Chalmers had filled his car up with petrol just outside Kirkcaldy on the evening before he died.

Heading around to the other side of the bed, McLean found another book, this one more modern. He'd seen it in all the bookshops and newsagents for months now. There was a movie coming soon or something. If he ever had the time to read, he might have picked a copy up, but it was more the sort of thing Emma would like, not him. And not the sort of thing he'd have thought a man like Chalmers would read either, although it was always possible. It wasn't so much the choice of reading matter that concerned him, though. It was the fact that there were two books, one either side of the bed. Two bedside lights, too, but only one alarm.

Bending down, he looked under the bed. Something lay at the foot end, dropped and forgotten. He reached in and pulled out the briefest of women's knickers, black lace and silk. As he held them up to the light, McLean caught that whiff of drains again, bent his head slightly to sniff the scant fabric.

'Wondered where you'd got to, sir . . . Oh.' Harrison took that exact moment to walk into the bedroom. Her normally ruddy face darkened even more. 'Sorry, sir.'

'I found these lying under the bed.' Heat spread across the tips of McLean's ears as he proffered the undergarment to the constable. 'Do they mean anything to you?'

Harrison gave him a look of utter horror, then seemed to understand. She took the panties with some reluctance, unwilling to touch them even though she was wearing gloves. 'Not my sort of thing, to be honest, sir. Something like this, well, it tends to get wedged uncomfortably if you wear it for more than a few minutes. If you know what I mean.'

'Designed to be taken off, rather than worn.'

'Exactly.' Harrison gave him a brief smile of relief at his understanding, and the knickers back. McLean guddled in his pocket for an evidence bag and dropped the offending article inside.

'So it would seem Mr Chalmers had a lady friend visiting, which might explain the sheets. I think tracking her down is a matter of considerable importance, don't you?'

'Yes, sir.' Harrison paused. 'Any idea how?'

The call came as they were heading on to the dual carriageway, just past Kirkcaldy. McLean fumbled his phone out of his pocket with one hand, reaching for the headlight switch on the way past as he handed it to Acting DC Harrison. She stared at it as if it were some kind of poisonous snake tossed into her lap.

'Well, answer it, won't you?' He peered through the windscreen at the dark road ahead as flurries of snow began to spatter against the glass. Harrison fumbled with the unfamiliar device but managed to accept the call before it rang off.

'Detective Inspector McLean's phone,' she said, in a voice that would make a temping agency receptionist proud. There was a pause while McLean tried to concentrate on the road rather than look at her, then she added, 'No, this is Acting DC Harrison. The detective inspector is driving right now.' Another pause, and then, 'No, I don't think hands-free is an option. I can put it on speakerphone if that helps, but it's a wee bit noisy in here.'

McLean spotted a parking area a few hundred yards ahead, indicated and pulled over, letting the engine idle to keep some heat in the car.

'Who is it?' he asked as Harrison handed the phone back to him.

'A woman. Think she said her name was Tennant? Ruth or something?'

McLean grabbed the phone, shoved it against his ear. 'Ruth?'

'Oh, thank Christ. I didn't know where else to turn.' Far from the calm and collected woman he had met at the offices of Morningstar just forty-eight hours earlier, Ruth Tennant sounded distraught, her words catching in her throat.

'Where are you now? What's the problem?' McLean glanced at his watch. By the time he got back to the city, rush hour would be in full flow.

'Oh God, it's such a mess. They've trashed everything.'

'Look, slow down a bit. Who's trashed what?' McLean asked the question even though he was fairly sure he knew the answer to at least the second half. 'Are you at the charity's office?'

'I was out all day chasing up sponsors. Thought Malcolm was OK here on his own. But he's gone. The front door was open and the place has been turned over. Oh God. First Bill, now this.'

'Have you called the police?'

Silence. And then: 'What do you think I'm doing now?'

McLean bit back the retort he wanted to give, counted to five in his head. 'OK. I'll get a squad car over as soon as possible. I'm in Fife at the moment, on my way home. I'll be there in less than an hour. You going to be all right?'

Through the corner of his eye, McLean saw that Harrison had already pulled out her airwave set. Thinking quickly, a good sign.

'I'll lock the door. Wait for you.'

'You do that, Ruth. I'll get there as soon as I can.' He hung up, rubbed his eyes, then turned to Harrison. 'Get on to Control will you? Need a squad car to the offices of Morningstar.' He glanced in the wing mirror, selected first gear and pulled back out on to the road, before adding: 'Oh, and I hope you didn't have any plans for this evening. Looks like it might be a long one.'

17

All things considered, McLean reckoned he made quite good time from Kirkcaldy to the West End. If it had been morning it would have been a different matter, of course. Fighting a way through the stop—start of the city's rush hour was never much fun, especially when the car you were driving was older than you. At least in the evening he was going against the bulk of the traffic flow.

Not one but three squad cars were parked on the double yellow lines outside the offices of Morningstar when he arrived. A couple of uniform constables were loitering outside, hunched into their fluorescent jackets and heavy fleece coats against the cold. They'd even stretched blue-and-white police tape in a cordon around the steps that led up to the front door, so he felt he was safe to pull in alongside. It was unlikely anyone would give him a ticket.

'Mrs Tennant. She still in there?' McLean asked of the first constable to approach him. The young lad looked a bit surprised to be asked.

'Aye, sir. Wasn't expecting anyone from CID to turn up. It's just a burglary. Sergeant Stephen's inside taking a statement.'

'No such thing as "just a burglary", constable.' McLean slapped the officer on the shoulder, then ducked under the tape and sprung up the steps, confident that Acting DC Harrison would not be far behind.

His first sight was of the door itself. He remembered it from his previous visit, but now the wood around the lock was splintered, fragments lying on the floor. It looked like someone had used a crowbar to jemmy it open, which was strange given that it should have been unlocked anyway.

Inside, the mayhem spread across the reception hall. All the magazines had been swept off the table between the two low sofas set out for waiting visitors. The reception desk lay on its side, the computer and phone tumbled on to the floor in a tangle of cables. Looking around, McLean couldn't see what had happened to the receptionist's chair, and then he saw it, knocked over and wedged into the doorway that led through to the kitchen area where Malky had made him his coffee. Low voices echoed through from the offices beyond the hall. He took a step towards them, foot crunching on the broken shards of a plant pot.

'I think we're going to need Forensics here, don't you?' he said to Harrison. She nodded, retreating to the doorway as she pulled out her airwave set once more to make the call.

He found them in the office where he'd spoken to Ruth Tennant the day before. Sergeant Stephen and a female constable sat in a couple of the mismatched armchairs, Tennant across the table from them. She looked up as he stepped in through the open door, haggard face creasing into a worried smile.

'Tony –' She stood up, glanced at the two uniformed officers. 'Inspector, I should say.'

'Ah, sir. You're here. Good.' Sergeant Stephen also sprang

to his feet, eyes flicking past McLean's shoulder to where Harrison was standing.

'You've got the scene secure I take it, Kenny?'

'Couple of constables on the back door. You'll have met the two at the front. I take it this is all connected to the Chalmers case? What with someone going over his house as well.'

'It would be bloody strange if it wasn't.' McLean looked around the room, seeing signs of turmoil everywhere. It wasn't quite as violent as the explosion in Chalmers' living room, but it was quite clear that someone had been through the office in a hurry, looking for something in a frenzy. A crazed drug addict hoping to find a fix? It didn't seem likely.

'Have you touched anything, Ruth?' he asked. Mrs Tennant looked a little startled, struggling out of her shock before she could answer.

'A bit. The doors. I may have stood a few chairs up and stuff. But no. I don't think so. I've not looked through any of the cabinets yet.'

McLean followed her gaze over to the row of filing cabinets along the wall behind the desk. Several drawers had been pulled open, files lying scattered around. The desk was largely as he remembered it from their earlier meeting, except for a large clear space in the middle.

'Your laptop?'

'They took it. Don't think there's much of any use to anyone on it, and it's so old it's hardly worth flogging for drugs.'

'You think that's what this is about? Someone stealing stuff to feed their habit?'

Mrs Tennant shrugged, a pained expression on her face. 'I don't know. We deal with drug addicts every day. It's what we do here, Tony. Help them come to terms with their problems, find ways for them to quit, give them support while they're recovering. I must have seen thousands over the years, and not all of them make it. Too many fall back into old habits.'

McLean wasn't convinced. 'What about the rest of the house? Chalmers' office? Upstairs?'

'We don't use much above the first floor. Well, except for storage. Used to have some rooms where folk could stay. Sort of a halfway house until they got themselves straightened up, but the offices around here didn't like it, so we moved that part of the operation. It's all empty rooms now.'

'We'll give them a quick check, make sure no one's hiding up there. I'll need to see Chalmers' office again, too.' McLean turned to Sergeant Stephen. 'You OK keeping an eye on things until Forensics get here?'

The sergeant nodded. 'Aye. And I've had a wee shuftie upstairs. It's all empty. Doesn't look like anyone's been up there in a while.'

'What about Malky? You said he was meant to be here?'

Tennant was staring off into the distance, the shock of the burglary beginning to take over. McLean reached out and gently touched her hand. She started, looked at him with wild eyes. 'What? Oh, Malky. Yes. Sorry. He often works late, getting the place tidy for the clients coming, that sort of thing. I don't think he really likes going back to his flat. He lives out on the Dalry Road.'

'And you've tried calling him?'

'He's not answering his mobile. Don't think they've got a working land line. I'd have gone round, but –'

'It's OK, Ruth. We've got this now.' McLean put on his best reassuring voice, hoping it would help. 'Why don't you give Malky's details to Sergeant Stephen here. We'll send a squad car round to check, and then get someone to take you home. That OK, Kenny?'

'Fine by me, sir. Always got time for Morningstar.'

McLean stood up, motioning for Tennant to stay as she went to do the same. 'Stay here, Ruth. I'll be back as soon as I can.' He turned to Harrison. 'OK, Constable, you're with me. Let's go and see what's missing.'

The damage and destruction seemed to get worse as they moved towards the back of the house. McLean recalled the corridor leading to Chalmers' office as a clutter of stationery cabinets and piles of cardboard boxes. Now the boxes were tumbled about the floor, the cabinets wrenched open and their contents thrown out, as if by a toddler impatient to get to their favourite toys. They picked a careful route through the mess, entering the office to find its light already on. It hadn't so much been searched as ransacked. Chairs lay on their backs, cushions slashed open and stuffing strewn all around. The photographs of Chalmers posing with the great and good had all been ripped from the walls. They lay in a pile in the middle of the room, snapped frames and broken glass speaking eloquently of a deep-rooted hatred for their subject. McLean looked for the picture of Dalgliesh and the other reporters that he had noticed before but if it was there, he couldn't see it. Harrison made to step into the room, but he put up his arm, held her back.

'Best not to upset too much before Forensics get here, aye?' They'd have their work cut out making sense of it all in any case. Whoever had been through the room had pulled out the drawers of the desk, one by one, and turned them upside down over the surface before throwing them aside. McLean pulled out a pair of latex gloves, knowing he was going to get a bollocking from Jemima Cairns for messing up her nice tidy crime scene. He picked a way through the detritus and edged carefully around the desk until he could see the holes where the drawers had been. Scattered over the surface and all around the upturned chair was everything McLean had seen the last time he had been here. It was impossible to get any closer without disturbing things, but amongst all the broken pens, old CD-Roms and power adapters for long-forgotten equipment he could see no glint of shiny silver, no cigar cutter with its curious inscription.

As he crouched down on his haunches, he caught a whiff of something unpleasant, too. Blocked drains, or something similar. He'd smelled it before, at Chalmers' house in Fife, so maybe it was something to do with the man himself. Then again, McLean hadn't noticed it the first time he'd been here, sat in that chair, gone through those drawers.

'What were you looking for?' He thought he'd asked the question under his breath, but the words must have carried across the silent room.

'Sir?' Harrison still stood in the doorway, arms by her sides in an uncomfortable stance as if she thought her mere presence might somehow contaminate the crime scene. Fair point: neither of them should have been mucking about here before Forensics arrived.

'Nothing. Just wondering what happened here, and where poor Malky Davison has got to.' He stood up slowly, stepped carefully back to the door. 'I've a horrible feeling it's not anywhere good.'

The house was dark as McLean pulled up the drive and parked his car by the back door. A quick glance at his watch showed that it was the wrong side of midnight: another long day. Mrs McCutcheon's cat stared up at him from her favourite winter spot in front of the Aga, blinking angrily as he flicked on the lights. She stood up, arched her back and then leapt on to the kitchen table, pausing only briefly to sniff at the plate of what looked like a healthy salad that Emma had left unfinished. Or perhaps barely started would be a more accurate description. For a moment McLean thought she might have left it out for him, but he dismissed the idea just as swiftly. He opened the fridge and pulled out the plate of cold pizza left over from the previous night, considered a beer to wash it down, then thought better of it. Bad enough to eat and then go straight to bed; drinking wouldn't help at all. Not even a dram from the drinks cabinet hidden behind a secret panel in one of the library bookcases. He had to be in the station in just a few hours' time for the morning briefing, after all.

Stifling a yawn, he sat down at the table and worked his way methodically through the pizza, not aware quite how hungry he had been until it was all gone and he found himself picking at Emma's wilted salad. He slid both plates away, sat back in his chair and glanced up at the clock on the wall. There really weren't enough hours left until he had to get up and go to work again, but his mind was still churning away, trying to make sense of the puzzle that was Bill Chalmers, his death and the events that had happened since. Maybe a dram and a few minutes of staring at the library wall would help.

Mrs McCutcheon's cat gave him an evil glare as he went to scrape the remains of Emma's salad into her bowl. She was right, of course. Lettuce, tomato and a few shavings of hard cheese were not a suitable meal for an obligate carnivore. Instead, he shoved them all in the bin before sliding the plates into the last spaces in the dishwasher. It hummed into life as he left the room and headed for the library.

Switching off the kitchen lights plunged him into total darkness. He didn't mind. This was his home, the house where he had grown up. He knew it as well as he knew anything, the way it creaked and groaned, the smells, the exact number of steps it took to get from one end of the corridor to the other, where it opened on to the hall. He walked on silent feet, relaxed in a way he couldn't be any-where else. It was madness, keeping this house. Just him and Em rattling around in a place big enough for the most promiscuous of Victorian families. But he could never think of selling, moving. Where would he go?

Enough light filtered in through the library windows for McLean to be able to see his way to his favourite arm-chair. A table beside it held a lamp, and he flicked it on, blinking as the dull brightness shattered the dark. Something moved on the sofa, groaning as if it were in pain.

'Em?' McLean hurried over as the shadowy shapes resolved themselves into a person lying on their back, head bent at an awkward angle. The television wasn't on, and the stereo was switched off. No hiss *thunk* of a record on the turntable left playing while she had fallen asleep. She hadn't wrapped herself in a blanket either, despite the unlit fire and the chill in the air. It looked like she had simply collapsed.

'Em?' He knelt beside her, reached a hand to her hair and gently eased it away from her face. She was dressed for work: sensible shoes, jeans, thick, woolly jumper over a cotton blouse. He could see she was breathing, but that was scant reassurance given what she had been through. Memories flickered in his mind, of finding her in a very different place, years earlier. Naked and bruised, handcuffed to an old iron bedstead, unconscious. It had taken the best part of six months for her to wake from that trauma.

'Em?' He brushed her cheek with the back of his hand, feeling a coldness there where she should have been vibrant and warm. She stirred at his touch, her lips parting to emit another low, pained moan. It sounded almost like speech, but no language he had ever heard. Under her closed eyelids, he could see her eyes flicking this way and that, like those of a terrified child.

'Em. Wake up.' This time McLean placed a hand on Emma's shoulder and shook her more firmly, willing her to wake. It took a long time, too long, but slowly the moaning quieted to nothing. Her eyes stilled, then slowly opened. A confused frown spread across her face.

'Tony? Where am . . . ? What . . . ?' She tried to move her head and sit up, then winced. 'Ow.'

'Careful. Think you must have cricked your neck.' McLean reached an arm under Emma's shoulder and helped ease her upright. She stretched gingerly, not risking another spasm, then looked around the library with wide eyes.

'How did I get in here?' Emma started shivering. 'Jesus, it's cold. What time is it?'

'Late.'

She looked around the darkened room, eyes wide so that the whites glowed in the lamplight. 'I don't even remember coming in here. I was in the kitchen, then . . .'

The words drifted away to nothing, but he could hear the tension in them, the worry. McLean put an arm around her shoulder and helped her up. She leaned into him, shivering more violently now. How long had she been lying there in the dark?

'Let's get you to bed, OK?' He steered her towards the door, all thoughts of a late night dram gone, along with the tumbling thoughts of the day. There was just one overriding worry now. 'And tomorrow we'll see about getting you an appointment with Dr Wheeler.'

18

The ringing phone was a welcome relief from a morning spent wading through paperwork. Somewhere else in the building, the investigation into Bill Chalmers' murder was chugging along, consuming resources without getting very far, overseen by Grumpy Bob and Acting DI Ritchie. McLean wanted to be in the action with them but, in truth, he knew there was none. The break-in at the offices of Morningstar so soon after the mews house suggested a line of enquiry that might be fruitful, but until Jemima Cairns had finished going over both scenes with her finest-toothed comb, they were stuck waiting.

'McLean.' He clamped the headset against his hunched shoulder, one hand closing the folder he had been working on while the other darted out to catch the pile it had come from to stop it tumbling to the floor.

'Control here. You put a request out for any sightings of Malcolm Davison?'

'Malcolm . . .' McLean took a while to join the dots. 'Malky. Aye. Have you found him?' McLean's excitement died almost as soon as it sparked; he wouldn't have been getting the call from Control if they'd found Malky alive.

'In a manner of speaking. Call's just come in about an unidentified male found in an abandoned flat in Muir-house. Drug addict. Looks like he's OD'd. No' sure if he's your man, but the description fits.'

'Muirhouse?' McLean pictured the concrete tower blocks, grey and foggy. One of the city's more spectacularly failed social experiments. An investigation had taken him out there just the year before. Another suspicious death, but not drugs that time. Or at least not any drugs the labs had been able to identify. 'Anyone from Specialist Crime assigned to it?'

'No' yet. Reckon if it's your man you'll be wanting to look into it yourself.'

McLean weighed the options. If someone else started investigating and it turned out to be Malky after all, then he'd have to go over everything the other detective had already done, which would waste time and add to the pile of shift allocation forms stacking up on his desk. On the other hand, if he found himself a spare detective constable, headed over to the crime scene now and it turned out not to be Malky, then he would have wasted a morning better spent concentrating on Chalmers. Except that a morning away from the paperwork was never really wasted, was it?

'Send me the details. I'll head over straight away.'

The trip to Muirhouse was mercifully swift, DC Harrison proving to be as skilful a driver as she was at finding a pool car in the first place. She wasn't too chatty either, which suited McLean just fine. He found it easier to think while moving, preferred to walk the streets in search of inspiration than sit at his desk and feel the weight of the bureaucracy crushing in on him. Sitting in a car was a good compromise; it would have taken all day to walk to the crime scene. As it was, light traffic meant the journey took little more than half an hour, and soon they were being shown through the police cordon and into a derelict council house, its windows boarded up in anticipation of redevelopment. Judging by the layers of graffiti and stinking piles of garbage in the mouldy hallway, the anticipation had been going on for quite some time.

'Scene of Crime here?' he asked of the uniform constable standing at the door. The young man nodded and pointed up the street a few paces. McLean almost didn't recognize the forensics van. It was new, for one thing, and sported a strange logo on the rear doors. If it hadn't been for the familiar sight of Dr Cairns in a full white body suit, he might have thought it was a council van or something from one of the utility companies. She greeted him with a surly scowl as he approached.

'You'll need a suit if you're going in,' she said, opening up the back of the van as he approached. She brought out a plastic-wrapped overall and a clipboard. 'And you'll have to sign for it, too.'

McLean raised an eyebrow. 'Sign?'

'Aye. Everything's got to be accounted for.' Cairns grimaced. 'Welcome to the private sector.'

'Private . . . ? I thought it was meant to be a public–private partnership.' McLean recalled a meeting, a couple of incomprehensible memos. Something to do with cost-cutting and rationalization and an empty assurance that nothing would really change. Was this what Emma had been moaning about?

'Don't get me started, OK?' Cairns waggled the clipboard at him, so he signed it. The paper overalls were no more comfortable than before, and he managed to rip the seam on one leg pulling it on. So the cost-cutting had started early.

'Where's the body?' he asked, as the forensic scientist continued scribbling away at her clipboard.

'First floor.' Cairns paused for long enough to point in the direction of one of the windows. Above ground level they hadn't been boarded up and the glass reflected grey clouds. A cold wind blowing in off the Forth made McLean glad of the thin extra layer as he trudged back to the house, where DC Harrison was still chatting with the uniform constable.

'You stay here. Get all the details down for the report.' He stepped into the hallway, nose wrinkling at the stench. Stone steps led up to the first-floor flats, bounded on one side by an iron handrail he wouldn't want to touch even with gloved hands. 'I'll go see if this really is our man.'

He needn't have worried. Surrounded by the city pathologist, his assistant, a crime scene photographer and another white-suited technician, Malcolm 'Malky' Davison didn't look all that different from the last time McLean had seen him, except that he was lying on his back and staring at the ceiling with dead eyes rather than handing him a cup of coffee. His face was still the colour of sun-bleached cardboard, a sallow sepia tint flecked with dark pockmarks. His mouth hung slightly open, revealing the jagged brown teeth of an addict, and his eyes were bloodshot and yellow. Lank hair splayed out on the cushion behind his head as if he were posing for some alternative fashion magazine, an image not helped by the way his right arm reached behind him, crooked at the elbow. Peering closer, McLean saw the left arm lying straight, a tell-tale tourniquet hanging around the scrawny bicep where it had been loosened once the vein had been found.

'Not much more we can do with him here.' Angus Cadwallader pushed himself back from the body, struggling off his knees and into a standing position with much groaning and creaking of joints. Only once he had steadied himself against the wall did he turn and notice McLean standing behind him. 'Oh, Tony. What a pleasant surprise.'

McLean was about to come back with a quip of his own when he noticed the crime scene photographer look up at him. She was wearing the full white bunny suit, complete with overboots and hood, which was probably why he hadn't recognized her before. He felt a bit of an idiot all the same.

'Emma? Is that you?'

She smiled, then stuck her tongue out at him before holding up the camera and taking a couple of pictures of his face. McLean opened his mouth to comment, concerned after the way he had found her the night before. This wasn't the time, though, or the place. He switched his attention to the pathologist as Cadwallader helped his assistant up from the floor.

'What's the story, Angus?'

'He's dead. Looks like an overdose. We'll know better once I've got him back to the mortuary.'

'How long, roughly?'

Cadwallader let out a weary sigh. 'You always ask. His core temperature's the same as the room and he's past rigor mortis, so more than a few hours at least. I'll get you a better idea as soon as I can schedule him for a PM. I take it he's not just some poor unfortunate junkie, then?'

'He was, but that was a while back. I was told he'd long since quit the habit. Name's Malky Davison. He works – worked I should say – for Morningstar. I met him just a couple of days ago. He made me a nice cup of coffee.'

Cadwallader looked once more at the dead body, nodded his head. 'Morningstar. I see. Well, I guess that would explain why a detective inspector would turn up to a place like this. I'll see if I can't get him to the head of the queue.'

'Thanks, Angus. I've a horrible feeling this is going to get messy.'

'Doesn't it always when you're involved, Tony?' Cadwallader's smile was genuine, but the sentiment rang too true for McLean to appreciate the joke. He shook his head gently and stepped aside so that the pathologist and his assistant could make good their escape.

'This how he was found?' he asked.

Emma was busy taking photographs, but she turned to face him at the question. 'It's how he was when I got here, for sure. No one from Forensics has moved him.'

McLean crouched down beside the body, seeing the all too familiar signs of overdose. Malky had kept his gear in a little zip-up wash bag, not unlike the one McLean had been given by his grandmother when he first went off to boarding school and which he was still using almost forty years later. It lay beside him, edges frayed, the apparatus of his drug-taking neatly arranged. By all accounts, this was a simple case; easy to guess why the reformed addict had slipped off the wagon, too. The high-profile death of his employer, sudden close scrutiny by the press and the police. That was enough surely to send someone back to their old, bad habits. So why did it all seem so wrong? So . . . staged.

'Don't think I'm going to find out much more here.' He rose up out of his crouch, knees protesting loudly. 'Think I'll go find Harrison and see what she's dug up.'

'Harrison?' Emma asked. 'New girl?'

McLean nodded. 'Nabbed her from Uniform when we first found Chalmers. We've drafted in a few others as well. It's not easy to run an investigation when half the trained detectives have left.'

'All change, and not much of it for the good.' Emma shook her head, then tried to hide the little sway she did to one side. McLean noticed it though, and the way what little of her face he could see went pale as the blood drained from it.

'Em, you OK?' McLean knew as soon as the words were out of his mouth that he shouldn't have said them. He could tell by the way her brow knitted into a deep frown, her lips pursing in suppressed anger. If she hadn't been holding an expensive digital camera, she would probably have folded her arms across her chest, maybe even started tapping her foot.

'I'm fine, and you know it, Tony McLean.'

'At least tell me you spoke to Dr Wheeler this morning.'

'Yes, I spoke to her. She asked how you were, actually. Something you're not telling me?'

It was a classic diversionary tactic; McLean knew that as well as anyone. 'Look, I'm only asking because I worry, OK? You took a nasty –'

'Yes, I know. I was the one it happened to, remember. And it was three years ago. If I was going to drop down dead, do you not think I'd have done so already?'

McLean opened his mouth to complain, but fortunately

Jemima Cairns stopped him from making a bad situation even worse. 'You two lovebirds know this is a crime scene, aye?' She walked into the room, followed by two technicians, ready to take the body away. McLean stepped aside, watching closely as they placed a stretcher on the floor alongside the body, gently folded the arms over the lifeless chest, and lifted it on in a well-practised manoeuvre.

As they left, Cairns stooped down and began carefully placing the items on the floor into clear plastic bags, labelling them as she went. Emma continued to take photographs, but he was fairly sure this was just an excuse not to have to talk to him.

'I'll be off then,' he said to Dr Cairns. 'Let me know if you come up with anything unusual.'

Cairns turned, ready to give him some sarcastic response, but both of them were interrupted by Emma's quiet 'oh'. They looked up just in time to see her puzzled frown turn to a blankness as her eyes rolled up into her head. Her knees buckled and before anyone could do anything, she toppled sideways into the pile of mouldy cushions.

19

'We're going to have to keep her in for observation. I want to get her into the CT scanner as well, have a look at what's going on in her head.'

It was all too hauntingly familiar. McLean stood at the corner of the hospital room, looking at Emma's sleeping form as Dr Caroline Wheeler went through her speech. How many times had he been here before?

'She's going to be OK though?' Even he could hear the desperation in his voice.

Dr Wheeler put a reassuring hand on his arm. 'I'd be lying if I said I knew for certain. Let's wait until the scans are in, OK?'

'You'll look after her, won't you?' McLean's gaze moved from Emma's slack, sleeping face to the comfortable chair by the wall. It was very tempting to sit there and wait for her to wake up. Not something that would go down well with his superiors though, especially in the middle of a major investigation that looked like it was getting more complicated by the hour.

'Go do your job, Tony. Let me do mine. I've got your number. We'll let you know as soon as she wakes up.'

As if it were taunting him, McLean's phone buzzed in his pocket, yet another in a long string of texts coming in from the investigation team – wanting to know where he was, no doubt. He should have switched the thing off when he came into the hospital, but they were far enough from the ICU and all the sensitive equipment he had thought he could get away with just muting it. Judging by the frown he received from Dr Wheeler, it was probably time to leave.

'I'll come back this evening. See how things are then.'

'You do that.' Dr Wheeler's touch was firmer now, turning him around and guiding him to the door. He risked a last glance back at Emma, still sleeping as peacefully as he had ever seen her, then nodded his thanks to the doctor and left.

A few of the junior nurses scowled at him as he walked down the corridor to the exit, phone out and scrolling through his messages. Most were too busy with their work to worry, or knew him anyway. Time was, this hospital had almost been his second home, after all. He even managed a couple of smiles and a polite 'Hello, Inspector' before he stepped out into the cold.

Despite an early start, the day was getting away from him, a weak yellow sun in a pale blue sky heading towards dusk already, even though it was only just gone three. McLean considered walking back to the station; it would take an hour, but the weather was good and he would have the rhythm of his feet on the pavement to help him think. Another buzz of his phone: another message from Brooks demanding to know where he was and what he was up to. It only made the thought of going off grid for a while more tempting. But he couldn't do that. Not if it meant the detective superintendent started taking out his frustration on the rest of the team. Reluctantly, he headed for the taxi rank.

*

'Where the fuck have you been, McLean? You're meant to be leading this investigation, not gallivanting off whenever you please.'

As welcomes went, it wasn't particularly fond, but nothing he hadn't heard from Detective Superintendent Brooks before. McLean considered ignoring his boss, but it was difficult when he was surrounded by junior officers and admin staff in the middle of a busy major incident room. The bustle and noise quietened almost instantly, all eyes turned to the pair of them.

'I'm surprised you noticed I was gone, sir.' He gave Brooks his best politician's smile. 'Still, I'm here now. Was there anything in particular you needed?'

Brooks was a fat man; there was no polite way of describing him otherwise. He liked his food and struggled to find a suit that could contain his ever-swelling flesh. His florid neck bulged out of the collar of his shirt, merging seamlessly into a head shaved bald and shiny with sweat despite the relative cool. Anger made him redden and swell even further, so that those not used to seeing it might think he was about to explode. Sometimes he did, at least metaphorically, and it was best to be elsewhere when that was happening. McLean had worked with him long enough to know when to back off, but they hadn't reached that point yet.

'Daily progress reports, McLean. Ongoing budgets. Cost projections. Or did you just think there was an endless pot of money for things like this?'

'I'm aware of the latest spending cuts, sir. I know we have to be smart with our investigation and not just throw resources at it in the hope something sticks.' McLean resisted the urge to add 'like some detectives I could name'.

'That's why I've not been in here as much as some lead investigators might. That's work best left to the project-management princes. As for progress reports, you'll have one just as soon as we've made some progress. We haven't even got the full toxicology results back from the lab yet.'

'I don't want your excuses, man. I want results.'

'Do you not think I want that too, sir? We're doing the best we can, but it's early days and it looks like someone else is interested in Chalmers, only they're not so fussy about due process.'

Brooks' face darkened, but at least the anger appeared to be subsiding. 'Someone else? What do you mean? Who?'

'I wish I knew. His Edinburgh house was broken into the night before last; looks like an interrupted burglary, but I'm not buying that. I've a suspicion someone's been through his place out in Fife as well, but that's been done a lot more subtly. Someone's ransacked the offices of Morningstar too. Turned them upside down, like they were looking for something. And I've just got back from Muirhouse –'

'Aye. Heard about that. Dead junkie. Could you not have left that to the drugs boys? Or even Uniform?'

'As I was saying, sir, before you interrupted, I've just got back from Muirhouse, where I was able to identify the dead man as Malky Davison, who worked for Morningstar. Yes, he was an addict, but he was recovering. He'd been straight for a couple of years.'

'So the shock of his boss dying knocked him off the wagon. Tragic, I'm sure, but it's not exactly relevant to this investigation, is it? I mean, unless you're telling me he had a helicopter pilot's licence or a tame dragon.'

McLean took a deep breath, let it out slowly in the hope that his growing frustration would go with it. 'He lived in Dalry, sir. So what the fuck was he doing in Muirhouse?'

'What are you on about, man?'

McLean bit his tongue, stopping himself from saying something that would stir the rage in the detective superintendent's breast once more. The entire major incident room was silent around the two of them now, breaths held so tightly that if someone didn't faint soon it would be a miracle.

'I've only just this moment got in, sir. I'm still waiting for the pathologist to come back to me with a time for the post mortem. All I can say is that if Malky Davison died from a drug overdose it was no accident, and I'd lay good odds it's connected to Bill Chalmers.'

Brooks held his stare for long moments, piggy little eyes almost vanished into the folds of his face so they looked like nothing so much as raisins pushed into unbaked dough. Finally, he shook his head.

'You're a bloody menace, McLean. This should have been a simple investigation.'

McLean knew bollocks when he heard it, and so, too, did Brooks. The detective superintendent turned away swiftly as his words sank in, stalking out of the incident room to a ripple of retreating officers. The bear having exited stage left, they all fixed their attention back on McLean, looking for guidance, as if he had any more idea what was happening than any of them.

'It's Stringer, isn't it?' he asked of one of the young detective constables nearby.

'Sir.' The young man nodded his head in confirmation.

'How are things coming along?'

A look of terror flickered across the detective constable's face at the question, which suggested to McLean that he didn't have much of a clue. 'How do you mean, sir? Things?'

'Aye, sorry. I should be more specific. Have we anything useful from the phone lines?'

DC Stringer's panicked look softened to one of relief. 'It's mostly rubbish, sir, but there's a few possible leads. Several callers say they were woken that morning by a strange noise near the Meadows, apparently, so there must have been something there. San— DC Gregg's gone off with Pete – sorry, DC Blane – to interview a couple of them.'

McLean looked around the room until he spotted a map of the city pinned to the wall by the whiteboards. 'Got them mapped yet?' he asked.

'I'm sorry?' Stringer looked panicked again, then he followed McLean's gaze to the wall. 'Oh, I see. No, sorry, sir. I'll get on to that right away.'

'You do that, Constable. See if we can't find out where our dragon came from. And while you're at it, give Ruth Tennant a call. I'd like to get her in for a formal statement. Meantime, if anyone needs me, I'll be in my office, making up a progress report for the superintendent.'

20

He had been meaning to head straight to his office, but somehow McLean's feet took him along the corridor of the station and down the stairs to the lower levels. It was a bit like travelling back in time. Smooth plastered walls painted institution beige and hung with motivational posters gave way to brickwork masked by a hundred and more years of leaded gloss white, so heavy it seemed to ooze like a child's ice-cream cone on a summer holiday in Portobello. The corridors were narrower too, their vaulted ceilings the undisturbed domain of spiders. Some of the more imaginative constables liked to pretend there were ghosts down here, the trapped spirits of condemned men who had died in the cells before they could be taken to the Grassmarket to be hanged. Never mind that the last public hanging in the city had happened before even this ancient part of the station was built, although perhaps not by much. It made for a good story to wind up the newbies.

It was ghosts and the searching of them that had brought him down here, McLean realized. The Cold Case Unit, of which he was still nominally in charge, lived deep in the bowels of the station, far away from the bustle of everyday investigations. It might well have been a great place to retreat when the major incident room was too demanding and the stacks of paperwork in his office too much to bear, were it not for the fact that nine times out of ten retired Detective Superintendent Charles Duguid could be found down here among the dusty archive boxes. For all the rapprochement they might have made in the past few months, McLean still found Dagwood hard to be around and he suspected the feeling was mutual.

'Beginning to think you'd forgotten all about us.' The detective superintendent leaned back in his leather chair, the same chair that had graced his office back when he was still a serving policeman and which McLean could have sworn was in Brooks' office until a couple of months ago.

'Thought you liked to be left to your own devices. And it's been a bit busy lately, chasing up your old chum Bill Chalmers.'

Duguid grimaced more than scowled, which was something of an improvement. 'Had much help from the top brass on that?'

'Funny you should mention it.' McLean pulled a chair out from one of the nearby empty desks and sat down on it. The Cold Case Unit should have had a half-dozen retired detectives working for it, backed up by a couple of constables and a sergeant, all reporting to him so that he could report to Call-me-Stevie, the deputy chief constable. So far, persuading retired detectives to join the team had proved harder than anticipated, and the DCC's enthusiasm for the whole project had waned, or at least been diverted elsewhere. Mostly, it was Duguid and Grumpy Bob, with occasional help from any detective constables who weren't quick enough with their excuses. Today it was only Duguid.

'Let me guess. Keeping their distance?'

'We've had two press conferences and nobody higher than a DI has bothered to turn up to either.'

Duguid stroked his chin with fingers that were far too long. 'Well, you can see it from their point of view. I'd be the same. First thing that'd happen if I was there, or Brooks or Robinson, there'd be a question about Bill's time on the force, about whether we'd worked with him and if we'd known about his drug dealing. Before you've got past the first question, the whole press conference is derailed. Smart move, really, only fielding officers who joined after the shitstorm blew over.'

Put like that, McLean had to admit Duguid had a point. 'Still doesn't explain why they're avoiding the incident room. Not that I'm complaining really. It's nice to be able to just get on with the job sometimes.'

'Tell me about it.' Duguid grimaced again, and McLean had the strangest feeling the man was trying to smile. 'That's not what you came to see me about though, is it?'

'No. Well, not unless you've any great insights into the case, and I kind of think you'd have told me if you had.'

Duguid said nothing, just nodded, so McLean went on.

'It's more about Tommy Johnston. We never solved that one, so I'm guessing it's still open.'

'And you reckon now's the time the CCU should have another look?' This time Duguid's smile was more recognizable, although still not friendly. Unless you too were an alligator.

'Everyone else will say it's entirely coincidental that Chalmers was found by Tommy's son. To be honest, I'd probably agree with them. I can't think why anyone would want to give a message like that to a ten-year-old boy, or even his mother.'

'Message?' Duguid leaned forward, steepling his fingers together and resting his chin on the tips.

'There has to be a reason Chalmers was killed the way he was. The only thing I can think of is to send someone a message. It's a particularly extreme way of saying "Don't fuck with us", if you like.' McLean slumped back in his chair. 'If that's the case, then someone out there knows who killed him and why. We're nowhere near to finding out either, not with the way the investigation's going at the moment. So I'm casting the net a bit further. Coming at it from a slightly different angle, if you will.'

'And if the CCU does all the work, then it's our budget footing the bill, which should keep Brooks happy.' Duguid did that half-smile half-grimace thing again. 'And here's me thinking you didn't care about the money.'

'Actually, I hadn't thought about that, but it's a good idea.' McLean stood up, scraping the chair legs against the flagstone floor. 'Can you make a start on reviewing the old case files?'

'On my own?' Duguid asked, waving a hand across the empty room.

'Good point. I'll track down Grumpy Bob.' McLean thought about the major incident room upstairs, the stalled investigation. 'See if I can find you a couple of constables, too. If you promise not to frighten them too much.'

Hunched over in the little circle of light from his desk lamp, McLean had no idea what time it was when his phone rang. It had been already dark when he started working through the overtime sheets, duty rosters and a thousand and one other things that needed his immediate attention, so a quick glance at the window didn't help. Only the twinge in his neck and shoulders when he reached for the handset suggested it had been more than an hour or two.

'McLean.'

'Call for you on the switchboard, sir. A Dr Wheeler?'

An icy chill ran down his neck and McLean scrambled in his pocket for his mobile. It let him know that it was near enough eight in the evening, but it also seemed to have decided there was no signal in his office. That would explain why the doctor had phoned the station, but not how he could have forgotten all about Emma's collapse that morning.

'Thank you. Put her through.' He tensed as the phone line went dead, then clicked as the call was connected. What possible bad news could there be that she would go to all this trouble to get in touch with him?

'Hello? Are you there?' Dr Wheeler's voice sounded distant, as if she were calling from the other side of the world, not the other side of the city.

'Hi. Caroline. Sorry, yes.'

'You're a hard man to contact sometimes, Tony.'

McLean fumbled with his mobile phone, peering at the screen and the little icon that told him he had one bar of signal now. It vibrated in his hand, a slew of messages and missed calls suddenly appearing. Dr Wheeler wasn't the only one who had been trying to contact him all afternoon and evening, it seemed.

'Sorry about that. My mobile seems to be acting up. Usually no problem with a signal in here, but for some reason it's not seeing anything.'

'That's karma, then. For when you should have switched it off in the hospital this morning and didn't.'

McLean relaxed a little. If Dr Wheeler was able to make jokes, then chances were she wasn't bearing bad tidings. 'What can I do for you? I take it this is about Emma?'

'The same. I'd say you could take her home and get her out of my hair but realistically we need to keep her in overnight for observation. I've got her booked for the MRI scanner at one and she should be able to leave after that.'

'Surprised she didn't call to let me know herself.' McLean thumbed the long list of mobile contacts his phone was only now admitting to having received. 'Oh, looks like she did.'

'That's probably one reason why she's been so . . .' Dr Wheeler paused, as if trying to find the right word. Or maybe trying to be diplomatic.

'Awkward?' McLean suggested.

'Unsettled, perhaps. I can see her point. I don't much like being cooped up in this place and I work here.'

'I'll swing past on my way home. Probably should be leaving now, anyway. It's been a long day.' He stifled a yawn, stretched his neck from side to side and winced as a spasm of pain shot up into the back of his head. He had definitely been staring at paperwork for too long.

'Actually, that was why I was calling. Em's going to need a fresh set of clothes for tomorrow. I was wondering if you couldn't fetch her something first.'

It made sense, even though McLean knew that whatever clothes he picked out would be wrong. Fresher than what she'd been wearing when she collapsed though, and everyone felt better after a change of underwear, didn't they?

'I'll do that then. Expect it'll take me a couple of hours.' He looked at his watch, even though he'd only just seen the time on his phone. 'Is that going to be a problem?'

'I wouldn't have thought so, no. It's not visiting hours, but you've never really been one for rules, have you Tony?'

21

Big Pants Ruthie Tennant clearly didn't like police stations. McLean had come to that conclusion even before
they made it to the nice interview room, but as things progressed it became more and more apparent. She played
with her fingers constantly, first in her lap, then on the
tabletop, then back in her lap. Each question prompted a
nervous start, as if someone had let off a firework unex-
pectedly behind her, and before she answered she would
push her spectacles up her nose with a shaky finger.

'It's all just getting a bit too much to take in. I mean,
first Bill and now Malky. Who's going to be next? Me?'

'Do you think your life is in danger, Mrs Tennant?' Acting DI Ritchie asked the question. McLean had brought
her in on the interview because hc thought Tennant would
be more relaxed with another woman in the room. It didn't
really seem to be working. If anything, she was even more
nervous when Ritchie spoke than when he did.

'I don't know. I can't think why, but then I can't understand why anyone would want to kill Bill in the first place.
And now poor Malky. I don't believe for a moment he had
a relapse, you know. Even if that's what they're saying.'

'How long have you known Malky, Ruth?' McLean
leaned forward as he asked the question, trying to keep
things calm.

'Malky? Well. Four years, maybe? No, five. He came

through the programme. Christ, I'm not sure how he wasn't already dead, given the stuff he was taking. But he responded well, and he and Bill hit it off too. You know part of the programme is finding jobs for recovering addicts, right? We work with businesses all over the city, teaching them how to cope with employees who might not be as reliable as most. At least to start with.'

'But Malky came to work for the charity,' McLean said.

'Aye. Like I said, he and Bill got on well. We've had a few others work in the offices or help out with some of the programmes, but Malky's the first one to stick around for more than a month or two.' Tennant interlocked her fingers, dropping both hands into her lap as she stared straight at McLean. 'And now he's gone.'

'You have other staff, though. People who can step in and keep things running?'

'Yes and no. Bill was the driving force behind it all, you understand. Most of the people running the programmes are volunteers. We don't have a lot of money for permanent staff. Just me and . . . well, Malky.'

'You say he got on well with Chalmers. Did they ever go off together? You know, after work, for a drink sort of thing?'

Tennant looked at McLean as if he was mad. 'Bill? With Malky? Go for a drink?' She shook her head. 'You really don't know anything about him, do you, Tony?'

'That's kind of why we're talking to you. So are you saying Bill was teetotal? Malky?'

Now Tennant laughed, which at least had the effect of relaxing her a little. 'Och, no. He liked a drink as much as the next man. Both of them did. But Bill would no' go out with the likes of Malky. No' in public. No. If he was going out, it was with much richer company.'

'So Malky, then. Did he have any friends you know of?' Ritchie asked.

Tennant's smile disappeared almost as soon as it had arrived. Her hands went back to fidgeting. 'I don't really know. Not outside of the charity. I mean, he had neighbours, in his wee tenement, but they'd hardly be what you'd call friends.'

'So no girlfriend then? Or boyfriend? I mean, we really don't know much about him at all.'

'I don't think he was gay.' Tennant stared off into the distance for a while, as if her thoughts were written in small letters on the far wall and she'd forgotten to bring her spectacles. 'No. I think I'd have known that. His mum lives out Granton way. You'd be as well speaking to her as anyone.'

'You got a name and address for her?' Ritchie asked.

'Aye. Should have. Rose. Rose Davison. Here.' Tennant produced a smartphone that had to be too big for her tiny head and hands, pecked at the screen until it came up with the details. McLean watched Ritchie write down the name in handwriting much neater than his own. Another person to talk to; another piece in what was turning into a very large jigsaw puzzle with no handy picture on the box for reference.

'Have you had a chance to look at the offices, see what was taken?' he asked.

Tennant shook her head. 'Your forensic people are still going over everything, but I wouldn't be surprised if there wasn't much missing. We didn't have much for starters – no cash lying around, and it's not as if we hand out drugs.'

'But you do operate a needle exchange,' Ritchie said. 'I take it people can come to the office for supplies?'

There was a fraction of a pause before Tennant answered. Not much, but McLean noticed it. 'No. They used to, but that part of town, it's not somewhere . . . Bill didn't like . . .'

'The other businesses in the street complained about junkies wandering past their offices, is that it?'

'Something like that, aye.' Tennant tilted her head in confirmation, a flicker of relief in her eyes as they darted from Ritchie to McLean and back again.

'How did you get needles to people, then?'

'Mostly through selected pharmacies across the city. A couple of outreach centres. I can give you the addresses.'

'So you don't do anything but admin from the offices in Rothesay Terrace?'

'We run some self-help groups, but only for people who've progressed far enough through the programme. Bill was always keen on outsourcing the work to other more local outfits. And we get a lot of our money from businesses in the West End. They don't much like it if we encourage too many drug addicts into the area. If only they knew the history of that part of town.'

McLean was about to ask Tennant what she meant, but Ritchie butted in.

'You keep mentioning this "programme". What exactly is it?'

Tennant's face broke into a broad smile. 'Ah, the programme. That was Bill's greatest achievement, I think. Did you know that most psychoactive drugs are only addictive within a particular set of environmental stress situations? There's been studies in rats where, if you give them a perfect playground with food and toys and no stress, they ignore it when you put heroin out for them. But if you lock them in a featureless cage with no stimulus and overcrowding, they're addicts within a day. Well, it's the same with people, really. You've seen the deprivation in some parts of the city. Folk who've never been employed and never will be. Living in squalid conditions with no hope of ever improving. Endlessly bombarded with images of a perfect life they can never hope to achieve. Hardly surprising they turn to drugs and then get hooked. So the programme tries to deal with both. It's a multi-disciplinary approach, tackling the problems behind the addiction at the same time as the addiction itself. All of our clients undergo one to one therapy sessions, as well as group and self-help classes, while they're weaned off whatever drug they've become addicted to through chemical and other interventions. There are fortnight- and month-long boot camps designed to remove the clients from the soul-destroying environment that led to their addiction in the first place, and –'

'I think we get the picture.' McLean interrupted before Tennant fainted from lack of breath. 'So what's going to happen to the charity now?' he asked. 'Will you soldier on?'

'I don't really see how I can do anything else. I'll have to get more help in, and we'll have to see what the lawyers have to say about the offices. I've got a meeting scheduled with the accountants, too. We sunk a lot of cash into the latest campaign and now we're going to have to pull the plug on it. At least for the time being.' Tennant had been almost happy for a moment, explaining the rationale behind Morningstar, but now her hands were back in her lap, fingers twisting together then releasing again.

'I'll have a word with the forensics team, see how quickly we can get you back into your offices.' McLean stood up, indicating to Ritchie and Tennant both that the interview was over. 'I'll speak to the duty sergeant, too. We can have a constable on the door for your protection if you want.'

Something like terror flitted across Tennant's face. 'Oh. No. That really won't be necessary.'

McLean let out a silent sigh of relief. He'd made the promise genuinely, but the cost of personal protection would have knocked a big hole in their budget. 'Well, if you're sure. We can give you a panic alarm for the office and your home. Hopefully, you'll never need to use them.' He held out his hand, gave hers a reassuring shake when she took it. 'If there's anything else we need to know, I'll give you a call. That OK?'

Tennant looked a little surprised. 'Of course. But do you think that'll be likely? I mean, I've told you just about everything I know.'

'I'm afraid so,' McLean said. 'I've a suspicion the investigation into Bill Chalmers' death won't be over any time soon. And Malky Davison is a complication we could well have done without.'

'Well, that was a bit of a waste of time, don't you think?'

Acting Detective Inspector Ritchie leaned against the wall opposite the open doorway to the nice interview room, watching as Ruth Tennant was led away to a waiting car by a uniform constable. McLean fiddled with his phone; he'd somehow managed to turn it off during the interview rather than simply muting it, and now he couldn't get it to switch back on.

'Oh, I don't think so. I thought it was rather illuminating, actually.' He let out an inaudible sigh of relief as the screen lit up, although soon enough it would start pinging all the messages and missed calls that had come in during the past hour.

'How so?' Ritchie asked.

'Well, we found out all we ever needed to know about Morningstar's programme, for one thing.'

'Aye, and some. I've read that story about the rats. Sure it's not the whole picture. But that's not what you're talking about, is it?' Ritchie twined her fingers together, in and out, in a parody of Tennant's anxious fidgeting.

'You noticed that too? I've had nervous interviewees before, but usually when we've hauled them in as suspects. Not when they're just giving us background information.'

'You think she was hiding something?' Ritchie pushed herself away from the wall, peered down the corridor in the direction Tennant had left.

'I'm fairly sure of it, just not quite sure whether it's to do with Bill Chalmers' death, the break-in, Malky Davison or all three. Odd that she was scared they'd come for her next but didn't want us to put a constable on her door.'

'You want to get her back in sometime? Have another go at her?'

'Could do. Maybe get you and Sandy Gregg to interview her once we've done a bit more background on both her and the charity.'

'Why us?' Ritchie asked.

'Because she's uncomfortable in the company of other women.' McLean wanted it to be that reason, but he couldn't kid himself it was only that. 'And because I was at school with her when I was five.'

The pale lines of skin where Ritchie's eyebrows had once been raised high. 'Is there anyone in this city you're not distantly related to?'

'I was at school with her, Kirsty. We're not cousins or anything.'

Ritchie laughed, something McLean hadn't heard in a while. 'Just kidding. But I guess you're right. Best to keep your distance if there's any connection. Even something as tenuous as that.' She paused a moment before adding: 'What was she like, though? Did you have a crush on her?'

'Big Pants Ruthie? Hardly.' It was McLean's turn to laugh.

'Big Pants?' Ritchie arched her missing eyebrows again.

'Her mum dressed her in dungarees. It's a long story. Not really relevant here. I'm more interested in finding out where these residential treatments are held if it's not at the offices in Rothesay Terrace. I'd like someone to speak to the pharmacists doing the needle exchanges, too. And I'd really like to know why a charity struggling to raise funds can still operate out of a building worth at least a couple of million.'

Ritchie had already pulled out her notebook before McLean finished speaking, and was jotting down notes. 'Why is it I feel like a detective sergeant all over again?' she asked, with only the ghost of a smile as she spoke.

22

'Poor lad must have had a miserable life if these are anything to go by.'

Mid-morning and outside the sun would just be beginning to show itself above the tops of the Pentland Hills, south of the city. McLean had entered the city mortuary in the pre-dawn gloom that lingered in the depths of the Cowgate far longer than in most parts of town. He hoped he'd get a chance to see natural light at least once today.

'Track marks?' He stood a short distance from the examination table, keeping out of Angus Cadwallader's way as the pathologist made his swift but methodical examination of Malky Davison's body. Stripped naked, he was skeletally thin, his skin an unhealthy tone even for a dead man. How he could have managed to lift anything with those stick arms, McLean had no idea, let alone pull tight a tourniquet and find a vein.

'There's some of that, yes.' Cadwallader picked up one of the dead man's hands, cradling his elbow at the same time and angling the arm to the light. McLean peered in, seeing a mess of scars, pinprick marks and pale yellow bruising at the crook. 'See here? That's the injection point he used yesterday. But the rest of these are ancient.'

'According to his boss he'd been clean at least three years. He came through their programme, then stuck around to help others out.' McLean remembered the interview with Ruth Tennant, a woman struggling to cope with the sudden disintegration of her life. Even with all the shit falling around her, she had been proud of Malky Davison, shocked at the way he had died.

'Yes, well. I dare say he stopped injecting heroin that long ago, but I don't see much evidence to suggest he was what you would call clean.' Cadwallader put the arm back down on the stainless steel table, moving around to look at the dead man's head. Gentle fingers teased away straggly hair, revealing a scalp as acne-spotted as Malky's cheeks and forehead. Whatever Cadwallader was looking for, he clearly didn't find it there, switching his attention first to the eyes, then Malky's mouth, and finally peering closely at his armpits.

'You think he was shooting up somewhere else?' McLean asked.

'Well, yes. At least, that was what I assumed, given his overall state ante mortem. But I can't find any obvious injection site. It's like he was taking in the drug some other way.'

'Like smoking it, maybe? Eating it?'

Cadwallader paused in his examination to stare at McLean, a curious expression on his face. 'Actually, yes. Very much like smoking it.'

He put down the leg he had been holding up to examine the inner thigh, and went back to Davison's head.

'A bit of light in here please, Tracy?' Cadwallader prised open the dead man's mouth, then fetched a tiny round mirror on the end of a slim telescopic pole from the table of instruments beside him. Bending low, he peered inside, using the mirror to look at the back of Davison's teeth.

McLean waited as patiently as he could, knowing full well that the pathologist would take only the time he needed.

'I did wonder about his teeth,' Cadwallader said, letting out a small groan as he straightened up. 'I mean, heroin addicts aren't noted for their dental hygiene, but if he'd really given up then these should be in a bit better condition. The rest of his mouth shows signs of prolonged dryness, too. You get that with all heroin use, but it can be particularly bad when it's smoked.'

'So he was still using, just not injecting?'

'Something like that, yes. We'll need to see what the toxicology screening comes up with, and I suspect that whatever was injected is going to mask most of what was already there. I'd hazard a guess, though, that this poor lad couldn't quite make the jump to clean living and instead swapped the needle for the pipe.'

McLean looked at the naked body once more, seeing the ribs poking through the skin of the chest, the tufts of hair sprouting around the nipples, the empty hollow of the stomach and the twisted, almost arthritic knobbliness of the joints. His mouth had not closed again after the pathologist's examination, and with his head tilted back he looked like some tortured soul from a Hieronymus Bosch painting.

'So you think maybe he did overdose? Couldn't cope with the strain of his boss dying like that and fell back into bad habits?' McLean tried to picture the room where they had found the body, the cushions spread out on the floor, the little washbag of drug-taking paraphernalia. He'd have to get that back from Forensics, check to see if there was anything unusual about it.

'That's not really my department now, is it, Tony?' Cadwallader grinned, though without much mirth. 'There is one thing that you might find interesting, though. Here.'

The pathologist beckoned McLean closer to the examination table, while at the same time lifting the body by the shoulder and rolling it slightly. Without being prompted, Dr Sharp ducked in to help, holding on to Davison's head. McLean stepped around the table until he could see the dead man's back.

'Look familiar?' Cadwallader pointed at a faded tattoo that nestled in between Davison's shoulder blades. It might have been a Celtic spiral or something Chinese, an abstract swirl of a pattern.

'Should it?' McLean twisted his head to one side, but it didn't make the image any easier to see.

'You've not seen the photos?' Cadwallader set the body back down again, a hurt expression on his face. 'Tracy, did you not send him the photos?'

'You know I sent the photos, Angus. They were attached to the PM report when you signed it.'

'PM?' McLean asked. 'Whose PM?'

Cadwallader shuffled over to the computer terminal on the counter that ran along one wall of the examination theatre. Above it, where the old X-ray light boxes had hung, were now a couple of expensive-looking flat-screen monitors, and they flickered into life as he poked at the keyboard with a latex-gloved finger.

'How do I get the bloody thing to work?'

Dr Sharp reached around him and tapped at the keys, swiping through a number of menus until some high resolution photographs appeared on the screens. McLean peered at them, not quite sure what he was seeing at first. Then he began to understand the scale, and it all started to make horrible sense.

'Bill Chalmers had a couple of tattoos, if you remember, Tony. He was quite badly cut up, so it took a while to get proper photographs. Good thing Tracy's such a neat hand with the stitches. This one was on his arm.' Cadwallader pointed at the first screen as he spoke. 'Nothing too unusual, I guess. If tattoos are your thing. But this one.' The pathologist tapped at the second screen. 'This was on his chest. It's not exactly the same, but . . .'

McLean took a couple of steps forward, peering at the image on the screen. Black ink described a series of arcs, lines jutting from them in a regular pattern that slowly resolved into a stylized image of the trailing edge of a wing. Curved around, it merged into a neck and then a head, jaws open, fangs protruding.

'A dragon?'

'Looks like it.' Cadwallader turned and pointed at the dead body on the slab. 'And it looks like your boy's got one much the same on his back.'

23

Bo's Inks sat between a disreputable bookies and a long-empty antiques shop in a quiet, dark street just off the Lothian Road. McLean remembered it from his beat constable days, back when Bo had still been alive. Then it had been a favourite stop on the daily rounds for old Sergeant Guthrie McManus, who had served in the Merchant Navy with Bo. Now it was run by Bo's son, Eddie, and his partner George and for all its down-at-heel appearance it was perhaps the best tattoo parlour in the city.

McLean pushed open the door to the sound of a jangling bell. The front of the shop might easily have been mistaken for a café in dire need of redecorating. Tables and chairs were dotted around an open space almost randomly, only whereas, in a café, they might have bowls of sugar and paper-napkin holders on them, here they were strewn with black leather-covered ring binders. Inside, he knew, were endless photographs and designs, a lifetime's work and potential inspiration for any would-be customers. The walls were lined with framed photographs too, with a general theme of tattoos.

'Finally come to get that excrescence on your shoulder properly sorted have you?'

McLean looked over to where an open doorway led through to the back of the shop and the instruments of torture used in the tattooing process. Eddie Cobbold grinned as he crossed the room, extending a warm hand to be shaken. If he had yet more tattoos on his bare arms and shoulders, McLean couldn't distinguish them from the mass of colourful swirls and abstract patterns that had been there the last time he visited.

'I've kind of got used to it, Eddie,' he said. 'And it's a handy reminder of the follies of youth.'

'I hope you're not disparaging the tattooist's art.'

'Only one particular tattooist, and I can't really blame him since I was the one asked for it in the first place.'

'Aye, but –' Eddie began to speak, then noticed DC Harrison standing in the doorway. 'Hang on. What happened to the wee ginger lad you had with you the last time?'

'He moved on, which means I have to break in a new detective constable. Be nice to her, OK?'

'As if I'd do anything else.' Cobbold smiled, revealing a single gold tooth in a line of perfect white. He gestured towards the doorway. 'Shall we go through? I take it you've not just popped in for a chat. And since you're determined to keep that sheep on your shoulder –'

'It's not a sheep, it's a Celtic symbol of peace. Well, it's meant to be.'

'It looks like a bloody sheep. Your only saving grace is it's wee.'

Cobbold led them through to the back of the shop, past a couple of reclining chairs that looked like they wouldn't have been out of place in a fifties dentist's. Industrial shelving piled high with inks of every colour, lined up like a captured rainbow. Neatly stacked cardboard boxes bore labels in Chinese script, and all around lay yet more of the leather-bound folders filled with designs. The walls in this room were covered in more photographs of tattoos and smiling, painted people.

'Quiet, isn't it?' McLean said, looking at the empty chairs and the distinct lack of customers.

'Afternoons always are. My clients are more your evening and weekend types. Least at this time of year they are. Come the summer there's students and tourists always popping in for a Prince Albert or a Heilan Coo on the buttock.'

'You do that?' DC Harrison's incredulity manifested itself in a voice pitched even higher than normal. 'Don't you, like, have to give people a chance to think things over before you . . .' She nodded at the chairs. '. . . Get to work?'

Eddie said nothing for a moment, his face creased into a deep frown. Then he broke into a broad grin. 'I like her, Tony.'

'Just don't get any ideas, OK?' McLean turned to Harrison. 'Unless you've got a thing for tattoos I don't know about.'

Harrison raised her hands in alarm. 'Me? No. I mean . . . Just . . . No.'

'It's OK. We don't strap people to the chairs and ink them. And it's not contagious.' Eddie turned his attention back to McLean. 'So what's this about? You want me to look at another dead body? I mean, Angus is a nice old man, but the smell of that place . . .'

'Aye, I know. It takes some getting used to.' McLean fished in his jacket pocket for the A4 prints he had made from the photographs Cadwallader had sent him, unfolded them and smoothed them out on to the table. 'Don't think you'll have to go back there any time soon, but I was hoping you might be able to shed some light on these.'

Cobbold bent over the photographs, peering closely for a moment. Then he stood up, went over to a set of small drawers over by one of the reclining chairs, pulling them out one by one until he found what he was looking for. Thin spectacles perched on his nose, he returned to the table and the pictures.

'This one I'm pretty sure I did about two, three years ago?' He placed a finger in the centre of the picture that showed Malky Davison's tattoo. 'Thin fellow, very dry skin for working on. Reckon he'd had a bit of a drug problem in his past, but he seemed clean enough.'

'You remember anything about the design?' McLean asked.

'It's not one of my own, so he must have brought it in. To be honest, Tony, I don't remember that much about it. Just recognized my handiwork. Customers quite often have their own designs and a lot of my job is persuading them not to use them. This though . . .' He picked up the photograph again and turned it this way and that. 'This isn't too bad, really.'

'What about the other one?' McLean pointed at the second sheet.

'The design's very similar, for sure. But I didn't do it. Could've been George, except I think he's better with colour work.' Cobbold picked up the second sheet and held the two together. 'Not the same body, is it?'

'Does the design mean anything?' McLean turned in surprise as Harrison asked the question. She had been so quiet he'd almost forgotten she was there.

'Mean anything?' Cobbold shrugged. 'Well, it's a stylized dragon. Both of them are. Dragons are a surprisingly popular tattoo, but they don't usually mean anything other than that the wearer's got a thing for fantasy. Unless you're a member of the triads or the Japanese yakuza, in which case it might be a badge of sorts, a clan marker.'

'You reckon these could be a gang thing?' McLean asked.

'Nah. These are too simple. Yakuza designs can cover half the body, and the triads' tend to be more intricate, too.'

'But they're similar enough to be related, would you say? Both done for the same reason?'

'Hard to say. Could be they just came from the same source. Which reminds me . . .' Cobbold put the two photographs back down, went over to the shelves and ran a finger along the spines of the black folders. None was labelled, but he selected one after a moment's hesitation, pulled it out and began flicking through the pages.

'I should really get these indexed properly. Maybe even put the whole lot on to an online database. Of course, it would help if I had even the faintest idea of how to do that. Ah, here we go.'

Cobbold opened up the folder and laid it out on the table for everyone to see. It was filled with designs, some ripped from magazines, some scrawled on scraps of paper, some neatly drawn on heavy artist's card. Each had been slipped into its own clear plastic binder, and the topmost showed an almost perfect replica of the dragon motif on Malky Davison's back.

'Is this your drawing?' McLean asked.

'No, this is what he brought in. Sometimes people want to keep their drawings. I usually make a copy then, and take a photo of the finished work.' Cobbold unclipped the binder, opened it up and pulled out the card. Clipped to the back of it was a photograph of the tattoo, presumably on Malky Davison, although it showed only a small amount of blotchy skin surrounding the actual image. McLean took them both, instinctively flipping the photo to see if there was anything written on the back of it. There wasn't, but the back of the card bore half of some corporate logo where it had been cut from a larger piece of headed paper, and beneath it some tiny, spidery handwriting he couldn't read.

'Can I take this? I'd really like the forensics experts to have a look at it.' McLean slipped the card with the design back into the plastic binder.

'Be my guest.' Cobbold shrugged. 'I don't imagine I'll need it anytime soon.'

The daylight had taken on a sepia tint that suggested it wasn't going to hang around much longer as McLean and DC Harrison left Bo's Inks and headed to the pool car he'd parked in a residents only space across the road. The air was brittle with cold, the sky overhead clear with the promise of a deep frost overnight. He glanced at his watch, surprised at how yet another day had got away from him.

'You couldn't deal with this, could you? Only I've got to get to the Western General.' He handed the clear plastic folder to Harrison, who took it with a surprised look.

'Of course, sir. Is there anything in particular we're looking for?'

McLean stopped in his tracks, unsure exactly how to answer. What was he hoping they might get from a piece of paper with a sketch on it that had been sitting around forgotten for a couple of years? Right now, he'd settle for pretty much anything.

'I doubt there'll be any usable prints on it. How about making a start on the handwriting, see if someone can't decipher that. And maybe try to track down that logo so we can see where the paper came from.'

'OK. I'll do an image search on the picture, too. It would probably help to know if it's got some meaning beyond being just a pretty design.'

'Good thinking. Get Stringer and Blane to help you. I'll be back in for the catch-up at six. See if you can come up with anything by then.' McLean pulled out the car keys. Harrison hadn't automatically gone to the passenger door, no doubt assuming he was going to make her walk back to the station again. For a moment, he'd been thinking exactly that, but it occurred to him both that it was the sort of thing DCI Spence would do, and that going to the hospital wasn't exactly work. He'd sat through enough lectures about the misuse of police resources to know he'd get a bollocking if Brooks found out. Hell, he'd even been the one lecturing some of the detective constables about it.

'Here you go.' He tossed the keys to Harrison, who caught them with surprisingly swift reflexes, even though she was still holding on to the clear plastic folder with her right hand.

'Umm . . . How are you going to get to the hospital, sir? You're not going to walk, surely?'

McLean considered it. He liked to walk, and the afternoon was cold but still. There just wasn't quite enough time to get there. 'I'll find a taxi at the conference centre. Don't mind me.' He walked a half-dozen paces away from the car before thinking of something else. Turned to see Harrison still staring at him with the keys dangling from her raised hand.

'And if I'm late for the briefing, just let everyone know what we've been up to, OK?'

24

'Well, the good news is it's not cancer.'

McLean sat in the small office in the neurosurgery unit that Dr Wheeler seemed to share with all the other residents and half of the nursing staff. Beside him, Emma looked crumpled, her hair awry and her face puffy, as if she hadn't really slept at all in the past twenty-four hours. He was beginning to regret his choice of a change of clothes for her now; the sweat pants and hoodie look didn't really sit well, and the waves of resentment boiling off her were enough to banish even the hard frost falling in the darkness outside.

'That's reassuring, I guess. So what's the bad news?'

Dr Wheeler leaned forward in her chair, elbows propped up on the desk amongst a clutter of papers, mercifully empty sample pots, a stethoscope and a couple of black felt-covered boxes that looked like they probably contained expensive equipment. A computer screen sat to one side, but the mouse and keyboard had been piled haphazardly beside it so it clearly didn't get much use.

'The bad news. Yes.' She let out a weary sigh that reminded McLean he wasn't the only one who operated in a permanent state of sleep deprivation. 'The bad news is I've no idea what it is.'

'It is something, though? I mean, the scans showed something, didn't they?' Emma fidgeted with the cords on her hoodie.

'Not exactly. We were scanning for signs of damage from your previous injury, and also looking for any sign of tumours. The simple truth of the matter is we found nothing. Your brain is as close to normal as any I've seen.'

McLean should have been reassured, but both Emma's nervousness and Dr Wheeler's dour face were enough to convince him otherwise.

'So what's the problem, then?'

'You mean apart from Emma collapsing for no apparent reason?' The doctor switched her focus to the woman in question. 'And it's not the first time, is it?'

McLean turned to face her, reached out to take her hand. Emma drew in on herself, quite clearly not wanting to be touched, and for a moment he was reminded of the days after she'd woken from her coma with the mentality and attitude of a teenager.

'Look, Tony, Emma. I'm a brain specialist. If there's something wrong up here –' Dr Wheeler tapped her skull with a bony finger, 'then I'll work it out. Can't say I can always cure what's wrong, but I'm pretty good at diagnosis. This time? I'm stumped.'

'So there's nothing in Emma's brain that's causing these blackouts?' McLean asked.

'Nothing at all. In fact I'm astonished at how well she's healed. If I didn't know better, I'd say there was no way she could have suffered such a massive head trauma just three years ago.'

'So what's causing it?' Emma's question was so sudden, so unexpected, that McLean almost jumped out of his seat. 'Why do I keep falling asleep? Why did I collapse in the middle of a crime scene? Have you any idea how embarrassing that is?'

'Em. Please.' McLean placed a hand on her shoulder. For a moment he thought she was going to push him away, but she calmed down, sunk back into her chair with weary resignation, and eventually reached up to place her own hand over his. She still didn't look at him, though.

'My best guess is something's causing your blood pressure to drop off the chart.' Dr Wheeler acted as if the angry outburst had never happened. No doubt she had suffered worse, for all that she was sworn to help people. 'Like I said, my speciality is brains and there's nothing wrong with yours. Not that I can see, anyway. I've sent some blood away for tests, and I'm going to refer you to one of my colleagues for further examination. Go home, the both of you. Get some rest. And don't worry. We'll find out what's causing this.'

'Good of you to drop by, McLean. Wouldn't want to think you'd forgotten us.'

The major incident room was quiet, most of the day shift gone home and the night crew snuck off for a quick brew in the canteen. McLean had managed to get Emma home, the questions still hanging unanswered in the back of his mind as they took the silent taxi ride across the city. She'd not been happy at all when he had explained that he had to go back to the station, and he'd almost called in to say he wasn't going to be able to make the evening briefing at all. As it happened, the whole thing was over by the time he arrived anyway. Just the stragglers still in the room. And Detective Superintendent Brooks. Strange how no senior officers had turned up to any briefings since the investigation had opened, yet now he was late, there was the boss man waiting.

'If I'd known you were coming, sir, I'd have . . .' McLean didn't finish the sentence, partly because he realized he was about to say something that would only make the situation worse, but mostly because Brooks being there had thrown him off balance.

'Never mind. That young detective constable of yours managed to fill me in on the situation. Off chasing random hunches again, it would seem. Whatever happened to proper detective work?'

'I'm not sure I understand, sir. How is following up a possible connection between Bill Chalmers and Malky Davison not proper detective work?'

'Do I have to spell it out? Your young addict with the overdose worked for Chalmers. That's your connection right there. No need to go pestering tattoo artists, or whatever you've been doing all day.'

McLean opened his mouth, but the words didn't come out. He was tired, worried about Emma, frustrated both at the lack of progress in the investigation and the lack of support from the senior detectives who had been so keen at the start. Perhaps it was no surprise it took his brain a while to catch on.

'Look, the DCC's given you a lot of responsibility heading up this investigation. It should be someone at least a pay grade higher, you know. And daily update reports to the chief constable himself, if it was up to me. But we've few enough DCIs as it is, and Mike's . . .' Brooks stopped midsentence, as if he couldn't quite bring himself to say what

Detective Chief Inspector Spence really was. He dispelled whatever thought it was with a shake of the head. 'It's no matter. He'll pull it together. Always has done, always will. But the point is, McLean, this is all on you. No one's going to pick up the pieces when you drop them, understand?'

'What makes you think I'm going to drop anything, sir? We've barely begun our investigation and quite frankly I think things are going reasonably well. We identified the body inside a day. We've tracked down his last known movements. Soon as I get hold of the bank statements we'll start looking into the financial side of things, and Forensics are working around the clock to process what scant evidence there is. If you've suggestions as to what else I could be doing, I'm all ears. Only this is the first time I've seen an officer more senior than an inspector in this room since the investigation began.'

Anger flared in Brooks' eyes. 'If you were ever here –'

'Don't pretend you've not been avoiding us, sir. I'm not stupid and frankly I'm used to being handed the poisoned chalice. I get it. You worked with Chalmers, so did the DCC and half of the senior officers in Specialist Crime. There's plenty of scope for embarrassment or worse to come out of this, so you're all keeping a distance. And you know what? That's fine. It leaves me to get on with the job without interference.'

A terrible silence had descended on the major incident room, all eyes turned to watch the war of words. McLean realized he had clenched his fists by his sides and slowly released them, letting the tension flow out through his fingers as he did so. Brooks didn't seem to have any such well-practised coping strategy.

'Just get a grip on the investigation, man. There's too much scattergun running around. No direction. You're senior investigating officer and I expect you to behave like it. Send a sergeant or a constable to do the legwork. Your job is in here.' Brooks looked around the room at the team, some of whom were staring with their mouths open. McLean couldn't help thinking there were better ways to motivate people than shouting at their boss in front of them.

'What are you lot looking at? Get on with your work.' The detective superintendent growled his rebuke, but his rage had subsided now. He stalked out of the room, muttering under his breath. Something was worrying him, it was clear, but McLean was fairly sure it wasn't the way the Chalmers investigation was being run.

25

'You got a moment, McLean?'

Heading down to the canteen in search of some late shift detectives, McLean was so surprised by the tone of the request it took him a moment to realize it was aimed at him. He was used to that voice barking the command, 'My office. Now!' with the promise of having a strip torn off him whether he complied or not. Quiet reasonableness was not something he could easily equate with Detective Superintendent Duguid, retired or not.

'Sir?'

'Not here. Come with me.'

McLean looked around the empty hallway, shrugged, and then followed Duguid down the back stairs and along the corridor to his lair. The Cold Case Unit was empty as ever, a single desk lamp throwing dark shadows into the corners. The detective superintendent slumped into his chair, running long fingers through his thinning hair before speaking.

'You're a magnet for all the weirdness and shit, you know that?'

'Things are rarely as straightforward as people would like them to be, sir. I'm sorry if that makes me seem awkward.'

'Oh, don't be such a fucking idiot, McLean. It's precisely your being awkward that makes you such a useful detective. That and the fact you're so rich you don't care if you get fired. Makes you hard to bribe, too.'

'Hard? I'd have thought impossible.'

'Oh, everyone has a price. And it's not always money. Remember that when they come for you.'

'They? I'm sorry, sir, I've no idea what you're talking about.'

Duguid stared up at him for a moment, the lamplight casting his features in dark relief. He shook his head and reached for a folder lying on the desk in front of him, tossing it towards McLean with a neat twist so that it landed facing the right way. 'No, I don't suppose you do. That's part of the problem, really. Tommy Johnston. Everything we have on him, which is to say pretty much bugger all.'

McLean picked up the folder, flipped it open and began leafing through the sheets within. Most of the pages were glossy photographs of Johnston as he had been found in his car and later laid out on the mortuary slab. It was easy enough to see what had killed him; the tiny round dot in the middle of his forehead was a dead giveaway. The post mortem report at the end confirmed that, apart from having his brains forcibly removed through a hole the size of a fist in the back of his head, Tommy Johnston had been in surprisingly good shape for a man of his age and reputation. He had just one identifiable injury that had occurred not long before his death, a rough abrasion on the skin of his left shoulder in a circle about two inches in diameter. In the photographs it looked like a burn, although the report was disappointingly vague about it.

'One of your friend Cadwallader's, fortunately.' Duguid had sat silently while McLean read through the very meagre documentation. Apart from the photographs and the

PM report, there was only a very short forensic summary sheet based on the initial analysis of the car in situ. It had been found parked up in a passing place on a one-track no through road south-west of Biggar.

'Fortunately?' McLean asked.

'He keeps copies of all his interesting cases. It's probably against the rules, but he's a bit like you in that respect.' Duguid slumped back into his seat as he spoke. 'That forensic report is all they could find in their files, and the photographs were on a back-up server no one remembered even existed until I asked the IT department if they could come up with anything for me.'

'So this folder's not from the archives then?'

'I can see why they made you a detective now. That keen intellect and insight. No, of course it's not from the fucking archives. There are no archives for the Tommy Johnston case. Nothing at all. The shelves are empty and there's no record on the system that they were ever filled. It's been wiped clean so comprehensively I'd have told you Tommy Johnston never existed if I'd not met the sanctimonious wee shite myself.'

McLean said nothing as the implications of Duguid's mini-rant sank in. He found a chair, sat down.

'So you've pulled this all together in the past day or so?' He held up the precious folder.

'No need to sound so impressed. I used to be a policeman, remember?'

McLean shook his head slowly. 'Sorry, I don't mean that. It's just . . . How the fuck can someone delete an entire unsolved case like that? And it's not even as if it happened all that long ago. What was it, ten years?'

'Aye, ten years last summer. Back when our old friend Sergeant Needham was still in charge of the archives and Brooks was only just a DCI. It wasn't our patch, but Johnston was an Edinburgh boy so we liaised with Strathclyde on the investigation. You know how well that went.'

'So who was involved at this end? Can we speak to them?'

'Well, Needy's dead, as I think you know. The only other detective I remember being on the case was John Brooks, which probably means Mike Spence was part of the investigation, too. Funnily enough, both of them have been avoiding me since I started asking questions.'

McLean opened his mouth to speak, then shut it again. He disliked Brooks and had even less time for Spence, but that was a long way from accepting that they might be bent enough to cover up a murder.

'I'll go see Brooks first thing tomorrow. See if I can't get a few Strathclyde names from him.'

Duguid looked up from his desk, the light reflecting off his spectacles in sheets of white. 'Not Brooks. Talk to Spence. And be subtle about it. Don't go charging in there accusing him and his best buddy of being anything less than fine officers. Play it right and chances are it won't come back to bite you later on.'

'You really think –?'

'The whole archive for the Johnston case. Gone. Like it never existed. That's not an easy thing to pull off. Whoever did that won't be too happy when they find out we're poking our noses into things they thought were dealt with already.'

*

Darkness filled the kitchen, and Mrs McCutcheon's cat stared at him with hostile eyes as he flicked on the lights. McLean knew what the problem was; he had brought Emma back from the hospital, then gone to the station again rather than spending the evening with her. She'd most likely be in bed now, possibly having worried herself to sleep wondering whether she was going to be able to keep her job. Bed would probably be the best place for him too, but he headed for the library and its secret cabinet of whisky instead. He needed time to think, some quiet away from the rushing jumble of events.

The house surrounded him with welcome familiarity, but there was a discordant note at its heart, as if it were sick. Something didn't feel quite right. It wasn't that the library light was still on, spilling out of an open door into the hall. The wrongness was on a different level that McLean couldn't easily put into words. He pushed through into the room, heart in his throat as he took in the details. Emma lay on the sofa, draped with a heavy eiderdown. She was still wearing the hoodie and sweatpants combo he'd brought to the hospital for her. The bag of dirty clothing and other personal effects lay on the floor beneath her feet as if she'd not yet gone upstairs to unpack it. For a moment he wondered if she'd collapsed again, but then she stirred, struggled out from under the covers, yawning, stretching, eyes bleary.

'Tony? What time is it?'

McLean glanced at his watch, even though he knew it was late and that was all that mattered. 'Gone eleven. You'd be more comfortable in bed, you know.'

'Aye. I didn't mean to fall asleep. Thought you'd be back earlier.'

'Me too, but Brooks . . .' He started to explain, realized it was a waste of time. 'You know how it is.'

'Not really, no.' Emma sat up, drawing the eiderdown around her like an old lady's lap blanket as she shivered at the cold. 'Knowing you, you'll have left for work at half six this morning, and now you don't come home until eleven at night. Once or twice, I'd understand, but it's every day. Do you ever stop?'

'I –'

'It was good, when you were on suspension. Just going in for the odd briefing or interviews and stuff. We had time to get to know each other again. But since this case started it's like you're a different person. Is this the real you, Tony? Was the other one a lie?'

McLean didn't answer. He wasn't sure that he could. Emma wasn't being entirely fair. Yes, he'd had three months of enforced leave just recently, but that meant there was a lot of catching up to do. And they were so short-staffed it was impossible to do the job in normal office hours. She was a forensic scientist, she knew that, surely? But of course that wasn't really what she was talking about.

'How are you feeling?' he asked eventually, knowing even as the words came out that they were the wrong ones.

'How do you think? I collapsed on the job, so chances are I'm going to get fired. The doctor hasn't got a clue what's wrong with me, which is only slightly alarming. And my boyfriend would rather be looking at dead bodies than me. Yeah, I'm fine. Peachy.'

McLean sat down on the sofa beside her, not really sure what to say. She shivered under the eiderdown again, her long grey hair shaking at the tips almost as if she were crying.

'I'm sorry,' he said, took a breath to try to explain, then opted instead to put an arm around her shoulders and draw her close. Emma still reeked of the hospital, but there was a reassuring mothball-and-dust aroma from the eiderdown that was doing its best to overpower the smell. She leaned in to him and he could feel her sobs. Not shivering with the cold, but scared at what was happening to her. Duguid's mention of Sergeant John Needham – Needy – had brought it all back to him; how Emma had ended up in a coma, how she had sustained major injury to her brain in the first place. But to think too hard about that was to invite madness in, so he held her a little more tightly and said nothing.

26

Early morning, after a better night's sleep than he'd managed in a while, and McLean found himself looking out over a sea of expectant faces. Not the ocean of the initial investigation briefing – numbers had dwindled as both public and media interest had waned – but still a good proportion of the station's full complement of officers and support staff had dutifully shuffled into the major incident room at the allotted hour. He felt that he should have been bringing them news, filling them with enthusiasm and encouraging them to ever greater efforts. Instead, he had very little to say.

'I'm sure I don't need to stand here and tell you all this investigation is getting away from us. It's gone a week now since Chalmers died and we're no closer to finding out who killed him, even how he ended up in that tree.' He glanced around, expecting to be interrupted, but there weren't any officers more senior than a sergeant in the room, apart from Acting DI Ritchie, and she was busy consulting her mobile phone about something.

'So, if anyone's got any smart ideas, don't be shy with them. In the meantime, we keep following up on those early phone calls and hope Forensics can come up with something. Questions?'

The silence would have been welcome, were it not a

reminder of how badly things were going. McLean didn't let it last too long. 'OK. Get to your work then.'

The briefing broke up swiftly, most of the officers filing out of the room rather than heading to the workstations or looking for assignments. He watched them go, only slightly worried that they might have turned up just to put something on their work recording for the week. He much preferred working with a small team anyway.

'Good pep talk there, Tony. Really motivational.' Ritchie had finished whatever it was she had been doing with her phone.

'Just telling it how it is. Unless something comes up soon, we're going to be reassigning most of this staff to other work. Can't justify this many bodies on an investigation that's going nowhere.'

'Aye, well. Those new detective constables have been busy with Sandy Gregg following up the calls to the hotline, and I saw one of them going over bank statements earlier. You never know, they might stumble on to a lead.' Ritchie nodded towards the far side of the room, where DCs Harrison, Stringer and Blane were huddled together, trying to look interested as DC Gregg pointed at the city map pinned to the wall. He remembered then what they had been up to, plotting the calls from the public about the morning Chalmers had died. If they'd found something interesting he was sure they'd have told him, but it was probably worth a chat all the same. First though there was another problem he needed to look into.

'Have you seen Jayne McIntyre recently?' he asked.

'Away over in Glasgow. Something to do with Special

Branch, or whatever the goon squad are calling themselves these days.'

'Why her? I mean, haven't they got anyone suitable over there already? God knows Strathclyde are always farming out their so-called experts to us.'

'Beats me.' Ritchie shrugged. 'But I can ask her if you want. That text that came in during the briefing was a summons. I've to head over this morning, help her out with whatever it is.'

'Did she say what?'

'She didn't say anything.' Ritchie pulled her phone out of her jacket pocket, swiped on the screen and held it up for McLean to see. 'Message came from the DCC himself.'

'Please tell me that's a flight plan you're plotting out, Constable.'

McLean approached the small group of detective constables as they clustered around the Edinburgh City map pinned to the major incident room wall. A big red arrow marked the spot where Bill Chalmers had met his violent end; two smaller arrows his mews house and the offices of Morningstar. DC Gregg was in the process of stretching as high as her short frame could reach to put a small white sticker somewhere in the north of the city. She stopped at McLean's voice, turned to face him.

'Sorry, sir. Didn't see you there. I was just beginning to mark things up.'

'And it didn't occur to you to ask DC Blane to do the top of the board?'

Gregg gave McLean a foolish grin, then handed the

sticker to the tall detective constable. 'You couldn't stick that in Muirhouse, could you, Lofty? Up there on Anderson Drive.'

Blane reached up barely above his shoulder height and placed the sticker with a surprisingly deft touch for such a large hand. McLean scanned the rest of the map, seeing all too few marks and those that were there spread randomly across the city.

'I take it the public aren't being as much help as we'd hoped,' he said.

'To be honest, sir, it's early days still. We've a mountain of callers, all claiming they saw a dragon or heard a strange noise. Some are easy enough to dismiss. Wrong time, impossibly wrong place, that sort of thing. They're all in the computer anyway, if we need to review it. We've managed to whittle the list down to people worth talking to, but it's not easy getting them to come into the station, and we're pretty short-staffed for going out to see them all.'

'Short-staffed?' McLean turned on one heel, opening his body out to the rest of the room where even now a couple of dozen uniform constables were doing a good impression of idling about.

'Aye, well.' Gregg shook her head from side to side a couple of times. 'I'm no' saying they're all completely useless but . . .' She let the sentence hang unfinished.

'How many have you interviewed so far, then?'

'Fifteen, sir. Of which only three are of any potential use.' DC Harrison clutched a freshly printed sheaf of papers to her chest as she spoke, and pointed at the map to indicate three yellow stickers. They were all close to the

Meadows, and formed a triangle around the end of Jaw-bone Walk.

'How many more have you got to work through?'

'Another twenty-five that might be relevant – going by the time they claim to have seen or heard something.' Harrison offered up her bundle of papers with a hopeful expression on her face, but McLean put his hands up to ward them away. There was plenty of that waiting for him in his office without adding to the pile. Her hope turned to disappointment in an instant, perhaps one of the best kicked-puppy faces he'd seen in a while.

'OK. OK. Three teams and we'll crack on with it. See if we can't get everyone spoken to by lunchtime. Gregg, you take Blane.' McLean racked his brain for the other constable's name for a moment. 'Stringer, isn't it? Go find Grumpy Bob and break the good news to him he's got a new understudy. Harrison, you're with me.'

Thomas Jenner lived on the top floor of a tenement in Sciennes converted into sheltered accommodation for the elderly. The last of the names on their list, he barely noticed McLean as he let them into his apartment, but his eyes lit up at the sight of DC Harrison. He welcomed them in with genuine warmth, ushering the detective constable through to a tiny kitchen to make coffee. For a moment McLean thought he might have to intervene as the old man insisted on physically helping her with the kettle and mugs. His lecherous eye and wandering hands did not go unnoticed.

'Three sugars for me, my dear. Need all the energy I can get. Don't suppose you'll take any in yours at all. You're sweet enough as it is.'

They all made it the short distance back to the front room without major incident, although Harrison flinched more than once as Mr Jenner's hands got out of control.

'Sit you down here, my dear.' He patted the second cushion of the narrow two seat sofa he had settled himself into, leaving McLean the armchair that was quite obviously where he normally sat. To her credit, she did as she was told, casting the inspector a glance that was angry and worried in equal measure.

'Mr Jenner, I'll get to the point if you don't mind. We're up against the clock with this one.'

'Oh, I imagine you are. What's it been, a week since that fella took a nosedive? Ten days? Reckon you must be getting it in the neck from your superiors if you're coming to talk to old blokes like me.'

'Well, you did call the hotline, and you gave us information that wasn't in the public domain. I'd like to hear about what you saw that night.'

Mr Jenner paused a while, looking from McLean to Harrison and back again before letting out a theatrical sigh.

'Take this will you, my dear?' He handed Harrison his mug, laying one gnarled and leathery hand on her thigh for rather longer than was appropriate before heaving himself out of the sofa with a groan of complaint. He limped a little as he crossed the small room to the window. McLean hadn't paid it much attention, distracted by the way the old man didn't so much flirt with Harrison as throw himself all over her. Now, as Mr Jenner drew the curtains all the way back, he saw that it wasn't a window but a set of doors with glass in their top half that opened on to a tiny balcony. A heavy overcoat draped over the arm of a nearby chair and Mr Jenner took a moment to struggle into it before opening the balcony window. Cold air spilled into the room, bringing with it the rumbling roar of the city. 'Care to join me?'

McLean stood a bit too quickly, wincing at the pain that lanced through his thigh. He tried not to limp too much as he crossed the small room and joined the old man on the tiny balcony.

'No' a bad view, really.' Mr Jenner had lit up by the time McLean stepped out on to a space barely big enough for the two of them. 'Only reason I like this place, really. Can't smoke anywhere in the building, no' even those new-fangled electronic doodads. I've few enough pleasures any more, but you're no' taking away my fags without a fight.'

McLean looked out at the view, over the rooftops of the nearby tenements and out across the Meadows towards the university and the hideous concrete bulk of Appleton Tower. Even if it was the opposite end from Jawbone Walk, it was as good a place as any to see something large fly low over the trees.

'That morning. You were out here having a smoke?'

'Quarter past five. Least that's what the clock on the telly said it was. Dark as you like and cold enough give a brass monkey a fright, but there's something about that first cigarette of the morning.'

'You usually up that early?'

'Aye, and before.' Jenner leaned against the iron railing without a care for the drop to the courtyard far below. 'Here's something they don't tell you about getting old,

Inspector. You don't need sleep as much as when you're young. You watch a lot of telly, read if you're lucky like me and your eyes are still good. And you stand out on your balcony smoking and watching the city wake up, if you've got a mind to.'

'What is it you did before you retired, Mr Jenner?'

'Me? Oh, I did a lot of things. Flew airplanes mostly. Freight 747s to places you've probably never heard of. Until they said I was too old for a licence any more. I miss the sky, though.' Mr Jenner blew grey smoke into the air, then hawked a noisy ball of phlegm up his throat and spat it into the void. It landed seconds later with a splat that put McLean in mind of nothing so much as Bill Chalmers doing a nosedive into the inflated canvas safety bag.

'Tell me what you saw, then. What you heard that morning.'

'It was odd, didn't sound like a plane or a chopper. Well, no ordinary chopper anyways. It came in from the north-east, low enough I thought it was going to crash, whatever it was. Maybe take out that tower and do the whole city a favour. Couldn't see anything much, and then it went behind the flat. If I didn't know better I'd say it circled around the Sick Kids Hospital and then went back the way it came. Could have been bringing in someone for treatment, only they've no helipad there, and no emergency services either. And anyway, the whole thing didn't take more than a minute, I'd say.'

'So what do you think it was? A helicopter? Microlight? Something else entirely?'

Mr Jenner stubbed the last of his cigarette out on the railing, then flicked it the way his sputum had gone. 'I've read the papers, seen the news on the telly. That wee boy saying it was a dragon, yes? Well, I can see how someone might think that, given the noise it was making.'

'But you and I both know dragons don't exist, don't we?'

'Truth be told, I don't know that much about dragons at all, Inspector, but I can tell you this much. I'm pretty damn sure they don't smell of aviation fuel.'

27

'Think I might need to have a shower when we get back sir.' DC Harrison hugged her arms around her chest, rubbed at herself as if she had been attacked by a swarm of biting insects. She was walking just a little bit faster than her normal pace too, trying to put as much distance between herself and Mr Jenner as possible.

'Sorry about that. I'd have told him to behave, only –'

'We needed him on our side. Aye, I got that. It's OK. I've had worse. You should hear the comments when you're working a match at Tynecastle or Easter Road. But there's something about a creepy old man with wandering hands. Just . . .' She shivered and said no more on the matter.

'Still, it was worth the sacrifice. He's a reasonably reliable witness, corroborates what the others have said about the time, and it opens up some interesting possible lines of enquiry.'

'It does?'

'Well, better than the ones we've got so far, which counts as a morning well spent, if you ask me. Mind you, I wasn't the one getting felt up by a lecherous old pilot.'

Harrison grinned at that, and they fell into step as they crossed Melville Drive and the eastern end of the Meadows. It wasn't the most direct route back to the station, but it was more pleasant than fighting up East Preston Street and past the memories of McLean's burned-out tenement block.

'I took that photo from the tattoo shop to Forensics, sir. After we'd scanned it for an image search,' Harrison said after they'd been walking for a minute or two.

'Let me guess, they told you to take it away and not be so daft asking.'

Harrison stopped walking, looked up at him in surprise. 'Not exactly. Well, sort of. At first, anyway. But I said you'd sent me and then suddenly they couldn't have been more helpful.'

'Really? That's not like them. You must have caught them on a good day. Maybe they all got paid or something.'

'Ha. Maybe. Anyway, they're going to do some analysis on the paper, check it for prints and stuff, even if that's a bit of a long shot. Chances are it's covered in partials that won't match anything on record. Should have a few preliminary results through in a day or two.'

'Great. That's good work. Thanks.' McLean started walking again, so pleased that Forensics were being helpful it took him a while to notice what hadn't been said.

'Was there something else?' he asked.

Harrison stared at the pavement and her boots as they covered a dozen more paces. 'Its . . . Well. It's not about the case, or work for that matter really. Only, when I was there I got chatting to one of the technicians. Amanda Parsons. Said she knew you.'

McLean's heart sank. What strange gossip had the over-enthusiastic Miss Parsons been spreading? Something about his car, probably. 'If she told you we first met in a shrubbery in my back garden, I've a perfectly good explanation for that.'

'What? No. Nothing like that. She said something about your car and how jealous she was that I'd been in it. But . . . Shrubbery, sir?'

'Forget I said that, Constable. Do I need to make that an order?'

'Umm . . . No. I don't think so.'

'So what did Miss Parsons have to say? This was what you wanted to talk about, wasn't it? The subject you were working your way around to?'

'Am I that obvious?'

'I've been interviewing suspects more than twenty years. You pick things up.'

'Aye, well. OK. It's just I got chatting, and she's looking for someone to share a flat with. Got the chance of a nice place up Bruntsfield way. I'm tempted, been living with my folks since I came back from college, but rents in the city are half my wages.'

McLean wasn't quite sure what Harrison was getting at, and neither did he have any experience of renting except from a landlord's perspective, when Phil had shared his Newington flat as a student. That was a long time ago now. He had no idea what it cost to live somewhere central these days.

'It sounds like a no-brainer to me then. If sharing brings the cost down enough.'

'And you don't think Amanda's . . . Well, a bit strange?'

'If by that you mean do I think she's a psychotic axe murderer, then no. I don't really know her well, but she seems very enthusiastic and focused on her job. I'm guessing she's the sort of person who comes and goes at all hours, but then, if you're serious about being a detective, that's something you'll have to get used to anyway.'

'So you don't think it's a totally mad idea then? Moving in with a complete stranger?'

'Mad?' McLean let the thought roll around his head a while as he recalled how he and Phil had first met, getting on for thirty years ago now. A pub had been involved, a mutual friend, some drunken conversation. And the next thing he knew, he had a flatmate. Unlike Harrison, there had been no great financial incentive, but it had been nice to have someone his own age to talk to after growing up surrounded by people of his grandmother's generation.

'No, I don't think it's mad at all.'

'OK, people. Let's see what you've all got.'

The major incident room was quiet, the bulk of the officers on duty all having nipped off for some lunch or a quick five minutes in the smokers' shed at the back of the yard. Only half of the phone stations were manned, and even those operators looked bored as they tapped actions into the computer or typed up notes to be filed and forgotten. McLean and Harrison had been the first of the teams of detectives to get back from interviewing the more likely witnesses of whatever it was that had brought Bill Chalmers to the Meadows and dropped him there like spoor, but they'd not had to wait long for the others to return.

'Pretty much a busted flush, I'm afraid.' Grumpy Bob spoke up for Detective Constable Blane, who seemed to be having difficulty getting his sheets of notes in order.

'Nothing at all?' McLean asked.

'Well, maybe. You get a special kind of crazy person who likes to phone in to things like this. Especially when the tabloids start mouthing off about dragons. Doesn't help that the world and his wife have seen that new series on the telly.'

'*Game of Thrones*,' Blane said.

'Aye, I know, son.' Grumpy Bob grabbed the notes and put them down on the table before Blane could drop them all over the floor. 'First two were definitely crazies. Claimed they'd seen a huge winged beast in the clouds. I might've believed the first one, but the second one said pretty much the same thing word for word. And neither of them could explain to me how they could see anything in the dark. Claimed they were up at six, but I reckon they meant six in the evening. Second one swore he didn't know the first, but it was obvious he was lying. I'd charge them with wasting police time, only it'd be a waste of police time.'

'Any others?' McLean asked.

'Aye, there was one. Young lassie said she had to catch the first bus every morning to get to Gogar for her work at six. Thought she heard something while she was waiting at the bus stop on Clerk Street, but she had her headphones in. Whatever it was had gone by the time she took them out, but she'd have been in more or less the right place at the right time.'

'Pin her on the map then, Constable.' McLean watched as Harrison fetched a wheeled stool and used it to reach high enough to put a sticker on the junction of Clerk Street and West Crosscauseway. The point in Sciennes where McLean's reliable witnesses lived had already been marked.

'What about you two?' He nodded to DCs Gregg and Stringer. 'You were a bit further north, right?'

'Our best hit's Broughton Street. Coffee-shop owner getting ready for the early crowd. Reckons he saw something fly overhead, very low. Would have been just the back of five. Then we've got Mrs Daley.' Gregg flipped through her notebook, looking for the relevant page. 'Here we are, Liz Daley. Works as a cleaner for some of those big old houses in Trinity. One of her customers is some kind of investment banker, apparently. Works Hong Kong hours or something, and likes to come home to a clean house, so she's in there between half five and six three mornings a week. She was just getting off the bus that usually drops her on Ferry Road at twenty-five past five. Thought she heard a "whooshing rumbling noise like something flying very low", but when she looked up she couldn't see anything.'

'Harrison?' McLean looked over to see the detective constable already putting little white stickers on the map. It wasn't much, some might say clutching at straws, but something of a pattern was beginning to emerge.

'OK then.' McLean stood up and went to the map. Each sticker had an approximate time written on it, and he traced his finger over the creased paper from one to the next, looping around the back of Mr Jenner's top-floor flat, across the Sick Kids Hospital to Jawbone Walk and then on towards Trinity. 'Total speculation, but we know Chalmers fell from a height. Regardless of how he got up there, someone or something had to bring him. And the last place we know he went to was just outside Elie, up here.' He reached up as high as he could, pointing towards the ceiling, where an interesting brown stain had leached through the tile and wept down the wall. Frustratingly, the map ended at Newhaven and the south coast of the Firth of Forth, Fife not being considered important enough to be included.

'If we discount the dragon theory for a moment, that means a microlight, helicopter or something similar. One of our potential witnesses says he smelled aviation fuel too, so unless that's what modern-day Smaugs are drinking, we're looking at an unregistered aircraft originating in Fife, bringing Chalmers to the city and dropping him in the Meadows before heading back the way it came.'

DC Harrison still stood beside the map, and now she raised a tentative hand, like a schoolgirl asking to be excused.

'Umm, is that not a bit elaborate, sir? I mean, why go to all that trouble just to kill a man? Why not just run him over with your car, or push him doon the stairs?'

Or put a bullet in his head. 'That's the very question, Constable.' McLean looked at his meagre crew of detectives, then out across the depressingly quiet incident room. 'Work that out, and we've half a chance of finding whoever did it.'

28

It wasn't really on his way home, and he could have called her. Should have called to warn her, if he was being honest with himself. And yet McLean felt that he really needed to speak off the record, face to face, and unannounced. And so it was he found himself driving slowly down an unfamiliar street in suburban Colinton, trying with little success to make out the numbers on the doors of the identical dormer bungalows. Perhaps it would have been easier in the daylight, but probably not. The streetlamps were well positioned, not too far spread in this prosperous neighbourhood and, unlike in some of the less salubrious parts of town, they all worked. Few of the houses had lights over their doors though, and the shadows made what numbers there were all but impossible to read.

In the end he decided it would be easier to park and walk, finding a space right at the end of the road. It was another clear night, his breath steaming thickly in air well below freezing. Slippery, sparkly crystals smeared the pavement, making the going far more treacherous than it should have been, and when he reflexively reached out for an iron railing to steady himself, the touch burned his skin with ice.

Fortunately the house he was looking for wasn't quite halfway back down the street, and sat on the same side he had parked. McLean looked around before he pushed open the gate, not really sure whether he expected anyone to be watching, following. A little paranoia wasn't unhealthy, given the circumstances, but as far as he could see all the nearby cars were empty, the drawn curtains untwitching.

So much time elapsed between his silent press of the doorbell and the noise of a lock being turned that he was beginning to think the house might be empty despite the light filtering past the blinds in the front window. McLean had been about to turn around and leave, just make the phone call he should have made in the first place, but the creak of hinges in need of oil stopped him. The door opened just a crack, held back by a stout chain, and a thin face peered through at him for a moment before withdrawing. A pause while the door was closed again, the chain unlatched and then it was opened wide.

'It's Lucy, isn't it? I think we met once at a charity function. I'm –'

'Tony McLean. Yes, I know. Is this about Jayne?' The woman standing in the doorway was perhaps a foot shorter than him, and thin as a rake. Her hair had been shaved off recently but was beginning to grow back in a grey fuzz that clung to her scalp like mould. McLean knew that Jayne McIntyre's partner had been undergoing chemotherapy, but the knowledge didn't make seeing her any easier. She looked so frail he was amazed she had the strength even to lift the chain off the door latch, and her eyes, red-rimmed and dry, had the haunted look he'd seen on many a recently bereaved mother. Only as the implications of her question filtered out from his reason for being there did he start to understand.

'It is, yes. But not what you think. I take it she's not here?'

Lucy's shoulders slumped in partial relief, although she still carried herself like someone with the weight of the world bearing down on her. She stood to one side of the open door. 'No, she's not. Won't you come in out of the cold?'

'Jayne's not usually so secretive about her work. I've security clearance, so it's not as if she can't tell me what she's up to. But this last week since they sent her off to Glasgow it's like she's . . . I don't know, really. Like she's a different person.'

They sat in the front room, drinking tea from elegant porcelain cups. McLean perched uncomfortably on the edge of a sofa that seemed somehow too clean and new to be something of DCI McIntyre's. She had always struck him as a make-do-and-mend kind of person. But then she hadn't done too well out of her divorce – one of the problems of marrying a lawyer and then leaving him for another woman, he guessed – and her demotion would have eaten into her salary too. If memory served, Lucy had worked at the Procurator Fiscal's office, though McLean assumed she had taken long-term sick leave for the chemo. Perhaps if he'd spent more time talking to his colleagues he'd know these things, but then McIntyre had always been very cagey about her private life.

'Well, I'm sure she's perfectly safe. She's a DCI after all, not some undercover sergeant. It's probably a big VIP protection deal or Serious and Organized want something done and think it needs to be all hush-hush.'

'Serious and Organized?' Lucy cocked her head to one side, a smile ghosting her lips. McLean was trying hard to remember her surname. Matthews, or something like that. And he was supposed to be trained to remember details.

'I lose track of what they call themselves now. It's bad enough trying to work out if we're CID or SCD or what the hell we're meant to be without worrying about other divisions. I think they're the National Crime Agency these days, but last time I had anything to do with them they were the Serious and Organized Crime Agency, so Serious and Organized is good enough for me.'

'And you reckon they've got Jayne working for them?'

'If she's not telling you what she's doing, then probably yes. I can't think of anyone else who'd demand that level of security. And I've no idea what she's doing, though it explains why she's not been around my own investigation much.'

'That'd be Bill Chalmers, I take it?' Lucy – Masters, that was it. Lucy Masters took a delicate sip from her cup. No milk in her tea, and barely seen the leaves.

'Yes, for my sins I've been put in charge of that. Thought I might have some support from the higher-ups, but so far they've been conspicuous by their absence.'

'Distancing themselves from the inevitable fallout?' Lucy tilted her head at the question again, an affectation McLean had seen before. It took him a while to remember where, but it was something his grandmother had done.

'It's always nice to meet someone as cynical as me. But yes, I think that's probably the measure of it. I'd thought better of Jayne . . . Well, I still do or I wouldn't have come here to see her. I don't think it's a coincidence she's been dragged off to the other side of the country though.'

'Isn't that, I don't know, a little paranoid?'

Given her earlier reaction to his arrival, McLean found the question surprising. 'Possibly. But of all the senior officers involved, Jayne's the one I would have gone to first. The DCC knows she's got my back, so who would be the first person to side-line if they're trying to isolate me? It's no secret that I don't get on with my current boss any better than I did with the last.'

'Really? I'd heard you and Dagwood had buried the hatchet.'

Dagwood, not Duguid, and Lucy Masters seemed to be very well informed about the current politics in the station where her partner worked. McLean couldn't help but like her for it.

'Let's just say retirement has mellowed him. And there's the small matter of my saving his life last year.'

'Way I heard it, you got him into that situation in the first place. Only the Charles Duguid I remember was never so easily led, so I don't believe a word of it. Shame about that young lass too. Don't think she deserved that.'

A chill settled around him as McLean remembered Heather Marchmont's face, her quietly whispered 'thank you' as her life ebbed away, the blood that months had not quite managed to wash off his soul.

'But that's not why you're here, is it, Tony?'

He looked up at a face much more energized than the one he had first glimpsed through the half-opened door. What was it she had done at the PF's office? More than clerical work, McLean was sure of that.

'No. And it's only really peripheral to the Bill Chalmers case. A . . . coincidence I didn't like. Funnily enough it was Dag . . . Duguid who was looking into it for me. Tell me, does the name Tommy Johnston mean anything to you?'

Lucy leaned back in her armchair, a knowing look spreading over her face. 'Ah. I think I understand now. And yes, Tommy Johnston. There's a name I've not heard in a fair few years. One I'd not expected to hear, to be honest.'

'You've read the papers about Chalmers, I take it? Or at least heard the story about the wee boy out walking his dog. Claimed it was a dragon come to get him, but it dropped the body into the tree instead?'

'The young have such vivid imaginations.'

'Yes, they do. And the television doesn't help much. But the boy was – is – Tommy Johnston's son. That's not common knowledge, by the way. I'd appreciate it if you didn't tell anyone else.'

'Oh, I can be discreet, don't worry about that, Tony. But Tommy Johnston? There's a name to bring back bad memories. And I had no idea he had a son, either.'

'Very few people did, least of all the boy himself. He's only just ten, born after someone killed his dad.'

'So how is this relevant to Bill Chalmers? Did they even know each other?'

'Quite probably, which is why I asked Duguid to dig out the archives on the Johnston murder. It's unsolved, ten years old. Ripe for a second look, and exactly the sort of thing the CCU's set up to investigate. The only problem is there's nothing in the archives. No records of interviews, no evidence, nothing.'

'How's that possible? Surely there must be something in the records.'

'You'd think so, but there's not. We've managed to pull a few things together, from the mortuary records and some stuff the forensics lab had misfiled, but mostly it's just memories of the officers who were around at the time.'

Lucy nodded her understanding. 'Which is why you wanted to talk to Jayne.'

'And why I'm only slightly surprised she's been side-lined. The only other name I can come up with is Brooks, and he was fairly junior back then. I'll talk to him about it eventually, but I'm not holding out any hope he'll be helpful.' McLean looked up at the carriage clock on the mantelpiece, realized how late it was getting. And he'd promised Emma he'd be home at a reasonable hour.

'I'm sorry to bother you with this. It's not really your problem,' he said. 'And I've got to get going.'

Lucy put her cup and saucer down on the table beside her chair, levered herself up with the effort of an octogenarian, not the forty-something she most likely was. 'Of course. How is Emma?'

The question shouldn't have surprised him as much as it did. 'She's . . . OK, I guess. Had a bit of a scare earlier in the week. Hopefully it's nothing.'

'I hope you're right.' Lucy escorted McLean to the front door, unlatched the chain and slid the bolts back as if he were being released from jail. 'I'll tell Jayne you popped round, what you've told me, too. Soon as she's back from Glasgow.'

She pulled open the door, ice-cold air falling in like a drowning wave. McLean stepped swiftly through, expecting her to close it behind him and keep in the heat, but she paused a moment.

'Thanks for the tea, and the sympathetic ear,' he said.

'I rather think I should be thanking you, Tony.'

'Really? What for?'

'For having faith in Jayne. You'd not have come here if you didn't.'

Bright light shone from the kitchen window as McLean pulled up outside the house. Emma's little blue-and-rust Peugeot must have still been at the forensic lab car park, but its place had been taken up by a brand-new BMW that looked like someone had taken a normal car, shoved an air hose up its exhaust and blown until it inflated almost to bursting. He didn't recognize it, but the 'Baby on Board' sticker in the back window gave him some small clue. His suspicions were confirmed when he pushed open the door into the kitchen to find it filled with people for a change.

'Hey everyone, it's Uncle Tony.' Phil Jenkins, newly appointed professor of bioinformatics and McLean's oldest friend, pushed back his chair from the kitchen table with a horrible scrape of wood on flagstone. His wife Rachel stayed in her seat, as did Emma beside her. Tony Junior, perched in a carrycot on the table, just waggled his chubby little legs, gurgled loudly and waved his arms around in infant delight at yet more attention.

'Phil, Rae. If I'd known you were coming I'd have got home sooner.' McLean risked a sideways glance at the big clock on the kitchen wall, all too aware that it was past suppertime. Even for adults.

'Just dropped in to see how you were getting on. It's been a while.'

'And you wanted to show off your new company car too, I bet.'

'You noticed.' Phil smiled at some joke only he understood. 'Of course you noticed. Nothing gets past the great detective.'

'If only.' McLean pulled out the last chair at the table and slumped into it. He really wanted a shower, a bite to eat, a dram and his bed. 'So how's things?'

'Busy. You know how it is. I spend more time mollycoddling students than actually carrying out any research. They seem to want everything handed to them on a plate, and when you tell them they've got to work for their grades they get all uppity and start shouting about how much they've paid for their degree and how they're going to sue if they don't get a first.' Phil paused a moment. 'What?'

McLean tried to suppress the smile that was fast turning into a chuckle, but he was too tired to put on his best poker face. 'You, Phil. You sound like a grown-up. They say fatherhood changes a man. Not sure who "they" are, but I guess they're right.'

'Em was telling us about the hospital and her scans, Tony.' Rachel broke into the conversation before Phil's protestations became any more coherent than spluttered indignation. 'You should have called us.'

McLean looked at Rachel, then to Emma. They were as different as chalk and cheese, except at that very moment they could have been sisters. Rae had let her hair grow long, and the stress of her time in California had given her a few grey streaks in the dark red. She had more flesh to her face than Emma, with her prominent cheekbones and thin nose.

'It all happened a bit quickly,' he said, knowing that it was a pathetic excuse. He should have called Phil as soon as he'd arrived at the hospital.

'Well don't forget us next time, OK?' Rachel fixed him with a matronly stare that slowly morphed into a horrified expression as she realized what she had just said. 'Oh God, Emma, I'm sorry. I didn't mean –'

'I know, Rae. It's OK. I'm fine, really. It was just a stupid faint. Been a while since I last saw a dead body is all.'

McLean watched Emma for the smirk as she spoke, but it wasn't there. Either she was being perfectly frank or two years' travel had perfected her dry humour. Beside her, Rachel turned pale before recovering herself.

'Of course, if this one ever made it home at a decent hour, we'd probably not be eating just before bed. As he doesn't, we barely eat at all. I probably just fainted with hunger.' Emma placed a hand on McLean's shoulder as she spoke, pinching him just a little more firmly than was necessary.

'I'm sorry. It's this case . . .'

'The body in the tree?' Phil asked.

McLean nodded. 'You know the score though, Phil. I can't say anything. Wouldn't really want to, not with Tony Junior there listening in.'

Phil looked up at the clock. 'True enough. And we'd better be getting home too. He really should be in bed sleeping, but sometimes a trip in the car's the only way to get him to zone out.'

'Ha. Dad used to do that with me in the Alfa. At least

that's what my gran told me. Maybe that's why I like the car so much.' McLean stood up as Rachel got to her feet and gave Emma a quick hug. How strange that the two of them had bonded in such a short time.

'Give us a call, Em. Or drop round if you're bored of an evening. It's got to be better than sitting around waiting for the menfolk to come home.' Rachel rolled her eyes as she spoke, not caring that McLean could see her.

'Thanks, Rae. I might well take you up on that.'

'And as for you, Tony –' Rachel gave him a peck on the cheek – 'stop running away from the best thing that ever happened to you.'

29

A hard frost had left McLean's car almost impossible to get into and even harder to warm up, which meant that he was late for the morning briefing. As he approached the major incident room, Detective Superintendent Brooks lumbered down the corridor from the opposite direction, followed a couple of steps behind by DCI Spence and a gaggle of detective constables, like so many obedient wives.

'Cutting it a bit fine aren't you, McLean?' Brooks growled like the bear had been drinking heavily the night before. Behind him, Spence looked like he'd been on an even more epic bender, his face drawn, sweat slicking skin so grey it might have been paper. If he hadn't been standing upright, McLean might have mistaken him for a corpse.

'You know what they say, sir. If I'm late, I'm wasting your time; if I'm early, I'm wasting mine.' He gave the detective superintendent his best innocent smile, another quick glance at the walking dead that was DCI Spence, and then he ducked in through the incident room door.

There was more of a buzz to the place than there had been at the catch-up briefing the night before, although on reflection it would have been hard for there to be less. Over on the far side of the room, McLean saw that the original map of the city had been joined by a large flat-screen monitor showing a smaller-scale image of the whole of East Lothian and South Fife. The same image appeared on a smaller monitor at a nearby desk, where DC Harrison was busy duplicating the white dots from the previous days' interviews, which would hopefully be supplemented by more from the late shift working their way through the phone contacts.

'Good work, Constable,' he said as he neared the big screen, seeing what looked more like the splatter from an incontinent seagull than any actual pattern. 'At least, I think it is.'

'Oh. Morning, sir.' Harrison tapped at her keyboard, shifted the mouse and tapped once more before she turned to face him, then her gaze darted past him and her eyes widened. 'Sirs.'

McLean turned wearily to see that Brooks and his entourage had followed him right across the room. The detective superintendent was staring at the big screen through narrowed eyes.

'What's all this, then?'

'All the people who contacted the hotline after the press release, sir. We've been weeding out the improbable stories and interviewing a few of the more plausible ones. Plotting time and place to see if we can't work out how Chalmers got to the Meadows, and where from.'

Brooks carried on peering myopically at the map, but behind him DCI Spence made a noise that sounded a bit like someone strangling a chicken.

'Is there a problem, Mike?' McLean asked. 'Should I ask a constable to fetch a glass of water?'

'Very funny, McLean.' Spence's voice told eloquently

the lie of his words. His eyes were watery and this close there was a scent coming off him that wasn't unpleasant but neither was it healthy. He flicked his head back, using his weak chin to indicate the spatter of white dots spread over the city. 'You'll be needing something a bit stronger than a glass of water if that's the best you can come up with. Maybe some of that ridiculously expensive whisky you're so fond of. Too fond of, I'll wager.'

McLean ignored the jibe as best he could. It was true he'd often sat in his favourite armchair with a small dram of whisky from a bottle that had cost the wrong side of a hundred pounds, but too fond? That was a bit strong.

'At least I've something to be fond of, Mike. It must be so difficult loving only yourself.'

'Are you two going to bicker like old women all day?' Detective Superintendent Brooks asked. 'Only if you are, can you not do it in front of the constables?'

'Sir.' McLean nodded, suitably chastised. It was too early for a proper argument anyway.

'This map.' Brooks tossed a hand in its general direction. 'Is it as useless as it looks?'

'That depends –' McLean began, but DC Harrison butted in.

'Sorry to interrupt, sir, but it's a bit confusing because it's not finished yet.'

Brooks made a low rumbling noise that might have been a precursor to the main earthquake or might have been an invitation to Harrison to continue. Whichever it was, she took it as the latter. She had stood up in the presence of the detective superintendent, but now she sat down again and began tapping at the keyboard.

'The white dots are the geographical locations of all the callers claiming to have heard something like a plane or helicopter that morning, barring the obvious crazies. This is everything we've got, regardless of time and bearing in mind that very few people have reported any kind of actual sighting.'

'We know he was dropped from an aircraft of some form. How does confirming that help us? Or have you still got teams out in the Pentlands looking for dragons?'

'Actually sir, we reckon whatever it was brought Chalmers to the city came from the north or north-east. Not the south.' DC Harrison tapped her keyboard again and some of the white points turned red. 'See?'

'What's this?' Brooks stepped closer to the screen. Forgotten to put in his contact lenses again.

'This is the points filtered by time, sir. Everything within a half-hour window of when we know Chalmers must have been dropped. Well, approximately. We don't know how long it took the wee boy to run home, or how long before his mum called after that, but I've made my best estimate and come up with this.'

McLean peered at the map on the big screen. The white points were still there, like second-hand pizza on a Saturday-night pavement, but the red points formed a much tighter group. They clustered around Newington, Sciennes and the Meadows itself in a squashed circle whose centre was just about near enough Jawbone Walk to be statistically significant. More interesting to him though was the tail on the circle, heading off over Dumbiedykes and the parliament before petering out as it curved north over Trinity and Newhaven.

'And what's this?' Brooks stabbed a pudgy finger at a single red point on the south coast of Fife. It was hard not to draw a line to it from the city.

'That's Bill Chalmers' house, sir. Where he was last known to be.'

'That's very good work, Constable. And thanks.' McLean kept his eyes on the big screen, not wanting to watch as Brooks and Spence stalked out of the major incident room, followed by a gaggle of sycophant detective sergeants and constables.

'Thanks? For what, sir?' Harrison asked.

'For this.' He gestured towards the mess of red and white dots. 'And for stopping me having a go at Spence, I guess. There's something about him that just winds me up. Even if he does look like something out of a horror movie right now.'

'Is it true what they say about him and the detective superintendent?'

McLean stopped himself from asking what it was that they said. He knew exactly who they were, the junior officers taking the piss out of their superiors whenever they could. He'd done it himself as a constable, less so as a sergeant. It was important for morale, but only so far. And it wasn't something constables were supposed to share with inspectors.

'I'll pretend I didn't hear that,' he said. 'Now, where are we with the interviews?'

Harrison blushed a little at the reprimand, but her embarrassment didn't last long. 'All done, sir, and all in the database. It was much easier once we got the big screen and the mapping software sorted. Not sure why we didn't have it here from the start.'

McLean took a sweeping look around the major incident room, seeing the busy horde of constables, plain clothes and uniform, carrying out the thousand and one tasks that were more about making sure the investigation ran smoothly and on budget than actually solving the case. He knew there was a need for the procedure, that simple and boring things like ploughing through endless phone calls from the public were what would give them the break they needed, but it still didn't feel like detective work to him.

'So what's next? Have we had forensic results back from the mews flat or the charity offices yet?'

Harrison looked slightly lost. 'I don't know, sir. I think DS Laird was in charge of that. Do you want me to chase them up?'

McLean stared at the screen for a moment. 'No. They'll get here eventually. I'm not holding out any great hopes they'll give us much anyway. I'm more interested in this.' His eyes glazed over as he let his thoughts wander, turning the image into a mess of greens and blues. They headed out across the Forth from Newhaven, and sooner or later he'd have to follow that lead back to Fife. But there was another case that needed his attention just west of there, a coincidence that didn't sit well. 'Do you know if the house where we found Malky Davison is still secure?'

'Sir?' DC Harrison's puzzled frown suggested he'd made one too many mental leaps. She was young and inexperienced. Hopefully she'd catch up soon.

'Muirhouse. You know. Where we found the dead drug addict?'

Harrison shook her head slightly. 'I know who he is, sir. Just wasn't sure how it fitted in with the interviews.'

'Never mind. Just find us a car, can you? I really don't fancy driving the Alfa over there and I'd like to have another look at the place before the locals start using it as a dosshouse again.'

The little red lights on the dashboard read minus two as McLean turned up the heater in the pool car to max. Outside, the air was clear, a pale blue sky threatening even lower temperatures as darkness fell. DC Harrison drove carefully, no doubt mindful of black ice. They were twenty minutes into the journey before she finally spoke.

'Why are we going back to Muirhouse, sir? Thought we'd come to the conclusion Davison slipped off the wagon after his boss died so publicly.'

'That sounds like Brooks talking. Find the simplest solution and fit the evidence to it.'

Harrison flushed slightly, her cheeks reddening as if she had been scolded. 'Isn't it usually the simplest solution, though, sir? I mean, Occam's razor and all that?'

McLean almost made a disparaging comment about standards in education but stopped himself at the last minute. 'You're right,' he said instead. 'But simplest doesn't mean ignoring evidence because it doesn't fit in with your solution. Take Davison. There's a logical explanation for what happened to him, sure. He was a recovering addict who was pushed back over the edge. It's not uncommon for people like that to overdose. Chances are his death was just another tragic accident. But we can't ignore the fact that his place of work was turned over, and we have to ask the question why he was in Muirhouse when he lived on the Dalry Road? What's so special about that derelict council house?'

As he spoke, they turned the corner into the street, seeing the house in question up ahead. Blue-and-white crime scene tape still covered the doorway, but the main deterrent to the locals was a squad car parked conspicuously across the road. Harrison pulled in behind it and killed the engine as a couple of uniform constables climbed out.

'Morning, Janie,' one of them said, then noticed McLean getting out of the passenger side. 'Sir. Heard you wanted another look at the place.'

McLean nodded. 'This part of your beat?'

'Aye. We cover the whole of Muirhouse, down the coast to Newhaven too, if necessary.'

'Know anything about these houses?' McLean indicated the row of council tenements, all with boarded-up ground-floor windows and an enviable collection of graffiti.

'Scheduled for demolition a while back, so I heard. There's meant to be new housing association blocks going up in their place, but planning and funding keep getting in the way.' The constable rubbed his hands together and blew on them for warmth. McLean couldn't blame him; it was freezing, and the icy wind whistling around the crumbling buildings didn't bother going around a person, just cut straight through.

'Any idea who used to live there? Before it was all boarded up?'

The first constable shook his head. 'Sorry, sir, before my time.' He turned to his colleague. 'You any idea, Andy?'

As McLean turned to face the other constable, an older man who might possibly have been working the area when people still lived in it, he caught movement out of the corner of his eye. A man, dishevelled and hunched over himself, had appeared from the gap between two of the blocks and was walking towards the cordoned-off entrance, head down. He looked up as if suddenly remembering something, a flash of pale face as he saw the policemen, then he swiftly turned and started to walk in the opposite direction. He didn't run, but his shuffle sped up and he disappeared back the way he had come. Quite clearly he didn't want to be anywhere near them.

'You see that?' McLean asked the constables. He stepped out into the road and hurried over, expecting them to follow him. By the time he reached the gap between the two blocks and glanced back, they were still standing beside their squad car, mouths open. DC Harrison was nowhere to be seen.

Shaking his head, McLean set off down the narrow passageway, coming out in a scrubby communal area at the back of the development that only someone with a very vivid imagination could call a garden. At first he couldn't see the man, but then he spotted him, heading away towards a similar passage on the other side. Suppressing the urge to shout, 'Stop! Police!' he hurried after him, careful to avoid tripping over the abandoned shopping trolleys, broken bicycles, discarded mattresses and endless other rubbish strewn around.

The man wasn't moving quickly, but he clearly knew where he was going, which gave him an advantage. McLean barked his shin against a metal post hidden in the

246

long grass, letting out a choice expletive at the pain, and limped on. He reached the passageway just as the man was approaching the other end and the street beyond.

'Wait. I just want to talk.' It was a stupid thing to say, but it seemed to work. The man stopped, turned and faced him. McLean didn't recognize him, hadn't really expected to.

'Fuck off, pig,' the man said, then turned away again. Straight into the path of DC Harrison as she stepped out to block the passage.

'You kiss your mother with that mouth?' she asked, and before he could say anything else he was in an arm lock on the ground.

30

'Why'd you run away from us? And what were you doing sniffing around our crime scene in the first place?'

McLean sat on the business side of the plain, Formica-topped table in Interview Room Three and wished he was in Interview Room One, where the ventilation worked, or even back in the observation booth and letting someone else do the interrogation. Sitting across from him, the man DC Harrison had so skilfully detained didn't look like a person so much as a mismatched collection of skin and rags. And smell. There was a miasma rising from him that even a powerful extractor fan would have struggled to cope with. In here, far from any windows or any other kind of draught, the effect was more powerful than any chemical weapon banned under the Geneva Convention. He had reluctantly given his name as Scotty Ferguson, and he had a record of convictions going back a decade. More interesting to McLean was the fact that he was currently undergoing one of Morningstar's rehabilitation programmes. That and the two medicine bottles they had found on him, their contents now on their way to Forensics for urgent analysis.

'Dunno what yez mean.' Ferguson coughed, dislodging something wet and slippery from his lungs that McLean hoped wasn't going to make itself known to the rest of them. Beside him, DC Harrison was getting her first suspect interview experience the hard way. Hovering a few paces back, Grumpy Bob had the benefit of being close to the door, should the atmosphere become unbreathable.

'These bottles we found in the pocket of your . . .' McLean paused, considering how best to describe the tattered rags that hung from the man's shoulders. '. . . Coat.'

'Dunno what yez talkin' aboot. 'Snot mine that. Never seen 'em before.'

McLean leaned back in his chair, partly to put as much distance between himself and the source of the stench as possible, partly because leaning forward was making his hip ache.

'I'm inclined to believe they're not yours, Scotty.' McLean lifted one of the bottles off the table, peering at the label through the plastic of the evidence bag. There were no words on it, just an abstract design that looked remarkably similar to the tattoos on Malky Davison and Bill Chalmers.

'I can go, then?' Ferguson made to stand up, but without much enthusiasm. The effort of lifting his body a few inches seemed to exhaust him, and he slumped back down in his seat with a noise McLean hoped wasn't a trump.

'Funny,' he mused. 'Like I said, I believe they're not yours. I don't believe you've never seen them before. What's in them, Scotty? What's the significance of these designs?'

A haunted look spread over Ferguson's face. Hard to see the true colour of his skin under all the grime and stubble, but McLean could have sworn he paled at the question. He said nothing, just folded his arms, his gaze flicking this way and that, avoiding McLean's eyes until it finally alighted on DC Harrison's chest. Staring at that seemed to soothe him. McLean put the bottle back down on the table. 'You know Malky Davison, don't you, Scotty?'

The twitch was almost not there, but McLean saw it. A momentary flick of the eyes away from the ogling, towards him and then back again. Ferguson muttered something that might have been 'Malky who?', but it was said with such lack of conviction McLean knew the man was on the verge of breaking.

'When was the last time you had a fix, Scotty? Yesterday? This morning?' He turned in his seat to speak to Grumpy Bob. 'What do you reckon, Sergeant? Stick him down in the cells for a few hours? Let him sweat it off?'

'There's only the lower cells left at the moment, sir. You know, the ones in the basement with no windows? We've got a few remand cases blocking up the nice ones. The electrics are on the blink down there too, but I don't suppose you'll mind sitting in the dark, will you Scotty?'

'You can't keep me here. I ain't done nothing. I swear it. I wasn't there. I didn't see –'

'Didn't see what, Scotty? Where weren't you?' McLean swung back around to face the man. The fear was in his eyes now, and they locked on to McLean's gaze with a terrible pleading.

'I . . . I can't. They'll know. They'll come for me.'

'Like they came for Malky? Like they did for Bill Chalmers?'

Ferguson sniffed, and McLean could see tears glistening in his bloodshot eyes. For a moment he thought the grubby man was going to say something. He swallowed, opened his mouth, and then the trembling started.

'Come on, Scotty. We can protect you. If you've got

information that's useful to us, we might even be able to turn a blind eye to all this.' McLean indicated the bottles. 'Why don't you tell us what those symbols mean, for starters, eh?'

'The . . . The symbols? On the bottles?' Ferguson's trembling was more violent now, his arms shaking as he pressed them into his lap. Where his face had been pale under the layers of grime, now it was florid, a vein bulging in his neck. McLean turned to tell Grumpy Bob to get medical help, but the detective sergeant was already at the door.

'I can't . . . I can't . . .' Ferguson stammered the words out as if something had a hold of his tongue. He was starting to foam at the mouth now, flecks of spittle arcing out and on to the table, sticking in the wiry hairs of his scrawny beard. 'Help . . . me . . .'

He stood up like a puppet on ill-handled strings, lunged towards DC Harrison, one outstretched hand reaching for her top. To her credit, she didn't scream, but stood swiftly, grabbed the offending hand and pressed it hard to the table.

'Jesus Christ. He's burning up, sir.' She shifted her grip as Ferguson collapsed across the table, body spasming. Knocked to the floor, the two bottles smashed in their evidence bags, and then with a scream that sounded more like a wounded bird than any man, he fell still.

'Poor bastard. You reckon he'll live?'

Grumpy Bob leaned against the wall opposite the open door to the interview room, far enough away to avoid the worst of the rank smell wafting out into the corridor.

McLean had moved further away still, watching as Scotty Ferguson was wheeled out on a stretcher. DC Harrison had already left, clearing out of the interview room to make space for the resuscitation team who had brought the drug addict back from the brink. Her first experience of a suspect interrogation was not one she would easily forget.

'Who knows? Can't even say what he was on at the moment, but he really didn't want to tell us about these.' McLean held up the evidence bags, now full of shards of glass. A dark, sticky liquid had oozed out into the plastic.

'You'd best be careful with that. Give it another few minutes and it'll have eaten through. You really don't want to get any on your skin.'

McLean looked up to see Harrison heading back down the corridor, a happier look on her face than when she had left minutes earlier. Amanda Parsons walked beside her, eyes fixed firmly on McLean and the broken bottles. She pulled a large evidence bag from her pocket as she approached, opening it wide so that he could drop his prize into it.

'And maybe another one, too.' Parsons doubled up the bags again before stepping into the interview room and putting the whole lot back down on the table.

'Dr Cairns is going to be very disappointed to find you've smashed up her bottles before she got a chance to look at them properly, Tony.' She smiled broadly, then wrinkled her nose. 'Gods, what is that smell?'

'Sorry about that. I think poor Scotty Ferguson may have lost control of his bowels when he had a seizure just now.'

'Would that be the same fellow whose wares you asked us to test on the hurry-up?' Parsons waved a sheet of paper in the air with a flourish. 'I was headed over this side of town, anyway. Wanted to check with Janie if she was still interested in sharing a flat. Thought I'd drop your results in and kill two birds. It's just the basics so far, but I thought you'd like to know asap.'

'Anything interesting?' McLean asked.

'Very. They're both opium based, but each bottle's slightly different. Some kind of tincture, like laudanum, only with more weird stuff added in for good measure. It'll take a bit longer to work out the full chemical composition, but whoever's using it needs to be very careful indeed.'

'Why's that?' McLean asked the question even though he was fairly sure he already knew the answer.

'Because its potency is off the scale. I've never seen anything like it. A couple of drops would kill an elephant, let alone a man.'

'Good thing I didn't get any on me then.' McLean couldn't help himself from wiping his hands on his thighs. 'Do you think this might be the same stuff we found in Bill Chalmers?'

Parsons wrinkled her brow, either in thought or because the stench was truly eye-watering. Outside in the corridor, someone's airwave set trilled and at the same time McLean felt his mobile phone vibrate in his pocket. He pulled it out as she answered, only half listening.

'We'll have to wait for the full spectrum analysis to compare, but if it is the same stuff then I'm buggered if I know how they got it into him. You'd need to water it down a thousandfold, and then some. Christ, there'd be enough in those two bottles to last someone a lifetime. Can't imagine what that would be worth.'

'Sir. Just got a call from Control.' DC Harrison stood in the doorway, her happy smile replaced with a worried frown. 'Some guy called Cobbold? Called in a burglary. Asked for you by name.'

McLean stared first at the message on the screen of his phone, then at Parsons, then at Harrison. Her frown had turned into a wide-eyed stare of surprise.

'Eddie Cobbold? Bo's Inks? Who the hell would want to burgle a tattoo parlour?'

31

'Fifty years this shop's been here. My dad set it up with his compensation money when they invalided him out of the merchant navy. Fifty years, and it's never been so much as broken into. And now this.'

Eddie Cobbold sat on an upturned wooden chest in the middle of the front room of Bo's Inks. It looked like someone had been through the place with an axe, or possibly a chainsaw. The tables were smashed to splinters, books of designs ripped open and pages strewn everywhere. The burglars had gone around the walls, methodically smashing the glass in all the picture frames. The front windows had fared no better, cracked and hazed where the safety lamination has stopped the panes from disintegrating entirely. What little floor McLean could see had been scuffed and scratched as if some giant beast had ripped at the wooden boards. Gouges and splinters shone white against the deep brown of generations of booted feet like broken bones poking from shattered limbs.

'You any idea who might have done this?' McLean picked his way through the carnage and into the back room. He couldn't get very far. The reclining chairs had been bent and twisted, shelves pulled from the walls and their contents thrown to the floor. Like the front room, all the pictures had been smashed and the books of designs ripped apart.

'I've asked around. But we're a tight-knit community you know. If I'd pissed someone off, they'd come and tell me to my face. Not smash up my shop like . . .' Eddie tailed off, as if acknowledging the extent of the damage was too much to bear.

'Nobody was hurt though? There wasn't anyone here? George –?'

'George is fine. He's away in the States. Big convention in Vegas. He's competing for Scotland. Christ but he's going to be pissed when he gets back.' Eddie reached into his pocket and pulled out a phone, held it up to the light. 'Don't know whether to call him and let him know, or leave it till he comes home. He's made it to the semi-finals so far. Be a damn shame if he pulled out now. Then again, what's the point in winning a big competition if this is all the shop you've got to come back to?'

'You know if much has been stolen?' McLean turned slowly in the doorway, his gaze taking in the ceiling, where cracks and holes in the plaster told of frenzy. It put him in mind of the destruction in Bill Chalmers' mews flat and the offices of Morningstar. Not so much a burglary as a demolition. Unleashed fury rather than any desire to steal.

'Hard to tell. We don't keep any cash in here, just the machines. They've been smashed up, which is just stupid.' Eddie slumped his shoulders in defeat. 'The whole thing's just stupid.'

'What about the alarm? Did that go off?' DC Harrison stood by the front door, inspecting the damage to the frame where something very heavy had battered the hinges out of the wood.

'If it did, I never got a call. Which reminds me.' Eddie

lifted up his phone again, flipped through some menus. 'I need to have a word with the alarm company about that. Pay them enough bloody money.'

McLean left him to make the call and went to join Harrison at the front door. She had crouched down, and was teasing something out of the wreckage strewn around the frame.

'Here, better put these on.' He handed her a pair of latex gloves. 'Wouldn't want you getting it in the ear from your new flatmate.'

'Hadn't made up my mind about that yet, sir.' Harrison took the gloves and snapped them on before going back to the pile of rubbish. After a moment she managed to pull out what looked like a badly smashed security camera. Looking up, McLean saw the holes in the wall where it had been fastened, a ripped coil of flex dangling from the ceiling cornice.

'Yeah. That should have been working too.' Eddie Cobbold joined the two of them, slipping his phone into his pocket as he did so. 'And according to Penstemmin Alarms, my system is still fully functional. Apparently it was set at nine last night, and then switched off at one in the morning. Nine's when I left, so I guess that gives you an idea of when . . .' He shrugged, raising both hands to encompass the utter destruction of his livelihood.

'We might be able to get something off this, sir. It's got a memory card in it.' Harrison held up the mangled security camera for all to see.

'It's meant to feed directly to our cloud service, so we can access it from anywhere,' Eddie said. 'George understands the tech better than me. He set it up.'

'OK.' McLean looked around the shop one last time, not seeing anything new. 'We'll get the place dusted for recent prints. Doubt we'll find much though; it's a fairly public space, after all. Anyone can come in off the streets while you're open.' He pointed at the security camera. 'I'll have some of our IT people take a look at that, see if we can't find anything on there. And could you give us access to the footage from the last couple of days, if you've still got it?'

'Shouldn't be a problem.' The tattoo artist let out a low sigh. 'Not as if I'm going to be doing any inking for a while.'

'I'm sorry, Eddie. We'll do our best to find out who's done this. Maybe even why. But first I think we need to have a chat with all your neighbours.'

The shops to either side of Bo's Inks were hardly worth bothering with. One was empty, just the sign above the door to suggest that it had once sold antiques. McLean could see through the glass that no one had been in there in an age; the pile of junk mail and final demands spread out from the door in a yellowing paper fan was another indication of its total abandonment. To the other side, the bookmaker's was one of those places he just knew was going to be unhelpful. It had that kind of air about it.

'Not open till ten, aye.' The man at the counter had a sour, thin face, skin pasty as if fresh air and sunlight were strangers to him. His lank, greasy hair had once been red but was leaching to grey like an old paint colour card left too long in the sun. He peered at the world through thick spectacles that would have worked better were they not smeared with fingerprints and other grot.

'I'm not here to place any bets, unless it's one on how long this place stays open after I've gone.' McLean held up his warrant card, pulling it back just out of reach when the man tried to take it. He left his grabbing hand hanging in the air a moment longer than necessary before flexing grubby fingers that sported too many heavy gold rings, shrugged and went back to studying his copy of the *Racing Post*.

'What do you want to know?' He didn't look up as he spoke.

'Next door. I'm sure you've noticed it's been broken into. You hear anything? See anything?'

'Only just got in, dint I?' The man sniffed. 'We don't open till ten, like I said.'

'What time do you close?'

'Depends, dunnit.'

'OK. What time did you close last night, then?'

'Back of ten, I think. Might've been a bit later if there was a fight on.'

'And was there?' McLean bit back his frustration, resisting the urge to grab the man's paper and tear it into pieces in front of him.

'No fight last night, sir. Least not one a place like this would be taking bets on.' DC Harrison approached the counter with a smile on her face that was as mischievous as McLean had ever seen. She tugged the paper out from under the man's nose, flipped it around and opened it up to a page that was just a lot of meaningless numbers as far as McLean was concerned.

'Hey, that's mine.'

'Don't reckon a place like this would have much reason

to be open past six. Just long enough to pay out the winners on the last race at Ayr, maybe close a little earlier to make the punters come back for their winnings the next day. You strike me as the kind of man who likes to keep his hands on the money as long as possible.'

'My hours is my business. Now give me back my paper, aye?'

'You live here? At the back of the shop? Maybe upstairs?' Harrison nodded to the single door behind the counter, closed at the moment. She folded the paper but didn't hand it over.

'Here? Nah. There's just a wee office and the cludgie back there.'

'So who lives upstairs, then?'

'Search me. Students most likely. Either that or bloody immigrants.' The man snatched his paper back, and Harrison let him have it. McLean stepped to one side as she turned her back on the counter and headed for the door.

'Nice speaking to you,' he said, then followed her out.

'Sorry if I overstepped over the mark there, sir. Only I know his type and he'd have strung you along for hours if he thought he could get away with it.'

Out on the pavement, McLean was looking to see where the most likely entrance to the flats above the ground floor shops was, and hardly heard DC Harrison's apology.

'What was that? Oh, no. No need to apologize. You're quite right. Probably would have been even worse if he'd had any punters in. Nothing like a bookie for playing to an audience. Nicking his *Racing Post* was a smart move. I was going to tear it up.'

'That might not have helped.' Harrison walked away down the street, past the wrecked frontage of Bo's Inks and the empty antique shop before calling back, 'Think this is the one, sir.'

A set of worn stone steps led up to a front door that could have done with a lick of paint. On closer inspection, McLean reckoned it could have done with being thrown in a skip and replaced with a new one. Cracked and squint, it didn't meet the latch properly, making the electronic door-entry system somewhat redundant. He pushed it open and stepped back in time to his undergraduate years.

The narrow, dark hallway led to a stone staircase at the back, an even narrower passage cutting underneath it to an opening on to a yard behind the building. There were no doors on the ground floor other than the one they had come in through, confirming what the bookie had said. The building was three storeys high, two doors leading off the first landing. McLean chose the one that would open up above the antique shop and Bo's Inks, knocked loudly on the door and, for good measure, tugged at the ancient bell-pull that jutted from the doorframe. He hadn't been expecting it to work, but he felt the weight of the wire, and then heard a distant tinkling in the flat. It slowly petered away to nothing, and then was swallowed up by the sound of a door slamming. Heavy footsteps clumped across the hallway and the door was yanked open.

'Youse any idea what time it is, aye?'

A young woman stood before them, dressed in heavy cotton pyjamas and with a tartan blanket wrapped around her shoulders. She had pulled on a pair of Doc Martens boots, the laces trailing across the floor behind her.

'Detective Inspector McLean. Specialist Crime Division.' McLean held up his warrant card and the young woman peered at it through bleary eyes. 'This is Detective Constable Harrison. We're investigating the burglary of the tattoo shop downstairs. Wondering if we might have a word, Miss . . . ?'

'Weir. Molly Weir. And before you ask, yes, I know. And no, I'm no' a witch.' She looked across at Harrison, and McLean reckoned there couldn't be much difference in their ages. 'Aye, come on in. I'll put the kettle on.'

Molly Weir lived in a surprisingly large flat. Like most Edinburgh tenements built before the war, it had high ceilings with nice decorative cornice work and ornate plaster roses around the light fittings. The hall was dark, walls lined with wood panelling to chest height. Its only source of natural light came from skylights above the doors leading off it, but the kitchen they went into was bright and warm. A tall window looked out on to the yard behind and the backs of more tenements beyond. Molly clumped in her heavy boots over to an electric kettle, took it to the sink and filled it, ignored all the while by another young woman, who was sitting at the kitchen table and staring intently at her laptop.

'Don't mind Karen. She's in her own wee world.'

McLean noticed the white headphone cords snaking up to the young woman's ears. It surprised him that she hadn't noticed any of them come into the room though. Maybe she had, and strange men appearing at all hours was nothing unusual here.

'You lived here long?' he asked.

'Couple years now. I work nights at the Sick Kids. Be nice to have my own place, but this is handy, and cheap for the area.' Molly Weir found mugs and teabags and set about making tea. Something about the pouring of boiling water was clearly a trigger, as the other young woman raised her head, noticing company for the first time.

'Who're you?' She pulled first one earphone out, then the other, releasing a surprisingly loud and tinny racket into the room until she tapped at the laptop to silence it.

'It's the polis, Karen. Nae bother. Someone's done over Eddie's place and they're looking into it.' Molly held up a mug in each hand for McLean and Harrison to take. 'That right, aye?'

'Eddie's place?' The young woman at the table closed her laptop down and stared up at McLean. 'When?'

'Last night. We think sometime after one in the morning. Were you here?'

'I was. Molly would've been at work. Ben and Eric were both in too, though.' Karen reached up and took the mug that was offered to her, and McLean only then realized that Molly had made four teas without asking.

'And I take it you heard nothing all night,' he said.

'No. Slept like a baby. Which is odd, now I think about it. I usually sleep really bad, like.'

'What about these others you mentioned? Ben and Eric?' Harrison asked. 'Are they in?'

'No, they're both at work. Left about eight. Didn't say anything about noise when I saw them. So your burglars must've been very quiet.'

McLean was about to tell the two young women exactly what kind of state the tattoo parlour was in, but he stopped himself at the last minute. It was impossible that someone could have trashed the place and not made a noise about it, but then nobody had called it in until Eddie had turned up to open the shop. No passers-by had noticed, and it seemed that the neighbours hadn't heard a thing.

'You mentioned Eddie. I take it you know him?'

'Aye, Eddie's all right.' Molly leaned against the kitchen counter, the sunlight silhouetting her unkempt hair like a saintly halo. 'I'm no' into all that body art and piercings and stuff, but all's fair in love and war, aye?'

'She's such a prude.' Karen rolled up her sleeve to reveal a beautifully rendered image of a leopard twining around her upper arm. 'Eddie designed this, but it was George who did the actual inking. He calls me Kitty.'

'That's gorgeous.' DC Harrison moved in close to peer at the tattoo.

'Thanks. You're no' so bad yourself.'

McLean couldn't quite decide whether Harrison blushed at that, but the ghost of a smile played around her lips. Perhaps she didn't get compliments often.

'The other flats, across the hall and upstairs,' he said. 'You know who lives there?'

'Upstairs is empty.' Molly looked up to the ceiling as she answered. 'Not sure who's on the other side at the moment. There was an old couple, but she died and he went into a home over Newhaven way.'

So much for witnesses, then. McLean took a long sip of his surprisingly good tea, mourning the lack of biscuits. 'Did either of you notice the shopfront this morning?'

Karen looked up from her seat at the kitchen table. 'No' been out yet. Sorry.'

'Can't say as I noticed anything either.' Molly knocked back her tea in one gulp. 'Mind youse, my walk home brings me in from the other direction. Don't remember seeing anything on the pavement that was unusual. Why?'

'Just trying to gather as much information as possible.' McLean went to his pocket to fetch out his card, but DC Harrison was quicker off the mark.

'See, if either of you remember anything, or if Ben and Eric saw anything, just give us a call?' She placed the neat white rectangle down on the kitchen table beside Karen's laptop, then flipped it over, picked up a stray pen and began scribbling. 'And here's my mobile too. Just in case.'

32

'You seemed very chatty up there, Constable. What was that all about?'

McLean followed DC Harrison down the stone steps to the cold, narrow entrance hall and out into the noisy street. A couple of squad cars had pulled up on the double yellow line, sandwiching a battered white van that most likely belonged to the forensics services. Someone had even unwound some blue-and-white 'Police: Do Not Cross' tape, but there weren't any pedestrians to warrant it.

'I don't know. Just seemed like nice people. And after the bookies, well . . .' The detective constable shrugged. 'And that was a stunning tattoo.'

'Talking of which, I'd quite like another look at the shop. You want to go see if we can get a ride back to the station in one of those squad cars?'

Harrison nodded her assent, striding off towards the nearest car as McLean ducked under the tape. Looking at the shattered window from the outside, it was hard not to come to the conclusion it had been smashed from within, the reinforced glass bulging outwards. Tiny fragments and shards scattered on the pavement crunched under his feet as he stepped in through the door, straight into the blinding flash of a camera.

'Oh, Tony. Sorry. Didn't see you there.' Amanda Parsons let her camera hang by the strap strung around her neck and moved carefully around an upturned, broken table to get a better position.

'Anyone would think you were following me.' McLean blinked and squinted until the bright yellow dot in the centre of his vision faded away to nothing. The sight it revealed was no better than before.

'Aye, well. I was closest when the call came in. Don't normally do the camera work, but we all have to muck in sometimes.'

'Tell me about it. You dusted for prints yet?' McLean couldn't help noticing that Parsons was kitted out in the full white overalls and bootees, whereas he had just brought glass fragments in from the pavement outside on the soles of his unprotected shoes.

'Just a couple of places where they might have been left by whoever did this. There's prints everywhere, but only a few that look fresh enough to be worth checking. They'll probably turn out to be you and Janic though. And Eddie, of course.'

McLean took a couple of careful steps until he was standing in the middle of the front room. It was impossible to move anywhere without dislodging pages ripped from the design books. They littered the floor like confetti at a Goth wedding. Parsons did her best not to criticize, but he could see that she wanted to shout at him for disturbing her nice pristine crime scene.

'You want me out of here, don't you?' he said.

'Am I that easily read?'

'No. It's just that I've grown so used to being told off by people in white suits. Kind of feels wrong not to be.'

'Well, I can yell at you if you want. You know, if it helps.'

Parsons smiled, raised her camera and took a photograph of him in one swift motion. McLean was fast enough to close his eyes against the flash, but not to turn his back. No doubt he'd be appearing in the forensics services Christmas party slideshow at the end of the year. Unless something more embarrassing came up in the intervening months.

'You make anything of this?' He swept an open hand through the air, indicating the room and its destruction.

'I thought the big picture was your speciality. I'm just here for the small stuff.'

'Humour me, why don't you?'

Parsons dropped her camera on to its strap again, letting out a long breath through her nose, as if thinking needed some outward physical sign. She turned slowly, then dropped into a crouch and began gently moving bits of broken chair, picture frames and other stuff out of the way. Finally she started to leaf through the ripped-out pages of the design books, piling them all together until she reached the dark wooden floorboards beneath. Unlike the area immediately in front of the door, where they had been splintered and cracked as if by some crazed lumberjack, here they were just dark and dirty, polished with the boots and grime of generations.

'Here's my theory. Whoever did this was looking for something. A specific design in one of these books. Either they found it and then trashed the place to cover themselves, or they didn't find it and trashed the place in a fit of pique.'

'Pique?' McLean gazed over the carnage, thinking that there was probably a better word but unable to find one.

'See, all these pages are underneath everything else.' Parsons tugged a few more from the pile. 'If I was just breaking stuff up, they'd be mixed in with it all. And some of these folders would still have stuff in them.' She reached down, struggled a bit before coming up with a black leather ring binder. Flipping it open revealed it to be empty.

'What about in the back?' McLean stepped more carefully through the detritus to the back room, with its twisted and shattered reclining chairs, toppled shelves and ransacked cupboards. A first glance suggested it was exactly the same as in the front, almost as if the floor had been lined with the designs before everything else was broken and heaped on top.

'Looks the same to me.' Parsons joined him in the doorway, pointing her camera at the mess and popping off a couple more flashes. 'I wonder if they found what they were looking for.'

'McLean. My office. Now.'

He had only just walked through the back door into the station, DC Harrison a step behind him as she struggled with her phone. McLean half expected to see Detective Superintendent Duguid glowering at him from the stairs; it was Dagwood's favourite barked command, after all. Instead, he saw Brooks leaning against the bannisters and looking for all the world like a man who's just eaten both his lunch and that of the poor thin fellow sitting next to him.

'Get that camera to the IT boys won't you, Constable? And see if there's any good footage from the public cameras in the street. You never know, we might get lucky.' He shrugged – well, it was worth a try. 'I'd better go and see what all this is about.'

Harrison's eyes were wide as she looked past McLean to the looming presence of the detective superintendent, but she nodded once, slipping her phone back into her pocket. The broken CCTV camera was in a clear plastic evidence bag they had borrowed from the forensics van, and she held it like a prize goldfish as she carried it off in the direction of the IT lab.

'Do you never check your messages, McLean? Been trying to get you all morning,' was all the greeting Brooks gave him. McLean was used to worse, but he pulled his phone out anyway, flicked on the screen.

'What messages would those be, sir?' He held up the handset for Brooks to see. It was unlikely the detective superintendent would have sent a text himself, which meant that some poor underling was going to get it in the neck soon.

'Never mind. What have you been doing all morning? You were told to lead this investigation from the incident room, not go gallivanting off all over the city. Where the fuck have you been, man?'

McLean was certain that Brooks knew exactly where he had been. Best to humour him though; he was clearly on the edge of a foul mood.

'Tattoo artist's shop up Lochrin way was done over last night.'

'A burglary? That warrants a detective inspector's personal attendance these days, does it?' Despite his bulk, Brooks could move at speed when he wanted to. He had set off up the stairs at an athlete's pace and McLean had to hurry to keep up. The twinge of pain in his hip was an unwelcome reminder of how unfit he was these days.

'I visited that same shop just a few days ago, sir. It was the place where Malky Davison got his tattoo. Bill Chalmers too. I don't think it's any coincidence it was broken into not long after we visited.'

'You could have sent your new girlfriend on her own, you know?'

'My new . . . ?' McLean took a moment to realize that Brooks was referring to DC Harrison. A warm flush spread across the back of his neck, heat burning the tips of his ears for no accountable reason. The embarrassment lasted only a few seconds before the anger kicked in. 'Really, sir? You think that's the sort of comment the most senior detective in the region should be making? I mean, I expect that kind of thing amongst the constables, but you're a detective superintendent for fuck's sake.'

It was Brooks' turn to redden, although his flush wasn't confined to his ears and neck. He stopped mid step and turned on McLean, hand raised and a stubby finger jabbing in his direction.

'I let you get away with that insolent tone with Mike because he's an arsehole and deserves it. I don't expect to hear it directed at me. You got that?'

McLean started to open his mouth, a perfect retort forming, but his instinct for self-preservation kicked in at the last moment. He'd been here with Duguid too many times before to fall so easily into that trap.

'I'm sorry, sir. I just wouldn't want as promising a detective as Harrison to be the brunt of more scurrilous rumour than she's going to be getting anyway.'

If Brooks was satisfied with the apology he didn't show it.

'Well, send her out with a sergeant then. Don't think you have to investigate everything yourself. You're management now. Act like it.'

McLean gritted his teeth against the response that wanted to come out, Brooks taking his lack of response as a challenge.

'Do I need to make it an order you don't leave the station?' The detective superintendent folded his arms across his barrel chest, eyes disappearing into the folds of his face as he scowled. McLean took a deep breath.

'No, sir. That won't be necessary.'

'Good. You need to be here so that we can reach you as quickly as possible. Senior officers don't much like being kept waiting.' Brooks turned away from him and carried on rapidly up the stairs. McLean only managed to catch up as the detective superintendent stopped to open his office door.

'Sorry about the delay, sir. Seems our favourite detective inspector is a hard man to track down.'

McLean's initial confusion at Brooks' words turned to surprise when he saw who was already waiting in the office. He'd not seen the deputy chief constable since the first briefing at the beginning of the Chalmers investigation.

'Ah well, he's here now. Come in, Tony. Come in.'

McLean knew what the condemned man must feel like walking to the gallows as he stepped into the room. There was an atmosphere about the place that had nothing to do with the tightly closed windows, the radiators turned to the max and the non-functional ventilation system. It might have had something to do with the way Detective Chief Inspector Spence was looking at him with undisguised hatred through rheumy eyes set in a face that would make a skeleton look fat, or it might have been the sight of retired Detective Superintendent Duguid glaring at him from the far side of the big conference table.

'Have a seat, Tony, won't you?' The DCC pulled one out and motioned for McLean to sit. Sensing it would be unwise to disobey, he did as he was told. No one said anything until they were all seated, and even then Call-me-Stevie dragged out the silence with unnecessary theatricality.

'I've been reviewing progress on the Chalmers case, Tony,' he said eventually. McLean couldn't help but notice that this was the third time the man had used his first name. That couldn't be a good sign, could it?

'It's not as far forward as I'd like, sir. But we've got some promising leads. Just this morning, I –'

'I'm sure it's all coming along fine, but like I said at the beginning, Tony, this is an important case. Important people are watching. The press not the least of them.'

'So what's the problem? Are we not moving fast enough? Moving too quickly? Only I can't help but notice no one in this room other than me has bothered to turn up to any press conferences. There hasn't been much input at all from anyone more senior than a detective inspector.'

'This isn't about Chalmers, McLean.'

Of all the people in the room who might have spoken, Duguid was the last McLean was expecting, and the only one who could actually make him shut up. Something about the massed ranks of senior officers, and the deliberate absence of DCI McIntyre, had put him on his guard. And the best form of defence was attack.

'This is about the CCU, Tony.' Robinson made it sound like an unfortunate rash caught from a dalliance with a lady of the night.

'You're meant to be reviewing cold cases but so far we've not exactly seen any results.' Brooks directed the accusation at McLean, refusing to meet Duguid's eye.

'Perhaps that's because you put me in charge of it and then suspended me for three months. Or maybe it's because you assigned only two serving officers to it and didn't even bother to replace the one who left the force shortly afterwards. I don't know, maybe it's because every time we open an old case someone comes up with a good reason to shut it back down again. Almost as if there are senior officers out there who don't want their past mistakes brought out into the open. Too much dirty laundry.'

'Tony, Tony. You're reading far too much into this as usual. Seeing conspiracies where there are none.' The deputy chief constable leaned forward in his chair, his tone that of a headmaster trying to be reasonable. 'I'm sure some of the cases you've resurrected might give a few retired officers red faces, but to suggest anyone has actively tried to shut you down . . .'

'Until now, of course.'

'Well, yes. I can see how this might look. But it's nothing to do with that at all. It's purely a matter of budget and staffing levels. You know as well as I do how short-staffed we are. You said it yourself: we've not replaced the officers who've left – and there's a good reason for that. It takes time to train up new recruits, and there's few enough of them wanting to work Plain Clothes these days. We have to prioritize current investigations over reopening old cases. Especially with Chalmers eating up all our resources, there just isn't the manpower to keep the CCU open.'

'What? You're shutting it down?'

'Let's call it a temporary halt on operations, why don't we? I'm sure when times are better we'll have the resources to start things up again.'

'What about Chief Superintendent Duguid?'

'Charles will stay on as a consultant. He's got the experience and the clearance so it would be a shame to waste that.' Call-me-Stevie smiled like a crocodile, his pearly white teeth just too perfect to be real. 'He'll be helping out with the Chalmers case now.'

33

Still reeling from his meeting with the DCC, McLean didn't much fancy going back to the major incident room and its air of listlessness. Instead, he headed for his office and the relative sanctuary of mindless paperwork. He'd been out all day, which meant there would be enough waiting for him to last a lifetime.

'Ah, sir. I was hoping I might find you up here.'

Lost in his thoughts, it took him a while to realize he was being spoken to. McLean looked up to see Detective Constable Stringer heading down the corridor towards him.

'And here I am. Was there something in particular you needed?' The DCC's words echoed in his mind. Too few new recruits wanting to work in Plain Clothes. It made sense: far easier to get regular overtime in uniform, and the shifts were much more predictable. Plus you didn't have to wade through quite so much of humanity's shit every day.

'We've managed to get something off that camera you and Janie brought in from the tattoo shop, sir. Thought you might want to see it.'

Given the alternative options, working through a slow mountain of duty rosters or captaining the rudderless ship that was the Chalmers investigation, a trip down to the basement and the IT labs was an easy decision to make.

'Pete's gone to speak to the CCTV guys about street cameras in the area too,' Stringer said as he and McLean walked down the stairs. 'Pretty sure we know what time they arrived so if we're lucky we might get a picture. Maybe a number plate if they came by car.'

'Pete?' McLean asked.

'Sorry, sir. Constable Blane. Most of the others call him Lofty, but it's not his fault he's that size.'

'Pete, eh?' McLean was uncomfortably aware both that he should really have known that, and that he didn't actually know DC Stringer's first name either. 'And what do they call you, Constable?'

'Stringer, mostly. If they're being polite.'

'Not much of that around here, but then I guess you've found that out already. Got used to it, too, or you wouldn't still be with us.'

They reached the door to the IT labs before Stringer could make any response to that, and McLean pushed it open without bothering to knock. He'd not been in there in a while, but it still had that odour of sweating male and air of organized chaos about it, even if some of the equipment looked a lot more modern. A cluster of technicians and detectives were huddled around one end of the central bench, staring at a flat-screen monitor. One of them looked up in surprise.

'Oh, Inspector, sir. We were hoping you'd still be around.'

'What have you got for me?' McLean asked.

'Your friend at the tattoo parlour did us a solid buying half-decent kit. The camera in the shop has its own memory card and a back-up power supply, so in theory, as long as it's still pointing in the right direction, it'll record anything that moves.'

'I don't like the sound of "in theory".' McLean joined the group, looking over DC Harrison's head to an image on the screen of Bo's Inks as he remembered it from before the burglary.

'Aye, well . . .' The technician reached for the mouse that was tethered to the monitor, no box of electronics visible anywhere on the desk. He clicked a couple of times and the image changed.

'It's on a two second time lapse, sir.' Harrison twisted around in her seat to face him. 'Not brilliant resolution either. But there's a timestamp says it's one in the morning, near as. See.'

McLean peered at the grainy image on the screen as a figure appeared in the middle of the room, followed by another. They moved in a series of awkward jerks as the images on the card were played as a movie. Clear enough what they were doing though: they pulled the black folders filled with designs off the shelves and tabletops, ripping out pages and tossing them to the floor. He was just about getting bored with the regularity of it, frustrated that the picture was too poor to make out any features beyond the black clothing the burglars wore, then something else blurred across the screen. One more image showed a smear of light and dark all but impossible to make out, and then it ended.

'That'll be when they noticed the camera and ripped it off the wall.' The technician pointed to the workbench where the camera lay in pieces. 'Jumped up and down on it in hobnail boots too, by the look of the poor wee thing.'

'It's just like the last time, sir. See?'

McLean had hoped to make an escape from the station

278

and for once head home at a decent hour, but a breathless Detective Constable Blane had caught up with him just as he was stepping out into the car park at the back of the station. McLean had reluctantly followed him back to the major incident room and the network-connected workstation that could tap into the city's CCTV footage. Now he looked at images from four different camera angles, each showing streets approaching Bo's Inks.

'What time is this?' He peered at the slightly fuzzy numbers at the bottom of each image. So much for new high-resolution cameras.

'Quarter to one, sir.' Blane loomed over him, having insisted McLean take the seat in front of the screen. At least his arms were long enough to reach the mouse and keyboard without getting awkwardly close.

The view wasn't particularly inspiring. There were no pedestrians and very few cars at that time of night. At one point McLean thought he might have seen a fox trotting down the pavement, but it disappeared as the image turned to foggy grey and white. A few moments later the picture reappeared, and one of the other views dropped. Then the third and the fourth.

'It does the same again about half an hour later. There's other cameras across the city the same. Technicians reckon it's a glitch in one of the substation hubs or something. All sounds like gobbledegook to me.'

McLean stared at the screen again as DC Blane tapped a few commands, navigating the system like a professional for all his protestations of technological ignorance. He tapped at his teeth with a finger for a moment, trying to work out what was bothering him. Through the corner of his eye he could see the original map of the city, with its white dots marking the potential helicopter sightings. Unless it really had been a dragon, of course.

'It's Pete, right?'

DC Blane looked a little surprised to be asked. 'Yes, sir.'

'Well, do me a favour will you, Pete? I'd like to see a map of where these cameras are and mark the exact times the pictures blank out like that for each one. Do it for the mews house burglary too, will you? And see if there's anything for the offices of Morningstar.'

'You think someone's what . . . jamming the cameras somehow? Is that even possible? They're all hard-wired, aren't they?'

'I've honestly no idea. It's just a hunch. Might not come to anything, but humour me, eh?'

Blane nodded his understanding, which made a change from the weary sighs McLean normally got whenever he asked a detective constable to do anything for him. 'There was one thing, sir. Not sure whether it's relevant or not, given the circumstances.'

'Anything you think's relevant is worth bringing up, Constable, however insignificant. Especially when our investigation's as bogged down as this one. What have you got?'

The detective constable reached for the mouse, clicked on an image in the corner of the screen to bring up a snapshot of a road and cars. 'This is the next camera along from the tattoo parlour, sir. Before it went on the fritz there were a few cars that I could put through number-plate recognition.' Blane clicked again and another image replaced the first one, remarkably similar except for a council bin visible at the road edge. 'There's not much of a pattern to the numbers in each of the locations. Mostly taxis, as you'd expect at that time of night. There's one number that appeared on more than one camera, though. Both the night of the mews house and the tattoo parlour break-ins.'

'You got a name for the owner, I take it?' McLean squinted at the image, trying to make out what model the car showing was, even though he had no way of telling whether that was the one to which DC Blane was referring.

'I have, and that's what so confusing, sir. See, it belongs to a reporter. Jo Dalgliesh.'

The house really wasn't what McLean had been expecting. It was in an expensive part of the city for one thing, although it was always possible that Dalgliesh had been living there since before it had become fashionable. He wasn't sure why he'd never bothered to find out where she lived before, except that for a long time he had hated her so much he couldn't bear even to speak her name. Time had softened that hatred into a dull acceptance, and recent events had brought them together for long enough to expose his prejudices for what they were. But still, he had never thought of the reporter as a friend, never needed to know where she lived.

Even so, he had to check twice against the address that Sergeant Hwei had dug out for him. Parked across the road from a detached two-storey-plus-attic Edwardian pile, he couldn't help thinking that Dalgliesh must rattle around in all that space. Granted, it was about a fifth the size of his grandmother's house. His house. But it was still big enough for a sizeable family and their servants.

Something from a bygone era that in any other part of town would have been split into three apartments, if not six.

The air was so cold and clear as he walked across the empty street that he could see stars overhead. There weren't many parts of the city where you could do that these days, although his own back garden was one. Approaching the front door, McLean confirmed his suspicions that this was indeed just one house, and he pressed the one doorbell to an echoing 'ding dong' from inside. He waited in the shivering cold, ears straining to hear any sound. Nothing broke the dull, distant rumble of the city. No lights appeared above the locked door or in any of the empty windows.

He crunched through thick gravel to the bay window that would have looked on to the front living room had the shutters not been closed. He could see enough to know that the room was unoccupied though. A narrow passageway took him around the back to a surprisingly neat garden overlooked by an elegant conservatory. Squinting through the glass revealed a faded wicker armchair and a glass-topped table, clear except for a copy of the *Edinburgh Tribune*, folded in half so he couldn't see what the date was. He knocked on the back door, but it was clear the house was empty.

'She's no' in.'

McLean spun around too quickly, almost falling over as a twinge of pain ran through his hip. There wasn't much light in the back garden, but enough filtered in from the streetlights for him to see a man peering over the nearby wall.

'I kind of figured that out. Have you seen her recently?' He moved away from the back door, stepping out of the deeper shadows so that the man could get a better look at him.

'Who's asking?'

'Tony McLean. Detective Inspector, I should say.' He pulled out his warrant card, even though the distance between him and the neighbour was too great for it to be seen.

'Oh aye. Heard of you. All that nonsense up at the old psychiatric hospital. Those bodies. That was you, wasn't it?'

McLean thought of correcting the man, but so far he'd been reasonably civil. 'My case, yes. So have you seen Ms Dalgliesh lately?'

'She's no' talking to the polis at the moment. Says she doesn't trust youse lot any more.' The man on the other side of the wall had a thick coat on, his head enveloped in a furry hat. His breath steamed in the lamplight as he spoke, spiralling upwards in a night so still it could only be a harbinger of storms to come.

'I'll take that as a yes then.' McLean stuck his hands in his pockets to stave off his shivering. 'Look. I know what she's like, and if she's avoiding us she's probably got her reasons. If you see her though, tell her I was here, will you? I really need to talk to her.'

34

A strange car was sitting outside the house as he pulled up the drive. For a moment McLean wondered if it might be Dalgliesh. She most probably drove something like the grubby silver Audi. Whoever it belonged to, they'd not been there long. Ice was forming over the windscreen but the bonnet still showed evidence of heat in the engine. He didn't hang around looking at it, the nip in the air enough to ache in his lungs as he walked to the back door.

A blast of welcome warmth hit him as he entered the empty kitchen. There was no sign of Mrs McCutcheon's cat, but the kettle sat on the hotplate alongside the cheap tin caddy the teabags lived in. McLean followed the scent of biscuits through to the front of the house. As he approached the library door and heard voices in relaxed conversation, he realized just how tense he had become. The case was starting to get to him, and the threats from Brooks and the DCC didn't help. Why they couldn't just leave him to get on with the investigation he couldn't understand, but bringing those frustrations home would only make things worse. He paused a moment, letting the tension in his shoulders ease as he twisted the door handle and let himself in.

'Tony, you're home. Look who just dropped by.'

Emma had been sitting on the sofa, the neatly folded

eiderdown beside her. She leapt to her feet on seeing him, a welcoming smile on her face. Sitting in the armchair beside her, Detective Chief Inspector Jayne McIntyre clearly felt that standing was unnecessary. She merely looked at him with tired eyes and raised her mug of tea in welcome.

'I see you've still not mastered the art of working only the hours you're paid for.' She cracked a smile that eased some of the weariness from her features. 'Good to see you, Tony. I understand you dropped by for a wee chat with Lucy last night.'

Emma almost skipped across the floor, gave McLean a warm hug and a kiss on the lips. 'You want a mug of tea? It's not long brewed. Or I can get you something stronger if it's been that kind of day.'

McLean stared at her, confused for a moment before it dawned on him that an answer was required. 'No, tea's fine. You sure? I can get it myself.'

'Sit, Tony. Jayne didn't come around to hear me prattle on. I won't be long.' Before he could answer, Emma had swept past him and out of the room.

'She's looking well.' McIntyre struggled to stand, but McLean motioned for her to stay seated.

'Better than this morning, I have to say. Much better than a couple of days ago.'

'The hospital? Aye, I heard.'

'And I heard you'd been dragged off to Glasgow on the hush-hush. What's all that about?'

'Bloody waste of time is what it's all about. Someone thought now was the best time to conduct an in-depth review into the impact of increasing numbers of women in the police force. That's why they dragged Ritchie in as well, or at least that's how it was explained to me. Why it has to be done now, and out of Glasgow rather than Edinburgh, I have no idea.' McIntyre laid the irony on thick and tried another smile, but the tiredness was back this time. She couldn't stifle the yawn that turned into a shiver. 'Scuse me. Your armchairs are far too comfortable. If it wasn't so chilly in here I'd probably fall asleep.'

McLean looked at the cold, empty fireplace. 'I keep on telling Emma to light the fire in the morning, but she doesn't seem to mind the cold. These old houses were designed to be draughty. Not much fun when it's minus ten outside.'

'Aye, well. That's what you get for living in a mansion when a wee bungalow would do.'

'Your place is very cosy.'

'It's Lucy's. My dickhead of an ex-husband got mine.' McIntyre remembered her tea, took a long drink. 'But that's not why you went around last night, is it? To see the place.'

McLean settled himself down into the other armchair, hoping Emma wouldn't be long with the tea. It really wasn't warm in the house, the ancient cast-iron radiators gurgling and rattling as the equally ancient monster of a boiler in the basement burned its way through the oil output of a small Middle East country without producing any discernible heat.

'I wish there were time for social visits, Jayne. I really do. But you and I both know there's something rotten going on. It's no coincidence you've been side-lined just as the most important case in years opens. No coincidence it's been given to me to lead, without any support from higher up.'

'Everyone above your pay grade worked with Chalmers in some capacity or another. They don't want to start digging into that mess because they know sooner or later they're going to come face to face with their younger selves doing something stupid.'

'And you? Why'd they have to send you away?'

'What's the common denominator among all the senior officers so studiously distancing themselves from your investigation, Tony? Use that keen intellect of yours.'

McLean stared at McIntyre for a while, thinking. 'They're all men?'

'I like the questioning in your voice. But yes, they're all men. Bill Chalmers was old school. Thought a woman's place was in the home. Or possibly his bed. He was right chummy with the lads, but he couldn't stand a female detective. Deep down I think he felt threatened by us. No surprise I never got asked to join them all in the pub after work. Didn't bother me. I never liked him. Still seems a bit much sending me off on handholding duties just to get me out of the way.'

'I don't think it's Chalmers they're worried about, to be honest. Wasn't him I wanted to talk to you about, in any case.'

'No?' McIntyre raised a quizzical eyebrow. 'Who, then?'

'Tommy Johnston.'

It was as if a light had gone on inside her head. The creases in McIntyre's forehead eased as the understanding settled across her features. 'Tommy Johnston. Well now. That puts a whole new complexion on things. I wasn't part of that investigation, you understand. I was back in uniform by then, on the fast track for the DCC's post, if you believed the pretty words.' McIntyre shook her head at a sudden realization. 'Christ, it would have been ten years ago, wouldn't it? I was young then.'

McLean knew exactly how few years older than him the DCI actually was. He'd never really considered her as anything other than his age, more or less. She looked much older now, sunk into his overlarge armchair and cradling a mug of tea like a granny.

'I knew about Tommy Johnston though. Everyone did. Even you'll probably have had some run-in with him. You remember how it was back then, the tacit agreement that as long as the girls were well looked after we'd look the other way? Of course, it went further than that, higher than that, but I don't need to tell you. It all changed though, when somebody put a bullet in his head.'

'I remember the chatter, but I wasn't involved in the investigation.'

'No, of course not. You wouldn't be asking otherwise.' McIntyre put down her mug, the tea unfinished. 'Why are you asking, anyway? Do you really think a ten-year-old unsolved murder is connected to Bill Chalmers today?'

'It could have just been a coincidence, that little boy being the one to find the body and him turning out to be Johnston's son. He was born after his father's death, so it's not as if he knew him. His mother never really made much of it either. Basically nobody knew. So yes, I thought it might have been a coincidence.'

'But you looked into it anyway.'

'You know me, Jayne. No stone unturned. And I didn't

waste a lot of resource on it. Just asked Duguid to review it as part of the CCU work.'

'I imagine Charles was delighted. He's in his element raking up the dirt.'

'Well he couldn't find much. All our archives on the case have mysteriously gone missing. The only stuff he's managed to pull together is from outside agencies. And surprise surprise, as soon as he starts digging, they shut down the CCU altogether.'

McIntyre's face hardened into a scowl and she sat up straighter in her chair. 'They what?'

'Yes, I thought that'd be news to you. Yet another reason for packing you off on some made up special assignment. I don't imagine you'd have let the CCU go without a fight.'

'Ah, Tony. I'm just a DCI now. If Call-me-Stevie wants to shut something down, there's not a lot I can do about it.'

'But it brings us back to Johnston. Even if his connection with Chalmers is coincidental, I can't let it lie now.'

'No, you can't.' McIntyre paused a moment, the thoughts wrinkling across her brow. 'But what if someone knows that about you? What if they're using that admirable if annoying characteristic of yours for their own ends?'

McLean looked away from those eyes that saw right through him and to the heart of the matter. The library door stood slightly ajar where Emma had left to fetch him a mug of tea. She'd been gone too long even to have made some fresh, but it didn't take a genius to work out why she was staying away. He glanced at the fake bookshelf that hid the drinks cabinet and its collection of fine malt whiskies. Perhaps a dram would help him think.

'Who was lead on the investigation? Was it Lothian and Borders or Strathclyde?'

'Far as I remember, it was a joint investigation. Johnston was Edinburgh based, but his body was found just inside Strathclyde's region. Out at the foot of the Pentlands, old Oggscastle Road.' McIntyre stared into the middle distance, her eyes unfocussed, as if she were reading the information from the inside of her head. 'Brooks was one of the principal investigators, but he was only a DI then. He'd have been reporting to someone higher up the food chain, especially for a professional hit like that. Don't quote me on this, but I think it was Bob Naismith. He was detective superintendent at the time. Or it could have been your old chum MacDuff, before he lost his mind to Alzheimer's.'

'Duff never got any higher than DCI before they pensioned him off. Besides, both Bob Naismith and him are rather too dead to ask for any details. Who was the Strathclyde lead?'

'Ah, that's much easier. I remember him being a bit of an insufferable git even back then. I've never trusted anyone who tries so hard to be everyone's friend. The years haven't really changed him much, even if he's moved from CID to Uniform.'

'The DCC? Stevie Robinson? Well that would certainly explain why he's not too keen on having the case reopened.' McLean reached up to the book shelf and pulled out the fake copy of *Whisky Galore* that triggered the hidden door mechanism. He opened up the drinks cabinet and pulled out the first bottle that came to hand. A twenty-five-year-old Teaninich from the Malt Whisky Society. He really should have something to eat first. Reluctantly, he put the bottle back, closed the door. 'I never took him for bent. A pain in the arse, yes. Prone to doing favours for his friends. But shutting down a murder investigation?'

'That bothers me, too.' McIntyre hauled herself out of her armchair with more effort than it should have taken a woman of her age. 'He knows something, though. I expect it's not something he's done but something he knew others were doing and did nothing to stop. That's fine when you're a DCI who just wants to get the job done. Not so good when you're deputy chief constable. And with the chief constable's job coming up, he'd not want anything awkward from his past resurfacing now.'

'So it's really just politics then?' McLean didn't believe it, and neither did McIntyre, if the sad shake of her head was anything to go by.

'I hope so, Tony. But hopes can be easily dashed.'

'Thanks for giving us space. Nothing said that you couldn't have heard, but it's always easier if there's fewer people involved.'

McLean had seen McIntyre out with a promise to keep her up to speed on the investigation until she could get out of her west coast assignment, then hurried to the kitchen and its permanent warmth. Emma and Mrs McCutcheon's cat had both greeted him with suspicious eyes, the latter only relenting when he went to the cupboard, fetched food and filled her bowl. While he was doing that, Emma had poured him a cup of very stewed tea.

'I figure it must be bad if McIntyre's coming here rather than talking to you at the station. This still about Bill Chalmers?'

'Sort of.' McLean took a sip of his tea, trying not to let his wince at its bitterness show. A bowl of sugar sat in the middle of the table, but he didn't think it would go unnoticed if he started shovelling teaspoonfuls in, so he went in search of biscuits instead.

Emma said nothing as he rifled through the cupboards until he found some digestives past their sell by date, just smiled at him, politely declining his offer of one from the pack.

'So how was your day?' he asked through a mouthful of soggy crumbs. 'You seem a lot cheerier than you did this morning.'

'I feel a lot better, thanks. It's . . . I don't know. As if something clicked and the headache just went away. I even got paid, see.' Emma pointed at the stack of post in the middle of the kitchen table, a torn open envelope on the top of the pile. McLean picked it up, pulled out the slip and glanced briefly at it.

'To be honest, I thought it was my P45. Technically I'm still in my probationary period so they could fire me without a bother if they wanted to.'

'What did Dr Wheeler say about going back?' McLean struggled to remember the conversation in the hospital; so much else had happened since then. 'She was going to refer you to another specialist, wasn't she?'

'Aye, I've an appointment for tomorrow afternoon. Should hopefully get to the bottom of it then.'

'You want me to come with you?'

For a moment he thought she was going to say yes, and McLean wondered how easily he could square that with the threats he'd received from Brooks about avoiding the incident room.

'No, it's OK. I reckon I can manage on my own. And besides, you've got bad guys to catch, right?'

'Bad guys?' McLean smiled at the words, fiddling with Emma's payslip as he did so. There was something about it that wouldn't let him put it down, and it wasn't the embarrassingly small figure of her salary.

'I thought you worked for the Scottish Police Authority,' he said after a while. 'Don't they provide all our forensics services?'

'Aye, they do. Those guys just manage the payroll. Least, that's what I was told. I reckon they're supplying some lab services too, though. Creeping privatization. I know most of the technicians aren't too happy about it. Double the paperwork and continuous professional appraisal. It's no' fun being watched all the time.'

McLean tapped the payslip against the rough wooden tabletop as he listened to Emma's words. Outsourcing was everywhere these days, although he wasn't convinced its cost-effectiveness was anything other than a trick of accountancy. He dropped the paper back on to the top of the pile of post, and that was when he noticed what his thumb had been obscuring. A tiny logo for the payments company, the letters beneath it almost too small to read in the poor light of the kitchen.

'Do you know the company name?' He pulled out his phone, brought up the photo gallery and flicked through it for the image he'd taken of the tattoo design. Right next to it was the photo of the reverse of the card, the partial logo and scribbled handwriting. DC Harrison had been looking into that, and he'd quite forgotten it, but now he could see a similarity between the two. Something like a coiled serpent.

'Yeah, someone told me. Think it might have been your friend Parsons moaning about it. Begins with an "S", I think.'

'Sai . . .' McLean picked up the payslip and squinted at it again, the chill spreading through his stomach as realization dawned. 'Saifre Incorporated?'

'That's it.' Emma's smile was quite incongruous, and turned into a frown as she saw McLean's face drop. 'You know it?'

'I know Mrs Saifre. You'd probably know her better as Jane Louise Dee.'

'The IT billionaire? You think this is one of her companies?'

'Almost certainly.' McLean placed the payslip carefully back on to the pile of post, treating it like an unexploded grenade. 'And I don't believe for a minute this is just a coincidence.'

35

Six o'clock in the morning wasn't McLean's favourite time of the day, but at least he was awake. The same could hardly be said for Detective Constables Stringer and Blane, sitting side by side in the empty conference room on the third floor. Puffy, red eyes spoke eloquently of a late night in the pub, a fact confirmed by the strong smell of stale beer rising off the two of them. He didn't know what, if anything, they had been celebrating, nor was he about to ask. They were here, and that was more than he might have expected.

At least DC Harrison was bright-eyed, though McLean wasn't about to see whether she was also bushy-tailed. Acting DI Ritchie had spent the past ten minutes trying to stifle her yawns as surreptitiously as possible, and failing. Grumpy Bob looked no different to any other time of the day, and the chances were good he'd slept in the suit he was now wearing. He had a large paper cup of the best smelling coffee in the world and had even managed to bring some extra along, just not enough for everyone in the meeting.

'You're probably all wondering why I've called you here, rather than the major incident room, for the main briefing.' McLean took a sip from his cup and wondered if he shouldn't have offered it to the two suffering constables.

'The thought had crossed my mind, McLean. I'm not

used to getting texts at midnight summoning me to secret meetings.'

Retired Detective Superintendent Duguid was pink scrubbed and clean, fresh out of the shower, no doubt. The young detective constables kept giving him sideways glances, which he was trying hard to ignore. A reputation could be a terrible thing to have to live up to.

'You at least will have some idea, sir.' McLean stumbled on the title. It felt strange calling the retired DS that, and yet he could never, would never, call the man Charles.

'Tommy Johnston.' It wasn't a question. 'You spoke to Brooks?'

'No. I was going to, but that was before the DCC shut us down. I did speak to McIntyre though, and she had some very interesting information. Did you know that Robinson was lead investigator for Strathclyde on that case?'

Duguid's face was answer enough. He opened his mouth to speak, but DC Harrison pitched in before he could say anything.

'Sorry, sir. But why is this important? Aren't we supposed to be tracking down how Chalmers got to the Meadows? I don't see how a cold case is relevant to that.'

McLean paused before answering, taking the time to collect his thoughts. He'd gone over it again and again in his mind, in the dark, staring at his bedroom ceiling with Emma's warm body snoring gently beside him. It still didn't make sense in any normal way, but then normal was something that happened to other people.

'Bill Chalmers was killed for a reason, and I'm fairly sure that reason was drugs. Not your usual street heroin — this is something new and different and very, very dangerous. I may be jumping to conclusions, but I think whoever did over Chalmers' mews flat and the offices of Morningstar was looking for it, and may well have been behind his murder, too. That's an aspect of the investigation we're already pursuing, but there's something else that bothers me.'

'The way he was killed. Where it happened,' Grumpy Bob said.

'Exactly, Bob. It's the manner of his murder that's key here. It's so brazen, and so bizarre, it can only be some kind of message.'

'Isn't that, I don't know . . .' Harrison began.

'A little far-fetched? Possibly. It gets better though. If his death was a message, then it stands to reason that both the nature of it – dropping him from a height – and the positioning are important. There's nothing in Bill Chalmers' past to suggest that the Meadows are particularly relevant to him, but he was killed just a few hundred feet from the house where Tommy Johnston's son and widow live. A son and widow very few people knew about.'

'On the other hand, it's only a few hundred feet more from where I live, sir. Is that not a coincidence too?' Grumpy Bob leaned against his desk, sipping from his cup.

'That's the thing though, Bob. You know me and coincidences, but even I was prepared to chalk this one up to blind luck. Then we found out the archives for the Johnston murder investigation were missing. And when the CCU kept digging anyway, they shut us down. Someone doesn't want that case looked into, and chances are it never would have been, had it not been for Chalmers pointing us at him in such a dramatic way.'

Silence filled the room, underscored by the noises of the day shift arriving and officers making their way to the major incident room. McLean would have to address them all soon, gee them up to carry on searching for clues, not to give up hope. He'd rather have thrown all those resources at tracking down what had really happened to Tommy Johnston on that forgotten back road in the Pentland Hills ten years ago.

'So what do you want us to do?' Ritchie asked.

'I need you to find out everything you can about Tommy Johnston that might possibly be relevant to Bill Chalmers. Where were his clubs? Are they still open? Who owns them now? What about the girls who worked for him – what happened to them? I'll speak to the boy and his mother myself, but any and all information about the man is going to be useful. Oh, and one other thing.'

All eyes turned to him, even the droopy, half-awake ones of Detective Constables Stringer and Blane.

'Let me guess,' Grumpy Bob said. 'There's no work recording code for this.'

'Exactly. Be very careful who you speak to, and don't tell anyone who isn't in here right now what you're doing. If you're asked, tell them it's background checks I specifically asked for. But really, don't get asked, OK?'

Heads nodded in acknowledgement, only Duguid making a low growl of assent.

'Good. Get to it. We'll have another meeting at shift end. See how far we've got.'

'You sure you can trust them all, Tony? Sure you can trust me?'

He'd watched as first the young detective constables, then Grumpy Bob and finally Duguid had left the CID room, leaving only Acting DI Ritchie and a deepening sense of doom behind.

'I'm more worried about getting those three into trouble, to be honest. They don't need a black mark on their records this early in their careers. Especially not Harrison. She's got a lot of promise.'

'Oh aye? Fancy her do you?' Ritchie's smile told him it was a joke, but still McLean felt that uncomfortable warmth spread across the back of his neck and over the tips of his ears.

'Don't. You're worse than bloody Brooks. And I'm old enough to be her dad, so no, I don't fancy her.'

'There's older detectives would probably take advantage of her keenness, never mind the age difference.' Ritchie shrugged. 'I've seen it happen before.'

'That why you left Aberdeen, Kirsty?'

It was Ritchie's turn to blush, the freckles on her pale face darkening. Her stare hardened with them. 'Just be careful, aye? I don't like where this is going. Setting up a secret team to work behind everyone else's backs. It's —'

'You're going to like it even less when I tell you Mrs Saifre's probably mixed up in all this too.'

From blush to faint in a heartbeat. McLean watched as all the blood drained from Ritchie's face. In that instant he could see the damage the mysterious disease had wrought on her, despite two years of recovery. She'd nearly died from her encounter with Mrs Saifre, and McLean still didn't want to think about what he had done to save her.

'How?' The word slipped out as the ghost of a whisper.

'I'm not sure, but the logo of one of her companies was on the piece of paper with the tattoo design we took from Bo's Inks before it was done over.' McLean told her about Emma's payslip, the horror on Ritchie's face turning slowly to anger as he did so.

'Too much to hope it's just a coincidence,' she said. 'But why's she running payroll for the forensics services?'

'She probably doesn't even know she is. There's Saifre companies all over the world. Financial management's just one of many pies she's got her sticky fingers in. It's the connection with Bill Chalmers and Malky Davison's tattoos that bothers me more.' McLean let out a long sigh. 'She's part of all this. I just wish I knew what "all this" was.'

'Any news from the hospital about Ferguson?'

McLean stood in the major incident room, staring at the whiteboards and maps in search of inspiration. It was one thing putting together a team to look into the Johnston angle without the high heidyins knowing about it, but there was still the small matter of finding out who had murdered Bill Chalmers, how and why.

'He's in intensive care, sir.' DC Harrison pushed her chair away from the workstation where she had been updating the electronic map. 'I spoke to a Dr Wheeler? Neurology specialist, I think she said she was.'

'Caroline. Yes, I know her.' It didn't surprise him that she would be dealing with Ferguson, although sometimes McLean wondered if there were any other doctors working in Midlothian NHS. That she was involved didn't bode well.

'They've got him stabilized, but he's unconscious.

Something about the seizure originating in his frontal cortex. Be lucky if he even remembers his name when he wakes up.'

'So he's unlikely to be much use to us then. Pity. I really would like to know where he got those bottles from, who they were meant for.'

'Aye, well. The doctor did say he'd been using, and fairly recently. The blood test results came back with a very similar profile to Malky Davison.'

McLean's gaze finally focussed on a picture pinned to the whiteboard with a magnet. Bill Chalmers' shattered body, still hanging in the bare branches of the tree over Jawbone Walk. Something clicked in his head as Harrison's words filtered in through the swirl of thoughts.

'What about Chalmers? Has anyone compared his blood tests with Malky's? And now Ferguson's?'

'I . . . I don't know, sir.' Harrison sat back down at her workstation, picked up the phone. 'I'll get on to the hospital and Forensics. Do you think it's likely they're similar, too?'

'They were all drugged, so why not the same drug? The stuff in those bottles – only I've no idea how you'd take it.' McLean turned away from the whiteboard, giving Harrison his full attention. 'While you're at it, ask the hospital if Ferguson has any tattoos. I'll lay good odds he has something very much like Malky's. Call me as soon as you've got some answers. I'll be out for a little while.'

'Yes, sir.' Harrison paused, still holding the phone handset. 'If anyone asks, can I say where you're going?'

'Only if I tell you.' McLean smiled, and then left without another word.

*

His phone rang as he was walking up Sciennes Place. Warmed by his exertion, McLean was surprised at how cold the handset felt in his hand. The air was freezing, his breath steaming as he answered.

'McLean.'

'Hi, Inspector. It's Amanda Parsons.'

'I'm not your boss, you know. You can call me Tony.'

'Aye, well. Maybe. I'm in a bit of rush so I'll get to the point. That shit sample you asked me to get analysed.'

McLean raked through his memories, coming up blank. 'Remind me again?'

'The manky hanky. You know. Shit splattered all over the railings and door?'

'Oh, yes. That. Sorry. I'd completely forgotten. It's been a busy time.'

'Tell me about it. But don't get your hopes up too much. The results back from the lab make no sense at all.'

'How so?'

'Well, there's some human DNA in there, but it's wee fragments. Like it'd been broken down by something. Only other time I've seen results like that's when we've been trying to see what's been eaten, not what's done the eating.'

'Umm . . .' McLean stopped walking, glancing up nervously for no good reason. The clear skies of the past week and more had gone, replaced with ominous clouds, tinged purple with the threat of snow.

'It's probably just a duff sample. Not exactly like it was taken in ideal circumstances. The DNA could be yours, for all I know. Had you used the hanky before you wiped your hands with it?'

'It's possible. It was a cold morning and that always gets my nose running.'

'There you are then. The rest of the sample's just random junk. Doesn't match up with anything on any of our databases, anyway. Hard to tell if it's animal or vegetable. Sorry.'

'That's OK. It was a long shot.'

'Well, I feel bad. Should've done a better job, but all that sort of stuff gets farmed out to a private lab now. Won't be long before we're all privatized, I'll bet.'

'All in the name of efficiency.' McLean didn't try to hide the irony in his voice.

'Aye, well, I'm sorry I couldn't come up with anything better. Reckon it's a dead end.'

'Never mind. Even a negative result's useful sometimes. Thanks, Amanda.'

'No problem, Tony. And it's Manda, by the way. Only my mum uses my whole name.'

36

Still considering Amanda Parsons' words, McLean almost didn't notice the commotion as he turned the corner into Marchmont Crescent. A cluster of people was moving slowly up the hill on the other side of the road, some walking backwards with video cameras on their shoulders. It reminded McLean of nothing so much as seagulls mobbing a poke of chips and at the centre of it all, barely visible in the throng, a small boy walked a terrified dog on a lead.

'Come on, John. Tell us what it looked like.'

'Smile for the camera, Johnny.'

'Did you see the body fall, kid? What did it sound like when it hit?'

'Hey. You lot. Leave him alone.' McLean rushed across the street, pulling out his warrant card as he approached the throng. They were so intent on the chase hardly any of them noticed him, so he grabbed the nearest one by the shoulder and spun him around.

'Hey, what do you think you're –?' It took a few seconds for the man's eyes to focus on the card held inches from his face. He took a step backwards, tripping over the heel of one of the other men, and they both fell to the ground in a cascade of limbs.

'Watch what you're –'

'What the fuck –?'

'Get up, take your cameras and get out of here. Before I have you all locked up for harassing a minor.' McLean pushed aside a third man, clearing the space to where young John Johnston stood with his dog Tilly. Whether it was the presence of a policeman in their midst or the blood lust had simply passed, the collected journalists dropped back, heads hung low.

'Go on. Get out of here. Go chase some real news.'

For a moment McLean had an image of himself as an irate father figure shouting at unruly kids in the kind of comic book his grandmother had frowned upon him reading as a boy. He could almost see the rolled-up newspaper brandished in anger, the strange lines radiating out from his head in Letraset dots. The assembled journalists gathered themselves, picking up dropped notepads and in one case a very expensive video camera, and stalked off in a bunch, muttering to each other. He'd probably pay for it in the early editions tomorrow, but it was worth the effort just to see the relief on the young boy's face.

'You remember me, John?'

'You're the polisman. See, Tilly knows you.'

True enough, the elderly dog had come out from where she had been cowering behind John's legs and was now sniffing carefully at McLean's trousers. He crouched down slowly, offered a hand and then gave her a scratch behind the ears. His kindness earned him a wag of the tail and a sloppy wet lick across the fingers.

'They been bothering you before?' He straightened up, looking around the street to see where the journalists had got to. A couple stood by a parked car and, further away, the one with the expensive camera was climbing into a white panel van.

'All week. Sometimes I can get out the back and away before they see me. But the gate's been locked the last couple days.'

'Well, let's go talk to your mum about that then.' McLean pointed the boy in the direction of his front door. 'And I'll have to see about getting those reporters moved on.'

'Oh, it's you. Thought it was another of those damned parasite journalists.'

As greetings went, it wasn't perhaps the friendliest. Given the circumstances, McLean was prepared to let it slide. Ellen Johnston looked a lot more tired than the first time they had met, an air of desperation about her dishevelled appearance. He'd seen it before in people who from no fault of their own came to the attention of the media.

'John was being hounded by a pack of reporters. Thought I'd see him home safely.' McLean watched as the young lad and his dog disappeared across the hall and in through an open door. It closed with a solid *thunk* behind them, the clack of the lock uncomfortably noticeable in the frosty silence.

'It's been like that every day since . . . well, you know.'

'Didn't you complain?'

'Aye, I complained. Nice wee lad on the phone promised me they'd look into it. I've not even seen a squad car cross the end of the road, let alone anyone come past. Not since you lot finished off in the park.'

'I'm sorry, Mrs Johnston. If I'd known, I'd have stationed an officer outside your door. Or at the very least had someone check the street regularly. I left you my card. You really should have called me directly. That's the whole point of giving you my number.'

'Aye, well. I've had enough of being told not to waste polis time to know better.' Johnston looked at him straight in the eyes. 'What were you doing in this street anyways? You don't live round here do you?'

'No. Though I used to have a place like this over in Newington, until it burned down.' McLean glanced about the hallway of Ellen Johnston's tenement flat. He'd come alone this time, not exactly following procedure, but then more often than not the sight of two police officers just made people clam up. This was about as far from a formal investigation as he could imagine, anyway.

'That was your place, was it? I remember that. Heard a lot of people died in that fire.'

'Everyone living there except me and a cat. But that's not why I'm here.'

'Why are you here then? Apart from helping wee John with those monsters from the press.'

'Actually, I came to speak to you.'

Johnston cocked her head to one side, much like her son's dog had done the first time he had met it. 'Me? Oh. OK. Why don't you come through to the kitchen? I'll make us a cup of tea.'

McLean did as he was bade, following Johnston into a surprisingly airy and modern kitchen. The far wall was dominated by a long window that looked out on to the shared back gardens of the block, or would have done, had the first spatterings of snow not begun to block the view.

'Thanks, by the way. For helping John.' Johnston pointed to a small table pushed up against the wall, indicating that McLean should sit.

'I've had a bad relationship with the press in the past,' he said. 'Don't like to see them picking on anyone, and going after a ten-year-old boy is just evil.'

'Aye, evil. That's just about the size of it. They were all over the place after that horrible . . . thing. In the park. My mistake for talking to that nice lad who came round that first afternoon. Should have known he wasn't from Social Services, but he was right convincing.'

'I'm sorry they even found out about you in the first place. Don't know how that happened, but if I could pin it on any particular officer, they'd be looking for a new job.'

Johnston brought over two mugs, set one down in front of him and then took the seat opposite. 'It's funny, but I actually believe you when you tell me that. Not many of youse lot I'd say that about.'

'Thanks. I think.' McLean looked briefly at his tea, insipid white with too much milk and too little time to stew. 'I'll get straight to the point, Mrs Johnston. I need to talk to you about your husband. John's father. Tommy.'

It was there in her face, the momentary freeze at the name. Ten years dead, and still it sent a shiver through her. She took a drink of tea to hide her reaction, using the mug as a shield against him. McLean couldn't really blame her. From what little he'd managed to piece together about Johnston, he'd been one of those men who was all charm until things weren't going exactly the way he wanted them to, and then the fists came out. Ten years of being a single mother had hardened the features of the woman sitting opposite him, but in her youth Mrs Johnston would have been quite the looker. A trophy wife.

'I was a dancer at Frou Frou. Down on the Grassmarket. And when I say "dancer", that's what I mean. I wasn't a sex worker or a stripper. Tommy had plenty of them on his books, but he had some legitimate income too. Frou Frou was one of his more upmarket places, believe it or not.'

'What happened to it? The club?'

'It's still there, far as I know. Different name of course, but the same clientele. Or the same type anyways. The lads who watched me dance are probably all married with kids and a mortgage now. There'll be a new generation of oversexed idiots though. Some things never change.'

'So what about Tommy then? How long were you together?'

'Long enough to father a child. Stupid arse got himself shot in the head before he could care for the lad though. Probably had it coming, mind.'

'Why'd you say that?' McLean took a sip of his tea, then wished he hadn't. The overwhelming flavour was washing-up liquid.

'Tommy was all charm. He'd promise you whatever you wanted to hear just so he could get what he wanted. It worked with the girls. Ha, it worked with me, didn't it? Even if I did manage to persuade him to do the right thing when he knew wee John was on the way. But he used the same technique on his business partners, the people lending him money, his suppliers.'

'Suppliers? I take it you don't mean the snacks and drinks.'

She smiled, softening some of that hardness of years. 'Are you always so polite, Inspector? No, I don't mean the snacks and drinks. I was just a dancer, that's all I wanted to do, and the money was good enough. If I'd wanted more, I could have done escort work. Lots of the girls did. And then there were the more specialized services. For select clientele.'

For a moment McLean thought she was winding him up, but there was something about the way Johnston said it that made him think she was being serious. 'So Chalmers supplied drugs to some of his customers. Hard drugs?'

'If you were part of the right crowd you could have anything you wanted. Well, anything you could afford. That's what I heard, anyways. Never saw much of that sort of thing myself.'

'And this took place in the club? What did you call it, Frou Frou? Down on the Grassmarket?'

'No. Not there. Tommy was too smart to let that side of his business mix with the other. Sure, he'd find new customers at Frou Frou, charm them with that winning way of his, hook them in. But the real action happened somewhere in the New Town. Some private club. I never did find out where.'

Thick white chunks of snow spiralled out of a bruised sky as McLean stepped out of the tenement door on his way back to the station. He'd remembered his coat on the walk over, but his hat was still at home, gathering dust in the front porch. His shoes weren't going to survive the walk without his feet getting soaked either.

'Little birdie tells me you've been looking for me. Wanted to see me about something.'

McLean looked around, rewarded for his efforts by a large flake of snow slipping perfectly down the gap between the back of his neck and the collar of his shirt. Normally the smell of smoke gave him warning, but Jo Dalgliesh was on the e-cigarettes now. She leaned against the metal railings, dragging whatever strange concoction was in the device deep into her lungs before letting it out in a gout of sweet-smelling steam.

'Wanted?' He shook his head. 'Needed is more like. You've been spotted at a number of crime scenes recently and you won't answer your phone. Suspicious types might think you've got something to hide.'

'You gonnae arrest me?' Dalgliesh held out her hands, wrists pressed together for handcuffs. McLean kept his stuffed into his coat pockets; it was too bloody cold for that kind of nonsense and the snow was only getting thicker.

'Would it make any diffcrence?'

'Prob'ly not.' Dalgliesh shoved the e-cigarette back in her mouth. 'So what you want to see me about? Sorry, *need* to see me about? Actually, fuck that. Let's get out of this snow before I freeze my balls off.'

The reporter stepped into a road rapidly turning white, leaving McLean with no option but to follow. He wasn't aware of any cafés nearby, but then Dalgliesh fished a set of car keys out of her pocket, hit the button and an expensive-looking Jaguar flashed its indicators, gave off a chirrup of alarm. She hurried around to the driver's side, popped open the door as McLean was peering in through the passenger window.

'Get in, won't you? Don't want youse getting the leather all wet.'

He opened the door, surprised not to see rubbish strewn all over the carpets and a smell of stale cigarette smoke in the air. Instead, that unmistakable new-car smell hit him full on.

'Hire car?' he asked as he slid into a soft leather seat, ran a hand lightly over the walnut veneer set into the dashboard. The heavy snow had dampened down the noise of the city, but an even greater level of quiet fell over them as Dalgliesh clunked shut the driver's door.

'Fuck off, hire car. This is my new toy. Was hoping for a chance to give it a bit of a run, maybe head out to Fife an' have a wee poke around Bill Chalmers' place. This snow's not what I planned for at all.'

She turned the key and McLean thought he might have heard the faintest whisper of an engine starting. The loudest noise was the fans blowing welcoming warm air at his face and feet.

'Not meaning to sound ungrateful or anything, but how can you afford something like this? Must be, what, fifty grands' worth of motor?'

'Aye, and then some.' Dalgliesh peered through the windscreen as the wipers fought with ever more snow, indicated and pulled out slowly. In all the years he'd known her, McLean couldn't remember ever seeing her in a car that didn't have a big yellow taxi light on the roof, and she dressed like someone who could only afford to buy their clothes in a charity shop. She'd worn the same battered old leather overcoat for nigh on twenty years. On the other hand, she'd written a bestselling biography of a serial killer, ghost-written a dozen more hatchet jobs. She lived in a large house in a posh part of town. Why shouldn't she have the money for an expensive car? Especially if she'd got herself a nice new project lined up.

'Chalmers. You've got a publisher for that book you were going to write about him.'

'See, that's why you're a detective inspector. Always looking for the bigger picture behind the wee details. This little puppy,' Dalgliesh patted the dashboard in front of her, 'is my way of raising two fingers to the Tories and their taxes. Say hello to my legitimate business expense.'

McLean found a button at the side of his seat, pressed it and was rewarded with a warm sensation around the buttocks that was both pleasant and slightly alarming. 'That might explain why you went to his mews house. What were you doing hanging around Bo's Inks though?'

Dalgliesh stared out through the windscreen as she inched the car forward through the swirling snow. 'Ah. You saw that.'

'Nothing gets past CNPR. You should know that.'

'Still, sloppy of me to use my own car. I guess I've only myself to blame.'

'You've still not answered the question.'

'And you've no' looked into Morningstar properly, or we wouldn't be having this conversation. If I didn't know better, I'd say you were deliberately avoiding the place, and I had you down as straight up. No' bent like your DCC and that fat bastard Brooks.'

'Bent? What about you and Chalmers then? You said you hardly knew him, but he's got a photograph of you in his office.'

Dalgliesh slowed the car right down, pulled to a halt at the side of the road and turned to face him. 'What the fuck are you talking about? Don't think I even met the man more than . . . oh.'

'Oh?'

Dalgliesh indicated and pulled out into the thinning traffic again. 'Yes. Oh. As in, I can't believe a trained detective can leap to such spectacularly stupid conclusions.'

'I saw the photograph, Dalgliesh. He had his arm around your shoulders.'

'Aye, 'cause I was the only woman there. Men and their bloody wandering hands. We were at some press awards junket his charity was involved in. And it was ten years ago. More. Fuck's sake, why'd you think that meant anything?'

'You go off radar. Nobody can contact you, but your car's spotted at several crime scenes related to our investigations. We even found a gift with your initials on it in his desk. Your initials are J D aren't they? Joanne Dalgliesh?'

Even as he said it, the doubts that should have been there before crept in. Why had he thought that when he'd found Chalmers' cigar cutter? Was it just because of the photograph he'd seen moments earlier? Dalgliesh was right, he was a trained detective. Leaping to such conclusions wasn't like him. Sure, there had been other things, adding up to a suspicion, but not the certainty that had filled him right up until the moment he'd opened his mouth to speak.

'I'm sorry,' he said. 'Now I say it, I can't believe how bloody stupid it sounds.'

Dalgliesh indicated again, and pulled the car into the side of the road. It was a measure of how bad the driving conditions had become that nobody tooted a horn at her. All the other cars were moving at a crawl as they negotiated the snowstorm.

'She has that effect on people. Thought you might have realized that by now.'

'She? Who?' McLean asked.

'The person with the initials J D. Or perhaps it should be J L D.' Dalgliesh twisted in her seat to face McLean. 'Look, Tony. The reason I've gone off radar is because right now I don't trust anyone. No' the police, no' my editor and certainly no' the new owner of the *Tribune*.'

'J L D?' McLean asked, the answer coming to him as he spoke the letters out loud. 'Jane Louise Dee. I should have bloody well known.'

'Aye, your old friend Mrs Saifre up to her tricks again. Thought she'd been quiet too long.'

'Too much to hope she'd be gone for good.' McLean let his head tilt back until it hit the soft leather headrest with a quiet *thunk*. Ever since seeing Emma's payslip, he'd not been able to put the devious Jane Louise Dee, aka Mrs Saifre, out of his mind. His last run-in with her hadn't exactly gone well.

'Going to have to walk the last wee bit. I'm no' ready to come in for questioning, and you don't want to be seen hanging out with the likes of me.' Dalgliesh nodded towards the view out of the windscreen. Part obscured by the falling snow, McLean could see the station a hundred yards down the road. He unclipped his seatbelt and opened the door, a blast of cold air tumbling into the warm cabin.

'You really reckon she's behind all this?' he asked as he stepped out of the car.

'I'd no' have said it if I didn't. Look at the Morningstar offices. See who really owns them. Follow the money, aye?'

37

'Where the hell have you been, McLean?'

Covered in snow from the short walk to the station, McLean took his time to dust himself off in the doorway before turning to answer. Detective Chief Inspector Mike Spence didn't have the same threatening deep voice as his immediate superior, nor could he carry the same sense of menace as Brooks' predecessor, Duguid.

'Outside, Mike. Hence the snow. Was there something you wanted? Only I was going to head to the canteen for a cup of tea. It's bloody freezing out there.'

'You think you're better than the rest of us, don't you? Rules are for the little people and you're oh so big with your money and your fine house and your stupid wcc car.'

'Is there a problem?' McLean asked. He'd known the DCI to be fractious at times, but Spence sounded like someone had just killed his cat.

'Too fucking right there's a problem. The detective superintendent and the deputy chief constable both told you – no, ordered you – to lead this investigation from the incident room. Send sergeants and constables out to do the legwork, collect it all together and look at the bigger picture. That's how it's done, McLean. But no. You have to go swanning off to interview people who've got nothing to do with anything. I report this and you're off the case, you know that? And after your wee fuck-up last year you'll be off the force too.'

He might have gone on. McLean knew the man was building himself up for an explosion, but something caught in the back of his throat as he took in a deep breath, and the next thing he was bent double, coughing his lungs out. Spence had always been thin; the word 'ascetic' sprang to mind, although it implied a certain gravitas the detective chief inspector lacked. Now he looked positively cadaverous. His skin was dry and tight over the bones in his face, as if he had spent the past two thousand years in a sealed room under an Egyptian pyramid. The hand that gripped the plastic-coated bannister of the stair looked more like the claw of some arthritic raptor.

'You OK, Mike? Only you look —'

With a gasp that might have been a death rattle, Spence breathed in again, thumping his chest to dislodge whatever had been choking him. Tears streamed from his eyes as he stood up straight, his cheeks showing colour more associated with his fat friend Brooks.

'I'm fine, McLean,' he wheezed. 'As if you'd care if I wasn't. Be much better if I didn't have to keep running around after jobs you're meant to be doing. You've a crew up there without a captain. Deal with it.' Spence stared at him a little longer than was comfortable, then turned and struggled back up the stairs, pausing every so often to cough like a teenager. McLean watched until he was sure the way was clear, then turned and headed to the canteen. Hang whatever it was Spence and Brooks and Call-me-Stevie wanted. Nothing was going to come between him and a hot mug of tea.

*

'Nobody else about?'

Mug of thick canteen tea warming his hands, McLean pushed his way into the CID room, hoping to find some detectives he could bully into doing some work. Only DC Harrison was there, sitting at the desk that had been Ritchie's before her promotion to acting detective inspector and the miserable little office that came with the title.

'Stringer and Lofty just left. I can give them a call if you want.' Harrison lifted her airwave set off the desk.

'No, that's OK. One detective's plenty.' McLean set his tea down and pulled out a chair, considered where to start. The conversation with Dalgliesh had unsettled him; any reminder of Mrs Saifre would do that, and two of them in quick succession felt like a pit opening beneath him, swallowing him down into the hell that was her natural domain. The richest woman in Scotland, and quite possibly the world, she was the great spider at the centre of a massive web, her influence everywhere. No wonder the CCU was being shut down, his investigation going nowhere and, for all their bluster, the senior officers content to let him run around in his usual ineffectual circles. That would suit Mrs Saifre perfectly. And meanwhile, she was slowly taking control. Or maybe she already had it.

'What do you want me to do?'

Harrison's question brought McLean out of his musing. There was too much competing information, too much that wasn't relevant. They'd allowed themselves to be hijacked by the bizarre nature of Chalmers' death and forgotten one of the first rules of detection. Good thing Jo Dalgliesh was there to show him how to do his job.

'Did we ever look into the ownership of the charity offices?' McLean asked.

'Not sure. I think Lofty might have been going to look into it. Shouldn't be hard to find out though. I can call the land registry, probably get quite a lot from a Google search first.'

'Do that. Thanks. I need everything you can find out about the building where Morningstar has its offices. Not just who owns it now – that's Bill Chalmers, if what I've been told is true. Who'd he buy it from and when would be useful information. Where he got the money from might be more difficult to trace, but if there's a mortgage that'll be registered on the deeds.'

'I'll get right on it.' Harrison pulled out the keyboard and mouse that had been piled up to one side of the monitor in front of her and started tapping away like a one-fingered woodpecker. 'Is this leading anywhere, sir?'

'I'm not sure, but something doesn't add up and as I was just recently reminded, when you're stuck for an answer then following the money's the best place to start.'

'You think this is about money? I thought it was drugs.' Harrison's fingers had found their rhythm now, her right hand darting to the mouse and back to the keyboard as she stared intently at the screen. Much as he hated to admit it, McLean wasn't as good at the whole connected world as he might have been, always reliant on others with the relevant skills to ferret out the information he needed.

'The two are usually linked,' he said. 'And Chalmers had more money than I'd expect for someone running a charity. More property, too.'

'What about the message angle? We still reckon his

death was meant to warn others? Stop them from doing whatever it was he was doing?'

McLean swallowed down a mouthful of tea. 'Actually I don't think that was what the message was about at all.'

'You don't?' Harrison paused in her typing, fingers an inch off the keyboard.

'No. It's far-fetched, I know. But I think it was as much a way of pointing us at Johnston as disposing of Chalmers.'

Harrison's fingers still hovered in mid-air, a look that was half puzzlement, half concern spreading over her face. 'But how would someone do that? I mean, anyone could have discovered the body, not just the wee boy. And what if he'd taken the dog out later that morning? Why do something so complicated?'

McLean almost said 'because that's how she operates'. He stopped himself at the last moment, knowing how stupid it would sound. He had no proof Mrs Saifre was behind any of this, no real idea what 'this' was, if he was being honest with himself. There was only the gut feeling that she was involved. It had always been only a matter of time before she came back, so why not now?

'Let's just concentrate on finding those title deeds, OK? If we ignore all the weird stuff, the fact is someone killed Bill Chalmers. If there's a reason to be found anywhere in all this mess, it'll be there.'

'Ah, Tony. I was hoping I might find you here.'

McLean looked up from his desk, over the neatly stacked piles of overtime sheets and resource-allocation forms, to see the surprising figure of Deputy Chief Constable Stevie Robinson standing in the open doorway. The one benefit of his tiny office being stuck at the back end of the station was that it attracted no passing traffic. He liked to leave the door open to lessen the feeling of working in a broom cupboard, but it did mean that if anyone really wanted to come and visit he never had any prior warning.

'Sir.' McLean struggled to his feet, grabbing at the nearest pile of papers before it toppled to the floor. The DCC looked around the room as if he'd never seen it before, eyes widening as they took in the shelves lined with folders, stacks of archive boxes piled against the walls, paperwork covering every inch of desk and the complete lack of a second chair for him to sit on.

'How the hell do you get any work done in this place?'

'I find it homely. Half of this stuff was in here when I was given the office – what, four years ago? No, must be five now. No idea whose case files they are.' McLean was only half joking. He'd never got around to sorting the rubbish left behind by the previous incumbent of the office, and had no idea who that had been or when he'd left. Certainly, the room had been empty and forgotten for some years. He stared at the dusty archive boxes, sagging and crumpled under the window and in the far corner. How ironic if they were actually the missing Tommy Johnston files.

'Well it's no bloody good, is it? We'll have to see about getting you a proper office, just as soon as this case is cracked.' Call-me-Stevie glanced over his shoulder, as if worried he might be overheard in this empty corner of the station. 'You got a minute? Only I'd like to have a chat about the case.'

'Of course. Here? Or would you prefer to go somewhere with a bit more space?'

The DCC considered for longer than should have been necessary. McLean knew well enough that he could have just phoned and ordered him to the top floor, or sent a constable to fetch him. Clearly Robinson wanted to talk alone, and without anyone knowing he'd done so.

'Here will be fine.' He stepped further into the room, closed the door behind him and then leaned against it. McLean perched on the edge of his desk in solidarity. It was easier to talk to someone when you were on more or less the same level, too.

'Was there anything in particular? Only we'll be having a daily catch-up briefing in about an hour. There's some promising results coming from the forensics side of things and we've got a team out in Fife going over Chalmers' house again. Acting DI Ritchie's heading up that side of things now she's back from Glasgow. Seems there was a bit of a cock-up and she wasn't needed over there after all.'

'Ritchie, yes.' Robinson cocked his head to one side like a puzzled spaniel. 'I'd really like to make her promotion permanent. Christ knows, she's more than up to the job and she's earned it. But we've so few sergeants left and not many DCs ready to move up a grade. It would help if I didn't have to find a couple of million in cost savings too.' He shook his head as if he'd just emerged from a stream with a proud stick in his mouth. 'But that's a discussion for another day. It's Chalmers I needed to talk to you about. And possibly Johnston.'

'Only possibly?'

'Yes, well. I remain unconvinced of the need to dig up

that old case just because of who first discovered Chalmers. But it's most odd that all the archives relating have gone missing. That's quite an effective way of making any investigation almost impossible and certainly expensive.'

'And shutting down the CCU before it really got started isn't?'

'That . . . wasn't my decision.' Robinson tried a smile but couldn't quite muster the energy for it. 'You might find this hard to believe, Tony, but I fought hard to keep the CCU open. The best I could manage was to get the board to agree to keep Charles on as a consultant. The screws are being tightened everywhere, you know. There's no money for these things.'

'What do you remember about Johnston, sir? I heard you were lead investigator on the Strathclyde end.'

Robinson stiffened, his hands closing together across his stomach in a reflex action that spoke volumes to McLean.

'Did you? Who told you that?'

'You mean it's not true? Who was the lead, then?'

'No, it's true. Up to a point. I was a DCI back then. Last case I was involved in before I moved back to Uniform. Probably the reason I moved back, to be honest.'

McLean said nothing. Sooner or later the DCC would get to the point, and he'd found it was always easier to get someone to speak if you just listened.

'A lot of people were very unhappy when Johnston died. Sure, he was a scumbag but by and large he was our scumbag. He knew exactly how far he could go, what he could get away with, and he never went past that line. And in return he kept a lot of worse things from happening.

'He wasn't the only one, of course. I mean, he mostly operated out of Edinburgh, a bit of Fife and that club of his in Perth. We had – how can I put it? – arrangements with other unsavoury characters over on the west coast too. Look hard enough, you'll probably find it's still going on. I'm sure there's a few petty criminals you could have arrested but didn't because they were more use to you on the outside. And you didn't want to think what might ooze up out of the mire to take the place they vacated.'

Robinson seemed to find it hard to meet McLean's gaze as he spoke. His eyes darted from window to wall to desk. McLean watched him for a while, trying to think of anyone he'd let walk free rather than having to deal with the mess their arrest would inevitably cause.

'Can't think of any. No.' He shook his head, perhaps a little over-theatrically.

'Maybe that's why you're still a DI with no promotion prospects then. Maybe that's why most of the other detectives don't want to work with you.' The DCC pushed himself away from the door, started pacing then found there was no room for more than a couple of steps before he'd have to turn around and head back the way he'd come.

'None of that really matters to you, does it, McLean? You don't care if you lose this job because you don't need the income. You don't lie awake at night wondering if your pension's going to be enough to live on once you've raided your savings to put two ungrateful kids through university. This is all just a game to you, isn't it? Fucking up people's lives.'

McLean bit his tongue to stop himself from lashing out. Robinson's words had a thin veneer of truth on them but like all politicians he twisted them into barbs that could get under your skin. It was clear that the DCC was very agitated about something, and McLean's best guess was that for all his protestations it was the failure to investigate Tommy Johnston's murder that weighed most heavily on Robinson's mind. He opened his mouth to speak again, closed it and finally let out a long sigh through his nose, shoulders drooped, before speaking.

'What's the point, eh? I'm near enough retirement. Not going to get the top job, however much my wife wishes it. But here's the thing. This job. Nobody ever comes through it squeaky clean. Mistakes are made, blind eyes turned, favours owed and given. We get the job done though. Most of the time.' Robinson shook his head slowly from side to side, then pinched the bridge of his nose as if that was the only way to stop himself. 'I don't know, Tony. This case is dragging up stuff that really should have stayed buried. Or never been buried in the first place. It stank back then, but it's really rotten now.'

'You know I'll keep digging unless expressly ordered not to, sir.'

Robinson let out a half-mad laugh. 'Really? When's being told not to do something ever stopped you before?' He stood up straight, smoothed down the creases in his jacket and pulled at the cuffs until they were just right. Presentation was everything. 'No, you carry on. Dig as deep as necessary. Just don't be surprised if you lose what few friends you have left in the process.'

38

He was still pondering the deputy chief constable's words an hour later when he left his office. The catch-up briefing would begin soon, but first McLean needed to check in on his other, more informal team. He found at least some of them in the CID room, clustered around DC Harrison's desk and peering at her computer screen.

'No, that's the column you need to look at, see? And it cross-references to this bit here.' DC Blane stabbed a finger the size of a small cucumber at the screen, mistiming and almost knocking it over. Harrison grabbed it before it could topple off the desk, catching sight of McLean as she did so.

'Ah, sir. Think we might have found something for you.'

'Oh yes?' McLean looked around the room, seeing a couple of other detective constables at the far end. There were no sergeants about, and a complete lack of acting detective inspectors, but then Ritchie had taken DC Gregg to Fife and Grumpy Bob would be in the major incident room with a mug of tea and a newspaper at this time of the evening.

'I got on to the land registry database like you asked, sir. Took a bit of searching, but the building where Morningstar are based does indeed belong to Bill Chalmers. Or to his estate, I should say. Not sure who stands to inherit.'

'This much I already knew.' McLean tried not to sound discouraging, hoping that the detective constable hadn't spent the past couple of hours finding out nothing. 'What about the neighbours?'

Harrison did a little half-smile, half-grimace that made her look about fifteen. 'That's where it gets complicated, sir. Well, it was complicated to start with, but it gets even more complicated. There's shell companies and overseas whatnots and all manner of stuff I don't begin to understand. Luckily for us, Lofty here spent eighteen months working for a bank before discovering he had a soul after all. He knows this stuff inside out.'

Detective Constable Blane blushed at the praise, which was when McLean first noticed just how large his ears were.

'What's the story then, Pete?' he asked.

'They've used a very sophisticated financial instrument, sir.' Blane stood up as straight as he ever did, towering over the seated DC Harrison. 'I'm really quite surprised, if I'm being honest. Those properties must be worth a couple million each, but this kind of thing's usually more common in companies worth hundreds of millions. Billions, even.'

McLean could feel his mind glazing over. 'The short story, Constable.'

Blane smiled broadly, Harrison looking up at him and giving him the gentlest of nudges with her elbow. It didn't take the insight of twenty years' policing to know that a bet had been placed and McLean was the target. Well, if his lack of technical acumen was something around which the team could bond, he could live with that.

'Short story is that the next-door buildings on either side also belonged to Chalmers. Or at least to the bank which lent him the money to buy them, since technically he never paid off the mortgage. Don't know if he had life insurance. That's something Jay . . . DC Stringer's looking into.'

McLean tried to picture the buildings in his mind. One side was the end of the terrace and had been offices of some form; he could check easily enough. The other was a guest house, run down and not the sort of place he'd choose to stay if he needed a bed for the night. 'Good work. No, excellent work. I think tomorrow we'll have to pay another visit to Morningstar and find out a little bit more about Bill Chalmers' property empire. Meantime, there's a catch-up briefing and then it's shift end. Go home the both of you. You deserve a night off.'

'It gets better, sir.' Harrison was trying to suppress her excited smile and failing badly.

'Better?'

'Yes. See, Chalmers bought the Morningstar offices not long after he came out of Saughton, about twelve years back. Then he picked up the end-of-terrace block a year later. He bought the guest house two years after that, so it looks like he was just taking his opportunities, building a property empire. It worked to his advantage; they're all worth at least twice what he paid for them. But the really interesting thing is here.' Harrison pointed at the screen, now showing a scan of some waffling document. McLean recognized the entry to the Sasine Register, recording the building's changes of ownership down the years. He had hoped that Dalgliesh's information would pan out, but even so it surprised him to see the name on an official document.

'Tommy Johnston. Well, well, well.'

The snow had barely eased up as McLean left for home. The car park at the back of the station looked like it had been made from royal icing, vague shapes of riot vans and squad cars turned orange and slippery by the streetlamps. His Alfa had fared a little better than most, sheltered by the lee of the wall that separated the car park from the lane leading to it. He only half froze clearing the snow from the windscreen and rear window with bare hands, but the engine came swiftly up to heat, filling the cabin with welcome warming air long before it managed to clear the fogging on the inside of the glass enough to be safe to drive.

He sat for long minutes, listening to the quiet growl of Italian horses and the whirr of the fan, staring at nothing as his thoughts flitted from one nugget of information to the next. The visit from the DCC had been unsettling, to say the least. McLean had been expecting to be taken off the case, made to do something else entirely or simply ordered not to stick his bloody nose in where it wasn't wanted. Instead, Robinson had seemed almost unable to make up his mind. The more he thought about it, the more McLean saw the whole event as a kind of confessional, with Call-me-Stevie as the sinner and him as the priest. That wasn't a happy idea at all. What was the absolution required? What was the sin?

And then there was this evening's revelation, the details of Chalmers' growing property portfolio. Dalgliesh had hinted at, and Ellen Johnston had talked about, a place in the New Town, a private club where her skills as a dancer were not required. He really should have followed the money earlier in the investigation; the connections between Chalmers and Johnston went far deeper than the proximity of Johnston's son and Chalmers' tree. But someone had gone to great lengths to hide those connections. Someone with influence over some very senior police officers. Someone with a great deal of money and no great qualms about using it.

Bright red lights across his vision brought McLean back to the present. A squad car drove slowly past and out into the snowy night. He took his opportunity, eased the Alfa into gear and followed.

The one thing to be said for the appalling weather was that the roads were largely clear. It was treacherous driving though, a mixture of churned-up slush, fat snowflakes and constantly trying to anticipate when the wheels would skid, the steering lock up. At least the Alfa was light compared to more modern cars, and its tyres were narrow, sinking down through the snow to get a grip on the cold tarmac beneath. It was still entirely inappropriate to the weather, and McLean dreaded to think what the salt on the roads might be doing to the very expensive paintwork. By the time he pulled up the driveway to his home he was determined to go out as soon as possible and buy something new, probably with four-wheel drive. He took his time to inch the car into the old coach house, promising himself he'd give it a good hose down with clean water once the weather broke.

The outside light was on beside the back door, but the

falling snow made it all but useless. It didn't bother him much, he'd lived here all of his life, could probably have walked from the coach house to the door blindfold and not tripped over anything. Except for an anxious cat twining itself around his legs and making a curious chirruping sound he'd never heard before.

'What's up with you?' McLean bent down, reaching out as Mrs McCutcheon's cat nosed at him. She nudged his hand once, then turned and trotted off to the back door, disappearing with a clatter through the catflap. All manner of terrible scenarios spun through his mind as he pushed open the door and hurried through to the kitchen, and as the cat leapt up on the table the worst of them seemed to have come true.

Emma sat at one of the chairs, her head slumped against the wooden tabletop. A broken mug lay on its side by her outstretched hand, the dark stain of tea leaching into the boards. She wasn't moving, even as Mrs McCutcheon's cat stooped down to sniff her head and then began licking at a puddle of pale liquid in a piece of shattered pottery.

McLean wasn't aware of dropping his briefcase, or the act of crossing the room. He was just there, by her side, one hand reaching for her neck to check for a pulse, the other digging his phone out, thumb sliding all over the screen in his haste to summon help. She was cold, too cold, and he couldn't see any sign of breathing. Her skin had always been pale, but now it looked almost translucent, waxy, like too many corpses he had seen at too many crime scenes. He paused, fingers just inches from her throat. He didn't want to touch her. Without that touch there was the possibility she was still alive, the faintest glimmering of hope.

Mrs McCutcheon's cat was not so squeamish, abandoning her tea and nudging Emma's head vigorously. McLean shooed her away and finally pressed his fingers to the curve of that neck, just below the chin. For a moment his worst fears were confirmed, his world plunged into a pit of despair. And then he felt the faintest of ticks, a distant heartbeat slow and weak and fragile. The phone in his other hand squawked into life as the call was answered, and he brought it up to his ear so fast he could almost hear the glass screen break. He relayed the information in short, efficient manner, just as his training had taught him, and then he gathered her limp body up to him in a fierce hug, waiting, waiting, for the silent arrival of the flashing lights.

39

'We've got her stabilized, but that was very, very close. If you hadn't found her when you did . . .' Dr Wheeler didn't finish the sentence. She didn't need to; McLean could see it in her tired eyes.

'How has she . . . ? What did she . . . ?' He stopped talking. There was nothing he could ask, nothing he could do except find himself a comfortable chair and wait. He thought about phoning Phil and Rachel, but it was late and the snow wasn't getting any lighter outside.

'We're doing what we can, Tony. I've booked her in for a full body scan tomorrow and I've got a couple of other consultants lined up to have a look at her. Something made her blood pressure plummet again, but I've no idea what. Young Miss Baird is something of a medical enigma.'

'Is it OK if I hang around, see if she wakes up soon?'

Dr Wheeler stifled a yawn. 'Sure. Knock yourself out. You know your way around this place as well as any nurse. I've got to get back to my rounds just now, but I'll look in on her again in about an hour.'

'Isn't it a bit late for rounds?' McLean asked.

'Welcome to the twenty-four/seven NHS.' Dr Wheeler had a clipboard thick with papers under her left arm, but she swept the right in a semicircle around the near-deserted corridor. 'Actually, we've had a spate of referrals recently. Vomiting, nausea, diarrhoea, really bad shakes. I'd say it was a virus, but none of the tests shows anything. And it's not the usual crowd who succumb to these things either.'

'No?' McLean tried his best to be interested, his mind still fixated on the scene in his kitchen and how he had been convinced he'd come home to a corpse.

'No. If it was a virus or some other infection, I'd expect a wider social spread of sufferers. Working class, maybe small-time clerical. These are all high income folk. Captains of industry. Friend of mine in the private place up by the zoo says he's had fifteen referrals this week. All similar symptoms and no easy diagnosis. We've got six senior lawyers and a judge in one ward here. They could almost have a trial.'

McLean laughed, but only because Dr Wheeler needed the boost. His worried mind had finally caught up with what she had been telling him, and now the pieces of the whole puzzle started to look like they might possibly all fit together.

'How many would you say you've had in with these symptoms? When did they first start appearing?'

'A week ago. Ten days maybe. Why?'

'And you'll have done blood tests, I take it.'

'Of course. That's how I know they're not all suffering from some virus or other disease. If I didn't know better, I'd have said they were in the early stages of drug withdrawal, but a judge? Six lawyers? A couple of my colleagues from the Royal are off sick, too, now I come to think about it.'

'Sounds like a bad case of yuppie flu.' McLean reached for his phone, then remembered he was in the part of the hospital where such things were supposed to be switched off. 'I'm sorry. I really have to go and speak to someone about something. It's to do with a case I'm working on.'

'I'll give you a call as soon as there's any change. Don't you worry, Tony.' Dr Wheeler smiled. 'Or should I say Detective Inspector?'

'You might just want to disown me entirely. Especially after my next suggestion.'

'Go on.'

'Your six lawyers and judge – maybe even your two colleagues too. Get their bloods screened again, only this time look for the metabolites of opium, maybe some other stimulants as well. I'll get Amanda Parsons over at the forensics lab to send you the analysis of some stuff we took off the streets a couple of days ago. I've a nasty feeling I know who it was meant for now.'

He couldn't remember the last time it had snowed this heavily in the city. Normally the worst winter could throw at Edinburgh was a light dusting on the pavements that turned swiftly to slush; you'd wake up to find the Pentland Hills painted white and a bitter cold seeping down off them like dry ice. The Firth of Forth protected the city from the worst extremes of temperature and when a snowstorm did hit, it usually blew through swiftly.

Not so this time. When had he stepped out of Ellen Johnston's tenement? Mid-afternoon, perhaps teatime, except that it had still been light. A glance at the clock on the dashboard showed him that it was fast approaching midnight, and still the snow drifted down in great chunks. Rush hour was going to be chaos, unless wisdom prevailed and everyone stayed at home. Schools would almost certainly be closed.

The drive across town was memorable mostly for the need to avoid abandoned cars, although the old cobbled road surface of Randolph Crescent taxed McLean's skills more than a little. Normally at this time of night he'd expect to make the journey in twenty minutes at the most, but it was getting on for twice that before he finally pulled into the station car park and slotted his car back into the space he'd left just a few hours earlier. He should have been tired, both physically and emotionally, but he knew that there was nothing he could do for Emma, and Dr Wheeler's words had opened up a possibility that needed investigation as soon as possible.

'Who's on night shift for SCD?' McLean surprised a sleepy uniform constable as she stared bleary-eyed at a computer monitor in the major incident room. He recognized her as one of the team who had first secured the Chalmers crime scene, but couldn't for the life of him put a name to the face. All of the other workstations were unmanned.

'Gru— DS Laird, sir. And Janie. DC Harrison, I should say. Think they're in the canteen.'

'Harrison? I thought she was on the day shift.'

'Aye, she was, but we've had to shuffle everything about since the DCI called in sick.'

'Spence?' McLean asked the question even though he knew there weren't any other detective chief inspectors involved in the case. The man hadn't looked well earlier in the day, but he'd never known him to take time off for anything. 'When did this happen?'

'Not sure, sir. Sometime this afternoon. They found him collapsed at his desk. Whisked him off to the Royal.

The detective superintendent went through all the rosters himself, offered overtime to anyone who was prepared to help.' The young constable yawned, only remembering to cover her mouth with the back of her hand when it was really too late. 'A few of us have pulled a double shift, but you can't say no to the money, aye?'

McLean nodded his agreement, thanked the constable and headed to the canteen. At this time of night the counter was closed, but the vending machines still supplied coffee, tea and something that claimed to be hot chocolate but lied. It was a sanctuary in the heart of the station, a place where you could go to escape the hurly-burly. Or catch forty winks on the late shift.

'Sir. I thought you'd gone home.' DC Harrison stumbled to her feet as she saw McLean enter the room. Across the table from her, Grumpy Bob merely raised an eyebrow.

'Bit of a change of plan. Emma's in the hospital and I didn't much feel like sitting in an empty house all night.'

'Emma?' Harrison asked, but Grumpy Bob spoke over her. 'She all right?' He shoved his seat back and struggled upright.

'To be honest, Bob, I don't know. But she's in the best hands right now, and I need to follow up on a hunch.' McLean pulled out a chair, pointed at the table for his colleagues to sit down. 'Look, I just heard about Mike Spence. Did either of you see him earlier today?'

'Didn't get in until after he'd been taken off to hospital,' Grumpy Bob said. 'Why?'

'Harrison?' McLean asked.

'He was in the incident room this morning. Not sure I saw him after that.'

'How did he look? Was he sweating? Feverish?'

'Sorry, sir. I didn't really notice.'

McLean shook his head, tried to bring himself back on track. It might just have been a coincidence that Spence was sick too, but there had been too many coincidences already, as far as he was concerned.

'It doesn't matter. Harrison, did you set up the visit to Morningstar tomorrow?'

Harrison looked surprised for a moment, a combination of tiredness and non-sequitur flummoxing her.

'How's that . . . ?' She shook her head. 'Sorry, not important. Yes, sir. It's all set up. Mrs Tennant is expecting us at nine.'

'Good. We'll head over there as soon as we can find a car better suited to this weather.'

'What, now?' Harrison glanced at her watch. 'But it's one in the morning.'

Grumpy Bob stood up again, reached over the table and patted her on the shoulder. 'Best do as he says, lass. There's no stopping this one when he's got a bee in his bunnet.'

It took less time to find a pool car than McLean had thought, but then the late shift rarely had need to leave the station. They even managed to find one with four-wheel drive, which proved a godsend as they negotiated the ever more treacherous streets across the city to the New Town. He sat in the passenger seat, Grumpy Bob in the back, as DC Harrison drove. It was obvious she had been on the advanced driver training course more recently than either of them.

'So how are we going to get in, then?' Grumpy Bob leaned forward between the two front seats like an impatient child as they parked in front of the imposing building. The snow showed no sign of easing off yet, piling up on the pavement at least a foot deep now.

'I really have no idea.' McLean pushed open his door and climbed out into the night. It was surprisingly quiet, the snow dampening all the noise the city had left to give. There was no wind here either, cut off by the high buildings all around. At this time of the night the street was deserted too, as if the city had survived some terrible apocalypse that had wiped out all the people. The orange of the streetlamps reflecting bright off every surface only added to the feeling that they had somehow stumbled into hell just at the moment it had frozen over.

'Might as well try the front door.' Grumpy Bob clumped up stone steps, his footfalls muffled, and reached for the heavy brass doorknob in the centre of the twin outer doors. McLean squinted through the steadily falling flakes to see what he was doing, but the detective sergeant soon turned and stomped back down again, shaking his bobble-hatted head.

'What about the guest house?' DC Harrison set off along the pavement towards the next terrace house along. McLean followed her, looking to see any sign of life in the dark building. He'd have expected at least a light in the front room, perhaps even a welcoming reception area, but it was as closed and dark as its neighbour.

'Can't see anything in the basement either, sir. Oh, hang on.' Harrison was peering over the iron railings into the narrow light well between pavement and house. She took a few steps further away and pushed at a section. A gate swung inwards and as it did, McLean could see the slight dip in the snow at its base where the tracks of many feet had been almost covered up. Stone steps led to a basement door, sheltered from the worst of the weather. A few crates were piled beside it, but they didn't look like they had been moved any time recently.

'Hold on.' McLean grabbed Harrison by the shoulder as she headed for the door. There was considerably less snow on the ground here, but he could see that the shallow depression made by passing feet didn't go the way they might have expected. 'You got a torch, Constable?'

'Sorry, sir. I wasn't expecting to come out tonight.'

'Never mind.' McLean fumbled around in his pockets until he found his pencil light, twisted it on and shone it over the darkness. Sure enough, opposite the door leading into the building was another, smaller door that seemed to suggest a room under the pavement, or perhaps even under the road. The scuff marks in the snow led that way.

'You two all right down there?'

McLean looked up to see Grumpy Bob peering down from street level. The white flakes tumbling down around him caught the light from the streetlamps and gave everything a Christmassy air. Bob Laird would have made a fine Santa, too, were he not a couple of months too late.

'Someone's been down here recently. Might still be inside. Get us some back up, will you, Bob? Me and Harrison here are going to have a wee nosey.'

'On it, sir.' Grumpy Bob's face disappeared and McLean turned his attention back to the door. It was a little shorter than he was, once gloss black paint flaking and peeling off the wooden surface. Back in the days when this building had been a private residence, it would most likely have opened on to a coal hole or cold store for foodstuffs. It had an old iron handle, round and smooth with use, and beneath that a simple keyhole.

'Let's see if this is open, shall we?' McLean took hold of the handle, twisted it with surprising ease and no noise. The lightest of clicks, and the door swung inwards on to darkness beyond.

40

The first thing he noticed was the smell. A sweet, cloying scent that went straight to his head and fuddled his thoughts. McLean peered into darkness for long, stupid moments before remembering the torch in his hand. He twisted it on to reveal a low, arched ceiling and a passage stretching away under the street. Alcoves in the brickwork held shoes, and on the other side a series of hooks were draped with coats. He reached out, felt the material of one. It was synthetic, cheap, and as he moved it a rank odour blotted out the heavier aroma that seemed to be coming from the far end of the passage.

'Follow me.' He whispered the words to DC Harrison, unsure quite why he felt the need for subterfuge. He could hear nothing except the almost silent shushing of snow-flakes as they drifted down outside. And then it came to him: a low moaning, a gentle susurrus of voices from the end of the passage. As his eyes began to adjust to the poor illumination from his failing torch, so he could see another door and the faintest of red glows at its base.

The cloying smell grew ever stronger as he moved down the passage. The ceiling was high enough to clear his head, but still McLean felt himself stooping at the oppressive weight of bricks above him. Something about the place seemed to push him down, mess with his head. He shook it off, standing up straight as he reached the inner door.

'Stay back,' he whispered to Harrison, who had crowded in behind him as if the darkness terrified her. Then he turned the handle and pushed the door open.

Beyond it lay an old cellar that looked like nothing so much as the crypt of some ancient church. A heavy rug had been laid out over the central aisle, covering the uneven flagstone floor, and at the far end stood a plain wooden table, piled with boxes and other rubbish. Small alcoves led off the main area, and in each was a low bed. Some were empty, but most were occupied by what at first looked like bundles of rags. Closer inspection of the nearest revealed it to be a man, asleep or comatose McLean couldn't tell. He smelled unwashed, his dirty face and unkempt beard suggesting someone more familiar with park benches than clean sheets.

'You. You shouldn't be here.'

McLean looked up swiftly, unsurprised to hear the voice. A short, round, middle-aged woman stood in the middle of the aisle. She must have been in one of the alcoves when he and Harrison had first entered.

'This is your programme, isn't it, Mrs Tennant? This is what you and Bill Chalmers have been doing all the time.' McLean made a swift count of the occupied beds. Fourteen people, all drugged out of their minds.

Tennant's shoulders slumped in defeat, head bowed. 'It's not what you think.'

'It never is.' Looking past her, McLean could see the top of the table more clearly now. There were needles and syringes piled up alongside some of the boxes, jars of pale liquid and all manner of apparatus he had last seen in chemistry O-level classes. And there in the middle of it all, like the communion wine on the altar, a glass medicine bottle with a plain white label. A stylized image that might or might not have been a dragon. McLean turned to DC Harrison, still standing in the doorway with her mouth hanging open. 'Got your airwave set on you, Constable? I think we might need a few ambulances here sharpish.'

'It's worst when the weather's bad. These people, they've nowhere to go. They don't trust the shelters, don't trust anyone, really. Life's kicked all of that out of them.'

Interview Room One was warm, a muggy scent of something exotic hanging in the air: the last remnants of the opium den still clinging to her clothes. Ruth Tennant looked tiny, sitting in the plastic chair on the other side of the table from McLean and DC Harrison. She had turned down their offer of a lawyer, which gave him high hopes for a full confession. He stifled a yawn, all too aware that he'd not slept in almost twenty-four hours. He really should have gone home, let Tennant stew in the cells until a more decent hour of the morning, but he knew he'd get no sleep.

'What exactly is it that you give them?' he asked. 'Not heroin. Certainly not methadone.'

Tennant shuddered. 'Methadone? That's more trouble than anything. No, this is something Bill stumbled across. No idea when or where; he's been using it since before I joined Morningstar.'

'So what does it actually do, this something?'

'It helps people cope with their shit lives. Takes away their pain.'

'Sounds a lot like heroin to me and last time I looked that was still illegal.'

'Everything's illegal, Inspector. We wouldn't be working out of an old coal cellar if it was all above board, would we?' Tennant leaned forward and rested her arms on the table. She looked as tired as McLean felt. 'Look, you know as well as I do it's not easy for people to kick the habit once they're hooked. Sure, some just need a little help getting back on track, but most people do drugs because they need an escape from a life that's frankly not worth living. Weaning them off the chemical is one thing, but nobody tries all that hard to address the cause of their addiction in the first place.'

'Like rats in hell.' McLean rubbed grit from his eyes, seeing DC Harrison stifle a yawn as he did so.

'Exactly. Wish I could make it heaven for them, but I can't. So I give them a place where they can get their fix safely. A warm room with basic medical facilities on hand. A supply of a narcotic that takes away their pain for a while without the worry it might be cut with poison. Or worse yet, actually pure.'

'Laudanum? It's hardly benign, is it?'

'Is that what you think we give them, laudanum?' Tennant almost laughed, but she clearly didn't have the energy for it. 'Trust me, Tony. It's a much safer drug than that. Don't ask me what's in it. I know it's opium based, but I'm no chemist. I just know that it's safe.'

'Because Chalmers told you so?'

'Because I've been helping people with their addictions for ten years now, and not one of them has died on the programme. A lot of them have cleaned themselves up completely through it, too. The drug lets them quit without withdrawal. If they want to. If not, then they're safe and they're not breaking into people's houses to get their fix.'

McLean saw the flicker of fire in Tennant's eyes as she spoke, the energy briefly squaring her shoulders and straightening her back. He had no idea if what she was saying was true but clearly she believed it was.

'It doesn't matter, anyway.' Tennant shook her head wearily. 'I've no idea where Bill got the stuff from. Malky did, but that's my last bottle. There's enough left for a few months more. Then our wonderful programme would have come to an end anyway. Ten years of working to help those who can't help themselves. And all for nothing.'

She wiped a tear from the corner of one eye, sniffed and ran her fingers through her greying hair. It was all very convincing, but there was the small matter of the reason McLean had gone out to the offices in the first place.

'So what about the others, then? The wealthy professionals. Are their lives so shit they need your programme, too?'

Tennant switched from tired to confused in the blink of an eye. 'Others? I don't know what you mean.'

'Six lawyers and a judge in the Western General, suffering from something that looks remarkably like cold turkey. Fifteen people in a private hospital in Corstorphine. A couple of senior consultants in the Royal Infirmary. All admitted since Bill Chalmers took his unfortunate tumble. That doesn't sound like a programme to help homeless drug addicts with their withdrawal to me.'

The confusion deepened. 'I honestly don't know what you're talking about.'

McLean studied Tennant's face as she spoke. He was too tired to think properly, but she was tired as well, and not very good at hiding her true feelings. He'd seen her energy and enthusiasm for helping the needy, and understood that she truly believed in that cause. His talk of affluent addicts had clearly baffled her. If she knew something, she wasn't trying to hold it from him. And if she didn't, then his hunch had been wrong, for all the unexpected result it had brought them.

'Where else do you run your programme? Apart from the basement where we found you?'

'We operate from several outreach centres in the more deprived parts of the city, but you have to understand, Ton . . . Inspector. Most of the programme is exactly what I told you it was the last time we spoke. All above board and perfectly legitimate. The drug . . . We don't give that out to just anyone.'

'How do you select who's going to be the lucky ones, then?'

Tennant shook her head. 'That was Bill's decision. He had a way with people. Talked to them. I don't know, he just seemed to size them up and make a decision.'

'And you'd no idea that he was doing the same with paying customers. Did you never wonder where the money for it all came from? Where the drugs came from?'

'You want this, sir? Don't think I need it now.'

DC Harrison held a steaming mug of coffee in a weak grip. She looked exhausted, but then, they all were. Ruth Tennant at least had the benefit of a warm cell to sleep in; the rest of them needed to get to their own beds. McLean hated to think how this was going to look on the overtime and duty rosters.

'How many sugars did you put in it?' He reached out for the proffered mug, never one to turn down a free coffee.

'None. One of the night-shift constables made it for me. Think he's got a crush on me.'

'Well as long as he didn't put a love potion in it.' McLean smiled, then took a swig. It wasn't the best in the world, a slightly bitter note on the finish that suggested cheap instant granules scraped from the bottom of a long-open jar, but it was warm and wet and might just wake him up enough to drive home safely.

'OK. Reckon it's near enough your shift end. Go home, get some kip and I'll see you back here in the evening.' He took another, longer swig of the coffee, the bitterness less noticeable now. 'You moved into your new place yet?'

Harrison looked a little startled at the question. 'Aye, just about.'

'Well, you're probably OK discussing the case with Manda if you see her, but keep it under wraps if you can. Reckon there's far more to this than meets the eye, so the fewer people who know we're on to it, the better.'

Harrison nodded her understanding, stifling a yawn at the same time. McLean watched her shuffle out of the room, then pulled out his phone, checked to see if there were any messages from the hospital. Should he head over there now? Hang around for the day shift to arrive and bring them all up to speed? He should probably go home and feed the cat, or maybe call Phil and Rachel and ask them to. Or maybe head back to New Town and check that the team of frozen constables he'd left guarding the crime scene were all under control.

The options piled up, each as important as the last.

McLean knew the symptoms of exhaustion well enough; he'd been here before. The most insidious one, though, was the inability to recognize any of them for what they were. He drained the rest of the coffee, then pushed himself up on to weary legs, stretched and yawned, looked around the empty CID room. Where was everybody?

He stumbled slightly, catching his foot on the edge of a loose carpet tile as he left the room. A little shock of pain ran up his thigh, reminding him of the broken bone that would never be truly healed. It always ached when there was a change in the weather, but at least the adrenaline woke him up a little. He moved swiftly through the station in the direction of Brooks' office, but when he got there the door was closed, no one home. Time for him to head to his own.

The snow had finally stopped falling as he stepped out into the yard at the back of the station. McLean's little red Alfa sat under a heavier dusting than the last time, but he spent less time cleaning it off. It wasn't that far, really, and as long as he could see out the front and back, glimpse the wing mirrors, he'd be fine. The engine purred like the masterpiece of Italian engineering it was, soothing him as he pulled out across the slippery tarmac and on to the street beyond.

It was strange driving across a city almost devoid of life. Normally at this time, the first tricklings of the rush hour would be starting to flow down the main arteries. He would expect to see people out on the pavements, battling their way through the snow to work or school, but there were precious few about. Even the buses were absent, trapped in the depot by the weather, he assumed. Snow ploughs had been hard at work though, clearing enough of the road for him to make a careful journey home.

Cocooned in the warm cabin, McLean drifted through a cityscape as alien to him as the moon. Somewhere in the back of his mind he was aware that something was wrong, but still he pressed on, through the silent white turned hellish orange by the streetlamps. He wanted to get home, needed to be there even though the house would be empty. It was safe there, protected by something he didn't fully understand. She was out there somewhere. Mrs Saifre. The devil. But she couldn't reach him as long as he was within those walls.

He was almost there now, peering through an ever darker windscreen as he inched past the church with its new roof and slightly tarnished reputation. The road here was more treacherous, snow still thick between the soft white humps of cars parked on either side. Just before the turn up to his drive, McLean sensed that something was amiss, his sleep-deprived brain too slow to process the information. He looked sideways, across the road to the driveway of the house opposite, just in time to see something massive and formless hurtling towards him. He slammed a foot hard on the brakes, but the car slid forward regardless, straight into the path of whatever it was that had somehow appeared from nowhere. A horrible, expensive crunching of metal, and he was thrown forward. His head clattered off the steering wheel, and McLean had just enough time to rue driving a car with no airbag before the blackness took him.

41

Something rough rasped at his face, scraping sore skin that tingled all over with a horrible sensation. McLean shivered against a cold that ached him to the core. He couldn't move, a dead weight on his chest, something holding his arms and legs tight and at awkward angles.

A noise like the distant revving of engines accompanied the rasping sensation on his cheeks, and the weight on his chest shifted. McLean risked opening his eyes a fraction and was greeted by the sight of Mrs McCutcheon's cat, far closer up than he would have liked.

'Get off, will you?' He groaned and struggled against the bonds holding him down as he tried to take in his surroundings. It made no sense. He was still in his car, in the road outside his house. The impact had smashed the front end almost completely, but somehow his seat had collapsed backwards, tangling his arms in the seatbelt. Wincing at the little stabs of pain that accompanied every motion, he slowly extracted himself from the straps, then lifted the cat off his chest and sat up. The steering wheel had folded on to his legs, pinning them against the seat, but he managed to shuffle backwards and extricate them. A tug on the handle proved only that the door had wedged itself closed as the whole car had concertinaed. McLean clambered out through the broken windscreen, barely noticing the shards of glass as they embedded themselves in his palms and scratched at his skin through the tattered fabric of his suit.

He stood on wobbly feet as the snow tumbled around him, and looked at the mess that had been his car. No amount of money was going to put it right this time. The front end was twisted and broken, as if some massive, taloned hand had reached out of nowhere and squeezed the car until it popped. The metalwork was not so much bent as torn apart, long gashes glistening silver and fresh against the red paintwork. A wave of nausea washed over him, followed by a bone-deep shiver. McLean put a hand out on to the crumpled roof to steady himself, and that was when he realized.

'What the fuck hit me?'

There was nothing else in the street. No vehicle with its front bent out of shape, no stone wall driven into in confusion and exhaustion. Just his crumpled and ripped Alfa Romeo sitting in the middle of a wide, empty road. McLean turned slowly on the spot, but there was nothing to see. Just a single pair of parallel tracks behind the car, already half filled with fresh snow.

'How . . . ?'

His voice sounded distant, drowned by the roaring in his ears. Mrs McCutcheon's cat had been twining herself around his legs, but now she reached up one paw and dug her claws into his thigh. The bright point of pain brought McLean back to himself, at least enough to act.

'Thank you. I think,' he said. Rubbing at the sore point seemed to help too. He reached back in through the broken passenger window, fetched out his briefcase and phone. Then, with the cat leading the way through the drifts, he limped through his front gate and up the gravel drive to safety.

The first squad car arrived just a few minutes after he'd put in the call about the accident. McLean heard the crunch of gravel under wheels as he sat at his kitchen table, nursing a large mug of hot tea. He'd heaped several teaspoons of sugar into it, even though he didn't normally take any, and now he was waiting for the shock to hit.

'Jesus Christ, Tony. What the fuck happened?' Acting Detective Inspector Ritchie swept into the kitchen without bothering to knock. Behind her, DC Stringer stood in the doorway, eyes wide as he looked around a room that was probably bigger than his entire tenement flat.

'Grumpy Bob and Harrison, are they OK?' It was the one thought that had been going round and round in his head since the accident. If it had been an accident at all. He remembered all too well the strange attacks his team had suffered the last time they ran in with Mrs Saifre and, given the bizarre nature of his accident, he was under no illusions now that she was somehow behind all this.

'They're fine, although Bob had a few choice words at being disturbed from his kip. We found him in one of the old cells down in the basement, sleeping like a baby. But what happened out there? You lose control and spin or something?'

McLean looked up from his tea. He'd been contemplating the perfect evenness of its beige surface, finding it hard to concentrate on anything else, but something in Ritchie's words sunk in.

'I don't know. It all happened so fast. Hit so hard I

bashed my head off the steering wheel, and then . . .' And then he had no idea.

'I think we'd better get you to the hospital. Get you checked up.'

'Hospital.' The words hit him like a bucket of cold water to the face. 'Emma.' He tried to leap to his feet, but somehow his legs were all tangled around the chair, and then the kitchen was tilting like a cheap special effect in a disaster movie. Strong arms caught him before he hit the floor, but not before his mug of perfectly beige tea toppled over. A shame, he'd been looking forward to that.

McLean was only vaguely aware of the journey across town. A gaggle of squad cars had blocked off the street at the end of his drive, protecting his broken Alfa Romeo like sentinels. Too late, of course, but he appreciated the gesture. Ritchie tried to question him a few times about what had happened; there was no sign of any other vehicle, and neither were any of the parked cars in the street damaged. Snow had obliterated a lot of the tyre tracks, the milling policemen the rest. There could be no denying that something large had collided with him, but it looked more like the car had been attacked than crashed. One for the forensics experts to puzzle out perhaps, except that poor old Amanda Parsons would be devastated when she learned what had happened.

Someone must have called ahead to the hospital; he was rushed through reception and into a private room in a huddle of uniforms and detectives. It all felt slightly unreal, as if it were happening to someone else and he was just watching.

'Looks like concussion. He's got a nasty bump on the forehead there.'

McLean focused his eyes and saw that Dr Wheeler was standing in front of him, an expression of weary concern spread across her face. He had no idea how long she had been there.

'How's Emma?' he asked. His voice sounded like a stranger's, cracking and brittle.

'Oh, so you're with us now, are you? Emma's fine. She's sleeping. Let's worry about you, Tony. What the hell have you been doing to yourself?'

'I crashed my car.' It seemed like such a simple thing, but the ramifications spiralled away from him in ever widening circles, threatening to stretch out into nothing. There was something important he had to remember, had to tell the doctor before he passed out.

'Coffee.'

'No, Tony. You're not having any coffee now. You need to rest.' Dr Wheeler laid a hand on his shoulder, pushing him firmly down on to the stretcher they'd wheeled him in on. 'I'll give you a sedative if I have to.'

'No. Not coffee now.' McLean struggled against the waves of exhaustion that pulled at his consciousness. 'This morning. I drank Harrison's coffee. Think someone might have spiked it.' He reached up to grab the doctor's arm, convinced that someone had slipped a few drops of Bill Chalmers' drug into the drink. The movement sent a spasm of pain through his neck and back, sweeping over him and dragging him back down into darkness.

*

Everything ached. His arms and legs were pinned down as if by some invisible hand, smothering him. McLean struggled to wake up, each breath laboured and unsatisfying. But at least he was warm.

Sounds slowly pushed their way into his attention, a rhythmic, gentle beeping of some distant machine, the quiet shush of air through a ventilation system, muffled voices in conversation, their words too soft to hear but their tone one of urgent concern.

'What . . . ? Where . . . ?' He forced open eyes gummed up with sleep, and saw above him a familiar pattern of ceiling tiles. The tone of the voices changed, an impression of motion on the periphery of his vision. He moved his head to see better, wincing in anticipation of a pain that never came.

'So you've decided to come back to us. Good.' A head appeared in his eyeline, followed by the rest of a doctor he didn't recognize.

'What happened?' McLean struggled weakly against the restraints that held him down, discovered that it was only the hospital blankets. He had no strength at all. Another face swam into view, this time one he did know. Dr Wheeler clutched a clipboard to her chest like a shield and he noticed for the first time that her fingernails were chewed down to the quick.

'You had some nasty toxins running through your system. Still trying to work out what they are. You've had a stomach pump, and we've been keeping you on a drip while your body sorts it all out.'

He relaxed his head back into the softest of pillows, blinking away the blurriness in his vision. As if words were power, he could feel his strength flowing back, but the pit of his stomach was an empty void and his throat was as dry as the wind.

'How long since I came in?'

'A day, more or less. I expect you'll have the mother of all hangovers. You were right about the coffee, by the way. What the hell was in that?' Dr Wheeler put the back of her hand to his forehead in much the same way as his grandmother had when he was a child. McLean wondered what she would have made of the neurosurgeon.

'I don't want to know.' He squinted against the dull pain beginning to blossom in his head. Very much like the feeling of having spent too long with Phil getting on the wrong side of a bottle of whisky. 'You'll have sent blood off for analysis, though? My guess would be some kind of opioid with traces of other unusual chemicals. The profile will be similar to your six lawyers and a judge, only they're in withdrawal, so maybe not.' McLean struggled upright, the weakness of sleep sloughing off him. He looked at the catheter in his arm, the rubber tube connecting it to the drip. In the movies, the hero just pulled the thing out and walked off, but he wasn't in a movie. Or a hero for that matter.

'How do you get this thing off?' he asked.

The still-unnamed doctor looked at him as if he was mad. 'What do you mean?'

'Trust me, Isobel. It's not worth arguing with this one.' Dr Wheeler handed over her clipboard and then went to a cupboard at the side of the room. She came back with cotton wool, a plaster and various other things that smelled of antiseptic, set about removing the catheter and taping up the hole in McLean's arm. Her touch was light, soft and warm, her scent as she bent close to him surprisingly pleasant.

'How's Emma?' he asked again.

'She's fine. We think we know what the problem was, and we've got it under control. She's . . .' Dr Wheeler paused, a strange, distant look in her eyes as she considered something. 'Well, she can tell you herself. We'll be sending her home either today or tomorrow. Probably tomorrow, since you seem intent on discharging yourself right now.' She pressed her thumb perhaps a little more firmly on the centre of the sticking plaster than was necessary, sending a tiny jolt of pain up McLean's arm. 'And now I suppose you'll be wanting some clothes.'

42

It took a surprisingly long time to get across town. If the taxi driver was to be believed, the snow hadn't let up much in the twenty-four hours McLean had been out cold, and while the council roads department was doing its best to keep the main arteries clear, there were still sidestreets that were impassable, cars buried under shapeless mounds of white. And all the while, it kept on fluttering down.

'That nice wee lassie on the telly reckons we've got this for another week. Something about a freak deflection of the jet stream. Don't understand a word of it, ken, but it's no' making life easy for the likes of me. Whole city's in gridlock.'

McLean only half listened to the monologue. He'd been in hospital for just a day but it felt like the world had changed completely. Who was looking after the investigations? Where were his team right now? What had happened to his car? Who was looking after Mrs McCutcheon's cat? He stared out at a world gone mad, draped in white, where beasts could appear out of nowhere and grab you while you were driving down the street.

The station was quiet as he walked in through the front door, but the look of surprise on the duty sergeant's face said it all. He was buzzed through without a word, even though McLean knew that everyone in the building would know he was here in the next couple of minutes. He toyed with the idea of going to his office, hiding behind his paperwork and using the solitude to get his head around everything that had happened. But if that had been his plan all along, then he would have gone home to his irate cat. Instead, he carried on up the stairs to the major incident room.

'What the fuck are you doing here, Tony?'

Maybe not the friendliest of greetings, still it was delivered in a tone of incredulity rather than hostility. DCI McIntyre stood in the middle of the room, surrounded by an attentive court of junior detectives and uniform officers. Whatever it was she had been telling them would have to wait, as all her attention focused laser-like on him.

'Thought I might be of some help,' he said.

'Help? You're barely standing, man. Nasty crash like that, you should be off for at least a week.'

The fact that she mentioned the crash and not whatever it was they all thought had caused it didn't go unnoticed. McLean had to admit he felt like shit, but he'd come into work feeling worse before, usually self-inflicted and in the company of either Grumpy Bob or Phil Jenkins. Now his mind was curiously clear; it was just his body that was wrecked.

'I'm fine . . . ma'am.' He held McIntyre's gaze as she scowled at the title.

'You're far from fine, Tony. But since you're here, I'll use you. God knows, we've few enough decent detectives as it is. And unlike some people you've had a day off.'

'I wish I felt like it.' McLean scanned the room, noting the buzz about the place. 'Something come up? Only last I was here it wasn't exactly a hive of activity.'

'Aye, well. That was before someone tried to poison you. Good thing the cleaners are rubbish. Picked up that mug you drank out of and parcelled it off to Forensics. Traces of some opioid in the dregs. It's a miracle you drove as far as you did.'

'Harrison. She's OK, though?' McLean scanned the room, looking for the detective constable, but his eyes were bleary and difficult to focus.

'She's fine. Grumpy Bob's a bit pissed off because someone broke into his flat and trashed the place, though.'

'Trashed it?' McLean had been there and for the life of him couldn't see how anyone could tell.

'Aye. He's fine. Probably just as well he crashed out in one of the empty cells. Might have been a different matter if he'd gone home.'

'So what's got this place buzzing?'

'Ritchie had a bit of a breakthrough.' McIntyre pointed at the wall with its maps and whiteboards. Photographs had been pinned up showing a snow-covered landscape, and as McLean approached so he could make out ramshackle hangars and the gutted remains of a control tower.

'The East Neuk's dotted with old airfields and stuff, left over from the war.' McIntyre laughed. 'Showing my age there. Most of these kids hardly remember the Balkans or Kuwait.'

'I know what you mean, but where is this?' McLean pointed at the photos.

'Just through the trees from Chalmers' place. Couple hundred yards tops. I've got that new lassie of yours, Harrison, looking into who owns it, but if you wanted somewhere to launch a chopper from . . .'

McLean stared at the photos more closely. A thin red line had been drawn from one to a point on the map to show exactly where the cluster of buildings was. 'There's no runway?'

'About a hundred feet or so. Then the main road goes through the middle of it, and the rest's been dug up. I wouldn't want to land a plane there. Maybe one of those microlight jobbies.'

'Ritchie about?'

McIntyre checked her watch. 'Should be in any time now. Unless she's stopped off at the hospital to see how you're getting on. You gave us all a hell of a fright, Tony.'

'Gave myself a hell of fright, Jayne. I still don't know what happened. One minute I'm about to turn up my drive, the next my head's clattering off the steering wheel and something's mashed up the front of the car like it's made of tinfoil.' McLean stared at the map without really paying it any attention, his mind trying to sort out the sequence of events and failing badly.

'Concussion does weird things to the brain.' McIntyre put a friendly hand on his shoulder. 'Perhaps you really should be taking the doctor's advice and going home, eh?'

He ignored her. Something on the map had finally registered. He leaned in close, tapped his finger on a rectangular shape. 'What's here?'

'What do you mean?' McIntyre pulled spectacles out of her cleavage, where they had been nestling on a gold chain. Perched on the end of her nose, they made her look much more grandmotherly than she would ever be.

'This.' McLean tapped his finger on the rectangle again, reading the words printed just beneath it. 'Corscaidin

Hall.' He slapped his head with the heel of his hand, then yelped as the bruise complained loudly. 'I should have bloody well seen it.'

'Seen what?' McIntyre was giving him her concerned matron look.

'Chalmers' house. Out by Elie. It's modern. Probably seventies, maybe a bit earlier. Concrete and glass and all designer flash. But it's set in old parkland.' McLean tapped at the photographs of the disused airfield again. 'These are through the woodland round the back, right? That's all young trees. Well, maybe the same age as the house. But at the front there's big old oaks and beeches, must be hundreds of years old. Metal fences along the roadside. They'd only be there if there was a big house to go with them. And there it is.'

'You sure you're not still concussed, Tony? Only I've no idea what you're talking about.'

'Where's Harrison? See if she can't find out who owns Corscaidin Hall. I'll save you the bother, though. It'll be Jane Louise bloody Dee.'

'Who?'

'Mrs Saifre? You must remember, surely. The Andrew Weatherly case?'

'I was a wee bit sidetracked then, if you remember? That was when I broke that journalist's nose and got into a spot of bother with Professional Standards.'

McLean stared at McIntyre, confused by the happy smile on her face. 'Aye, right. I'd forgotten. Saifre's a devil, though. So rich she reckons she's untouchable, and she's probably right. She likes to collect people, corrupt them. Get them to do her dirty work, and when things start to go wrong she just lets them go.'

'If you mean Chalmers, then quite literally so?'

A commotion at the far side of the room stopped McLean from answering. The pieces of the puzzle were all starting to come together now, but his addled brain couldn't quite make them fit. Not yet at least. He needed some time to think, but he had the horrible feeling time wasn't something going spare right now.

'McLean. Heard a rumour you'd slunk back here.' Detective Superintendent Brooks didn't even try to hide the sneer in his voice, but he wasn't angry. There was something else bothering him though, a look in his eyes McLean had never seen before. 'Ah well. If you're here it saves a call. You'll need to know, same as everyone else.'

'What's up?' McIntyre asked the question that was clearly on everyone's lips. Brooks didn't answer at first, and for a moment McLean thought the big fat man was going to cry.

'Mike . . . Detective Chief Inspector Spence underwent emergency surgery following complications from his . . . illness.' Brooks swallowed down a lump in his throat. 'He died about half an hour ago.'

43

'Are you really sure you should be here, McLean? You look like shit.'

Detective Superintendent Brooks' office felt strangely cold, as if the endless snow still falling outside had sucked all the warmth and life out of the room. McLean sat with his back to the nearest radiator, but still he shivered. Acting DI Ritchie and DCI McIntyre sat across the table from him, Brooks himself at the head. The empty chair to his right had been pulled away from the table slightly, as if it were still occupied.

'I'm fine, sir. Really. And you can't afford to send me home. Not now.'

All the fight seemed to have gone out of Brooks. His chubby face looked flaccid, like a party balloon the morning after. McLean had always considered the two of them, Spence and Brooks, Little and Large, as a bit of a comedy double act, but he'd never thought the detective superintendent had relied so utterly on the support of his right-hand man. Then again, he couldn't believe Spence was dead either.

'Are we expecting anyone else to join us?' McIntyre asked. It was a fair enough question; there were plenty of other senior detectives in SCD, after all. None of them had been much involved in any of Spence's cases though.

'I was expecting the DCC, and I asked Duguid if he'd

come along too, but this weather's not helping much. Can't hang around waiting for them. We need to put together a plan to cope with this mess.'

'Well, most of Mike's workload can be picked up by the DIs and sergeants. It'll be up to the individual committee chairs what they do about replacing him on the steering boards and the liaison committees he was on. Not sure he was doing any actual beat work these days, so that's something we don't have to worry about.'

As McIntyre spoke, McLean studied Brooks' face with a kind of grim fascination. Something had gone out of the detective superintendent. Normally he would be in charge, ordering people about. Now he seemed fine letting an officer junior to him take over. It made perfect sense, of course. McIntyre had once held his position, albeit in a differently organized Lothian and Borders Police. Still, McLean was surprised at how swiftly the big man had crumbled. He nodded once in affirmation of McIntyre's suggestions, rubbing at his face with pudgy hands.

'What about you, McLean? How are things progressing in the Chalmers case?' The growl in Brooks' voice was back now, his red-eyed stare leaving no uncertainty in McLean's mind that he blamed the investigation, and probably his own part in it, for Spence's death.

'We think we know where he was flown from, and I've a good idea both why he was killed and by whom. The problem as ever is going to be proving it. I was hoping to head back out to Fife this afternoon and check something out.'

'You were?' Brooks looked genuinely surprised. He raised his gaze past McIntyre and Ritchie, to the plate glass that made up one wall of his office. Outside the snow filled a sky the colour of a week-old bruise. 'And just how did you think you were going to get there? Half the city's ground to a halt, and it only gets worse when you hit the countryside.'

'There's plenty of four-by-four vehicles in the car pool, sir. I'm sure I could use one of those.'

Brooks stared at him again, silent for long moments before finally shaking his massive head just ever so slightly. 'No. Not looking the way you do right now. I can't afford to lose any more officers, even if they are a fucking pain in the arse sometimes. It's not so important it can't wait until the weather clears.'

McLean opened his mouth to complain, but Brooks shouted him down.

'No arguments. Chalmers isn't going to get any less dead in the next few days, and the press are too busy talking about the snow apocalypse to care. We need to concentrate on picking up all the work Mike was doing. Smooth transition to a new team. I'll be heading over to HQ just as soon as I can make the trip. Need to see about successional planning, promotions, making some of these temporary transfers permanent.'

'You really think you know what this is all about, Tony?'

The meeting with Brooks had broken up swiftly, no one keen to wait around for either Duguid or the DCC to show up. McLean had hoped to get a minute alone with McIntyre, but Brooks had insisted on taking her to his meeting with the top brass. Instead, McLean and Ritchie had gone first to the major incident room and then, seeing

368

it was back to its previous lack of activity, headed down to the CID room. As usual, it was mostly empty, but one desk showed signs of work in progress.

'I've a theory, let's put it that way. I don't think you're going to like it though, and I need to see what DC Harrison has dug up on that house in Fife Brooks is so keen I don't go and visit again.'

'Did I hear my name . . . Oh, sir. Didn't know you were back.' DC Harrison walked into the CID room, laden down with a stack of papers that, by their smell, were fresh from the printer across the hall. She stumbled slightly as the door caught her arm, dropping half of them with a muffled curse that would have made Grumpy Bob blush.

'Here, let me help you with those.' McLean strode over and stooped down, scooping up pages that looked like printouts of scanned documents. A quick glance showed him only that they were old, frayed edges highlighted in glossy black ink, ancient handwriting loopy and difficult to decipher. 'What have you got here?'

'Land registry records mostly, sir. It's all online, but sometimes it's just easier to print stuff out.'

'Find anything interesting so far?'

Harrison dumped her papers down on the untidy desk, then began sorting through them, peering closely at some of the more faded images. 'Not an easy thing to put together, sir. We know Chalmers owned the offices of Morningstar, the guest house next door and the end-of-terrace block on the other side. It appears he owned the mews house too, but the place in Fife must be rented. Ownership's in the name of a Jane Dee.'

The silence that followed lasted for a long time. Out of

the corner of his eye, McLean saw Ritchie sink into a chair and then very quietly say, 'Oh fuck.'

'Is it something I said?' Harrison asked.

'No. It's just that we've had a run-in before with Miss Dee, or Mrs Saifre as she prefers these days. I knew she was involved somehow, but this confirms it.'

'She's the devil.' Ritchie spat the words out, her voice cracking.

'She's very dangerous,' McLean added. 'And extremely well connected as well as incredibly rich.'

'Wait, what? Jane Louise Dee? The IT billionaire?' Harrison's voice notched up a couple of notes higher than normal.

'The same, although I fear that's only one of her many faces.'

'But what's she got to do with all of this? Why would she be interested in drugs?'

'Power and influence are her two favourite things. What better way to build up both than supplying the elite with narcotics of their choice? Providing them with a safe place to indulge and then holding that knowledge over them when she needs a favour?' McLean pulled out a seat and slumped down beside Ritchie. 'I couldn't see it before, but now it all starts to make sense. Horrible, cold, killing sense.'

'It does?' Ritchie and Harrison asked at the same time.

'Think about it. We know Chalmers was running a programme that was basically giving addicts their drugs for free and a safe environment in which to take them. That kind of operation's going to cost money, though, isn't it?'

'The charity –'

'Doesn't have two beans to rub together.' McLean interrupted Ritchie before she could break his train of thought. 'It's a front, or a partial front. I don't know, maybe it was even the original intention. But somewhere down the line Chalmers came up with a better idea for raising funds than chugging the tourists on the Royal Mile.'

'Supplying to a wealthier clientele?' It was Harrison who spoke.

'And a more boutique experience, I'll bet. What's the word? Hipster? Everything's artisan-baked or sourced from some obscure village in the high Andes. You've got idiots who'll pay five quid for a shot of coffee just because it's got a name they can't pronounce and it's served to them in an eggcup. Why not a hipster opium den? Somewhere they can get high on good old-fashioned drugs, taken the old-fashioned way?'

The silence that followed suggested McLean had hit upon something. Either that or they thought he'd finally lost it.

'And you think Mike Spence was one of their customers?' Ritchie asked after a while.

'Not only that, I think Brooks knew. Possibly Robinson too, although he'll deny it of course.'

'So what went wrong? I mean, if DCI Spence died of withdrawal, then something made the supply dry up . . . Oh.' Harrison's eyes widened as she put the pieces together.

'Chalmers supplied the drugs, probably got Spence into them in the first place. When he got thrown into the tree, that buggered things up. I've a suspicion the stuff we found on Scotty Davison might have been the last of it. Ruth Tennant seemed to be suggesting there was nothing left for the junkies, so why not the same for the paying clients?' The more McLean spoke it out loud, the more outlandish it sounded. But it also had a horrible ring of truth.

'So, this yuppie flu that's going through the city's wealthy elite is really just cold turkey?' Ritchie's face broke into a broad grin that was a welcome light in the darkness.

'What's all this got to do with Jane Louise Dee, though?' Harrison asked, and the very mention of that name snuffed out the light.

'Chalmers must have done something to piss her off. Maybe a bit of dealing off the books; maybe he just slept with her and she regretted it. She's the money behind it all, I'm certain of that. And whatever drug they're using, I'd lay good odds it was cooked up in a lab owned by one of her companies. She likes to be the power behind the throne. What better way to influence the movers and shakers than to have them hooked on a drug only you can supply?'

'But why stop it now? If you're right, she must have known what killing Chalmers would do?' Harrison asked.

'That's the bit I don't understand yet.' McLean rubbed at his face, the weariness and headache dulling his thoughts. 'My guess is Saifre's just reminding them who's in charge. She really doesn't care if people die in the process.'

44

Silence filled the house when McLean let himself in through the back door and on into the kitchen. He'd cadged a lift in a squad car to the end of his drive, but the trudge through calf-deep snow to the door had left his feet wet and numb with cold. The heat of the Aga was a welcome relief as he pulled off his shoes and opened the bottom oven to dry out his socks. The glare from Mrs McCutcheon's cat was less welcoming.

'Some way for me to repay you, eh. Sorry about that.' He fetched the cat food from the cupboard and filled up the empty bowl before setting the kettle to boil and making tea. He was both dog-tired and oddly restless, still coming down from the accident and trying to fit together all the mismatched pieces of the puzzle. Nothing made sense. But then if Mrs Saifre really was involved, nothing would.

How long he had been staring into the distance when his phone rang, McLean couldn't have said, but his mug of tea was empty, as was the packet of chocolate digestives he'd found in the back of the cupboard, even though he had no recollection of drinking or eating. He recognized the name that popped up on his screen.

'Harrison? You still at work?'

'Aye, sir. Night shift, remember?'

He'd forgotten, but it wasn't really important. 'I take it you've some news for me. Not that I don't mind the occasional social call.' McLean could almost hear the blush down the phone and wondered why he was teasing her. She was too good a detective to scare off.

'I ... Er, well. That is, yes, sir. I found something interesting.'

'Well?' McLean suppressed the urge to drum his fingers on the table. The combination of good tea and an entire packet of chocolate digestives had fired him up, driving off the fug of the past thirty-six hours and more.

'Well, it was after what you said about Jane Louise Dee. I was tracking down the deeds to the big house out in Fife – Corscaidin Hall?'

'Let me guess, it belongs to her as well.'

'Apparently it's been in the family for ever. I did a bit of background work, digging up a history of the place and all that. Seems the current hall was built by a chap called Nathaniel de Chauncy, back in the eighteenth century, but there's been a big house on that site for a lot longer. He was a notorious fellow, by all accounts. Leading member of the Beggar's Benison.'

'I'm surprised you'd know anything about that, Constable.'

'We did a project in school. That's how I recognized the name.'

Three cheers for the Scottish education system. 'So, did you manage to find anything more recent about the place?'

'Well, I looked up the de Chauncy family on the internet. There's tons of stuff because of the Dee connection, but most of it's pretty unreliable for the same reason. Seems the family fell on hard times. Same old story, son of a rich man gambling away the family fortune kind of thing. The last de Chauncy only had a daughter, so when she married the family name died out. But she did OK for herself Her husband was Roderick Dee. Made a fortune in coal. At one point he owned most of the East Neuk, and a lot of the west end of the New Town was built with his money. But his son blew most of his inheritance on the horses. They've been selling off the family silver ever since, but kept a hold of the house and the Mains. That's where she was born and brought up, apparently.'

'Jane Louise Dee.' McLean hadn't meant to say the name out loud, but it hung in the air between him and Mrs McCutcheon's cat like a curse. Something didn't add up though. 'I thought she started from nothing. Built her fortune from scratch.'

'Aye, well. There's nothing and nothing, right? Dare say the family didn't have much money to spare when she was growing up in a ruined old mansion in Fife.'

McLean stared into the middle distance, his eyes focused on a point in the darkness outside the window. 'That's good work. Thank you. Let's see if we can't flesh it out a bit tomorrow when we've got the whole team working on it.'

He killed the call, placed the phone back down on the table and carried on staring out at nothing. He'd wondered how Mrs Saifre fitted into all this, but now it started to make an approximation of sense. She'd groomed Chalmers, just as she had groomed Andrew Weatherly, only to toss him aside when he no longer pleased her. Had she done the same with Johnston? It was entirely possible there were legions of men caught up in her web. That's what she did, after all, collected people who might be of use to her. McLean shivered as he remembered how close he had come to being one of them.

He glanced up at the clock; not late, really, only the foul weather and his antisocial work habits making it feel like the middle of the night. He scooped up the phone again, dialled the number from memory rather than waste time flicking through the menus to find who he was looking for. Two rings and it was answered, the crying of an angry baby in the background.

'Hey, Phil. It's Tony here. Was wondering if I might ask a huge favour.'

By the time he reached the bridge, McLean had almost convinced himself that a shiny new BMW tank might be just the car for him. The comfortable leather seat warmed his backside and soothed away the aches and pains, while the high driving position and four-wheel drive meant he could navigate the abandoned cars and snow-drifted roads with relative ease. At least until he turned off the dual carriageway and entered bandit country. Fife lay under a thick white blanket and the further from the main roads he strayed, the more treacherous the conditions became. By the time he turned into the driveway to Chalmers' house, the darkness was complete and a fresh flurry of heavy flakes had begun to fall from a windless sky.

'Police: No Entry' tape had been pinned across the front door, but either the wind had ripped it away or someone else had been here before him. The ground gave no clue, too much snow obliterating any signs. McLean pulled the 'Welcome to Fife' keyring out of his pocket, feeling a slight twinge of guilt that he had never checked it in to the evidence store. He should really have let the rest of the team know what he was doing. No, he should really never have come out here at all, since he was under strict orders from Detective Superintendent Brooks not to. But he'd never been good at following orders. Particularly not those that ran counter to reason.

The headlights on Phil's car had stayed on for a while after he'd climbed out, a handy safety feature. They switched off just as McLean was bending to the lock. The sudden darkness enveloped him totally, his eyes taking time to adjust. He straightened up, looked around the snow-filled parking area, getting his bearings. The abandoned airfield would be through the trees, a couple of hundred yards to the north-west. Over to the east, perhaps half a mile away, was Corscaidin Hall, family seat of the de Chauncy and Dee families. Was she there, Mrs Saifre? Jane Louise Dee? Was she even now reaching out through her intricate web of corruption and influence to bring the investigation to a halt? Was there more to her than that? McLean shuddered at the memory of their last meeting. He knew that she was evil incarnate, and yet she fascinated him too. Like poking at a loose tooth, he couldn't help himself from digging deep into anything she was involved in.

The faintest of sounds brought him back to reality. McLean couldn't be sure in the dampened silence of the falling snow, but he thought it had come from the house. The key was already in the lock, so he turned it, then paused once more. Pulling out his phone, he swiftly tapped out a text message, sent it winging into the ether. Then he slipped the handset back into his pocket, turned the door handle and stepped into the darkness beyond.

45

The smell hit him like a slap to the face; sulphurous rotten eggs and a horrible burning of hair. McLean guddled with one hand in his pockets until he found his torch, and cursed under his covered breath as he remembered how poor the batteries had been when he and Harrison found the basement den where Morningstar ran their programme for recovering addicts. He could have switched the lights on; there shouldn't have been anyone here, and the house was in the middle of nowhere in a snowstorm, so he would be unlikely to be seen. Still, there was something about the illicit nature of this visit that made him reluctant. Instead, he twisted on the weak beam and played it over the entrance hall.

It was clear that someone other than a Scene-of-Crime team had been in here recently. True, when Forensics went over a place it could end up looking like a bomb had hit, but there was a method to their searching, and the mess here was different. Coats had been pulled from their hooks and thrown to the floor, presumably after their pockets had been rifled in search of something. The neatly rowed pairs of walking boots were all jumbled up in a pile now, and some of the storage cupboard doors hung slightly ajar, as if whoever had been through them had been in too much of a hurry to put anything back. Treading carefully, McLean followed the signs of searching through the rest of the house. They had been thorough in their ransacking, these burglars. At least, he assumed that was what they had been. It was always possible this was the work of some other agency; it wouldn't be first time the Secret Service goons had mucked up one of his investigations, after all.

The chaos petered out towards the front of the house, only the kitchen cupboards gone through. A few books on the shelves looked like they might have been moved, but it wasn't until McLean stepped through into the master bedroom suite that the mess resumed. The bed itself had been slashed open, as if Chalmers had kept his secrets sewn up within the mattress. In the bathroom, all the toiletries had been thrown into the bath, the medicine cabinet empty. Even the lid of the toilet cistern had been pulled off, the porcelain cracked in two where it had been dropped on to the floor. There was only water inside. And still that smell lingered on the air.

Retracing his steps, McLean headed for the utility room and the garage beyond. The cars were gone, presumably put on a flat-bed and taken away to Amanda Parsons' forensic lock-up. He'd have to follow up whatever secrets they revealed, although McLean didn't hold any high hopes for a breakthrough there. More likely, he'd find something through the door on the far side of the garage. It had been locked when he and Harrison had visited before, and he had assumed it simply opened out on to the garden beyond. But now it stood ajar, and there was no snow billowing in from outside. As he swept the failing beam of his torch away from it, he noticed for the first time a dull red glow coming from the opening.

It wasn't all that surprising to find steps descending

from the door. McLean was fairly sure he knew what he was going to find, but still he paused at the top, listening for any hint of a sound, any clue that there might be people down there. The air smelled cleaner here, the taint from the house little more than a hint. The scent of two rocks banged together. With a start he remembered Harrison's comments the first time they had come here. And in the mews house, too. It was something he had encountered before, the lingering odour of something wicked this way come. Brimstone. Shaking his head at the distraction, McLean stood at the top of the steps and listened a moment longer. If there was anyone in the basement below, they weren't making any noise. Twisting off his torch, he let his eyes adjust to the dull red light, then set off into the bowels of the earth.

A large basement room echoed the shape of the garage above it, a single light bulb of the kind used in photographic darkrooms hanging naked from a short cable in the centre of the ceiling. Metal shelves lined the walls, piled with cardboard boxes and the collected detritus of years. A couple of bicycles were abandoned in a corner, but most of the room was taken up by a large square table, its top clear and wiped clean. On the other side of it from where he stood, McLean saw another door, again slightly ajar. He was all too aware that he was being drawn ever deeper into the mystery, quite likely on purpose, and yet he was unable to resist. He had come this far; he needed to confirm what he was fairly sure he already knew.

Through the door, a narrow corridor ended in a bead curtain, soft red light seeping through the cracks and painting the dull concrete walls in blood spatters. The taste of the air had changed again, the sulphur stink over-laid with a sweeter, smoky aroma that pricked tears from the corners of his eyes and muddled his senses. McLean covered his mouth and nose with one hand, swept the beads aside with the other and stepped silently into the room beyond.

A couple of steps led down to a low room the same size as the entire house above. Beds were lined up along both long walls, and his first thought was of the dormitories at his hated boarding school. But these were more low plat-forms with thin mattresses and darkly colourful rugs on them than the sturdy iron bedsteads and neatly turned-down linen sheets of terrible memory. The painted brick construction was much older than the modern con-crete house above, the feeling enhanced by wall lights that sprayed red on to the vaulted ceiling like blood from a cut throat. McLean walked slowly down the centre of the room, seeing that each bed was laid out slightly differently, as if each was tailored to a particular need.

'Each one is, Tony. This one's yours.'

He spun around at the voice, his heart leaping in his throat. There had been no noise, no indication that any-one had entered, and yet there she stood, not two paces behind him. Mrs Saifre looked exactly as she had the last time they had met, immaculately dressed, her pale skin flawless, deep black eyes glinting in the low, red light. She pointed at the nearest bed with an open hand, and McLean couldn't help himself from looking that way. It was no more or less unusual than the rest, a dark heap of cushions and soft blankets where a person might lie comfortably in a drug-induced haze.

'None of these is mine.'

'No?' Mrs Saifre cocked her head to one side, made a slight sniffing motion, nostrils flaring as she stared deep into him. McLean had the horrible feeling his soul was being weighed, but he stood his ground, stared her down.

'No. You're right. But you came to me anyway. You got my message, dear, sweet Tony.' Mrs Saifre dropped her gaze, lifted her hand up to her mouth and pressed her lips against her palm. McLean took a step back, all too aware that behind him was only brick wall and solid earth. The only way out was past her. She might have seemed slight, but he knew better than to judge by appearances. He tensed, expecting a physical fight, or even the arrival of the bodyguards who usually accompanied her everywhere. A quick glance towards the door showed a huge bear of a man blocking it entirely, dark suit, hands crossed over his flat stomach, dark glasses even though there was not enough light to see properly.

Too late, McLean realized the guard was just a distraction. He turned his attention back to Mrs Saifre as she dropped her hand flat, palm upwards in front of those perfect, scarlet lips. She blew at him across it, and it seemed a ridiculous gesture. A blown kiss could hardly be deadly, could it?

The full force of her breath hit him like a desert storm, hot as hell and rough with sand. It stripped away his reason and, as it went, so the woman seemed to change. Her skin bulged and cracked apart, fingers turned to talons, eyes burned with oil flame and black, black smoke. His legs could no longer hold his weight, knees giving out, but he didn't fall to the floor. A claw as big as his torso grabbed him so hard the wind burst out of his lungs in a long scream, ribs cracked and back threatening to snap in two.

'Come. It's time we put an end to this nonsense.' Mrs Saifre's voice was inside his head, surrounding him in deafening noise. No longer the seductive, sultry tones of a woman but something deeper, harsher, much older. The low ceiling disappeared as he felt himself being carried upwards through it, through the house, and out into a night sky of snow and infinite darkness.

46

Lights strobed, white and red through closed eyelids. He could scarcely breathe; each gasp a spark of agony in his cracked lungs. McLean felt the lurch of regular motion as he was bumped up and down. Something held him tight around the waist, and all around him was a bitter, enveloping cold.

How could he have been so stupid, to come out here all alone? He should have known Mrs Saifre would have been watching, waiting for him to show up. But what did she want with him anyway?

'Wh– ?' He tried to speak, almost threw up with the pain. The motion stopped, bringing some small relief.

'Awake? My dear Tony, you are so full of surprises. That dose should have knocked you out for hours.'

McLean felt the grip around him loosen, then he was lifted upright. He risked opening his eyes, but it was mostly darkness, black trees and the fluttering of slow-falling snow. Then a pale face swum into view.

'I could put you back under, you know?' Mrs Saifre held him up by the front of his suit, which was just as well, as McLean couldn't have supported his own weight alone. She licked her lips slowly, the point of her tongue running first from side to side on the upper, then back the other way on the lower before disappearing back into her mouth.

'All it would take is one kiss.' She pouted like Hollywood's finest. 'But where would be the fun in that? No. Awake it is. Let's see how well you fly.'

Quite how a woman so slight could have the power to drag him, McLean didn't know. He had the vague sensation of others around him, the bodyguard perhaps, and maybe one other, but he couldn't see them, couldn't focus on anything except for Mrs Saifre and her heady, intoxicating, disgusting scent. It knocked all the fight out of him, rendered him compliant even though inside he was struggling to escape. Only the cold was his ally, making him shiver and burning up the toxins pulsing through him. With each dragged step his head cleared a little, so that by the time they emerged from the trees it began to make something approximating sense.

The airfield was difficult to see in the darkness, but enough light came from the helicopter sitting beside the dilapidated control tower for him to pick out the sides of the nearby buildings. It was like no machine McLean had ever seen before, all odd angles and paint that seemed to absorb light and heat. It had no markings on it, but as they approached its engines fired up and the rotors began to turn slowly with an oddly muted and rhythmical sound.

'This is how you killed Chalmers.' He forced out the words through chattering teeth, each one a stab of pain in his chest. It felt like all of his ribs had been snapped off and were working their way into his vital organs.

'Perhaps. Or maybe I just picked him up and carried him there. Dropped him right where he belongs. Marked the place of his death with my spoor.'

'But why? Weren't you supplying him?' McLean coughed, spat, expecting a dark, bloody patch to appear on the snow at his feet. To his relief it was only phlegm.

'Oh, Tony. You are such a naïf.' Mrs Saifre pushed him towards the helicopter, heaving him up into the open door at the rear as if he weighed no more than a half-empty glass of Château Lafite. He stumbled on the ledge, sprawling on the floor with a crash that knocked the wind out of him and sent more burning agony through his ribs. He could do nothing but curl up in a ball as she climbed in beside him and pulled the safety-harness straps over her shoulders.

'I am chaos, didn't you know? I thrive on disorder and frenzy. Why do you think I pointed you at Tommy Johnston in the first place? So many people who thought they were safe, that the mistakes they made were buried and forgotten. Well, we can't be having that, can we? It's time to sweep the board clean and start afresh. So many young talents to mould, to corrupt.'

Mrs Saifre made a whirling gesture with one finger and the noise of the helicopter rose. It wasn't the *thwup thwup thwup* of rapidly rotating blades McLean was expecting, instead the sound was somehow muted and distorted into something that sounded much more like the soft beating of a vast wing. An improbably large bird perhaps, or even a dragon. Coupled with the red glow of the navigation lights on its belly and the otherworldly sound of the engines, he could understand exactly why a frightened young boy might have thought it a dragon. He still couldn't account for his broken ribs, though.

'They'll never find you,' Mrs Saifre continued as the

helicopter lifted off. 'There's nothing to be gained by turning your death into a message. Somewhere over the Isle of May will do, I think. A thousand feet over the water should be more than enough. The fish will feed well tonight, and then I will pay a visit to the lovely Emma. Living in sin. My kind of person.'

McLean had no idea where the rage came from, nor the strength it brought with it. He wasn't tied – clearly, Mrs Saifre thought him incapacitated – and she was more than strong enough to overpower him. He knew that attacking her would be futile, but someone had to be piloting this helicopter. He gritted his teeth against the inevitable pain, drew his knees up tight to his chest and then rolled on to his front, using his momentum and the strength of his legs to propel himself upwards. In the near darkness it was hard to see anything, but the instrument panel ahead of him gave him the bearings he needed. He reached out, wrapped his arms around the back of the seat in front of him and the neck of the pilot sitting in it. The whole helicopter lurched sideways. McLean gripped tight for as long as he could manage, but he was weak from the crash, the drugs and nothing like enough sleep.

'Stop! What do you think you're doing?'

The voice grabbed hold of him like a vice, forcing him to its will. McLean fought back, kept his arm tight around the pilot's neck. He glanced around to see Mrs Saifre tugging at the restraints that held her to the seat, a look of fear and uncertainty in her eyes that was all the encouragement he needed. The helicopter tilted violently, throwing her to one side. McLean lost his grip, and fell against the door. The impact drove the wind out of his lungs and he felt something snap as the pain threatened to overwhelm him.

And then the door gave way, swinging open on to the void.

47

Cold air, flashing lights, falling. The wind whipped tears from his eyes as he tumbled head over arse over head over arse. He tried to spread his arms, for all the good it would do him; if you're already falling, might as well try to learn how to fly. How high had they climbed? Were they over trees? Would he hit the road, or maybe smash through the roof of Corscaidin Hall? For an instant, he wondered if this was how Bill Chalmers had felt in his last few seconds, panicked and terrified and so, so sorry for all the things he had done wrong in his life. He thought of Emma, and at the same moment something impossibly bright blossomed in the night sky, lighting up the underside of the clouds, reflecting off the million million snowflakes as they tumbled their lazy way to the ground. He had just enough time to hear the roar of an explosion like a distant dream of a thing, and then the ground engulfed him.

Motion, noise, terror. He was enveloped in darkness, soft, cold hands dragging at him, pulling at his clothes. His fall slowed as if he were running through icy water. Arms wide, face to the distant sky, he came to a stop with far less of a jolt than he had been expecting. Enough still to snap his head backwards until it collided with something solid.

And everything went black.

*

The cold woke him first. Or was it the panting sound, the frantic digging of paws and desperate barks? McLean couldn't feel his arms or legs. There was only cold. Freezing cold. It covered him completely, smothered his face and seeped into his mouth, his nose. He coughed, and the barking increased in its frenzy. Something soft and warm and wet nuzzled his face, bringing with it an odour of damp dog.

'What is it, Jess?' A voice he didn't recognize called in the distance as he tried to summon the strength to fight off the pack of wolves that were trying to eat him. Nothing made sense. Was he dead? Was this hell?

'Over here. I think she's found something.' The voice was closer now, and the beast on top of him whined. Another wet, warm slap on his face and McLean risked prising apart his eyelids. It was too dark to see, and then flickering lights outlined the shape of a massive maw, whiskers right in his face. Hot breath, smelling of fish and tooth decay, warmed his frozen skin as the beast began to lick him with renewed fervour, digging away at his chest and side.

'Come away now, Jess. What've you got there, eh?'

'Christ, I think it's a man. Is he alive?'

McLean screwed his eyes shut as the lights shone more brightly, torches directed at his face. The dog gave him one more lick, and then was gone. The weight off his chest fooled him into thinking he could move, but when he tried to sit up, nothing worked. He couldn't feel his feet or hands. Just cold that was turning warm now, and a small part of him knew that was a very bad sign.

The rest of him no longer cared.

'It's Tony. Quick.'

More movement, and then he felt someone kneeling beside him. McLean recognized the voice, but that wasn't possible. She was in Edinburgh, surely. Not out here in the snow.

'Emma?' The word came out as little more than a feeble moan, and at the same time he felt someone else slide down on his other side. He cracked open his eyes again, tensed against the brightness he knew would be waiting. Two faces peered down at him, lit by the reflection of their torches in the snow that seemed to tower above them all. 'Kirsty?'

A soft but insistent electronic beep broke through the dreams of rest and warmth and Kirsty's flame-red hair on a summer morning. McLean struggled into consciousness and immediately wished he hadn't.

Everything hurt. He was lying on his back and while the bed in which he lay was soft, it wasn't soft enough to ease the pain. His head pounded in time with the beep and his heart. His arms were heavier than lead, his legs aching as if he'd walked the Highland Way without stopping to eat or drink or sleep. But they were nothing compared to the pain in his chest and back. The only solace he could take was that if it hurt that bad, he must be still alive.

'I think he's awake now.'

He knew that voice, but it took a long time to place it. McLean tried to roll on to his side, almost screamed in agony, and decided that on his back would do for now. He blinked open his eyes to the familiar sight of hospital ceiling tiles and the tired, worried face of Dr Caroline Wheeler.

'Thought we'd lost you there, Tony,' she said, cracking a smile that was the best thing he had ever seen.

'Where . . . What . . . ?' His voice was an alien thing, dry and feeble.

'Don't try to speak. You've a fair bit of healing to do yet.' Dr Wheeler's head withdrew from his field of vision and McLean found he didn't have the energy to move. A moment later the familiar face of Acting DI Ritchie replaced it.

'You're a fucking idiot, you know that, Tony?'

'I . . . What?'

'Going out to Chalmers' house on your own. We're supposed to be a team, aye?'

'Sorry.' He swallowed hard against a throat as dry as a Wee Free Minister's Sunday sermon.

'Good thing Emma's as pig-headed as you are. The two of you are clearly suited to each other.'

'Em?' McLean frowned at the ceiling. He'd seen her, hadn't he? Out in the snow. But she was meant to be in here, waiting for the experts to decide what was wrong with her.

'Aye. She discharged herself. Went home expecting to find you there. I got your text about the same time as she called to see if I knew where you were.'

'And you both came out to find me?' McLean tried to lift his hand, but the movement sent a jabbing pain down his side that made him wince. A spasm washed through him on a wave of agony. He thought he might have heard a voice say, 'Oh shit, here we go.' And then the darkness welcomed him again.

*

The next time he woke, the pain had dulled down to no more than a horrible ache. When he coughed it was just unpleasant, not life-threatening, and the noise sparked motion across the room. McLean found it easier to move his head without the world exploding around him, even if he was still bone-weary.

'I was beginning to think you'd never wake up.'

He struggled to focus on the voice, eyes gummed and blurry. Blinking helped a bit, but it wasn't until she stood up and walked across the room that McLean was able to see DCI McIntyre properly. She looked exhausted, her face lined, dark suit crumpled. Had she always been that grey? He couldn't remember noticing it before.

'How . . .' He coughed as the word forced itself out through a throat as dry as a dead camel. 'How long have I been asleep this time?'

'Forty-eight hours, give or take.' McIntyre looked at her watch. 'And it's been fun, too.'

'Fun?'

'Aye, fun. Thought the EU referendum was a balls-up, but Edinburgh SCD could teach them a thing or two.'

McLean frowned, too weary to push for answers. He let his head relax into the soft pillows.

'Brooks has been arrested. The DCC's under investigation. The military are all over that helicopter crash in Fife. You surely know how to make a mess, Tony.'

The helicopter crash. He remembered now, grabbing the pilot by the neck, everything tilting sideways, falling. 'What the hell happened?'

'We were kind of hoping you might be able to tell us that. Ritchie got your text, so we knew where you were.

And thanks to DC Harrison, we even managed to work out what it meant. She's a good one. Reminds me of another young DC, oh, a couple of decades ago.'

'Poor girl. I hope she doesn't turn out to be quite such an idiot.'

'That would be difficult. Didn't realize how stupid you could be, to be honest. Though in your defence you'd been drugged with some particularly powerful opiate, so there's that.' McIntyre pulled up a chair, sat down beside the bed. 'And you did solve the Chalmers case. Ha, and to think you even suggested it might be some kind of helicopter with stealth tech right at the beginning. That stuff's so classified they've cordoned off the entire estate.'

'Brooks. You said he'd been arrested? And the DCC?'

'That's all Charles' work, not mine. Seems he took exception to them closing down his beloved CCU. He found some of the old Johnston case files. In your office, as it happens. Buried under about a decade's worth of junk. Seriously, Tony, that place is a pigsty. How do you get anything done in there?'

McIntyre's smile gave the lie to her criticism, but McLean knew there was a truth in what she said.

'Most of the files are still missing though. Someone cleared the archive, just didn't know what was stashed away in that office. But it was enough to point the finger at John. Mike Spence was involved, too. And Needy. That's how they wiped everything. Others must have known and turned a blind eye. Professional Standards have picked it up now. What a fucking mess.'

McLean stared at the ceiling, hoping to find answers in the random patterns of stains on the tiles.

'It's what she wanted all along,' he said after a while.

'What who wanted?'

'Mrs Saifre. Jane Louise Dee. Whatever you want to call her. She killed Chalmers, Christ only knows why. Not for the money or the drugs. Maybe for the leverage it gave her. She dropped him where she did as a message to the people who knew about Johnston. That's where it went wrong. He was meant to land on Johnston's doorstep, not in the tree. Maybe Chalmers learned how to fly on the way down.'

McIntyre looked at him as if he was mad. 'Save it for the debriefing. There's some spook from MI6 or somewhere equally vague wanting to speak to you. You'll need all your strength to get through that.'

McLean groaned at the thought of dealing with the Secret Service. He'd run in with them before, and it hadn't gone well. That had been Mrs Saifre's fault as well. Too much to hope the crash had killed her.

'How did I get here? How did I survive? I fell out of a helicopter for fuck's sake.'

'The gods must have been smiling on you.' McIntyre grinned as if she was one of them. 'When Kirsty and Emma turned up half the airfield was on fire from the crashed chopper. Local farmer came out to see what all the noise was about. His dog found you a ways off in a deep snowdrift. Way I heard it you couldn't have picked a better place to land. A few yards either side and you'd have ended up like poor old Bill Chalmers.'

48

Utter helplessness didn't sit well with him. McLean was used to getting on with things, not spending time lying on his back and staring at the ceiling until he fell asleep. His cracked ribs made breathing difficult, moving impossible without a great deal of pain. And above all else, he felt as weak as a newborn. His strength was returning slowly, he'd managed to eat something and could lift the glass of water by his bedside now, but the thought of standing, walking, dealing with people, left him exhausted.

His only visitors were police, which was perhaps unsurprising, as he didn't have many friends outside of work. Emma dropped by, her hugs making him wince, her anger at his stupidity more so. She'd left tearful but mollified, promising to return every day until they released him, but he didn't plan on staying any longer than necessary. Just enough time to get his strength back, his thoughts straight.

Duguid's visit was something of a surprise, although after his briefing from McIntyre, McLean had been expecting some kind of contact. Like pretty much everyone else, he'd called McLean a fucking idiot, but there'd been a glint of approval in the retired detective superintendent's eyes. Perhaps the fact that he was more or less full-time as a consultant to Specialist Crime Division while it picked up the pieces of its Edinburgh operations helped. Detective Inspector Ritchie was no longer acting, either. Her position had been made permanent. Now all they needed was to poach some more seasoned detectives from other regions and hope no one committed any serious crimes while they rebuilt the team.

'You've a nasty habit of upsetting the apple cart, Inspector.'

McLean must have been half dozing, as he hadn't heard the door open. He looked down from the ceiling to see a man standing at the end of his bed. Average height, average build, wearing an average suit and with a face it would be very easy to forget. He held a brown A4 envelope in one hand and pinched the bridge of his nose with the other.

'I did wonder when you might turn up.' McLean grimaced away the pain as he hauled himself upright against the pillows. The last time he had seen this forgettable fellow was a couple of years back, when the Andrew Weatherly case had opened up a can of worms. Funny how he appeared again now. Must be sensitive to the smell of scandal.

'I had thought I might wait until you went home, meet you there and try some more of your fine collection of malt whiskies. But I wouldn't want to upset that nice girlfriend of yours.'

'I take it this is about Mrs Saifre. You want to know what happened.'

'We know what happened, Inspector. Probably more so than you do. I just thought you'd appreciate a little update. Since you've done us all a bit of a favour.'

'I have?'

'Oh yes. That little operation of Chalmers', supplying

designer drugs to the rich and powerful. He was getting too much influence over key players. The last thing we needed was Mrs Saifre coming in and taking it all over.'

McLean tried to suppress his mirthless smile. 'You've got it all wrong. She was in charge from the start. I'll take the thanks though. Everyone else tells me I'm an idiot.'

'Oh you are, Inspector. I know you went out to that house alone because you didn't want to get any of your team in trouble, but that doesn't make it any less stupid for being noble. You're a loner in a team game, but you're also one of the few people we can trust to do the right thing. And if you're right about Saifre, then you've done us all more of a favour than we thought.'

'Is she dead?' McLean asked.

'Dead? Why would she be?'

'Because she was in that helicopter when it crashed. Or are you denying it even existed? I understand it's all hush-hush secret technology.'

A puzzled frown spread across the man's face. 'There's no way she could have been in that helicopter. She's in New York. Trust me, if she'd come back to Scotland, we'd know about it. We only recovered one body from the crash, and I'd appreciate it if you didn't tell the world about the helicopter. It's very secret technology and there are a lot of red faces in defence research right now.'

'Let me guess, though. One of her companies was involved in developing the thing.'

'I really can't comment.' The man dropped the envelope on to the bed. 'I lied, by the way.'

'You did?'

'Yes. The last time we met I said you wouldn't see me

again. I won't say it this time, but the sentiment's there. Goodbye, Inspector.' The man nodded once, then turned and left without another word.

McLean stared at the envelope sitting on the blanket at the end of the bed. Trust bloody MI-whatever-it-was to be so cryptic and shadowy, but worse yet, the average man had left his little prize just out of easy reach. Bending over with cracked ribs was a non-starter, but there was no way he was going to let someone else get a hold of whatever was in there before he did.

They'd given him some industrial-strength painkillers, so it wasn't so much agony as a lack of mobility that hindered him. Still, McLean managed to inch himself up into more of a sitting position, then swivel his battered legs around and finally lower himself to the floor. On balance, he thought he preferred not falling from a helicopter into a snowdrift, but once the room had stopped swaying like a boat in a storm he felt reasonably confident to take the two small, shuffling steps to the end of the bed.

The envelope was thicker than the last one the spook had given him. That had contained photographs of Mrs Saifre's Edinburgh house up for sale, her leaving in a chauffeur-driven Rolls, boarding a private jet and departing for the USA. This time it was a copy of a confidential Security Services report into the investigation of the murder of Tommy Johnston. Flicking through it, he felt a certain sympathy for Detective Superintendent Brooks. They had fairly swiftly identified the most likely killer, a professional hit man who had served time with Bill Chalmers. The motive was obvious to someone with all the facts, too. Johnston had tried to muscle in on Chalmers' little drug operation, threatened to go public with the names of some of his more influential customers. The list of names in the file was marked 'incomplete', but still it caused McLean to raise first one eyebrow and then both. Some of the more idiotic decisions of the top brass made a lot more sense in the light of it. And there at the bottom was Detective Inspector Mike Spence. The date on the report was ten years earlier, so Spence would not long have been promoted, and already he'd been corrupted. Brooks would have known, Robinson should have known, but they'd decided to hide his addiction rather than face up to it. Or if he was being charitable, they'd pulled together to protect one of their own. And so they'd become corrupted too. Had they known what Chalmers was up to? Tolerated it because he had been a detective and was now doing good works?

The twinge of pain that stabbed through his chest was almost lost in the surge of anger that coursed through him as he scrunched the report into a creased mess. It wasn't that long since he'd been hauled over the coals, faced suspension and possible charges on a falsified blood test that suggested he had a long-standing drug problem. And yet all the time that was happening, Mike bloody Spence had been trotting off to Bill Chalmers' hipster opium den for his regular fix. Irony wasn't a strong enough word.

'Oh, you're up. That's . . . good.'

McLean looked around to see Dr Wheeler standing in the doorway.

'I just . . .' He turned slowly, putting the report behind him like a guilty schoolboy caught in the dormitory with a porn mag. 'Yes. I'm feeling much better. Should probably go home and get some rest there.'

Dr Wheeler raised a single slim eyebrow. 'I know better than to argue with you, Tony. Maybe you and Emma can convalesce together. I've had a word with your boss though. I'll hear about it if you're back at work in less than a fortnight.'

49

The snow would take a long time to melt, but at least the roads had been partially cleared. The taxi still dropped him at the end of the drive, unwilling to venture up the slight slope, even though twin tyre tracks showed that someone else had tried and succeeded. McLean watched it slither over the slush as it fishtailed down the street and turned the corner at the end. He shivered at the chill wind that blew through his tattered coat and suit as if they weren't there at all.

The walk up the drive was a struggle for his weary legs and bruised back. The straps holding his ribs in place chafed with each slight slip on the compressed snow. It occurred to him halfway up that he could have called Phil, got his old friend to fetch him from the hospital in his shiny four-by-four. Then he remembered that the car would still be parked outside Bill Chalmers' house in Fife, or maybe even have been impounded by the military. That would be an awkward conversation to have.

Except that the BMW was parked outside his front door. Out of habit, McLean held a hand over the bonnet as he limped past, felt the latent heat of the engine rising into the frigid, still air. Not long arrived then.

Light spilled out of the kitchen window, and soon the warmth engulfed him as he pushed open the back door. Mrs McCutcheon's cat gave him a look that asked how dare he be saved by something as common as a sheepdog, but she got up and came over to him, arched her back and wrapped her tail around his leg anyway.

Voices from the front of the house led him to the library. McLean wasn't sure whether he was ready for a crowd. He really wanted to see how well a dram would mix with his painkillers to send him off to oblivion. But he'd borrowed Phil's car; the least he could do was talk to his friend, make the first of what would doubtless be many apologies.

A peel of laughter, high-pitched so most likely Rachel, was cut short as all eyes turned to face him. Emma sat in his favourite armchair, Rachel on the sofa nearby. Phil sat at the other end, Tony Junior asleep on his lap.

'Tony, you're back. You should have called. We'd have come to get you.' Phil almost leapt to his feet then remembered his bundle of joy and slumped back into the seat.

'They didn't want to let me go, but you know me and hospitals, aye?'

'Can't seem to keep out of them?' Rachel stood up and took her child from its father, hefting the baby to her shoulder with a practised ease.

'Something like that. Maybe.' McLean leaned against the armchair as Phil clambered to his feet too. 'You got the car back OK? I'm really sorry about that.'

'Some strange bloke delivered it to the university yesterday. Said he reckoned you'd probably not remember where you'd left it.'

'Average size, average build, easy to forget?' McLean felt the suit pocket where he had shoved the folded report.

'That's probably him. Anyway, you're fine, and that's all that matters. Cars can be replaced, eh?' Phil crossed the room and slapped McLean on the shoulder as he spoke. It was a gesture his friend had made countless times before, but never while McLean was nursing several cracked ribs. He tried to hide the pain, but something must have shown.

'Christ, sorry. That was a bit thoughtless of me. We just dropped by to make sure Em was OK. But now you're here, we'll be off. Don't want to get in your way. Sure you've lots to discuss.' Phil winked, but before McLean could ask him what he meant by it, Rachel had grabbed her husband by the arm and was pulling him to the door.

'We'll drop by tomorrow. See how you're getting on,' she said. Then as McLean started towards them added: 'Don't worry. We'll see ourselves out.'

He watched them go, the library door pulled closed behind them. It might have been his imagination, but he was sure he heard Rachel chuckling as she walked across the hall.

'Sit, Tony. Before you fall over. You look worse than me, and I'm a sight.'

Emma's hand on his arm broke the moment. He hadn't noticed her standing, but now she was close by, and guided him to the armchair before taking Rachel's spot on the sofa nearby. The fire was lit, he noticed, and judging by the warmth in the room, it had been for some time.

'How are you feeling?' They both asked the question at the same time. McLean's laugh was cut short by the stabbing pain of his ribs.

'Bruised, tired. Nothing much broken though, so I'll be fine. I just need some rest,' he said. 'What about you? Dr Wheeler said they'd worked out what the problem was.'

Emma said nothing for a while, just sat there staring at him. McLean hadn't noticed the crow's feet around her eyes before, or quite how much the grey had set in to her hair. She was a few years younger than him, but right now she could have been a decade his senior.

'We did get to the bottom of it, eventually. Can't believe I didn't realize a couple of months ago, but it was all too strange. Being back after so long travelling, settling in here.' Emma made a gesture that encompassed the library and the whole house. 'It's a bit of a step up from what I'm used to, really. It was fine while you were on suspension, but when you went back to work it all got a bit overwhelming.'

McLean said nothing. His mind wasn't at its best, too tired and battered by the pain in his body to think straight. But even he could see what was coming. Not for the first time he wondered why he kept on living in this big old house, rattling around its cold rooms, occasionally managing to surround himself with people, only for them to leave, or die.

'Your face, Tony. Honestly, how you can be a good policeman when you're so easy to read.' Emma leaned forward, placed her hand over his where it lay on his knee. He flinched a little as the movement sent a twinge through his ribs, but her touch was warm and reassuring. It lent him strength.

'You don't get rid of me that easily. I'm not leaving any time soon,' she said.

'I didn't . . .' he started, then accepted that he did. 'You're not?'

'No. Not before, and certainly not now. You'd better get

all the rest you can in the next couple of months. You're going to need it.'

'I am?' McLean asked, his thoughts struggling to work out what was going on. 'Why?'

'Because I'm pregnant, Tony. You're going to be a father.'

Acknowledgements

So here we have it, another Inspector McLean novel. If you'd told me ten years ago, when I wrote the first draft of *Natural Causes*, that I'd be sat here typing up acknowledgements to Tony's seventh solo outing, I'd probably have laughed at you, and yet here we are.

I am hugely indebted to the team at Michael Joseph, both past and present, who have taken my rough-around-the-edges early drafts and helped me polish them into something presentable. The success of these books has been in no small part due to them and their tireless efforts. You are too many to name, but an honourable mention must go to my editor Emad Akhtar, for his insight, encouragement and sage advice on this one. I only wish we could work together on some more.

Thanks as ever to my agent, the irrepressible Juliet Mushens, and to her tireless assistant Nathalie Hallam, of whose organisational skills I am in constant awe.

Eagle-eyed readers will have noticed a few changes in Tony's team. I am forever indebted to my godmother Janie, whose annual birthday and Christmas presents of book tokens set me on the path to reading and kept me on it down the years. This is one small way of saying thank you.

And finally my thanks to Barbara, who somehow manages to keep things running smoothly while I'm away in my imaginary worlds. I really couldn't do this without her.